Christmas at Mistletoe Cottage

LUCY DANIELS

HODDER

First published in Great Britain in 2017 by Hodder & Stoughton
An Hachette UK company

2

Copyright © Working Partners Limited 2017

Series created by Working Partners Limited

The right of Working Partners Limited to be identified
as the Author of the Work has been asserted by them in accordance
with the Copyright, Designs and Patents Act 1988.

A CIP catalogue record for this title is available from the British Library

Paperback ISBN 978 1 473 65390 0
eBook ISBN 978 1 473 65389 4

Typeset in Plantin Light 11.75/15 pt by
Palimpsest Book Production Limited, Falkirk, Stirlingshire

Printed and bound CPI Group (UK) Ltd, Croydon CRO 4YY

Hodder & Stoughton policy is to use papers that are natural,
renewable and recyclable products and made from wood grown in
sustainable forests. The logging and manufacturing processes are expected to
conform to the environmental regulations of the country of origin.

Hodder & Stoughton Ltd
Carmelite House
50 Victoria Embankment
London EC4Y ODZ

www.hodder.co.uk

Special thanks to
Sarah McGurk BVM&S, MRCVS

To Charles, John, Anna and Andrew

Chapter One

Mandy Hope glanced up as she walked beneath the Running Wild banner. Today was the official opening for the new Outward Bound centre at Upper Welford Hall. Her heart lifted at the sight of the brightly coloured bunting whipped by a gusty wind under the grey November sky. It felt like ages since she'd had a day off.

For the past three months, Mandy's every waking moment had been consumed by her work. Animal Ark, the veterinary practice she shared with her parents, Adam and Emily Hope, would have taken up enough time on its own. In addition, she had set up a brand-new business in the field behind the clinic. Hope Meadows was the animal rescue centre Mandy had always dreamed of creating, and she still felt a glow of pride every time she entered the handsome glass and stone building. But between her clinical work and the construction project, she'd had almost no time for herself. There was also the distraction of trying to purchase Lamb's Wood Cottage, the run-down smallholding on the edge of Welford that she dearly wanted to buy.

There had been a queue of cars lining up in the lane leading to the Outward Bound centre that Sunday afternoon so Mandy had parked some way off and walked up the narrow road with her beloved collie, Sky. Joining the crowd that was gathering in the paddock, she squeezed to the edge, with Sky at her heels, and admired the rope course that had been built at the edge of some ancient woodland. The rope constructions looked sturdy and safe, and the soft sandy colour of the materials blended into the trees until they seemed almost part of the growing forest. For today's ceremony, a rope was strung between two trees on the platform where the course began. A microphone and a pair of speakers stood on the wooden structure.

Mandy crouched to hug Sky, who was behaving remarkably well given the number of people who were here. It was a sign of Sky's rehabilitation that she could be comfortable among a busy crowd. Mandy let her mind drift back to her crazy, breathless summer, when animals in need of help had seemed to appear from every corner. Back then, the field she was standing in had been filled with rescued animals, thanks to the generosity of Sam Weston, the farmer who owned the land where Running Wild was situated. Mandy smiled as she pictured Bill, the enormous Shire horse, grazing among the sheep and cows she had rescued from Lamb's Wood when Robbie Grimshaw, its previous owner, had been taken ill.

Now there was a brand-new wooden shelter in the corner where six shiny quad bikes stood in a row. Both the shelter and the rope course had been built by Jimmy Marsh, Running Wild's owner and manager. Looking at the neatly constructed bike shed, Mandy was reminded of how much help Jimmy had given her over the hectic summer. In her mind's eye, she could still see him standing at the top of a ladder, carrying out repairs to the barn for her rescue animals. And if she was honest with herself, it wasn't just his woodwork skills that she admired . . .

A movement at the front of the crowd caught her eye. There he was, climbing confidently up to the platform in the trees: Jimmy Marsh himself. In his waxed jacket and corduroy trousers, he was almost invisible among the moss-covered branches and brown leaves. Another man climbed up beside him, reaching the top of the ladder with a grin that Mandy instantly recognised from TV. *So this is the famous Aira Kirkbryde*, she thought.

The attendance of Aira Kirkbryde had been the talk of Welford ever since Jimmy had invited him to the opening ceremony. Mandy had lost count of the clients who had come into the practice gushing about his survival programme on the BBC. Aira too was wearing a waxed jacket and cords. The two men could almost have been bookends, with their broad shoulders and cropped hair. They had been at school together in the Lake District, apparently. Mandy watched as Aira said something to Jimmy that made him laugh, creasing his wind-tanned face until his eyes nearly disappeared.

Jimmy turned to face the crowd and held up his hands

for silence. Stepping up to the microphone, he bent his head and spoke. 'Hello and welcome to Welford Hall,' he said, then paused for a moment, looking out over the crowd. His eyes seemed to rest on Mandy and she thought she detected the ghost of a smile, but then he was talking again, his magnified voice echoing beneath the iron sky.

'I hope that the rain holds off, for the sake of my good friend Aira here,' he said. A wave of clapping ran through the crowd, tailing off almost as soon as it began. 'Not that he isn't used to a bit of rain.' A murmur of earnest agreement from the people beside Mandy. 'Anyway, I don't think he needs any further introduction. I am delighted he agreed to come along today to our opening ceremony. So here he is . . . Aira Kirkbryde.'

Now the crowd clapped in earnest. There were a few yells of 'Aira' and an ironic wolf-whistle, and then Aira was holding up his arms like a rock star on a very small, high up stage. Gradually, the crowd fell silent.

'Thank you,' he said and smiled. Even from this distance, Mandy could sense the magnetism in that grin. 'It's my pleasure to be here today,' he went on, 'at this opening ceremony for the wonderful new Running Wild Outward Bound Centre. It's good to see so many people committed to exploring our fabulous British country-side.' A pause for cheers, with nods to individuals in the crowd. He certainly knew how to work his audience. 'Much as he'll hate it, I want to say a few words about my good friend Jimmy Marsh.' He held out his hand, indicating Jimmy, whose ears were turning red. Mandy felt a stab of sympathy, but was also curious to hear what Aira was going to say. She felt there was still a lot to learn about Running Wild's owner.

'Many years ago, Jimmy and I went to school together.' Mandy saw Jimmy glance down at the wooden platform under his feet. 'Back then, Jimmy was forever getting into trouble for climbing trees,' Aira said. 'It seems he has decided to make a career of it.' To Mandy's relief, Jimmy was grinning. 'Before he came here, he was a park-ranger in the Lake District National Park. It was his job to make sure that the local wildlife and the general public could both enjoy the countryside. I know that here in Welford he wants to do the same thing, especially for people who haven't been lucky enough to experience an outdoor life the way that we have.'

He stretched out his arm to take in the whole crowd, and Mandy sensed people nodding earnestly around her. There had been a rumble of opposition to the Outward Bound centre because of the fear that 'city kids' would run riot across the lovely moors. Aira was making the local community feel as if they were being incredibly generous, and doing a vital public duty.

'Anyway, I'm not going to talk for long. I know that many of you have come here today to try out the wonderful rope course behind me, so I won't keep you hanging any longer . . .' He paused as a mixture of groans and scattered laughter rose. Then he turned to Jimmy, who handed over a sturdy-looking hunting knife.

'Without further ado,' Aira announced, taking hold of the rope that stood in place of the more traditional ribbon, 'I declare that the new Running Wild Outward Bound Centre is officially open!' With a flick of the knife, he sliced through the rope.

There were a few cheers, a burst of clapping and then the crowd began to surge forward. Looking down, Mandy could see that despite the chilly wind, Sky had begun to pant. From the tension in her face, Mandy knew that the noise and movement was disturbing the sensitive dog. She reached into her pocket and crouched down beside the collie. 'Here you go,' she whispered, slipping Sky a chew. As the crowd continued to mill around them, Mandy stayed with her pet, running her hands through the soft fur on the sides of Sky's neck. 'What do you want to do now then?' she asked. Sky looked at her, her liquid brown eyes filled with trust. 'Should we head home? I'm guessing Jimmy will be too busy to speak to us today.'

'Guess again!' A pair of lightweight climbing boots with wasp-striped laces had come to a standstill in front of her. Mandy's eyes followed upwards, past the dark trousers and the new-looking Barbour to the familiar face that was grinning down at her. With a last caress of Sky's ear, Mandy took the hand he was holding out and pulled herself, rather awkwardly, to a standing position. She felt breathless, even as the heat rose in her face. Back in the summer, when they had first met, Jimmy Marsh had always seemed to catch her off-guard and now here she was again, blushing like a sixteen-year-old.

His grin widened. 'Sorry,' he said. 'I didn't intend to creep up on you.' Close up, he looked as friendly as ever, his frank green eyes surrounded by laughter lines.

The wind whirled against Mandy's cheeks and a shiver ran through her as she caught the scent of Jimmy's aftershave. 'I thought you'd be on duty all day,' she said.

He shrugged, his eyes apologetic. 'I'll have to go in a minute,' he admitted. 'Aira's keeping them entertained for now, but the rope course is free today so there's a bit of a stampede. I'll need to supervise.'

'It all looks great.' Mandy glanced around. 'I can see how much work you've put in.'

Jimmy nodded. 'You and me both,' he said. 'The new buildings at Hope Meadows seemed to spring up overnight. We've both had our hands full.'

'How are Abi and Max?' Mandy asked. She had met Jimmy's eight-year-old twins briefly when he had been caring for them during the summer holiday.

Jimmy's face softened. 'They're great, thanks,' he said. 'They'll be over next Saturday.' He paused for a moment. 'How about all your charges?' he asked. 'Did you ever manage to find a home for Rudolph?'

Mandy smiled. The adorable pygmy goat had been one of Hope Meadows' first residents. 'He's gone to a smallholding on the far side of Walton,' she replied. 'They've got loads of goats . . . and very tall fences,' she added. Jimmy had been driving past when Rudolph had taken a daring leap out of his pen and escaped onto the road. Happily for Mandy, Jimmy had caught the spirited goat – who really did seem to fly like one of Santa's reindeer – before he had a chance to cause an accident.

'Do you have many other inmates just now?' Jimmy asked. 'Only I know someone who's looking for a cat.'

'We've lots of lovely cats,' Mandy was always delighted to hear of any potential new homes. She glanced sideways at Jimmy, teasing him with a smile. 'How about you?' she said. 'Wouldn't you like one, too?'

'I'm sure they're lovely, but I'm more of a dog person. I'd love to come round and see them though – and you, of course,' he added.

Mandy felt herself going red again. She had been so busy recently that she and Jimmy had barely seen each other. He was very good company and made her laugh, but she had so little time to spare. She'd already cancelled more than one date when work had intervened. Understanding as he was, she wondered whether she was really being fair to him.

'Mr Marsh?' A young woman with dark hair and a smart black raincoat appeared behind Jimmy. Mandy recognised the farm secretary from Upper Welford Hall. 'We're going to let people onto the rope course now.'

Jimmy flashed Mandy a wry smile. 'I have to go,' he said, 'but I'll see you soon.' He reached out a hand and gave Mandy's fingers a brief squeeze. 'Bye,' he said, then turned and strode off towards the large queue that was waiting at the foot of the first net.

Mandy sighed and looked down at Sky. 'Guess it's just you and me again,' she said.

'Hello.' Before she had a chance to move off, a cheery voice accosted her. 'Lovely to see you here, Mandy.' It was Mrs Jackson, who lived in Rose Cottage, just up from Mandy's grandparents. Mandy was impressed to see that as well as wearing sturdy boots and a warm hat and coat, the old lady was sporting a hefty pair of binoculars. Was she hoping to birdwatch from the heights of the tree-house that stood at the end of the rope course?

'Just going to take a wander through the woods.' Mrs Jackson adjusted the strap on her binoculars. 'I'm glad that Jimmy Marsh seems to be taking his wildlife protection duties seriously,' she went on. 'Though I'm sure if he didn't, you'd put him straight.'

Mandy smiled to herself. She had lectured Jimmy more than enough about the local environment when they had first met, but she knew now that he was just as invested as she was. 'I'm sure he'll be very careful,' she replied.

Mrs Jackson nodded as if the reply was quite satisfactory.

'Hi, Mandy!' Rachel Farmer, the Animal Ark receptionist, came over to join them. Dressed warmly in an eye-catching red scarf and knitted hat, she was arm in arm with her fiancé, Brandon Gill from Greystones Farm. 'Are you going to have a go on the rope course?' Rachel asked.

Mandy shook her head. 'I've got Sky with me,' she said, by way of explanation.

'We could hold her for you, couldn't we, Brandon?' Rachel looked up at the young farmer, who flushed red before giving a single nod.

'That's very kind of you,' Mandy said. 'But I think we should be heading home.' She glanced down at Sky, whose fur was lifting like feathers in the wind. She was looking up at Mandy, her eyes expectant. Mandy slid her hand into her pocket and gave her a treat. 'Bye, Mrs Jackson. See you on Monday, Rachel,' she called, and then to Sky, 'Come on, girl.'

They got as far as the gate to the paddock before she was hailed again.

'Hello! Mandy?' The voice came from the farmyard next door. It was Graham, the dairyman from Upper Welford Hall. He was wearing his usual faded blue boiler suit and his hair stuck up on end, as if he had rubbed his hands through it. 'I was just about to take the stitches out of the cow you saw last week. She's healed beautifully. Want to take a look?'

Even though it was officially her day off, Mandy couldn't resist following Graham to see the black and white Friesian she had treated ten days earlier. As she passed through the archway into the Welford Hall court-yard, her eye was caught by the twinkling white lights of a huge Christmas tree that stood in the centre of the yard. The row of little shops specialising in crafts and home-made produce were also trimmed with greenery and lights and a mobile stall had been set up to roast chestnuts. For the first time, it crossed Mandy's mind that Christmas was not too far away. She felt a shiver of excitement. Christmas in Welford had always been magical.

Graham was disappearing into a passageway at the far side of the cobbles. Hurrying after him, Mandy followed him into a shed close to the milking parlour where her patient was being kept. She had carried out an operation to move the abomasum, the fourth chamber of the cow's stomach. It had become displaced to the left side of the cow's abdomen. Mandy had shifted it back to its normal position and sutured it in place. The cow had been unable to eat and would have died without surgery.

It was the first time Mandy had performed the op. Now, she was pleased to see the animal tucking into hay as if nothing had happened. The cow turned her head to gaze at them, a few wisps of hay hanging from her mouth.

'She started eating straight away,' Graham told Mandy. 'It's like a miracle.' Mandy could see that the cow's flanks had filled out and her eyes were bright and curious. The wound on her right side was, as Graham had said, impressively healed. 'Would you mind holding her tail while I take the stitches out, or would you like to do it?' he asked.

'I would quite like to do it,' Mandy said.

'Be my guest!' Graham smiled before handing over the small curved blade that would be used to remove the stitches. With a well-practised hand, he took hold of the cow's tail and leaned on her hind end until she swung round against the wall. Absent-mindedly, he scratched the placid animal's rump as Mandy approached. The wound site was smooth and clean, to her relief. The hair around the scar was already beginning to regrow. In a few months, there would be only a thin line to mark the operation. With a steady hand, Mandy clipped the thick suture material at the top and bottom of the wound, then unpicked the interlocking stitches in between.

'We've made some adjustments to the feeding routine after calving for the rest of the herd, as you suggested,' Graham told her. 'We've increased the fibre intake and we're supplementing with calcium and phosphorus. We don't want another one getting ill.'

'That's great.' Mandy stood back from the cow as Graham moved up towards the animal's head, loosening the halter from behind her ears, then dropping it free over her nose. Slipping the rope over his shoulder, he followed Mandy out of the pen and swung the gate shut. For a moment they stood side by side, watching as the cow pulled another mouthful of hay from the rack.

'We should go,' Mandy said. She could have stood there all day, breathing in the sweet scent of hay and clean bovine, but there was a lot to do back at Hope Meadows. Untying Sky's lead from a ring on the wall of the byre, she leaned down and stroked the collie's soft domed head. She would buy some of the delicious chestnuts she had smelled earlier on her way through the yard, she thought. They would warm her up as she walked back to the car. Pulling open the door, she stepped back outside into the chilly November wind.

Chapter Two

Mandy stood behind the glass wall of the rescue centre and stared out. The trees in the orchard were bare in the late afternoon light and the fellside had faded to its muted winter hue. The beauty of the landscape, the serene grasslands and endlessly climbing dry-stone walls lifted Mandy's heart. Hope Meadows, and its furry occupants, still felt like a wonderful dream to her. From the earliest days of helping animals with James, she had known she wanted to spend her life working with and for them.

Closing her eyes and inhaling deeply, she could still detect the fresh scent of sawdust clinging to the wooden beams. With the help of an architect, Mandy's father Adam had come up with the design for the centre. The reception area was dominated by a soaring glass window which flooded the building with natural light, even on the greyest days.

Despite the hard work Mandy had to put in at all hours, there was nowhere else she would rather be.

She opened her eyes and walked behind the counter she used both as an office and as a reception area when clients visited. There was a letter waiting for her on the desk. Rachel must have put it there yesterday. Picking it up, she saw the Harper's Supplies logo on the envelope and for a moment she felt uneasy. Her adoptive parents had made a generous investment in Hope Meadows, but in spite of their help, there were still occasions when the size of the feed bills and all the other expenses made her wince. Ripping open the envelope, she pressed her lips together. The invoice was far higher than she had anticipated. There was a letter attached and she flipped it open.

'Dear Amanda,' she read. 'I am sorry to let you know there was an error with your invoice from October and therefore the outstanding amount is rather higher than usual. Should you have any problems meeting this account, please do get in touch and we will discuss possible means of payment. Many thanks. Sally Harper.'

She looked up. The scene beyond the window was unchanged, but for a moment, the joy it brought her was dimmed. She had checked over the Hope Meadows accounts the day before and her bank statement had told her that without additional funding, she would soon be eating into her overdraft. She had calculated that she had enough to cover the November feed bill, but with the extra payment, there was no way she could afford to pay immediately. She would have to ring Sally, but it was Sunday evening. There was nothing she could do for now.

Pulling herself upright with a sigh, she walked through

to the room where she kept her smallest inmates. She was greeted by the welcoming *wheek, wheek, wheek* of two guinea pigs who had been brought in last week. Their previous owner had gone to university and her mother had felt unable to give them the care they deserved. The sight of them lifted Mandy's heart again. Despite the difficulties, this was all she had ever wanted. She smiled at the sight of a blunt little nose twitching. A pair of bright eyes peered out from the cage. 'Hello, Snowie,' she said to the rough-haired white cavy, 'and hello, Bubble,' as the second little creature appeared. Opening the fridge, Mandy pulled out a packet of rocket and posted a few leaves through the bars of the cage. She had been working with Snowie and Bubble every day, getting them used to being handled by someone different. They were mostly calm now, though if Mandy made a sudden noise or movement, they would still make a scrabbling dash for their bed.

Crossing to the other side of the room, Mandy gave some rocket to a pair of delicate, tiny Himalayan rabbits. She opened the door and stroked them each in turn. Their slim faces were almost comical with their twitching brown noses and soft dark ears, which contrasted so strikingly with the silky white fur on the rest of their bodies. Taking out her phone, Mandy took a few snaps of them in their newly cleaned cage. She would put the pictures on the rehoming page of her website later, alongside the profiles of the guinea pigs.

When Mandy returned to the reception area, Sky

stood up from where she had been lying on her bed in the corner and came to greet her. Mandy bent down to give the collie a cuddle, burying her face in the soft fur. How sweet she smelled.

'I'll be with you in a minute,' Mandy promised. 'I'm just going to check on the cats.' She walked over to the soft basket and dropped a chew for Sky, who snuffled up the treat and lay down with a sigh that made Mandy want to laugh. 'I know,' she said. 'You need *so* much patience to be my dog, don't you?' The sound of shuffling paws and Sky's tail flickering up and down was her reply.

There were currently six cats in the centre, three adults and one mother who was nursing a pair of three-week-old kittens. Despite Mandy's best efforts, the black and white mother cat was still very nervous about being handled and was inclined to hiss at the slightest provocation. She would, however, allow Mandy to remove her kittens from the nursing kennel. Since their eyes had opened, Mandy had been lifting them out at regular intervals, getting them used to being placed in different positions and learning to play simple games that would help with their training.

Mandy opened the cage of the oldest cat. Tango was a sweet ginger tom whose owner had died three weeks ago. The old lady's relatives hadn't been able to take him because they lived in a high rise flat and Tango had been used to going outside. He had once been very handsome, they had told Mandy. She thought he still looked splendid. His face held the quiet dignity of the aged feline: all prominent cheekbones with hollows in front of his ears. Tango butted his head against her, purring as she scratched behind his ear. He hadn't taken all his food, she noticed. At least half of it was still in his bowl. With a last stroke for his nose, she ushered him back into the cage and swung the door closed.

It was time to take the dogs out. There were currently four dogs in the canine section. There was a brief burst of barking as Mandy entered the kennel area, but it stopped as soon as she called out. She worked as hard as she could to keep the dogs quiet, though it could be a problem with any new inmate, and one or two never seemed to stop. She took out the two crossbreeds first. The slightly larger male was called Albert, the female Twiglet.

With Sky watching through the window, Mandy led them into the orchard and put them through their paces, working them both on the lead and off, giving them time to play together and interact as well as working with them individually. With their smooth coats and endearingly long noses, they reminded Mandy of Seamus and Lily, the two muscular little dogs that belonged to James Hunter, her best friend.

Back in the summer, Seamus and Lily had been ring-bearers at James's wedding to Paul. Their marriage had lasted only a few short months before James's new husband had succumbed to the devastating bone cancer that had torn through his body. Despite the pain, Mandy still felt privileged to have known Paul. He had named Hope Meadows and Mandy felt that with every animal she helped, it honoured the memory of a wonderful man. Seamus and Lily had been so dear to Paul, and Mandy knew that they had comforted James. She hoped she would find an equally special home for Albert and Twiglet.

Next it was the turn of the other two dogs, Melon and Flame. Melon was a two-year-old West Highland White terrier. His owners were due to have a baby. Mandy had offered to provide them with behavioural support when the baby arrived, but the couple seemed to feel that it was unsafe to have a dog in the house at all. Mandy hadn't had the heart to argue with them. It was better for the characterful little dog to come to Hope Meadows than to be left with a family who didn't really want him. Melon's eyes were bright in his white fluffy face. He looked sweetly cheeky when he put his head on one side, his short tail aloft. Mandy was sure that someone would fall in love with him very soon.

The last of the four dogs was a gorgeous golden brindle lurcher with the most piercing bronze gaze Mandy had ever seen. Even after several weeks of training, Flame was highly excitable and not easy to control. Mandy had spent a lot of time ensuring the fences and the hedge that ran along one side of the orchard were secure, but she still worried about Flame's safety. Although the fences were tall, the gate that led out into the field was slightly lower. If Flame spotted anything outside the paddock that she might view as prey, Mandy had a feeling that she might prove to be a talented escape artist.

As yet, Mandy had not found a way to practice Flame's recall reliably. She knew it was important never to call the lurcher to come until she was certain Flame's attention was on her and she would obey. There was no point setting the dog up to fail. Mandy had begun the training inside, where it was easier to keep Flame's focus on her. But as soon as they moved outside, sniffing around the paddock had proved to be far more exciting than anything Mandy could offer. Nor was Flame motivated by food, not when there was a whiff of prey scent on the air. While Flame gambolled around, sniffing at every tree and clump of grass, Mandy did not dare to call her. If she did and Flame failed to come, then the lurcher would be learning the wrong lesson. Mandy had a thin nylon wire on a harness that she could use to pull the lurcher in if Flame's training proved truly impossible. But she preferred not to use physical methods of attracting attention or to enforce obedience. They could, on occasion, give the animal unpleasant feedback. It was important to Mandy that Flame was able to enjoy their sessions.

For the time being, Mandy worked with Melon and kept her eye on Flame. On the odd occasion when the right moment arrived, and Flame did react positively, Mandy made sure she encouraged her as much as possible, both with treats and play.

Throughout the session with Melon and Flame, sometimes wandering round the orchard, but more of the time watching and joining in, was Sky. Mandy had worked hard to ensure the collie was as thoroughly socialised as possible. It was safe now for almost any dog to interact with her, and seeing Sky perform and receive treats often helped to raise the value of the rewards she gave to the other dogs. There was no question of Sky going anywhere, that was for sure. Hope Meadows would be her home forever.

Mandy thought back to the moment when she had plucked up the courage to ask her parents if she could keep Sky. Throughout her childhood at Animal Ark, Adam and Emily had maintained strict rules about taking on any of the stray animals that Mandy and James rescued. But Sky had been different from the beginning. Mandy hadn't been sure what to expect when she sat Mum and Dad down and asked them outright whether she would be able to keep the collie. They had looked at one another with half-smiles, as if they found her question amusing. Then Adam had pointed out she was an adult now, and more than capable of electing to have a pet. Emily had added that she was delighted Mandy would have company when it was time for her to move out.

Mandy felt a familiar knot of worry inside her stomach. When she had first enquired about Lamb's Wood Cottage, back in the summer, the estate agents had been encouraging and helpful. But when she had approached a mortgage company about the purchase, all kinds of problems had sprung up. Mandy had known how run down the cottage was, but she hadn't realised that it might affect her ability to get a loan. It was three months since Robbie Grimshaw's trustees had accepted her offer, and Mandy had her fingers crossed that next week might bring the news that her application had been granted. Much as Mandy loved her parents, there had been times in the past months when she been painfully aware that she had much less independence living under their roof.

A loud yelping jolted her back to the orchard. Mandy looked up to see Flame being catapulted tail over paws over the fence. The lurcher had tried to jump the gate, but one of her paws had caught on the railing. For an instant, Mandy thought she had broken her neck, but a moment later, the long-legged creature was back on her feet and racing across the field. Far beyond her on the green grass, a rabbit was in flight, its white tail receding at speed.

'Flame!' Mandy shouted. The lurcher did not check, even for a second. 'Flame!' Mandy called again, almost a screech. Running to the edge of the orchard, Mandy scanned the field, but Flame had already disappeared.

She called to Melon, who came trotting over at once, and took him back to his kennel. When she saw Flame's empty cage, Mandy almost wanted to cry. It was her own fault. She had let her attention wander when she should have been focussed on a sensitive, reactive dog who was entirely her responsibility. Rushing into the cottage, she found Adam at the kitchen table.

Her father stood up as she hurtled in. 'Is everything all right?'

'It's Flame!' Mandy panted. 'She's run off.'

'Okay.' Adam took off his reading glasses. 'What would you like me to do?'

Mandy thought fast. 'I'll go out in the car to look for her. I don't have a chance of keeping up on foot. I think it's best if you stay here in case someone spots her and rings on the landline.'

Adam nodded. 'Right you are. Don't forget to take your phone so you can let me know if you find Flame.'

Mandy grabbed her car keys, rushed outside, and jumped into her RAV4. Adam had followed her outside and she wound down the window.

'She'll turn up,' said her father. Mandy pressed her lips together. She hoped he was right.

But after half an hour of driving around the lanes and the village, there was still no sign of the distinctive lurcher. Mandy headed back to Animal Ark with a sense of despair. What else could she do to find Flame? The short November day was ending and the darkening sky echoed Mandy's gloom. She sighed as she turned off the engine and undid her seatbelt.

She was still sitting in the driver's seat when the back door of the cottage burst open. Adam rushed out, the phone in his hand. 'I've just had a report about a wild dog attacking some children's rabbits! It sounds like

Flame!' he gasped. 'This is the address.' He handed over a sheet of paper.

Mandy read the note with a sinking feeling. Had Flame really attacked someone's pets? For a moment she pictured the awful scene, but she dragged her mind back and read the note her father had handed her. *Geoff Hemmings, 21 Norland Way*. That was in the new estate on the edge of Welford. It wasn't too far away. Putting the car into gear, she set off.

Chapter Three

The modern estate looked peaceful in the gathering dusk. One or two houses had Christmas lights along their gables and there were a few decorated trees already in windows. Their twinkling brightness felt inappropriate. Mandy's head was throbbing. If Flame had killed the rabbits . . . Pulling on the handbrake outside number 21, she climbed out.

She walked up the path on shaking legs and rang the bell. The door swung open as if someone had been waiting. A man in a blue jacket glared at her.

'I'm Amanda Hope.' It was hard to get the words out. 'About the dog.'

'Come in.' Mr Hemmings' voice was curt. 'We called the vet because we didn't know what else to do. But the man we spoke to said it was from the rescue centre.' He spat the words over his shoulder as he walked through to the back of the house. Two girls, both dressed in pyjamas and dressing gowns, stood in the living room, their hands against a glass door that led into the back garden. Both had their eyes fixed on the golden dog that was attacking the rabbit hutch in the garden.

Flame looked frantic, snapping at the wire and chewing the wooden frame. As Mandy watched, the dog grabbed the wire mesh with her teeth and shook her head as if trying to rip it free. There was no sign of the rabbits, who were presumably hiding in the sleeping area. The younger of the children gasped. The older had tears running down her face. 'Daddy! Save Nibbles!' she cried.

'Does this door open?' Mandy almost shouted. Without a word, the man turned the key in the handle and slid the glass aside. As Mandy walked through, he pulled it closed behind her. It was clear he didn't want to go anywhere near the snarling dog.

Mandy stood at the edge of the lawn, trying not to panic. Should she take hold of Flame and drag her away from the hutch? Would she bite? The lurcher was like a possessed thing, and hadn't even noticed Mandy come into the garden. The thought of Flame ripping the mesh away and killing the rabbits in front of their owners gave Mandy courage. As she walked forward, to her relief, Flame's eyes swivelled towards her. Letting go of the wire, she bounded off around the garden. Mandy stood very still. If Flame jumped the fence again, they would be back at square one.

Flame bounced towards Mandy as if she wanted to play. Although she had a pocket filled with chews, Mandy wished she had brought a tug toy. Reaching into her pocket, she took out a treat but Flame raced off again. Mandy winced as she rushed across a flowerbed, leaving deep paw-prints in the soft earth. She didn't want to call Flame until she had the dog's attention again. But the family watching her through the windows would think she was a complete incompetent if she didn't do something. More rushing from Flame, more mud, a snarling dash at the hutch.

'Flame!' Mandy yelled in desperation and was relieved when the lurcher stopped, her ears pricked. 'Flame!' Mandy called again. Flame bounded up, thrusting her long nose into Mandy's left hand. Mandy lunged at Flame's collar and clung on. She reached across her body and pulled the rope lead from her other pocket. Without letting go of the collar, she slid the leash over the dog's slim neck and pulled it close, but not tight. Flame shook her head once, making her ears flap, then stood still.

For a moment, Mandy waited in the darkened garden, trying to catch her breath. Then she heard the patio door sliding open.

Mr Hemmings was marching towards her. 'About time!' he roared. 'Thought you'd let your stupid dog have a run in our garden, did you?'

'I had to . . .' Mandy began, but he was yelling again.

'Dangerous animal like that shouldn't be on the loose . . . could have attacked anyone . . . what if it had been the children . . .' Mr Hemmings was red-faced and incoherent with rage.

'She wouldn't attack the children.' Mandy was fairly sure that was true. Flame had never shown any signs of aggression towards people or dogs, just prey animals. But Mr Hemmings wasn't listening.

26

'I know exactly where your rescue centre is. I'm going to call the police and tell them that you have dangerous animals running all over the countryside.'

There was nothing Mandy could say. Even if she was ninety nine per cent certain Flame wouldn't attack a child, there was every likelihood that she would have killed the rabbits if she had broken into the hutch. Even without the rabbits, she could have caused a road accident while she was running around loose. There was no way Mandy could ignore how serious this incident had been.

Flame stalked back through the house on her lead with her tail between her legs. Mandy tried to look calm and cheerful, but she was horrified by the trauma on the faces of the children. She wanted to get down on her knees, to let them get to know Flame, so they wouldn't be afraid. But their father was glaring at her, daring her to say another word.

He opened the front door and Mandy squeezed past him, gripping the lead in her fingers. She was halfway down the path before he spoke again. 'The police will have that dog put down,' he hissed. 'Just you wait and see.'

'Oh, Flame,' Mandy sighed as she put the dog in the car. 'What are we going to do with you?' As she navigated the quiet streets of the estate, she told herself that she had caught Flame with no harm done. Surely the police wouldn't take action against a dog for briefly getting loose? Mandy would double and triple check the fences and maybe put up some extra high bars for the dog training area. If Mr Hemmings did report her, she needed to show she had done everything possible to prevent another escape.

Back at Animal Ark, she put her head around the door to tell Adam that she and Flame were back safely, then walked out to the rescue centre. Despite a warm welcome from Sky, she started her evening tasks feeling very gloomy. After a few minutes, she heard the door open and close.

'Hello, love.' It was her dad. 'Mum's back,' he said. 'I thought you might like a hand out here.'

'That would be lovely,' Mandy said. She was glad to have some human company. Together, they worked through the dogs and the small furries, feeding and cleaning in the endless cycle of care. They finished together in the cat ward. Despite Mandy's worries over Flame, she wasn't too distracted to notice that her dad made a beeline for the ginger cat Tango.

She watched as they purred at one another through the bars before Adam opened the door. Although Tango was affectionate towards her, he seemed particularly taken with her dad. With his eyes half closed in an expression of pleasure, the old cat rubbed his face against Adam's fingers. When Mandy's father bent down, the cat lifted his head, blissfully pushing himself against Adam's cheek.

'You're a sweet old chap, aren't you?' Adam murmured, rubbing his hand along Tango's spine.

Mandy smiled. She was glad she wasn't the only member of the Hope family to be reduced to a puddle by some cute animal interaction.

When all the cats were clean and fed, they made their way back through the veterinary clinic and into the oldest part of the cottage. Kicking off her shoes by the kitchen door, Mandy waited for Adam to finish washing his hands before she took his place at the sink.

There was a pan bubbling on the stove. Emily was stirring it with a wooden spoon, her cheeks flushed with the warmth from the hob.

'Hungry?' Emily asked, looking up with a smile.

'Fairly,' Mandy replied. Even if she wasn't, she knew she had to eat something.

'It's penne Arrabiatta,' Emily announced. 'Everything's ready.'

'I'll serve if you like,' Adam said. 'You two can sit down.'

'I hear you've had a tough afternoon.' Emily's eyes were sympathetic as she took the chair beside Mandy.

Mandy sighed. 'It wasn't great,' she admitted.

'What happened?'

As Adam handed out bowls of pasta, Mandy told her parents everything, from Flame's flying leap out of the orchard and her dash through the field to the horrible showdown in the Hemmings' garden.

When she had finished, Adam reached over and rested his hand on top of hers. 'Poor you,' he said. 'It sounds as if Flame will need a lot more work before she can go off lead again. We could think about raising the height of the fence too, if you like?'

Mandy managed to smile. 'You read my mind,' she said. The telephone rang in the hallway. 'I'll get it,' said Mandy, pushing back her chair. She closed the kitchen door behind her and lifted the handset. 'Animal Ark Veterinary Practice.'

'Hello,' said a brisk female voice. 'This is PC Ellen Armstrong. Is it possible to speak to Amanda Hope, please?'

'I'm Amanda Hope.' Mandy felt her stomach lurch.

'Hi, Amanda. We met up at Lamb's Wood earlier this year, didn't we? You were very helpful with Mr Grimshaw, I recall.'

Mandy pictured the friendly, freckle-faced police officer who had driven her up to Robbie's farm. 'Of course, PC Armstrong, I remember you,' she said.

'Call me Ellen, please. Look, I'm calling about a phone call we've had this evening. I understand a dog escaped from the veterinary clinic and was causing a nuisance. I need to ask you a few questions, I'm afraid.'

'She didn't escape from the clinic.' Mandy tried to keep her voice steady. 'It was from Hope Meadows Rescue Centre.' She gave a potted summary of Flame's adventure, emphasising that she had done everything she could to find and retrieve the lurcher. 'As soon as it's light tomorrow, I'll increase the height of the gate that she jumped over,' she promised. 'And Flame will be kept on a leash until she's had more training.' Would that be enough? Mandy wanted to assure the officer that she was taking the problem seriously. Increasing the height of the gate wasn't too difficult, but if she had to make all the fences higher, it would be expensive.

There was a pause on the other end of the line. Perhaps PC Armstrong was taking notes, Mandy thought. 'Right.' The policewoman's voice was more sympathetic than she had dared to hope for. Mandy unclenched the fingers that were gripping the phone. 'Well, so long as you do everything you can to keep Flame under control, I don't think we need to take this any further,' PC Armstrong went on. Mandy felt a surge of relief. 'But you understand that the escape of a dog is fully the responsibility of the owner, don't you? If there had been a road accident, you would have been liable.'

'I do understand that.' Mandy knew the law only too well, and the potential consequences. Back in Leeds, where she had worked for a year after qualifying, she had sometimes been called out to horrifically injured animals that were too badly hurt to be moved. The police had always been in attendance to oversee the legal issues.

'Just one other thing,' said Ellen.

What else could there possibly be, Mandy wondered. She stifled a sigh. Surely there was nothing else she could actually do, short of promising to keep Flame indoors all the time?

'When Mr Hemmings made his complaint, he told me he wasn't the only one who was concerned about your rescue centre.'

Mandy swallowed, feeling her palm grow clammy against the phone. Animal Ark had been in the village for years without anyone getting upset. Why would there be a problem with Hope Meadows?

'He mentioned people had been talking in the Fox and Goose. They were annoyed about noise from the dogs, it seems?' Again, PC Armstrong didn't sound hostile, but Mandy's heart sank. The question of barking had always been a potential issue. An occasional patient would bark in the clinic overnight, but it was inevitable that with several healthy dogs in the same building it could become more of a problem.

'The dogs do bark sometimes,' Mandy admitted. 'I work hard to train them to be quiet, but it's never going to be perfect.' Although she kept her voice calm, her mind was in turmoil. Who on earth would be complaining in the Fox and Goose? Their nearest neighbours, the ones who would be most affected, had been enthusiastic about Hope Meadows from the start. Mandy spoke to them often. As far as she had known, there had been no ill-feeling whatsoever.

'It's only something Mr Hemmings mentioned.' Ellen's voice sounded reassuring. 'I thought I should give you a heads-up. Just in case.'

'Thank you.' Mandy was still worried. Why didn't people get in touch directly if they had a problem? Hope Meadows was supposed to be a benefit for the local community. The last thing she wanted was for her centre to cause problems.

'Try not to worry about it.' PC Armstrong was speaking again. 'People often mutter to each other. They're much less likely to actually do anything.'

'I just wish they would mutter to me instead.' Mandy closed her eyes and leaned her weight against the wall.

'I've only had one complaint,' Ellen pointed out. 'The Fox and Goose thing is uncorroborated. Please don't take it too much to heart.'

That was part of the problem, Mandy thought. The rescue centre was at the heart of everything that was important to her. 'Thanks for letting me know,' she said, trying not to sound too despondent.

'Thank you for your time, Amanda. I'll let you know if anything else comes up.'

Thank goodness PC Armstrong was so nice, Mandy thought. She knew that conversation could have been much worse. Taking a deep breath and letting it out slowly, she walked back into the kitchen.

'Police?' Adam asked.

Mandy nodded.

'What'd they say?'

'Not a lot.' Mandy sat down and fiddled with her fork. 'I told them I'd check everything and be more careful. That I'd make the gate higher. PC Armstrong agreed that would do for now.'

'Not much else you can do,' Adam replied.

'That's good at least,' Emily put in. 'That they aren't taking it further.'

Mandy was about to mention the barking, but when

she looked at her mum, she was struck by how exhausted she looked. Ever since her return to Welford, Mandy had tried not to be alarmed that her mum seemed so worn out and pale all the time. But on the odd occasion she had asked, Emily had always denied there was anything wrong.

'Tired?' Mandy asked, studying the dark rings around her mother's eyes.

'Oh.' Emily looked almost guilty for a moment. 'Yes, I am actually.'

'Why don't you go up and have a bath?' Mandy suggested. 'Dad and I can clear up. One of us can bring you a cup of hot chocolate later, if you'd like.' Despite her own awful day, she still felt better than her mum looked.

Emily smiled. 'How good you are,' she said. 'Thank you. I will.' Pushing herself upright with an effort, she stood still for a moment, then trailed across, opened the door and disappeared. Mandy listened as the slow footsteps dragged up the stairs.

'Dad?'

Adam, who was ploughing through his second plate of spicy pasta, looked up.

'Is there something wrong with Mum? She seems so tired all the time.'

Adam frowned. 'I know,' he said. 'Sometimes I wish she would take things a bit easier. I should have run out and bought a takeaway so she didn't have to cook tonight. I didn't even think about it.' He ran one hand through his hair, making it stick up.

'But do you think there's something actually wrong?' Mandy didn't like to persist, but she was worried enough about Emily to push on.

Adam shook his head. 'No, your mum's as fit as the proverbial butcher's dog! It's not surprising if she feels more tired these days. It's always been a tough job and we're not getting any younger. I'm slowing down myself, to be honest.'

Mandy felt a slight sense of shock at his words. Somehow, her parents had always seemed ageless. They barely seemed to have changed with the passing of the years.

'Your mum's an adult,' Adam went on. 'If she needs help, she'll ask for it.'

Mandy knew he was right. She had to trust her mum to take care of herself. But meanwhile, she could do more around the house so that Emily could rest properly when she wasn't working. Standing up, she stacked the used plates, opened the door of the dishwasher and started to fill it.

Chapter Four

It was Monday morning. The rush of pets that had become unwell over the weekend was almost over. The Animal Ark waiting room had filled and emptied again. Mandy was working on the last patient of morning surgery.

'If you can just hold his head . . .' she smiled at Mrs Nolan, who was sitting in a chair beside the long-haired collie.

'He's such a good boy,' the older woman commented as she steadied the dog with one hand on each side of his neck. Mr and Mrs Nolan had once run Manor Farm, which lay outside Welford on the same road as Animal Ark. Now they ran the farmhouse as a bed and breakfast and rented the fields to a neighbouring sheep farmer.

Charlie the collie dog was quirkily handsome with one blue eye and a grinning face. Mandy had been delighted when Mrs Nolan specifically asked to see her. When she had first returned to Animal Ark, there had been a few clients who had seemed reluctant to try out a new vet, but that had passed. Grasping the loose skin on the back of Charlie's neck, Mandy slid the needle into place and in a moment had injected the vaccine.

Charlie didn't seem to have noticed. Reaching up, he licked Mrs Nolan, who fended him off with a laugh.

'Here you are, sweetie.' Mandy handed the dog a treat, which he wolfed down, then turned to look for more. 'Oh, go on then,' Mandy said, reaching for another chew. She crouched down to stroke the thick fur on Charlie's chest and without missing a beat, he reached over and licked her ear. Laughing, she pulled herself upright, wiping away the dampness. It was wonderful to work with animals who liked to visit. There were few things she relished more than helping a nervous patient learn that a trip to the vet could be a positive experience.

Mrs Nolan and Charlie left the room, and Mandy sat down at the computer to update the history and write the bill. Once she had finished, unless more clients came in, there would be time to see to a couple of inpatients and her rescue animals before her next call. When she stood up and walked through, Rachel was on the phone at the reception desk. Helen, the veterinary nurse who normally worked during the day, was away for a few days. Rachel mostly worked in the evenings and at weekends, but this week she was working in Helen's place.

She smiled at Mandy as she put the phone back down. 'That's a call for this afternoon,' she said. 'A sheep with a sore foot.'

Mandy walked over and looked at the book in which the large animal appointments and house visits were recorded. 'Mr Thomas,' she read. 'Ainthrop.' She looked at Rachel with a frown. 'Is Mr Thomas a regular client?' she asked. 'I haven't come across him before.'

'He's not been in recently,' Rachel replied, 'but he was here a while back, asking for worming medicine. I think he has a few pet sheep, but I don't know any more than that.'

'Okay.' It didn't surprise Mandy that Mr Thomas's sheep were pets. It was rare for any of their farm clients to call out the vet for a single lame sheep nowadays. Most of them would manage the situation themselves, or bring the sheep into the clinic in the back of a Land Rover. She glanced at the clock. It was already eleven and her next call was at twelve. She sighed.

'Is everything okay?' Rachel was looking at her quizzically. 'That was some sigh.'

Mandy leaned her hands on the desk. 'Everything's fine,' she said. 'Just sometimes there aren't enough hours in the day.'

'Could I help?' Rachel offered. 'If you like, I can clean out Snowie and Bubble at lunch time. The rabbits, too.'

Mandy thought for a moment. Whilst she felt guilty about accepting help from the Animal Ark staff, the small pets in the rescue centre did need cleaning. Rachel was looking hopefully at her, not unlike Charlie waiting for another treat. Rachel always had loved guinea pigs and Mandy had fond memories of helping her with her pets when they were both much younger. 'Thanks,' she said. 'It really would help, just this once.' She was going to have to think about finding a more permanent solution though. If she couldn't afford to pay, perhaps she could find some volunteers.

Half an hour later, she stood outside in the paddock. Melon the West Highland White was galloping back and forth on his short little legs, chasing a tennis ball. He was surprisingly good, dashing across the paddock each time Mandy threw the toy, capturing it, then racing back over to drop it at her feet. Twiglet was outside as well, zooming around, full of energy. It made Mandy smile to watch them. They'd have no trouble finding a new home, she thought.

The mobile phone in her pocket vibrated and she pulled it out. It was Jimmy. Melon dropped the ball at her feet. Mandy threw it again and at the same time clicked the button on the screen. Distracted by the call, she hurled the ball much higher than usual, but Melon, concentrating hard, pursued it as it flew across the paddock. Mandy watched in amazement, then burst out laughing. The little dog, without taking his eye off the missile for an instant, had jumped into the air and turned a complete somersault before landing back on his paws with the ball in his mouth.

'Sounds like someone's having fun!' Jimmy's voice sounded as if he was smiling.

Melon hurtled back to Mandy and sat at her feet looking up at her, shining eyes expectant in the fluffy white face. 'Sorry, I'm playing with one of my rescue dogs.' Mandy lifted the ball and flicked it away.

'No need to apologise. I was just wondering whether you'd like to come back over to the centre. You didn't get a chance to try out the rope course on Sunday. Would you like to have a go?'

Mandy's eyes followed the little Westie as he sprinted across the grass, but this time he had competition. As Mandy watched, Twiglet appeared seemingly from nowhere, grabbed the ball and hared off. She weaved a figure of eight around two of the gnarled apple trees and then dropped to the ground and started to chew. 'That would be lovely,' Mandy gasped, rushing across the paddock to try to rescue the ball. Melon stood staring at the larger dog. There was so much consternation in his expression that Mandy had to stop herself from laughing again.

'The centre is closed on Wednesday . . .'

As Mandy approached, Twiglet dropped the ball on the ground. Making a grab for it, Mandy brought her attention back to Jimmy's words.

'. . . so if you'd like to come over then, we could have a go together.'

'Sorry, Jimmy,' she panted. 'Did you say Wednesday?' She straightened her back, holding on tightly to the ball.

'Yes,' he replied. 'Wednesday afternoon, if you can get away.'

Mandy turned it over in her mind. It had been so long since she'd seen him properly. With all her commitments, she was constantly short of time, and she hadn't felt it was fair to suggest meeting up when her schedule was so hectic. But she was longing to see him. His voice on the other end of the line tugged at both her heart and her conscience. 'I'll ask Mum and Dad if they can spare me for a couple of hours,' she said a few seconds later. 'Would that be enough, if I can get it?'

'That would be fine.' There was a moment's pause. 'I know she won't be able to tackle the rope course, but Zoe and Simba were wondering whether Sky would like to come over as well.'

Mandy laughed. 'Well, she's inside right now, but I think I can answer on her behalf. That would be absolutely lovely.'

The drive out to Ainthrop was exquisite. The sky soared high and blue over the fell tops. Piercing winter sun made the bare trees show up black and stark against the horizon. Not for the first time, Mandy thought how much she loved the Yorkshire Dales in every season. Even with a gun to her head, it would be impossible to choose her favourite time of year.

Ainthrop was a tiny smallholding, its white-painted house set against a backdrop of undulating fields. Putting a few things in the pockets of her jacket, Mandy made her way down the front path. The man who came to the door was wearing a Harris tweed suit with a waistcoat, and looked about a hundred years old. Mandy found herself thinking he looked like something from a film set. He was the perfect image of a 1940s country gentleman with his checked shirt and green tie.

'Mr Thomas?' she asked.

'I am indeed,' the man replied in a surprisingly brisk voice. 'You must be the vet?'

'Yes,' Mandy replied. 'I'm Mandy Hope. You have a lame sheep that needs looking at?'

'Ah yes. Perhaps you could come to the back door?'

Mandy looked down at the wellingtons and waterproof trousers she had already donned. The hallway of Mr Thomas's house looked spotless. She turned around, walked back up the pathway and followed the track that led round to the back of the house. She found Mr Thomas, now resplendent in a drop brim tweed hat, pulling on a pair of immaculate boots on the back doorstep.

'The sheep are out in the barn,' he announced, standing up very straight and gesturing with one hand. There was a stone-paved area at the back of the house: a miniature version of the traditional farm steadings that were scattered throughout the valley. Directly opposite, on the far side of what appeared to be a garage, was a large, brightly painted sliding door. Mandy could hardly believe the old man would manage to open it, but he set his shoulder to the handle and pushed the heavy door until it moved smoothly aside.

Inside was an old-fashioned building of exactly the type Mandy loved most. The thick stone walls had been whitewashed at some time in the distant past. There was hay in a manger and a thick layer of straw on the floor.

Best of all were the three horned ewes that stood there, gazing at them with curious eyes. They were an attractive cream colour and their broad faces and legs were a very pale golden tan.

'How lovely!' Mandy exclaimed. 'What breed are they?' They were quite different from the Swaledales and Blackface sheep she was used to.

'They're Portlands,' Mr Thomas said proudly. 'I've had them since they were lambs.' He and Mandy leaned on the wooden gate that separated the door from the pen. 'It's Daffodil I'm worried about.' He pointed to the smallest of the three, which was standing furthest from them. 'My son came on Saturday to get them inside and we noticed she was limping. I gave her a day or two, but she's still not using it properly.'

Looking closely at Daffodil, Mandy could see that she was indeed taking less weight on her right foreleg. 'Okay.' She smiled at Mr Thomas. 'Let's take a look, shall we?'

The old man unclipped the gate, holding it open for Mandy and closing it once they had both stepped through. The straw was thick and springy underfoot. It was lucky the barn wasn't too big, Mandy thought. She didn't fancy chasing a lame sheep all over the place. Although Daffodil was small, she was eying them warily, her body still but tense with restless anticipation.

Arms outstretched, Mandy and Mr Thomas moved towards the little ewe. For a moment, it looked as if they would trap her easily in the corner and the game would be over, but as they closed in, just as Mandy was about to launch herself, Daffodil shot forwards underneath Mandy's hands and in an instant was gazing at them from the far corner of the byre.

It happened so fast, Mandy wanted to laugh. Daffodil had looked so placid. She still looked fairly chilled out, though she was watching them intently. Again, Mandy and Mr Thomas lined themselves up. This time Daffodil didn't even wait for them to close in before she skipped away. It was amazing what a turn of speed she could build up. *And with only three feet fully functional,* thought Mandy. *Goodness knows how Mr Thomas's son managed to get them inside.*

After three quarters of an hour, Mandy was starting to worry about the old man. While Daffodil was still fresh as a daisy, Mr Thomas was looking exhausted. Even Mandy herself was running out of steam. 'Is there someone else that can come and give us a hand?' she panted.

The old man limped over and leaned against the wall. 'I am sorry,' he wheezed. 'I thought with her being lame, we'd be able to get hold of her easily.' His blue eyes were troubled. 'I don't think there is anyone. My son works, you see. Only in Welford, but he won't be finished till later.'

Mandy leaned on the wall beside him. The three sheep were, by now, thoroughly stirred up. There was no way they could catch Daffodil without a change of plan. 'Do you have any gates or boarding?' she asked after a few moments thought. 'We could build a kind of tunnel for her.' She thought of the pathway of pallets she had built in the summer with the help of Seb Conway, the local animal welfare officer. She should have thought of it half an hour ago, but they had been so close to catching the wily sheep so many times that she'd thought it was only a matter of perseverance.

'We could lift off the gate to the yard,' Mr Thomas suggested, straightening up. Mandy was amazed that he seemed to have recovered so quickly. Despite his sprightliness, Mandy couldn't help but hope the gate wasn't too heavy. When they walked outside, she was pleased to see it was relatively small. Fortunately, the bars were close together. To Mandy's relief, it lifted easily off its hinge and between them they carried it back into the byre.

'We can prop it here,' Mr Thomas said, wedging one end between the bars of the manger. Working together once more, Mandy and the old man drove the ewe into the gap between gate and wall. This time, as she made her dash for freedom, Mandy propelled herself forward and to her relief, caught the ewe by the neck, hauling the wriggling body towards her before moving the animal into the brightest area of the barn.

It was the work of a moment to turn the ewe's head and tip the lightweight body up, so that the sheep was sitting on her rump with her back against Mandy's legs. Her compact feet were black and shiny from the clean straw. Grasping the right fore, Mandy looked closely at the hoof. Both cleats were well shaped and clean, but when she pulled apart the toes, she saw that the area between them was inflamed and looked sore. The red swollen tissue was covered by a thin layer of white.

'She's got scald.' Mandy showed the painful-looking lesion to Mr Thomas. 'Was it muddy where she was outside? It has been raining a lot lately.'

'It was, I'm afraid. We should have got them in earlier, but it was so mild for November, I thought I'd leave them out a bit longer.' The old man studied the little hoof. 'Can you cure it?' he asked.

Mandy checked the foot again. The horn looked healthy and there was no foul smell. 'I think so,' she said. 'Scald is caused by a bacterial infection. It's local-ised, so it should clear up with an antibiotic spray.' She pulled a can of Oxytetracycline from her pocket, glad she'd had the foresight to bring it from the car. Shaking it, she sent a jet of the blue-green aerosol in between the cleats onto the affected skin. 'Would your son be able to help you to treat it again?' she asked.

Mr Thomas nodded. 'He comes here most evenings on his way home,' he said. 'He says he comes to see the sheep but I suspect he's checking up on me!' His blue eyes twinkled under bushy white eyebrows.

Mandy couldn't help but be relieved. It was good to hear that Mr Thomas and the sheep were being looked after.

'Would you like a cup of tea? After all your hard work.'

Mandy sighed as she set the ewe carefully back on her feet. She would dearly love a cup, but she had been ages already. 'Can I just wash my hands?' she asked. 'I'd love to have tea with you, but I really should be getting back.'

The old man smiled. 'Another day then,' he said, and Mandy nodded.

'It's a date!' she promised.

Kicking off her boots at the cottage door, Mandy was pleased to see her mum sitting at the kitchen table with a mug of tea. 'Where's Dad?' she asked.

Emily smiled up at her. 'He's seeing a dog that's cut its paw,' she said. 'How was your call?'

'It was fine.' Mandy walked over and pulled a mug out of the cupboard, then put the kettle on. 'A sheep called Daffodil with mild scald. Her owner, Mr Thomas, was an absolute sweetheart.'

'Lovely. I don't think I've met him yet.' Standing up, Emily grabbed a sizeable box from the counter and placed it on the scrubbed pine table. 'What do you think of these?'

Mandy watched as she slid the lid off. Inside, there was a pile of Christmas cards. Emily pulled one out and handed it to Mandy. On the front was a frosty picture: thick-furred cows and a scattering of sheep in a snow-filled landscape. Beams of wintry sunlight sloped across the scene.

'Beautiful!' Mandy said. 'Are these the practice Christmas cards?' Every year since she could remember, cards had been sent out to their regular Animal Ark clients. Looking down at the picture, Mandy felt a surge of regret. She should have sent out cards for Hope Meadows to her suppliers and contacts. It was too late to order them now for this year. 'I should have had ordered some for Hope Meadows,' she said with a sigh.

Emily's smile widened. 'Look inside,' she urged.

Mandy opened the card and felt her heart lift. '*Merry Christmas and a Happy New Year from Animal Ark and Hope Meadows.*' She was constantly amazed by how much her parents did for her. She couldn't be more proud to have her rescue centre included in the official practice card. Reaching over, she gave Emily a big hug. 'Thank you so much, Mum,' she said. 'These are perfect!'

Chapter Five

'I'm sorry I'm so late.' Mandy stood on the doorstep of Lilac Cottage, where her grandparents had lived for as long as she could remember. Thank goodness she had finished work for the day. She had been called out to a calving after her chat with Emily, then got stuck behind a tractor on the way back. This had made her late for evening surgery, which had been Monday evening crazy.

Dorothy Hope, Mandy's grandmother, smiled. 'At least you're here now,' she said, holding out her arms for a hug. She led Mandy inside.

Grandad Hope, who was waiting in the hallway, took her coat and hung it up. 'You're so busy these days,' he said.

'I hope I haven't ruined your lovely food,' Mandy said apologetically.

There was laughter in Gran's eyes. 'I had enough years of your dad being late for meals that I know not to cook anything that would spoil when I have a veterinary surgeon coming for dinner,' she said. Mandy followed her grandparents through into the dining room. 'I've made some soup,' Gran told her.

Tom Hope pulled out a chair and ushered Mandy into it. There was a crusty loaf on the table. How Gran still managed to find the energy to do so much baking seemed like a minor miracle to Mandy, whose cooking skills were woefully basic. She really should try to learn, she thought, as Gran brought in the soup. It was winter vegetable, filled with onions and sweet potatoes, and with an unexpected kick of chilli.

Tom Hope finished buttering a slice of bread and looked up. 'Anything interesting happen today?'

'I only went on two calls,' Mandy said, 'but they were certainly challenging.' Gran and Grandad were looking at her with both sympathy and interest. 'The first was to a lame sheep up at Ainthrop,' she continued.

'Oh. The smallholding up near Jack Mabson's place?' put in Tom Hope.

'That's the one.' Mandy nodded. Her grandfather's local knowledge never ceased to amaze her. 'It took ages to catch the ewe with the sore foot,' she said. 'Then I had a calving just before surgery.' She flexed the hand that was now grasping her spoon. The muscles of her forearm protested. The calf had been breech and it had been painful working inside the cow as the uterus contracted down on her arm. She had managed to get the rope around the foot eventually, but there had been times when she felt as if her arms had turned to putty.

'Was the calf okay?' Grandad was looking at her proudly, as if he was already confident that everything had been perfect.

'It was fine.' Mandy smiled. Once she had corrected the breech, the calf had slipped out easily. The cow had turned and started to lick the little creature, which in turn had lifted its head. It had started to make its first wobbly attempts at standing up before Mandy had left the farm. She had popped her head back inside the byre after washing up. The calf had managed to stand up with its hind legs and was trying, in ungainly fashion, to co-ordinate its front end.

'Well done you. Should I cut some more bread?' Grandad offered, reaching for the bread knife.

'Yes, please.' Mandy watched as her grandfather carved off a thick slice and moved the plate towards her.

'I was in the post office today.' Gran pushed away her empty bowl and leaned back in her chair. 'They had the most wonderful handpainted Christmas cards. And Gemma Moss was telling me that Reverend Hadcroft has invited the nursery children to perform this year's Nativity in the church. That's something else to look forward to.' She looked at Mandy, who had finished her soup. 'Would you like some more?'

'It's delicious.' Mandy handed her bowl over for a refill.

'I can't believe it's getting so close to Christmas!' Gran exclaimed. 'It feels like no time at all since you were coming back from Leeds and now here you are, quite settled.' It was true, Mandy thought. The time had just disappeared.

'We're so proud of you,' Grandad put in. 'Getting

Hope Meadows up and running without a sniff of trouble. We always knew you could do anything you wanted!'

For a moment, Mandy toyed with the idea of telling them about Flame escaping and all the trouble with Geoff Hemmings. It was remarkable that Gran hadn't been told about this juicy piece of gossip when she was in the post office. It would be better not to tell them, she decided. She hoped the matter had been sorted out now that she had spoken to PC Armstrong. It was old news already.

'So how are things going with that nice young man from Running Wild?' Gran was sitting back in her chair still, but Mandy could see that this was a topic that was close to her heart. Both her grandparents had been wonderfully supportive when she had parted from Simon, the boyfriend in Leeds, with whom she had been planning a very different life before her return to Welford. Though they hadn't actively encouraged her to rush into a relationship with Jimmy, she knew that they had heard good things about him.

'I'm seeing him again on Wednesday.' Mandy felt a warm glow inside when she saw the approval on the two old faces that were gazing at her. Grandad, in particular, had been uneasy about Simon. She was pleased that he seemed to like Jimmy.

'How lovely,' Gran smiled as she held out her hand for Mandy's empty bowl.

'I saw him yesterday,' Grandad put in. 'He was coming

out of Harper's. He'd been buying food for those two gorgeous dogs of his.'

Harper's? The feeling of warmth drained from Mandy as she remembered the unpaid invoice.

'What's wrong?' Grandad was looking at her closely. He knew her too well. Gran had taken the dirty plates to the kitchen, but there was no way she could avoid telling her grandfather.

'There was a mistake in the Harper's bill,' she admitted. 'They hadn't charged me for October. There's not enough in the account to pay the whole thing. I meant to call Sally Harper today but I forgot all about it.' Even as she spoke, she felt guilt rising. How could she have forgotten something so important?

But her grandad was smiling his reassurance. 'It's hardly surprising you forgot,' he told her. 'It's easily done when you're so busy, but it's easily rectified as well. It was their mistake and Sally is lovely. I'm sure she'll do everything she can to help.'

Mandy sighed. 'I know,' she said. 'When I opened Hope Meadows, I knew that it wouldn't always be plain sailing. Things have been ticking over up until now, but it's just thrown everything out a bit.'

Grandad reached out a hand and gave hers a squeeze. 'Try not to worry,' he said. 'Get in touch with Sally tomorrow and if there is any problem, give me a ring. You know we love helping you out.'

For a moment, Mandy felt tears prickling the backs of her eyes. Her grandparents had always been so supportive, but she wanted so badly to prove herself capable of managing. 'Thanks,' she said.

The door swung open and Gran walked in with a delicious looking pink and white Battenburg cake. 'I know it isn't quite Christmas yet,' she told Mandy, with a roguish grin 'but I thought a practice run was quite in order.'

Mandy found her smile again. Gran loved Christmas almost as much as she did and her baking had always been one of the highlights of the season. Grandad was right. Worrying wouldn't help. She would call Sally in the morning and deal with whatever came her way.

She watched as Dorothy Hope carved a generous slice of the cake and took the plate her grandmother held out to her, 'Thank you. It looks wonderful,' she said.

It had started to rain by the time Mandy set out to walk back to Animal Ark. She strode up the lane, the droplets chilly on her face. Her leg muscles were aching, not just from today's work but from a hard session yesterday evening, replacing a prolapsed uterus in a cow. It had taken ages to manipulate the swollen organ back into place. Her back was sore too. It hadn't felt so bad earlier, but Mandy found herself wishing she could go straight into the cottage and fall into bed. Instead she had to go and check her rescue animals. Thankfully, everything was quiet. She stood for a moment with the lights off, gazing out of the rain-smeared window into the darkness, then made her way back over to the cottage and up the stairs.

She met Emily on the landing. Her mum was in her dressing gown, obviously also on her way to bed. 'Good dinner?' her mum asked.

'It was lovely,' Mandy replied. The earlier phone conversation with Jimmy popped into her head. 'Mum, could you and Dad spare me for a couple of hours on Wednesday afternoon, please?'

'I don't see why not,' Emily replied. 'I think you've earned a few hours off.' Mandy was glad when Emily didn't ask for more details. Both she and Adam had been very good since Mandy had moved back in. They rarely interfered or pried into her private life.

Emily gave her a tired smile and Mandy was reminded of her concern for her mother's health. The thought leaped into her mind that perhaps she should cancel Jimmy's invitation and spend the afternoon with her mum instead. Emily had turned away, heading for her bedroom and for a moment Mandy toyed with the idea of calling her back, but it was too late tonight to call Jimmy anyway. She stood on the landing, gazing at the now closed bedroom door, then opened the door to her own room and went in.

Chapter Six

The week went so fast, Mandy was startled to realise it was already Wednesday, and time to meet Jimmy at the rope course. After a hasty lunch, Mandy headed upstairs to her bedroom and inspected herself in the mirror. She needed a haircut, she thought. She could wear her blonde hair tied back, but the layers that framed her face were far too long and were beginning to resemble spaniel's ears.

Pulling the door open, Mandy peered into her wardrobe in the hope of inspiration. Although the November sun was bright, there had been frost on the grass that morning and it was still chilly. She decided on jeans that didn't normally get worn around the animals, and a soft woollen jumper with a matching red hat. To complete the outfit, she pulled on a short padded jacket. Whatever she wore, it had to be practical. They were climbing ropes, not going out on the town. But she wanted to make some kind of effort so she pulled out the mascara she had bought in the summer. The somewhat clumpy results were a marginal improvement, she decided.

Sky was sitting nearby, watching with her head on

one side. Sky's lashes were long enough for anyone. 'You're just lucky in the eyelash department,' Mandy told the collie. Sky tilted her head even further. Mandy smiled. 'Now you're rubbing it in,' she teased.

Mandy took the car up to Welford Hall and pulled into the parking area beside the gate. Stopping the engine, she jumped down and walked round to open the door for Sky. A sharp, cold wind whisked across Mandy's face, lifting her hair and sending a shiver down her spine. There was the slightest hint of wood smoke in the air.

Jimmy was on the far side of the closest paddock. He was wearing his waxed jacket and faded jeans over sturdy hiking boots, with a knitted hat pulled down over his ears. He was bent over a pile of rope, pulling it into a tidy coil.

Mandy let herself into the paddock and set off across the grass, feeling butterflies in her stomach. Apart from the short meeting at the opening ceremony, and their brief chat on the phone, it had been more than a month since she had seen him, she realised. He had been in touch twice since and both times there had been an animal that needed her attention. Not that he would be angry with her. He wasn't like that. The first time she had been unavoidably delayed helping Emily with a gastric torsion operation. The second, she had rushed through to York to help James with a kitten he had found. She hadn't felt able to let her old friend down. Hope Meadows was important to James too; Paul's legacy was inextricably linked to the centre.

But Jimmy had sounded very disappointed when she'd told him. Hopefully he wouldn't bring it up but it was complicated. Sometimes she felt she was investing so much time in her project that there was no space in her head for anything else.

Sky had no such reservations. As soon as the gate swung open, she floated off across the field, a black and white streak racing to meet Zoe and Simba, Jimmy's husky and German Shepherd. The three dogs greeted one another like old friends, tails high in the air, sniffing and circling. Mandy was glad of the distraction.

When she looked up from the dogs, Jimmy was coming towards her, beaming. For a moment, Mandy wondered if he would try to kiss her, but to her relief he stopped short and nodded. 'Hello,' he said, and leaned down to stroke Sky, who had run over to greet him.

'Hi.' Mandy's attention was instantly claimed by Simba and Zoe, who bounced around her demanding a fuss. Mandy bent over them, burying her fingers in their thick fur. As the two dogs licked her face, she could feel some of the tension dissipating.

Jimmy waited until Zoe and Simba had launched themselves after Sky, leaving Mandy alone, before speaking. 'Are you feeling fit?' he asked with a grin.

Mandy flexed her arms. 'Just about!' She took the light-weight leather gloves that Jimmy was holding out to her.

'These will prevent any rope burn,' he explained, pulling on his own pair. 'But this isn't going to be a serious test of military fitness, I promise!'

Side by side, they walked towards the wooden steps that led up to the platform at the start of the course. There was wind in the upper branches of the trees, and Mandy had to duck a waving branch as she climbed. A stray leaf whirled through the air, landing on the ground below. Mandy felt a moment of dizziness.

'Try not to look down!' Jimmy called from the platform. 'If you feel a bit dizzy, just stop and take a few deep breaths.'

Mandy joined him on the wooden ledge. 'I'm fine,' she said, trying not to puff. She gazed around at the treetops. 'What a stunning view!'

Jimmy nodded. 'It gets even better.' He moved to the edge of the platform where a short, sturdy net stretched upwards, higher into the trees.

Jimmy stepped off first, clambering expertly using the horizontal ropes as footholds and pulling himself up with the vertical pieces. Mandy watched him for a couple of moments, then followed. Below, the dogs circled the platform, tipping their heads back to look up. Mandy was tempted to call out but didn't want Sky to try climbing the steps to reach her.

The netting felt rough under her fingers, and she was glad of the leather gloves. Thank goodness her arms were strong from all the cattle work she had been doing. At the top, Jimmy was sitting astride a thick wooden pole. He nodded approvingly as Mandy hauled herself up to stand beside him, wobbling slightly as the net swayed.

'Well done,' he told her, the corners of his green eyes creasing as he smiled.

Mandy grinned back. Jimmy already seemed less like a stranger, and although the ropes were taking Mandy a long way out of her comfort zone, she definitely felt better knowing he was there.

'Now to get over,' he said. 'Come a bit higher so you can get your arm right over the top. Then grab one of the ropes on the far side with your right hand.' He swung himself down so that he was standing next to Mandy and demonstrated. 'Then,' he continued, 'grip one of the ropes on this side with your left hand. That way, you keep yourself stable as you climb over.' He braced himself on either side of the net, then swung his legs effortlessly over the pole and ended up facing Mandy from the other side.

Mandy followed, slightly less elegantly and with a bit of a scrabble to find the net with her left foot, but without losing her handholds.

'That's great,' Jimmy said.

From there, it was an easy scramble down the shorter side of the net to another platform. In front of them was a rope bridge.

'You first.' Jimmy nodded at Mandy to go ahead. His face was flushed from the exercise, and curls of brown hair were escaping from under his hat. Mandy had a glimpse of the small boy he must have once been, climbing trees around his home in the Lake District. It seemed odd that they had grown up more or less at the same time, either side of the Pennines, immersed in the countryside that would become their way of life.

Mandy took hold of the parallel ropes above the knotted bridge and clung on to them as she worked her way across, stepping on the thickest parts of netting and using her core muscles to stop herself from swaying too much. She was halfway across when she felt Jimmy set off behind her. Despite her increasing confidence, she didn't dare turn round and look. When she reached the far side, she felt a sense of breathless achievement. 'This is wonderful,' she enthused as Jimmy joined her on the wooden planking.

Jimmy smiled at her, his head on one side. 'Glad you like it,' he said.

Mandy studied the rest of the course which stretched around the edge of ancient woodland. She couldn't help noticing that Jimmy had kept to his promise and stayed well away from the red kites' nest, and from the centre of the copse where there was the greatest density of wildlife. There was another cargo net to be tackled first. Beyond it hung a series of rope swings, followed by a narrow ladder.

Mandy felt a surge of enthusiasm. 'I can do this!' she whooped. She began pulling herself up the second net, glancing back down to where Jimmy was waiting. He gave her a few moments' start and began to climb just as she slipped over the top. He made it look so easy, hand over hand, feet finding the outer edge of the gaps, close to the knots. As quickly as she could, Mandy made her way down the far side. When her feet touched the ground, she looked up as Jimmy was reaching the top.

Instead of holding the net on both sides and rolling his body over the wooden pole, he leaned over to grab a horizontal rope with each hand, then launched himself head first over the top. For a moment, he hung there, facing outwards. Then with barely a pause, still facing Mandy, he began stepping down the ropes as if they were nothing more challenging than a staircase. Left foot, right foot, he descended, grinning. Mandy watched, marvelling at how nimble he was, and then all at once, Jimmy's foot snagged and he lurched sideways, catching one of the vertical ropes just in time to stop himself landing headfirst on the bark chippings that covered the woodland floor.

The look of alarm on his face was comical. Despite her fright, Mandy found herself laughing. She held out her hand and steadied him as he stepped onto the ground between the net and the next obstacle.

Jimmy shook his head with a rueful grimace. 'That's what I get for trying to impress you,' he said.

'You should know better than to try and impress me near netting,' she said. 'You should have known someone would have to be rescued. First a startled deer, now a clumsy human!' The very first time they met, they had freed a deer that had become tangled in some of Jimmy's ropes.

'Maybe next time I can rescue you,' Jimmy murmured. He reached out a hand, brushing her waist, then his arms were round her, the firmness of his body pressed against hers as he leant down and kissed her, gently at first and then more deeply. His arms tightened. For a moment she felt the beat of his heart against hers, and her mind whirled with pleasure. Then a long furry nose was thrust between them and she found herself pulling away, breathing hard, as Sky tried to burrow into the non-existent gap between them. Her hands were shaking slightly. The kiss had been wonderful – but it had deepened so quickly, and the feelings it had churned up had been almost too intense.

Jimmy grinned, oblivious to the strange feeling that was washing through her. 'Your dog doesn't approve,' he said. His eyes were filled with amusement, but the nervousness Mandy had felt when she first saw him had returned. 'I've thought a lot about you over the summer, Mandy,' Jimmy admitted. He reached out his hand to take hers, and with an almost involuntary movement, Mandy took a step backwards. To her dismay, there was a lump in her throat.

'Is something wrong?' Jimmy asked. He looked worried.

Mandy felt a rush of confusion. She swallowed and gave a tiny shake of her head. 'Not really,' she managed. 'I wasn't . . .' She trailed off, then began again. 'I'm not sure that I'm ready,' she said. She stopped, the lump in her throat making it difficult to speak.

She had to explain, otherwise Jimmy would think she didn't want him in her life and that wasn't the case. There were just so many other things going on with the animals,

her worries about how she was going to fund Hope
Meadows, the complicated bookwork that she was having
to learn. Plus there was the way she was still feeling about
Paul's death, and James – and all those big emotions had
been mixed up even more by the kiss. 'I'm just not ready,'
she said again, swallowing hard. 'It's too soon.' Her toes
were curling. She wanted to explain how she felt, but as
happened so often when thoughts of Paul came into her
head, she found herself fighting off tears.

Jimmy's eyes searched her face. Mandy wondered
what he saw there. She knew she felt hot and flustered.
Her cheeks burned. 'It's okay,' he said after a long pause.
'I wasn't proposing marriage or anything. I just thought
we were getting close. I'm sorry if I misread the situation.' He glanced at the rope swings with their wooden
planks. 'Do you want to go home?' he offered.

Mandy shook her head. He had kept his voice steady,
but she could see hurt in his eyes. 'I don't want to go
home, but can we take things very slowly?' she said. 'It's
just, with Paul and everything and I've been so busy
and . . .' She trailed off. The last thing she wanted was
to use Paul as an excuse. She turned away as a salty
droplet escaped from her eye, and she wiped it from
her face with fingers that trembled.

'Of course.' His face when she turned back to him
was filled with compassion. 'We'll only go as fast as you
like,' he told her. Another tear escaped and he reached
out and wiped it from her cheek with his thumb.

'Can we change the subject please?' Her voice was

thin, but he smiled again and he did as she asked with a look of determination.

'How are you getting on with Lamb's Wood Cottage?' he asked as he helped her up onto the next platform, then showed her how to grip the rope and swing across to the first plank.

For the next few moments, Mandy's attention was taken up by her wobbly navigation across the rope swings, but when they reached the other side, she couldn't help but wish he had chosen another topic of conversation. 'I'm not getting on with it at all,' she admitted.

Jimmy raised his eyebrows. 'I thought everything would be settled by now.'

'It's not.' Mandy shook her head. 'There've been so many problems with the mortgage application.' There was a long pause while he obviously cast around for yet another topic of conversation, but with a sudden sense of pulling herself together, Mandy blurted out, 'I'd have had better luck applying for a mortgage on a house built of straw, even if the cottage was in a wood filled with big bad wolves.'

To her enormous relief, the tension dissipated as Jimmy laughed. He put his hands on his hips, addressing her in a mock serious tone. 'Well, Little Red Riding Hood,' he said, 'unless you want to be running around the forest in the dark, we should think about tackling the rest of the course.'

Mandy smiled back, relief flowing through her. 'Lead on!' she declared, gesturing with her gloved hand.

'That's the last,' Jimmy said half an hour later as they scrambled down one final net onto the hard-packed earth under the trees. 'For today, at least.' Mandy knew there were different elements in other parts of the forest, but the light was beginning to fade. 'Can I interest you in a cup of tea to warm up?' Jimmy asked.

'Yes, please,' she said, glancing at her watch. There was still time before she had to get back for evening surgery. They walked across the paddock with the dogs leaping around them.

Mandy had often wondered where Jimmy lived. Despite her professional visits to Welford Hall, she had never been aware of staff housing near the main yard. After a few minutes' walk along the main road, they turned into a small lane edged with stone walls and tangled verges. Tucked away a couple of hundred yards beyond the junction, Mandy saw a neat redbrick house with a dark slate roof. As they came nearer, she realised it was a pair of old-fashioned farmworkers' cottages. Each house had a white-fenced front garden containing a tree: a leafless cherry on one side, and an ancient, gnarly apple tree on the other, laden with white-berried mistletoe.

Jimmy stopped as they reached the gate of the cottage on the right-hand side, which had the apple tree. He pushed open the gate and stepped back for Mandy to go through. A path led to the white-painted front door. The three dogs pushed past Mandy to race ahead and stand panting on the step.

'Welcome to Mistletoe Cottage,' Jimmy announced.

'What a perfect name!' Mandy said as she admired the bountiful tree.

'Jared Boone, the estate manager for Welford Hall, lives in Cherry Tree Farm.' Jimmy nodded to the neighbouring house before turning to put his key in the front door. It opened with a scraping sound and the dogs rushed forwards as Jimmy stepped in and turned on the light.

The hallway was painted white and there were red tiles on the floor. Mandy wiped her feet on the rough doormat and reached down to pat Sky, who had hung back, suddenly wary of being inside a strange house.

'This way,' murmured Jimmy, heading towards a kitchen at the back. The room looked sparse but functional. There were white-painted wooden cupboards with dark worktops, and an old gas cooker stood near the curtainless sash window. Beyond the glass, the landscape was thrown into shadow by the kitchen light.

Zoe and Simba swirled around the floor while Jimmy stood at the sink to fill the kettle. Opening a cupboard, he pulled out two cream-coloured mugs and from another, he retrieved two teabags from a box. Then he turned round to lean against the counter and smiled at Mandy. He pulled a rueful face as he saw her glancing around the room. 'Sorry about the lack of interior design,' he said.

Mandy, who had pulled out a kitchen chair and sat down, shrugged. 'My interior design skills are much the same,' she confessed. 'Hopefully James is going to steer me in the right direction.'

Jimmy laughed. 'Maybe I should ask James for advice

as well.' He turned away, waiting for the kettle to switch itself off, then poured boiling water into the mugs. 'Milk?' he asked, opening the fridge.

'Yes, please.'

'Come through.' Lifting the mugs, Jimmy headed back out into the hall, waiting for Mandy and Sky to catch up before turning into the living room. It had light blue woodchipped wallpaper and an old-fashioned brick fireplace. 'I need to get the fire lit,' he said. Mandy noticed there was already paper and wood in the grate. Striking a match, he set the paper alight and as it caught, began to place coal from a scuttle onto the sticks. 'I'm afraid it'll take a while to warm up,' he told her.

Mandy stepped across the worn carpet and sank into the sofa. A faint scent of dogs greeted her. 'It's very nice,' she said.

Jimmy's green eyes held relief. 'Just need to wash . . .' He waggled his coal-blackened fingers. 'Back in a minute.'

Mandy sat back and studied the room, with one hand resting on Sky's head. The only ornament was a pewter pot on the mantelpiece that seemed to be filled with pens. In the corner beside the fire, a small TV stood on a pine stand. There were two dog beds on the far side of the fireplace, though for now, Zoe and Simba were sprawled on the rug in front of the fire.

'Would you like a bun?' Jimmy appeared in the doorway, clutching a round cake tin. Removing the lid, he held it out to Mandy. Inside there was a small pile of fairy cakes. They were all different shapes and sizes and garishly iced. Some were green, some pink, with multi-coloured hundreds and thousands scattered over the tops. 'The twins were over at the weekend,' he explained. 'We made them together.'

Mandy tried not to smile at the thought of Jimmy painstakingly decorating fairy cakes with eight-year-old Abi and Max. She helped herself to a pink one. 'Thanks,' she said. The little sponge cakes tasted better than they looked, she decided a moment later as she chewed. 'They're lovely,' she declared.

Jimmy looked pleased as he sat down beside her. 'They are, aren't they?' he agreed.

'How long did it take you to make them?' she asked. 'Last time I made a cake it took me all afternoon. Even then, it was barely edible. You'd think after all those years watching Gran I'd be an expert.' She took another bite.

Jimmy reached out and took one of the pink fairy cakes, holding it aloft on the palm of his hand as if it was a work of art. 'Magnificent, isn't it?' He grinned. 'It took us all afternoon as well,' he admitted, 'but at least they taste good.'

There was a flurry of black and white fur and Jimmy found his hand suddenly empty. The look of consternation on his face was so comical, that Mandy laughed. 'It appears that Sky agrees with you,' she said.

Jimmy looked over at the fireplace, where Sky had retreated, having wolfed the cake straight down. She looked pleased with herself, thought Mandy. 'I guess she still needs a bit more training around food,' she said.

Jimmy considered Sky, his head on one side. 'She was so thin when you got her, she probably had to take all the opportunities she could,' he said. Reaching out, he took another cake from the tin. 'Will she be all right after eating the paper case?' he asked.

Mandy watched as Sky edged closer to Zoe, who was lying as close to the fire as possible. Her beloved collie seemed to be feeling much more at home as she curled up beside the other dogs. She did too, she realised. It was cosy sitting together in front of the warming blaze. 'She should be fine,' she replied. 'It's not the first time she's eaten something she shouldn't.'

'At least she's in good hands if anything does go wrong.'

Jimmy held the cake tin out to her again. Mandy, hungry from her exertions on the rope course, took a green one and bit into it. 'Have you been busy with visitors yet?' Mandy asked. She had been so busy herself that she hadn't had much time to wonder how Jimmy's new venture was going.

'Not bad at all. Especially considering it's November,' Jimmy said. Mandy lifted her mug from the scratched coffee table and took a mouthful of tea. Although the cakes were charming, they were sweet. 'I've a big group coming in next week from Leeds,' Jimmy said. 'How about you?' he went on. 'I guess you're rushed off your feet trying to run Hope Meadows as well as working as a vet.'

'You could say that,' Mandy agreed. 'Mum and Dad have mentioned the idea of getting a new vet in. They haven't made up their minds yet. I guess they'll see how busy it is in spring with the three of us and then decide.'

'Is your work very seasonal?' Jimmy asked.

'Well, there's more farm work in the autumn and winter, then even more in spring,' Mandy said. She felt very much at home, talking to him about Animal Ark. 'Summer is the easiest time, which was helpful for setting up Hope Meadows.' She glanced at her watch. 'I'm afraid I'm going to have to get back,' she said with a sigh. 'It's been lovely, though.' It was absolutely true, she thought, in spite of the moment of awkwardness earlier. Jimmy was so kind and funny, and she had enjoyed a few hours away from the pressures of the surgery and her rescue animals.

Mandy finished off the last of her tea and shifted to the edge of the sofa. He had been so understanding earlier when she had asked if they could take things slowly. She should probably suggest something suitable, but her mind was blank.

'Will you have dinner with me on Friday?' To her relief, Jimmy spoke first. 'Not here,' he added. 'How about the Fox and Goose?'

Mandy smiled at him. The Fox and Goose was familiar and comfortable. It was hard to imagine anywhere she would feel more at home. 'That would be perfect,' she said. Together they walked out to the hall and Jimmy held out her jacket. Rather awkwardly, she slipped her arms into the sleeves. 'Thanks for the tea,' she said. 'And the lovely afternoon.'

As she turned back towards him, Jimmy reached out and with only a moment's hesitation, she slid into his arms. There was none of the intensity there had been earlier, but Mandy still felt as if she was floating by the time he released her. His green eyes searched her face as he released her and he seemed satisfied as he smiled his friendly grin.

'Okay?' he asked.

'Very okay,' she replied. Calling to Sky, she made her way to the gate and turned back for one last glance. Jimmy was standing in the open doorway. Giving him a wave, Mandy tugged the gate closed behind her.

Sky looked up at her expectantly. 'Come on, girl!' said Mandy. 'Time to go home.'

Chapter Seven

Mandy took a deep breath and bent down to unclip the lead from Flame's collar. Even though the height of the gate had been raised, she still felt anxious every time she let Flame run loose. Mandy swallowed the urge to call to the golden lurcher as she zoomed around the paddock. It was important for all the rescue dogs to be able to run off lead; human legs couldn't give them enough exercise on their own. Mandy dug her hands in her pockets and watched Flame pick up a scent. With her nose fixed to the ground, the long-legged animal made a dash towards the hedge that separated the paddock from the road.

Mandy's breath caught. Where there had been solid bushes before, now there seemed to be a flat patch of shadow a third of the way up the hedge. Could it be a gap? She sprinted over just as Flame launched herself at the hole, her furry body wriggling with excitement. Mandy lunged forwards as if she was tackling a rugby player and felt her fingers close around Flame's collar. Her knees thudded to the ground and she stayed there for a moment, panting. When she had caught her breath, she began to disentangle Flame from the branches. The lurcher backed out, snuffling and shaking scraps of leaf from her ears. She was still straining to follow the scent so Mandy kept a firm grip on the collar as she clipped the lead back on. She peered at the gap in the hedge. She was sure it hadn't been there yesterday. Once Flame was indoors, she would have to come back and look properly.

Flame looked crestfallen when Mandy shut her back into her kennel. The lurcher circled on her bed a couple of times and then flopped down with a sigh, as if she felt life was very unfair. 'Better to be shut in here than roaming the streets of Welford,' Mandy told her, slipping a treat through the bars. She headed outside, crossed the paddock, and crouched down to investigate the hole. It was hardly bigger than a flowerpot, but Mandy could see straight through to the lane on the other side. In a way, it was lucky it had been Flame trying to escape. One of the smaller dogs would have been through and away.

Mandy frowned. The gap was very strange. If it had been made by an animal trying to burrow through the hedge, she would have expected a hole at ground level and the earth at the base to be scraped. This was higher up, above the level that a rabbit or even a badger would reach. Some of the branches seemed to have been bent back deliberately, threaded in among the other twigs to leave a clear break. Had someone actually tried to make a hole in Mandy's hedge?

She gave herself a mental shake. Was she just being paranoid after her conversation with PC Armstrong? Even if some of her neighbours didn't like the noise of barking, was that enough to make them want to help the dogs escape? The thought that someone would be willing to risk the life of any of her animals made Mandy feel sick. Working with her fingers, she bent the wood back into place and did her best to cover the hole. Until the branches grew back, she would need to cover the gap. For the moment, she pulled a pallet into place. Later she would find something more permanent. As she shoved the pallet into position, the phone in her pocket began to ring.

'Hi, Mandy. Seb Conway here.'

'Seb!' Despite the distractions of the morning, it was always good to hear Seb's voice. 'What can I do for you?'

She could hear a smile in the animal welfare officer's voice as he replied. 'Can you meet me in Walton? I've got a bit of a challenge for you . . .'

Half an hour later, Mandy drove into one of the older roads on the far side of Walton. In spite of her worry about the hole in her hedge, she was interested to see what Seb had in store for her. He had received a report about two donkeys being kept in a back garden, and Mandy couldn't help hoping that the information was wrong. The houses here were detached and the gardens were large, but donkeys needed at least half an acre of land each to provide sufficient grazing. The area seemed so pristine that she couldn't imagine anything so homely as a donkey fitting in. Had Seb's witness been mistaken?

She was almost at the address Seb had given her. Turning the final corner, she spotted Seb's blue and white council van standing outside a sizeable house with a tidy garden. A small tree stood in the centre of a clipped front lawn. As she pulled up, the door of Seb's van opened and the welfare officer, looking smart in his black waterproof jacket, climbed out and locked the door behind him.

'Morning!' he called as Mandy opened her car door and hopped out.

'Hi, Seb.' Although she had done a good number of welfare visits before, Mandy still felt a surge of adrenaline. Most owners resented or feared the appearance of the welfare officer, and situations could quickly become tense, aside from any problems with the animal. Side by side, Mandy and Seb walked up the driveway to knock on the glossy white door.

The bell chimed inside and there were sounds of frenetic claws and agitated barking. A woman in a red sweater and fitted black trousers opened the door. As well as the toddler on her hip, there were two slightly older children dancing about behind her. The barking came from a brindle Staffie, half-hiding behind the woman's legs.

'Can I help you?' she asked. Mandy felt a burst of sympathy for the woman. She looked tired out and now, seeing Seb in his black jacket, there was alarm on her face too. 'Is something wrong?'

Seb smiled. 'Good morning. Mrs Powell? My name

is Sebastian Conway, and I'm from the local council. We've had a report that there are two donkeys being kept in your back garden,' he said. 'Is it possible for us to have a look, please?'

The woman frowned as she opened the door wide. 'You're welcome to look at them,' she said. From her expression, Mandy couldn't help wondering whether the woman had enough to do without two donkeys added into the mix. As they walked through the house, Mandy glanced around. There were toys on the floor, but the carpet looked new and well maintained. A real Christmas tree stood in one corner of the living room, surrounded by boxes of ornaments and tinsel. The Staffie bounced beside Mrs Powell, barking, but it looked fit and in good condition.

To Mandy's surprise, one of the children rushed up and took her hand. She had a large green bow in her hair and a sweet face. 'Are you here to see Robin and Holly?'

Mandy looked down, feeling like a giant. 'Are they your donkeys?' she asked.

'Yes,' the child replied. 'I'm Mia.'

'Well then, yes, Mia,' Mandy said. 'We've come to check how they are.'

Mia's older brother reached up for Mandy's other hand. He had dark hair and dark eyes with a slightly wary expression. 'What's your name?' Mandy asked, half delighted, half taken aback by the friendly children.

'I'm Stephen.' He stared up at her. 'Come on,' he said. 'We'll show you.' One on either side, they tugged Mandy towards the back door. Glancing over her shoulder, she could see Seb following behind. He looked as if he was trying not to laugh.

Mrs Powell looked even more strained once the back door was open. No wonder, Mandy thought as she looked around. Where there should have been neat flower-beds, there were millions of tiny hoof-prints. The lawn had been churned up, sticky November mud showing through the shorn grass. Worse, there was a privet hedge along the back fence. Although there was no sign that it had been eaten, it was completely unsuitable to enclose animals. Fortunately the berries were past, but the plant itself was poisonous to donkeys. The heather plants in the rockery hadn't been so lucky. There was no sign of living creatures, but Mandy noticed a small garden shed in one corner. Were the donkeys in there, she wondered?

Mrs Powell noticed the direction of Mandy's gaze. 'The kids love them,' she said, her voice hollow with resignation, 'but I had no idea how much trouble they'd cause.'

In one respect, it was a relief that she was willing to admit that there were donkeys in the back garden; Mandy never ceased to be astonished by what people tried to hide from Seb. They had found a bull mastiff crammed into a bathroom cupboard before now, with the owner swearing blind he'd never had a dog in the house. But it was so frustrating to look at the mess these donkeys had made of the tidy suburban garden without the house-holders realising they needed somewhere completely different to live.

Mandy bit back the flood of words that tried to burst out. Why didn't people do some research before rushing out to buy pets? Or even just engage their brains? 'The garden's not suitable for donkeys, I'm afraid,' she said, once she had full control of her tongue.

Mrs Powell shook her head. 'They're miniature donkeys,' she said. 'The breeder told us they'd only grow to the size of a large dog. He told us it would be fine.'

Mandy narrowed her eyes. Even miniature donkeys would need more space than this.

Mia let go of Mandy's hand. 'They're in here,' she announced, stepping up to the shed with a proud smile. Pushing down the latch, she stepped back and let the door swing open.

Two grey fluffy shapes rushed out of the shed, kicking their heels and tossing their heads. Despite the sweetness of their furry faces and dark eyes, Mandy felt a jolt of alarm. Although the donkeys were not much bigger than a Labrador, they looked slim, their muscles not yet fully formed. Their legs seemed overly long. 'How old are they exactly?' she asked.

'The breeder said they were two years old,' Mrs Powell said.

Mandy studied the donkeys. They were rushing in circles, skidding to a halt leaving hoof marks in the lawn, then trotting off again, delighted to be outside. Mandy hadn't come across many miniature donkeys, but her instinct was telling her this pair didn't look anything like two years old. 'I'll need to check their teeth,' she said. She would keep her doubts to herself until she was sure.

'Are you able to catch them for us?' Seb sounded dubious as he addressed Mrs Powell.

To Mandy's surprise, Mrs Powell was surprisingly efficient. She walked inside the shed and shook some food into a metal bucket. At the sound of the pellets, the two skittish animals made a bolt past them and rushed inside. Mandy and Seb slid in as well, pulling the door shut behind them. Though the shed was clean, it was very small for the donkeys to live in.

Two little headcollars hung on the wall, one pink, one blue. In the cramped space inside the shed, she and Seb managed to trap first one and then the other of the donkeys. It was obvious they didn't like having the head-collars in place and were not used to being led. It wasn't bright enough in the shed for her to examine them properly, so holding tightly to the ropes, they opened the door and manoeuvred the reluctant animals back outside. As far as Mandy could see, they were both in good health. Their fur was soft, especially behind their outrageously long ears. Holly in particular seemed to love being stroked. Mandy was not surprised when she lifted Robin's tail to discover that the little animal was uncastrated. If they were as young as she thought, it was better for his health that he had not been neutered yet, but it was likely to make him harder to handle as he grew.

All that remained was to check their age. Mandy's

suspicions were confirmed when she finally managed to check Holly's mouth and discovered that the little donkey still had milk teeth. The outermost incisor was not even through. A quick check in Robin's mouth showed the same thing.

'They're not miniature donkeys,' she announced, straightening up. 'They are foals.' And not really old enough to be weaned, she thought with a wave of anger at Mrs Powell's ignorance and the deliberate deception on the part of the breeder. He or she was at least as much to blame for these baby donkeys ending up in such an inappropriate home.

'I'm afraid it's not suitable for livestock to be kept in such a small space,' Seb told Mrs Powell, who was still holding the baby.

'But they aren't foals,' Mrs Powell objected. 'They're miniature.'

'They are not miniature,' Mandy insisted. 'They're young. In eighteen months' time, they'll be fullgrown donkeys.'

'Well, it isn't our fault.' Mrs Powell's mouth was set in an obstinate line. 'The breeder lied to us.'

Mandy looked at Seb, who let out a sigh before speaking. 'It doesn't really matter who's at fault,' he said. Mandy was impressed by his patience. 'They need a proper field.'

'And a shelter,' Mandy put in. 'The garden shed's not big enough even now. Donkey's coats aren't waterproof. And they probably still need milk. Have they been wormed?' She came to a halt. Mrs Powell was starting to look horrified.

'We can't afford anything fancy like that,' she protested. Mandy found herself wondering how much they had paid for the donkeys. Very likely they hadn't been cheap.

Behind them, a door slammed. Mandy turned to see a man in a black jacket and designer jeans striding across the churned lawn. He walked straight up to Seb, stopping so close his nose was almost touching the welfare officer's face. 'What's this?' he demanded, glaring round from Seb to Mandy, to the children and then back. Mandy noticed that the children had fallen silent and were staring at the man with worried eyes. 'What're you doing with my donkeys?'

Seb took a discreet step backwards, keeping his expression bland. 'We heard that there were donkeys being kept in a back garden,' he explained. 'I'm Seb Conway. I'm the welfare officer. And this is Amanda Hope. She's a veterinary surgeon.' Mandy was impressed by how calm Seb seemed to be. 'I appreciate that you bought these donkeys with the best intentions, but I'm afraid the garden isn't a suitable place to keep them.'

Mr Powell seemed to swell inside his clothes and the back of his neck turned red. Mandy froze, wondering whether she should try to do anything, but she had no idea what.

'They're my donkeys and they're fine!' Mr Powell shouted.

Holly, the little jenny, backed away. Mandy let her go,

though she kept hold of the rope. Robin, who was standing with Seb, also retreated to the end of his lead rope.

'Think you can just walk in here and start ordering us round, do you?' Mr Powell continued in a growl. 'Pair of do-gooders. You country types are all the same.' By now he was jabbing his finger at Seb.

Robin suddenly jerked his head backwards before skittering off to the side. Mandy only just jumped out of the way as he barrelled past, then tried to stamp on the rope as it slithered after him. She missed and only succeeded in splashing herself with mud. Robin rushed off across the lawn, leaving a trail of fresh divots.

Mandy clenched her hands, digging her fingernails into her palms. She reminded herself that the Powells hadn't done any deliberate harm to the donkeys, and they had bought them in good faith that they would be tiny pets. *But you can't keep any kind of donkey in a garden!* Mandy raged internally. She was again impressed by Seb, who merely moved away from Mr Powell, turned to her and said, 'Give me a hand getting him caught, would you?'

Mandy handed Holly's rope to Mrs Powell. 'Hold that tightly,' she told the alarmed-looking woman. 'Don't wrap it round your hand. You might get hurt.'

With the lead rope trailing behind Robin, it wasn't too hard to catch the little jack. Both Mia and Stephen looked tearful now, as if they realised their donkeys were in trouble. Once Seb had hold of Robin, Mandy went back and took Holly's rope from Mrs Powell.

Mr Powell shook his head. 'I want you to leave now,'

he ordered, gesturing to the side gate. 'I've had enough of your interfering.' His eyes flashed when Mandy and Seb didn't move at once. 'Did you hear me?' He seemed to be coming closer and closer to boiling point. Mandy stood motionless, clutching Holly's rope, hardly daring to breathe.

'You're still here.' Now Mr Powell was shouting directly in her face. From the corner of her eye, Mandy saw a head appear at the fence, then another. Great. They were attracting a local audience.

Seb had his phone out and was dialling a number.

Very slowly, holding her hands palm outwards, though still clinging to Holly's rope, Mandy backed away from the angry man. She needed to talk to Seb about what they were going to do. The donkeys weren't safe here, with too little space and that privet hedge, but Mandy didn't want to provoke Mr Powell any more than they had already done.

There were now about five heads looking over the fence, staring at the tableau of donkey welfare. The situation seemed ludicrous. Mandy moved as close as she could to Seb. 'Should we leave?' she asked.

'You're probably right,' Seb replied quietly. 'We should put them back in the shed,' he suggested. 'Leave the headcollars on. Give Mr Powell time to calm down.'

But as Mandy started to lead Holly forward, the air was split by the noise of sirens from the street outside.

Chapter Eight

Mandy froze. Squinting over at Seb, she saw him glance in alarm towards Mr Powell.

'I said it wasn't an emergency,' Seb said in a thick voice.

Mr Powell strode across the lawn, swearing under his breath. Mia and Stephen had retreated behind their mother.

'Maybe you should calm down, Jason.' Mandy looked at Mrs Powell in surprise. Her words made no apparent difference to her husband, but Mandy was amazed that the woman had said anything at all.

A handsome dark-skinned face peered over the garden gate. Mandy, who was not far from the fence, tugged Holly over and opened the latch. Two police officers stepped into the garden, hats tucked under their arms. 'I'm Sergeant Dan Jones, and this is PC Ellen Armstrong.'

Mandy didn't know whether to feel relieved or alarmed at seeing PC Armstrong. On one hand, it was nice to see a familiar face. On the other, yet again Mandy and her rescue animals were at the centre of trouble which required police attention. She studied the officer with

Ellen. She was pretty sure Sergeant Jones had been at Lamb's Wood too, but she hadn't had a chance to speak to him. Despite the intensity of the situation, she couldn't help but take an interest in the man who she knew was married to Jimmy Marsh's ex-wife. He looked fearless, she thought, and intelligent.

It didn't take long for Mr Powell to react. He marched towards them, his head extended like a gamecock about to attack. 'This just gets better, doesn't it?' he grunted. He held out his wrists. 'Well go on then,' he taunted, 'arrest me, why don't you?'

'That won't be necessary,' Sergeant Jones said calmly. 'We're only here to support Mr Conway.'

Both of them turned to look at Seb, who was looking faintly incongruous, holding on to a knee-high donkey. Seb in turn looked at Mandy, his eyebrows raised.

'The foals can't stay here,' she said. 'The garden isn't big enough and there are poisonous plants.'

'Utter rubbish,' Mr Powell objected. 'You've no idea what you're on about. They're not even foals, they're miniature donkeys.'

Mrs Powell, however, straightened up as if she was relieved to hear what Mandy had said. Looking down at Mia and Stephen, who were standing as close to her as they could, she began to explain. 'I know you love Robin and Holly,' she said, 'but this lady,' she pointed to Mandy, 'she's a vet and she says we haven't got enough room. They're not as old as we thought. They're still growing and they won't be able to fit in the garden.'

Mia's lip began to wobble. There were tears in Stephen's eyes. Mandy crouched down at the end of Holly's lead rope, looking at the children on their own level. 'I won't be taking them far away,' she promised. 'You can come and visit them while they're staying with me, if you like.'

Stephen blinked, and Mia nodded bravely. But Mr Powell hadn't finished. 'I don't know how you've got the nerve to talk to my kids,' he said. 'Those donkeys were their Christmas present and you're stealing them before Christmas is even here. Christmas is ruined now. Your fault. Stupid interfering cow.'

First Mia's mouth opened and a loud wail burst out, then Stephen screwed up his face and began sobbing loudly. The toddler in Mrs Powell's arms joined in too.

Mandy reached into her pocket and took out her mobile. 'Could you hold Holly for a minute please, Ellen?' she mouthed at the PC and held out the lead rope. Ellen stepped forward and took it. Dialling the Animal Ark number, Mandy turned away as far as she could, pressed the phone against her head and stuck her finger in her other ear to block out the sound of howling children and Mr Powell's chuntering.

She was glad when Adam answered. 'Hi Dad,' Mandy said, as clearly as she could manage. 'I need you to bring the trailer to Walton, if you can. I need to pick up a pair of donkeys.' She had bought the secondhand trailer from Brandon Gill for a very reasonable price and she was glad of it now. Otherwise, they could have been scrabbling round all night, trying to find transport.

'Is everything okay?' Adam asked, having taken down the address and repeated it back to Mandy.

'Fine,' she assured him. 'There's a bit of a fuss going on, that's all.'

After another tense thirty minutes, she was heartily glad when her father arrived. Mr Powell had finally tired of throwing insults, but was telling the children and the neighbours and anyone else who would listen that nobody had the right to take away his Christmas donkeys. What they were doing was theft. Mrs Powell hadn't tried to argue with her husband any more. She looked defeated, Mandy thought.

With the help of her dad and Seb, Mandy ushered first Holly and then Robin up the ramp into the trailer. She was glad the two little animals weren't any bigger. She and Adam almost had to lift Robin on board, linking hands behind him and pushing as Seb stood in front with the lead rope. When the donkeys were safely inside the trailer, Adam climbed into the front seat of the Discovery.

Seb spoke to Mr Powell once more. 'I know you don't agree, but we're not stealing your donkeys,' he explained. 'We're taking them away,' and now he was talking over the aggressive man's voice, 'to somewhere suitable until you can find somewhere better for them to live. They need a properly fenced field and a watertight shelter, at the very least.'

'What if we can't find anywhere?' Mrs Powell's face looked unexpectedly hopeful at the idea the donkeys might not have to come back. 'Will you keep them?'

Mandy glanced at Mr Powell, who was turning purple again. 'Let's not think about that now. I can have them for four weeks,' she said, 'which gives you plenty of time to look for a field.'

'Can we go inside?' Seb said to Mrs Powell. 'There's some paperwork we have to complete.' Mrs Powell headed back to the door with her children trailing after her. Sergeant Jones and PC Armstrong stood beside Mr Powell while Mandy climbed into her car. As she drove off behind her father with the trailer, she glanced in the rear-view mirror and saw Mr Powell glaring after her. She took a long, shuddery breath. They hadn't trained her for baby donkey conflict at vet school!

It was a relief to get back to Hope Meadows. Fortunately, for the moment, the two donkeys were the only large animals Mandy had in so there was plenty of room. Adam backed the trailer into the paddock and by the time Mandy had parked up and joined them, he and Helen Steer, who had returned from her holiday, were lowering the ramp.

'Oh, they're so sweet!' Helen gasped as the two grey shapes trotted out from the back of the trailer. Robin looked around the paddock, comically long ears pricked. Holly dropped her head to the ground and snorted at the grass. After a pause, the pair skipped around the paddock, exploring every corner.

'I'll help you get the straw,' Helen offered after they had watched the donkeys make a complete circuit of the orchard. She and Mandy gave the empty field shelter a thick layer of bedding and filled the water tub. When they returned, the foals were staring through the fence at the fellside as if they were dreaming of even bigger adventures.

'We'll give them a day or two to settle in,' Mandy said, 'then we can make a start on getting them trained.'

When she turned to go back in, she caught sight of the pallet that she had leaned against the hedge earlier. 'Could you give me a hand?' she asked Helen. 'There was a hole in the hedge this morning. I put that pallet over it, but I need to find something better.'

Helen frowned. 'A hole in the hedge? How did that happen?'

'I really don't know,' Mandy admitted as she led Helen over. Together, they pulled away the temporary barrier and crouched down to inspect the strange gap. 'Do you think it looks man-made?' Mandy said. 'It doesn't look as if an animal did it.'

'I see what you mean.' Helen's voice was doubtful. 'But who on earth would want to do that? Don't the locals think our dogs are wild and unsafe?'

Mandy could tell that Helen was trying to make a joke, but she was finding it hard to see the funny side. It was bad enough that Flame had been in danger once, running loose on the roads. If it happened again, Mandy's reputation would unravel faster than an old sweater.

'I don't think you should worry.' Helen's voice had sobered as if she had realised Mandy wasn't in the mood for humour. 'Surely nobody would be mean enough. It must have been some kind of accident. Maybe it was a car?'

It would be odd if there had been an accident of any sort in the lane without them knowing about it, but it wasn't impossible, thought Mandy. Perhaps someone had run off the road and their car had done the damage. But she couldn't see how a car could have struck the hedge and made such a neat hole. With a mental shrug, she helped Helen stuff the gap with short pieces of plank and tie them in place with wire.

'Jimmy's invited me to the Fox and Goose for dinner tonight,' Mandy said as she rotated her pliers to hold two ends of wire together.

'Great!'

Mandy felt her cheeks turn pink as Helen stared at her. 'We're taking things slowly,' Mandy told her.

'Really?' Helen looked as if she was trying not to smile. 'I thought you liked him.'

'I do,' Mandy admitted. 'There's just so much going on here,' she waved her pliers towards the rescue centre, 'and with trying to buy the cottage and . . . well, we've both got too much going on.' She didn't tell Helen she thought Jimmy deserved someone less busy. The nurse would tell her she was being daft. And she couldn't even begin to explain the complicated guilt she felt when she wasn't putting Hope Meadows and James first. Her friend needed her, but even he would tell her to go ahead. She closed her mouth, feeling the silence grow.

Helen didn't seem to notice. She reached up and

Lucy Daniels

patted Mandy's arm with her gloved hand. 'I can see it might be difficult,' she said. 'You're right to take your time, but don't . . .' She paused for a moment, frowning. 'Don't close yourself off too much. I know this job can be all-encompassing, but you have to pace yourself. Jimmy seems like a really nice person,' she pointed out. 'Think of how much he helped with the rescue at Lamb's Wood. And we both know he's gorgeous!' There was a smile in her eyes. 'I almost turned down Seb,' she added, 'because I didn't feel ready. But I'm not having any regrets at all.'

Mandy knew Helen was right. She would be a fool to push Jimmy so far away that she missed the opportunity altogether. Being a grown-up was so complicated! Then she thought of James, wracked with grief for his husband Paul, and she reminded herself how lucky she was that no one she loved dearly had died.

'Okay then, oh Wise Woman,' she said with a grin as she twisted the last wire into place and straightened up. 'I'm not going to rush into anything, but I won't rush in the other direction either. Is that good enough for you?'

Helen stood up too, rubbing her spine. 'That'll do nicely,' she said.

92

Chapter Nine

Looking in the mirror several hours later, Mandy frowned. How come other people looked so good in make-up? It changed the outlines of her face in a way that made her uncomfortable. Reaching for a paper hankie, she blotted off some of the lipstick, blurring the hard lines, and peered at herself again. Better, she thought. She looked more like her normal self.

She had worked and socialised with Simon, her previous boyfriend, before they had started dating. By the time they became a couple, Mandy had felt totally comfortable around him. Not that she hadn't wanted to look decent, both for herself and for him, but she had felt confident that Simon liked her just as she was. She felt like she needed to make more of an effort for Jimmy, especially as tonight they would be indoors, in the pub, rather than striding around the fells. Mandy knew his ex-wife was a beautician. There was no way she was going to match up to professional standards!

Glancing at her watch, she stood up. At least she didn't have to worry about cold wind and rope burns today. She was wearing a cream cashmere sweater that she loved, over a pair of skinny black jeans that made the most of her long legs. A smart pair of black boots completed the outfit. It wasn't as if she and Jimmy didn't know one another already, she reminded herself. They'd even kissed. And he had been kind afterwards when he could have made things awkward. Tonight would only be a big deal if she chose to make it one.

Mandy walked downstairs with Sky at her heels, trying to ignore the butterflies in her stomach. Going to the Fox and Goose should be like visiting an old friend, but Mandy couldn't help remembering the phone call with PC Ellen. Were people in the pub really gossiping about the new rescue centre?

Adam and Emily were sitting at the kitchen table, finishing dinner. Both looked up as she entered the room. 'You look lovely,' Emily said with a smile. Mandy found herself smiling back.

'I hope the young man in question will have you back at a reasonable hour,' Adam teased.

'I'll let him know that you'll be waiting up with a rolling pin,' Mandy joked. Bending down, she gave Sky a hug. 'You need to stay here,' Mandy told her. Sky gazed up at her and gave a little whine.

'Don't worry, Sky,' Adam said. 'We're getting left behind too.'

Emily seemed to sense that Mandy was feeling jittery. 'You go and have a lovely evening,' she urged. 'We'll look after Sky for you. Come here, girl.' With a last glance at Mandy, Sky crept over and lay down at Emily's side with a sigh.

'Thanks, Mum.' Mandy pulled on her coat and stuffed her purse into the pocket. 'See you later!'

Jimmy was waiting for her outside the Fox and Goose. He was dressed in a tight-fitting black polo neck with a jacket over the top and straight-leg jeans. Mandy couldn't help being impressed. Get a grip, she told herself, trying to ignore the flush that she could feel creeping across her cheeks.

Jimmy seemed very pleased to see her. 'You look lovely,' he said, with a gentle smile. He made no attempt to kiss her, but reached out and gave her hand a squeeze. His fingers were warm. 'Come on in,' he prompted. Opening the door, he ushered Mandy inside.

As they entered, she felt a flicker of alarm. The pub was packed, even for a Friday. She had been glad to come to the Fox and Goose, expecting its familiarity would help put her at her ease. She had pictured a simple meal with Jimmy in a quiet corner, but there was no chance of that now. Together they pushed their way over to the bar.

Bev Parsons looked up from the pint she was pulling. 'Jimmy!' She had to shout to make herself heard over the babble of voices. 'And Mandy Hope!' Mandy thought she detected a note of surprise in Bev's voice but the landlady's smile looked genuine enough. 'Have you come for our grand ceremony?' she bellowed.

'What ceremony?' Jimmy was shouting too.

'Switching on our Christmas lights,' Bev yelled. 'We decorate every year, but this time, we thought we'd make a real night of it.'

They certainly had, Mandy thought as she turned and gazed around the bar. The place was heaving.

'We actually came in for dinner.' Jimmy had to lean right over the bar to make himself heard. 'What are the chances of getting a table?'

For a moment, Bev looked troubled, but then her face brightened. 'We could open up the little room through the back,' she bawled. She raised her eyebrows suggestively at Jimmy, then glanced at Mandy, who felt her stomach contract. 'It'll be a bit more private.' Bev winked at Mandy, who, with some difficulty, managed to smile back. Up until now, she and Jimmy had only met outside or in private. Back in September they had gone walking together twice, but Bev's knowing looks were making her feel self-conscious. Before leaving for university, she hadn't dated anyone in the village. She should have remembered how much fascination kicked off when any local couple started 'courting' as Gran would have called it. Half hoping Jimmy would refuse, she peered out over the thronged heads. But there was obviously no chance of a table in the public bar coming free any time soon.

'That would be great, thanks,' Jimmy said.

The little room at the back was usually only used for private parties. There was no hope that their exclusive seating arrangement would go unnoticed by the rest of the pub. With reluctant feet, Mandy followed as Bev led them through the main seating area to the door on the far side of the room.

Mandy felt as if she had a neon sign over her head, letting people know she was here. Passing a table of four, Mandy recognised Christopher and Lola Gill, who lived at Greystones Farm with their brother Brandon. She didn't know the other two people at the table, but all four of them were looking from her to Jimmy and then back again. After a moment, the Gills remembered to nod, and Mandy nodded back. Then she caught the eye of one of the men sitting at the bar. It was Mr Farmer, who ran the local garage. He had turned almost all the way round in his seat to watch, making no attempt to hide his curiosity. To top it all, as they walked through the packed room, the sound levels suddenly dropped. Mandy wondered if they were waiting for her and Jimmy to perform a quick song and dance act.

To her relief, Bev was quick to unlock the door to the private room. Once they were inside, Mandy felt less like she was in a goldfish bowl. She pulled out a chair from the table by the window and sat down. Jimmy sat opposite her, his eyes twinkling with amusement.

'Can I get you a drink?' Bev was standing in the doorway, beaming at them.

'That would be great,' said Mandy. For a moment, she toyed with the idea of asking for a double. The strength of the reaction to her presence there tonight was unnerving. She had been in often enough over the years with different friends; normally, no one batted an eyelid. Was it the just the fact that she was with Jimmy, she wondered, or had they all been gossiping about Hope Meadows? Her shoulders tense, she looked across the table at Jimmy. He didn't seem at all bothered by the stir they had caused.

'I'll have a long vodka, please,' she said, turning back to Bev. At least Bev knew how to make her drink. In strange places, she sometimes had to explain.

'And I'll have a pint of John Smith, please,' said Jimmy. Pushing his chair out, he stood up. 'I'm just going to hang up my coat,' he said. 'Can I take yours too?' Mandy pulled off her jacket and handed it to him. As he left the room Mandy smiled at Bev, wondering whether she was waiting for their food order. But after a conspiratorial squint over her left shoulder, Bev turned to Mandy and gave her a thumbs up. 'Lovely young man,' she whispered.

Mandy felt her face turn red. 'We're just here for dinner,' she blurted out, then stopped in dismay. What other reason would they be here for? Did Bev think they were going to get up to all sorts the moment she left the room?

'I'll fetch you some menus,' Bev told her. She arrived back at the same time as Jimmy. 'Come and order at the bar when you've decided what you want,' she said, handing over the typewritten paper that held today's selection. With another dazzling grin, she left them alone.

'Do you know what you want?' Jimmy looked up at Mandy a few moments later.

'Apart from a hole to open up in the floor that we could hide in?' she suggested.

She wondered if Jimmy would tell her she was being daft, but he nodded, sending her a rueful look. 'Ah yes,' he said. 'Now I know what celebrities feel like!' He put his head on one side, his green eyes serious. 'Would you prefer to go somewhere else?' he asked. 'There's still time.'

Mandy wrinkled her nose, thinking. However much she loved Welford, there was a lot to be said for the anonymity of Leeds or even York. But she shook her head. Leaving now would draw even more attention to them. 'I can live with it,' she said. 'At least they haven't followed us in here!' She glanced down at the menu again. 'I think I'd like the Yorkshire pudding with onion gravy, please.'

'Of course.' Jimmy took her menu and stood back up. 'Celebrity is a burden I have to bear,' he intoned. 'Wish me luck!' His eyes were full of amusement.

Mandy laughed. 'Good luck,' she said.

He disappeared, leaving Mandy alone, but a second later a shape filled the doorway. Gary Parsons was bringing their drinks on a tray. Like Bev, he took a quick look out through the open door, then leaned in towards Mandy. 'Very nice to see you two here,' he whispered. 'He's a lucky man.'

For a moment, Mandy considered running away. Was everyone in this place giving them marks out of ten? To her relief, Gary set the drinks down on the table and retreated quickly, leaving her no time to respond. She felt relieved when Jimmy returned. Whatever was going on, it was easier to deal with it together. She took a slug of her drink, hoping it would help her relax.

Jimmy took a gulp from his pint, then set it down on the table. 'What have you been up to today?' he asked.

Mandy paused for a moment, recalling her morning's adventures. 'I went on a welfare visit with Seb Conway,' she said. 'To a pair of donkey foals.' Although it should have been an easy topic of conversation, talking about her job in public was always complicated. She could mention the visit but Mandy had to keep her mouth shut about the details, especially when it was a welfare case. 'It all got a bit heated and the police showed up,' she added.

Jimmy's eyebrows had migrated upwards. 'Really?' he said. 'Were the donkeys feral?'

Mandy pulled a face. 'Not the donkeys, no. The man who'd bought the foals got upset when we had to remove them,' she explained. 'It was a bit of a storm in a teacup. The donkeys can go back if the owners find a suitable field, but I got the feeling the man's wife isn't going to try very hard,' she added. 'Donkeys make a pretty terrible Christmas present!'

Jimmy grinned. 'Does this mean you have a couple of fluffballs hanging around Hope Meadows? Maybe I should come over to see them.'

'Oh, do,' said Mandy. 'Robin and Holly – those are the donkeys – are pretty adorable but they're just babies so Helen and I will do lots of handling and groundwork before they can be rehomed.'

Jimmy's eyes creased up as he smiled. 'Cows, sheep,

dogs, donkeys . . . Are there any animals that you aren't an expert in, Amanda Hope?'

Mandy felt her face turn pink again, but this time it wasn't from embarrassment. 'I probably could do to read up on arachnids,' she said with a grin.

'Hmmm, I can imagine it would be tricky to treat a spider with eight broken legs,' mused Jimmy.

Outside in the bar, there seemed to be some kind of upheaval as people stood up and pushed back their chairs. Presumably the time had come for the switching on of the lights. Before Mandy could suggest going out to join them, the lights in the main bar area went out. Mandy felt horribly conspicuous as light from their room spilled into the main bar, casting them in spotlight. To her relief, Jimmy reached up and flicked a switch on the wall so that they too were in darkness.

Pushing out her chair, Mandy stood up at the same time as Jimmy. She felt him move close behind her as she shifted into the doorway to get a better view.

Bev's voice came from behind the bar. 'Sorry we don't have anyone famous to turn them on!' she joked. 'You'll have to make do with me. One, two, three . . . Happy Christmas, everybody!'

With a flash, the bar lit up with hundreds of coloured lights and the crowd made the sort of appreciative noises that Mandy associated with firework displays. Tiny twinkling bulbs attached to netting covered the ceiling, and bigger lights were twined into garlands on the walls. The Christmas tree beside the hearth was a triumph of

festive decor, the tinsel and baubles glittering in a complicated sequence of flashing fairy lights. Mandy felt herself
grinning. Despite the awkwardness of the evening, this
was beautiful. Jimmy's hand touched her shoulder, warm
and steady, and Mandy leaned into him.

A moment later, the main lights came back on. Jimmy
sat down at their table and reached up to flick the switch
again. Mandy blinked as her eyes got used to the brightness.

'Well, that was rather lovely.' Jimmy smiled across the
table.

'I feel quite Christmassy now,' Mandy admitted.
Lifting her drink, she swallowed down the last mouthful.
Should she go and buy another? Jimmy was only half
way down his pint.

Just then Gary appeared in the doorway carrying two
giant Yorkshire puddings. Marching over, he set them
in front of Mandy and Jimmy with a flourish. 'Enjoy,'
he declared, then picking up Mandy's empty glass, he
asked, 'Can I get you any more drinks?'

'Same again, please,' Mandy said.

'Me too.' Jimmy lifted his glass and tossed back the
remainder of his pint. He held out the glass to Gary,
who raised his eyebrows.

'Sure I can't tempt you to a bottle of sparkling wine?'
he prompted. 'Might even have some champagne at the
back of the fridge, if you want me to take a look.'

Mandy opened her mouth to protest that it was just a
friendly dinner, but Jimmy spoke first, with a cautioning

glance at Mandy. 'Just the two drinks will be fine, thanks,' he said. Gary looked disappointed but headed back to the bar.

'I'm not sure I fancy some champagne from the back of the fridge,' Jimmy said impishly. 'Not a vintage I'm familiar with.'

Mandy let out a long breath. 'I shouldn't think anyone's ever ordered champagne here except on a special occasion.' With a stab of pain, she recalled James and Paul's wedding that summer, full of sunlight and joy and, yes, glasses of fizz. She pushed the sadness away. 'I really didn't think we'd cause such a fuss tonight.'

Jimmy winked. 'Everyone in Welford seems to have known you since you were knee-high to a Labrador. I'm not surprised they take an interest in you. I just hope I measure up!'

'Oh, don't worry, you do,' Mandy said without thinking. She paused. 'Eat up! Bev's Yorkshire puddings are legendary, and I dread to think what would happen if we let them go to waste!'

Despite Jimmy's delightful company, it hadn't been the most comfortable of meals, Mandy reflected as she walked out through the door of the Fox and Goose an hour later. The evening had been enjoyable, and she would have been happy to linger over drinks and dessert. But by the time they had finished the delectable Yorkshire puddings, the bar had become so full that people had started to spill into their side room. Once again, Mandy had found herself being stared at, and she was convinced she heard her name being muttered. She had toyed with the idea of asking Jimmy about any rumours he might have heard about the rescue centre, but she shied away from telling him about Flame's misadventures and the hostility she seemed to be stirring up among the locals.

Jimmy pulled the door to the pub shut behind them. For the first time that winter, the air was chilly enough for their breath to make little clouds in the night air. There was frost on the breeze. Standing close, not quite touching, they looked up at the outside festive lights.

'Do you think it can be seen from space?' Jimmy murmured in Mandy's ear.

She grinned. 'It's possible. Especially the world's fattest Santa.' She pointed to the generously-proportioned Father Christmas perched on the roof of the pub, resplendent in scarlet and white lights. She hoped he was tied down firmly; he looked as if he could do some damage with the right gust of wind.

Mandy turned to Jimmy. She wanted to say that she'd had a great time, but it was only partly true. The more time she spent with Jimmy, the more comfortable she felt, but tonight's events had all been a bit too weird for comfort, as if they'd been displayed under a microscope for all of Welford to marvel at. But she did know that she wanted to see him again.

'Maybe next time we should meet in York,' she suggested.

Jimmy smiled. 'Or out in the middle of the fell,' he said. 'It was still lovely to see you though. Could I persuade you out again sometime?'

'Maybe you could,' Mandy said. She felt suddenly warm inside. Despite the difficulties of the evening, he still wanted to see her as much as she did him.

'I'm afraid I can't see you this weekend.' Jimmy zipped up his jacket. 'I'm taking Abi and Max up to Keswick to see Mum,' he explained. 'Then I'm taking a party of businessmen out for a trip on Sunday. But I'll give you a call next week, if you wouldn't mind.'

'That would be perfect,' Mandy said. 'Perhaps you could bring the twins to see the donkeys.'

'They do love donkeys,' Jimmy said. Mandy had a fleeting sense of disquiet. She had expected him to jump at the chance. Didn't all children love donkeys? Her eyes flitted to his face, but he turned away and started walking.

Side by side, they headed down the lane. When they arrived at the entrance to Animal Ark, Jimmy bent to give Mandy an all-too-brief-kiss, then stepped back. 'I'll ring you,' he promised, before striding on up the lane. With an unexpected swoop of disappointment, Mandy watched as he disappeared round the corner and then listened until the noise of his footsteps died away.

You're being silly, she told herself. *It was you who told him you wanted to take things slowly*. Then she pulled herself together. If she had changed her mind, it was up to her to let him know. Next time they were together, she would make sure she did.

Chapter Ten

'What's the plan?' Helen asked. She was standing beside Mandy at the window of the rescue centre, looking across the paddock. Outside, Holly was watching a thrush peck at something on the ground, and Robin was galloping at full tilt around the orchard, his ears back, tail cocked high in the air. 'I don't know much about donkeys,' the nurse added.

Mandy was fascinated by the difference between quiet Holly and Robin's crazy antics. She watched him complete another circuit, his compact little hooves thudding on the packed earth. Just as well the paddock wasn't muddy or it would be like a ploughed field.

'I'm no expert myself,' she admitted. 'I had to do some research.' Robin skidded to a halt and was sniffing at Holly. Mandy wanted to laugh. 'We need to find out what they enjoy and spend time making friends. It will be very difficult to get them to do things they don't want to. It's all about persuasion.' She pulled a face. 'Not sure how easy that's going to be with Robin,' she said as he started hurtling in the other direction. 'Once we're sure he's six months old, we can get him castrated. For now,

I think we have to concentrate on getting them used to coming to us and being handled.' She turned to tidy a stack of worming leaflets on the counter. 'I'll spend time with them every day, but only do official training every other day. It helps if they have time to mull everything over.'

Helen laughed as the little jack careered past the window again. 'Robin is doing a whole load of mulling right now!'

Mandy laughed too, then looked at Helen. 'You want to come and give me a hand?' she asked.

Helen shook her head. 'Sorry, I'm meeting Seb,' she said. 'Otherwise I'd love to.'

'Another day then,' Mandy said.

When Helen had gone, she went to the food prep area and pulled out a chopping board. Grabbing a pear and some turnip, she chopped both into sticks that were small enough not to be a choking hazard. She had bought a belt with a pouch attached to it and she clipped it on, slipping the pieces of fruit and veg into the pocket before going outside. Finally, she grabbed two lead ropes and the pair of little headcollars supplied by the Powells.

When Mandy entered the orchard, Robin stopped mid-trot, his hooves splayed. One of his long fluffy ears twitched and his eyes opened wider. Mandy stood still for a moment, then moved back a step. The last thing she wanted was for the little jack to see her as a threat. Meanwhile, to Mandy's delight, Holly walked over with her ears pricked and started to snuffle at the pouch of treats.

Mandy stretched out slowly and touched the soft grey fur just below Holly's ear. With her other hand, she reached into the bag and pulled out a piece of pear. Carefully, she allowed the donkey to take it. Holly's ears were so soft, Mandy could hardly feel the fur against her fingertips. Her coat was coarser and fuzzy, but would improve with grooming. Holly blinked as if she was trying to decide whether she enjoyed being petted. She nibbled the pear, then moved closer to Mandy until her forehead was resting against Mandy's thigh.

Mandy tried not to squeak with delight. Being hugged by a baby donkey was pretty close to heaven. 'Hello, sweetpea,' she murmured. She ran her hand along Holly's tufty black mane and traced the dark line that ran the length of her spine and down each shoulder. Mandy had always loved the story that donkeys earned their distinctive dorsal cross markings because they carried Jesus into Jerusalem on Palm Sunday.

There was a tiny snuffle close by. Robin was staring at them, his nostrils flickering. 'Do you want some pear, too?' Mandy called in a conversational tone. Robin twitched one ear back, then forward again. He took a tentative step forwards, and another. Mandy turned back to Holly, watching Robin from the corner of her eye. She slid her hand into the bag at her waist and pulled out a piece of pear and one of turnip. Robin stretched out his neck but he was still too far away. He jumped back and snorted, tossing his head.

'Come on, poppet. You can do it,' Mandy whispered.

The donkey took two little steps, then reached out his muzzle. Mandy let him sniff at the treat and take it with his teeth. At the same time, she fed the piece of turnip to Holly. The little jenny crunched it up and nodded to ask for more. Robin ate more slowly, then stepped towards Mandy again. She moved away inch by inch until Robin walked more purposefully, gaining confidence. Then she stopped and fed him another treat while stroking his neck with her free hand.

'What a brave chap,' she praised him. She could see the whites of Robin's eyes which meant he was still on full alert, but he didn't shy away when she ran her fingers along his back and down his shoulder.

The next step was to re-introduce them to wearing a headcollar, which had seemed a pretty terrifying experience in the Hemmings' garden. When Mandy walked over to the post where she had hung the halters, both donkeys skittered away, their ears flattening in alarm. Mandy kept her breathing calm and steady as she picked up the halters and slung them over her arms. She put a piece of turnip in each hand and held them out towards Holly and Robin. Even Holly was suspicious this time but Mandy talked to them reassuringly until the donkeys came forward and snuffled up the treats. Then Mandy walked around for a few minutes, offering treats when the little animals came up to her but making no attempt to put on the headcollars.

When both Robin and Holly seemed comfortable with her holding the halters, Mandy decided to end the session. Giving the donkeys a final stroke and scratch, she headed back inside.

She wanted to do some individual training with the dogs next. With the exception of Sky, it would be the first time any of the dogs had come into contact with the donkeys. The two crossbreeds stared curiously at the fluffy grey creatures to begin with, but soon focused on Mandy. Their training was far enough that Mandy was able to do sit, stay and recall exercises with them to keep them distracted.

Holly and Robin seemed fascinated. At the beginning, they stood a safe distance away, but by the time Mandy had been working for a few minutes, they were standing under the apple trees, watching intently. Keeping Twiglet close beside her, Mandy walked the dog over to meet them. The donkeys blew down their noses at the dog, and with a wagging tail, Twiglet politely sniffed them back. When Mandy called Twiglet's name, the little crossbreed trotted alongside her into the rescue centre. Robin, apparently thrilled with his new friend, stuck his tail in the air and ran a celebratory circuit all round the paddock.

Next Mandy took Melon out of his cage. She had become very fond of him, with his shining eyes and feisty personality. He was wary of the donkeys at first, giving a worried little bark and swerving away from them. Mandy kept him on the lead and made him walk at heel until he had relaxed. Holly and Robin seemed to be bored with watching dogs now, and both put their heads down to nibble the grass. Mandy had unclipped Melon from his lead and was throwing his favourite ball for him when she heard a car pull up outside the rescue centre.

She looked over to see who it was. She wasn't expecting anyone, but it wasn't unheard of for people to turn up at the weekend. Calling to Melon, she clipped his lead on and let herself through the gate before heading to the front of the building.

All four doors of the car opened and a middle-aged couple climbed out, followed by two children, a boy of about ten with short hair and dark eyes and a teenaged girl. Unlike the rest of her family, the girl wasn't wearing jeans and a thick winter coat. Instead she sported a long black dress over scarlet Doc Marten boots. Her right ear was lined with earrings and a green stud gleamed in her nose. Her raven hair was spikey, standing up from her head as if it was terrified of the black circles she had painted around her eyes. *It's a look*, thought Mandy, secretly admiring the girl's conviction in her image.

'Can I help you?' She walked up with Melon trotting at her heels. The little Westie took one look at the family and singled out the girl at once. Forgetting his training, he lunged forwards to the end of his lead. His tail was wagging furiously, his button eyes merry. The girl looked startled for a moment, opening her eyes wide, but then crouched down to rub the top of Melon's head. He squatted beside her, mouth open in a doggy smile, wagging his tail frantically.

The man stepped forward. 'Hello,' he said. 'I'm Peter Dillon, this is Annie, my wife, my daughter Sam and this young man is Buddy.' Reaching out a hand, he ruffled the boy's hair. 'Sorry to disturb you,' he went on, 'but we were out this way and saw your sign. We've been looking for a dog for a while. We were thinking of a puppy, but when we saw you, we wondered if it would be okay to pop in. We can come another time if it's not suitable.'

'It's fine,' Mandy said. 'I have time. Were you thinking of any particular type of dog?' She looked down with interest at Melon and Sam. Melon was playing to his captive audience, sitting down with a pleading face, then jumping up in excitement when Sam praised him. Mandy was impressed when the girl didn't flinch as Melon licked her cheek. She just hoped he hadn't got a mouthful of foundation.

'Does this little fellow need a home?' asked Mrs Dillon. 'He's a livewire, isn't he?'

'He is,' Mandy agreed. 'And yes, Melon is ready for rehoming. I have some more dogs inside. Would you like to come in and see them?'

'That would be great.' Mr Dillon pushed his hand through his hair. 'What d'you think, Sam?'

'Did you say his name was Melon?' Sam looked up at Mandy.

'That's right. You can bring him inside if you like, and give him a treat.' Sam stood up slowly, shaking out the folds of her dress. Mandy got the impression she would happily have spent the whole day scratching Melon behind his ear. She handed over the lead and Sam's cheeks flushed pink as Melon started trotting beside her.

'There are three others available,' Mandy explained as she opened the door into the kennel room. A feeling of pride washed through her as the dogs, without a bark between them, stood up and came to the fronts of their cages, tails wagging.

Mandy popped Melon into his kennel and took Flame out of her cage, firmly attached to a lead. As the Dillons made a fuss of the golden lurcher, Mandy heard the main door open and close. She checked that Mr Dillon was happy to hold on to Flame, then slipped into the reception area.

'Hello, love!' It was Grandad. Bending over, still supple despite his years, he removed the cycle clips that were holding his trouser legs and dropped them into his pocket.

Mandy smiled. 'Hello. It's lovely to see you.'

'I've come to help,' Tom Hope announced. 'Dorothy and I are worried that you are doing far too much, so I thought you could use an extra pair of hands.'

'You don't need to,' Mandy told him. 'I'm fine, honestly!'

His eyes were twinkling. 'I know that,' he said. 'You've always been very capable.' He reached into his jacket and pulled out an envelope, holding it out to Mandy. She took it feeling pleased. She already had a couple of Christmas cards on the desk. 'Open it,' Grandad urged her.

With a smile, she did so, pulling out a beautiful card with a glittering picture of a graceful deer amongst snowy trees. 'It's beautiful,' she said, opening it to see the greeting inside. There was a piece of paper folded inside the card and she took hold of it and opened it up, wondering what it was. She gasped when she saw that it was a receipt. 'Harper's Stores,' she read. 'Paid in full.' She lifted her eyes to Grandad's face. He was grinning.

'I spoke to your gran about what you told me the other night,' he said, his voice gruff. 'She agreed with me that we couldn't think of a better early Christmas present.'

Mandy rushed over and put her arms around him and he hugged her tight. 'You are both wonderful,' she said. She had spoken to Sally Harper on the phone about the bill. Sally had agreed to let her pay in instalments, but Mandy had felt uneasy that so much was still outstanding. Despite her determination to stand on her own feet, the thoughtful gift really would make things much easier in the lead up to Christmas.

'Anyway,' Tom Hope went on, 'as I said when I arrived, I'm here to do some work.'

'You really don't need to,' Mandy told him, though his easy company always made her feel blessed.

'I want to help,' he said in a firm voice 'And your grandmother would love to get me out from under her feet!' Tom Hope grinned as he patted Mandy's shoulder. 'Don't even think about sending me home again. There's nothing I'd rather be doing than helping my favourite granddaughter.'

Mandy hugged him again. 'How could I turn down my favourite grandfather?' she teased. 'There are lots of things you can help with, but could you wait a minute or two? I'm just showing some clients the dogs.'

'Are you indeed?' Grandad looked pleased. 'Don't let them leave empty-handed! And I don't need a list of instructions, sweetheart. If you need me, I'll be sorting out the rabbits.' Without pausing, he headed for the small pets section. Mandy glanced out of the window. Harper's were due out this morning to deliver some feed, but there was no sign of them as yet. She would have to get on.

When Mandy went back into the kennel area, the Dillons were stroking Flame, who was soaking up the attention. Mandy noticed that Sam was watching Melon through the bars of his cage, and the Westie had his nose pressed against the metal, wagging his stumpy tail.

'How are you getting on?' she asked.

Mr Dillon, who had been crouching beside Flame, pulled himself upright. 'They're all lovely,' he said. 'It's hard to pick just one.'

Mandy laughed. 'I know that feeling,' she replied. 'You don't have to decide right away. If you think you might like one of them, I can take down your details and give you some time to think about it. Taking on a dog is a big commitment, and we only want to rehome these dogs once. I'll need to visit your house to check that everything is suitable, too. Why don't you fill in a form, and if you make a decision, give me a call.'

'That would be great,' said Mrs Dillon.

Putting Flame back in her kennel, Mandy took the family through to the reception area. As Mr Dillon wrote down his details, Mandy noticed Sam's gaze wandering back towards the dog room. When she turned back she had a dreamy expression on her face. Catching Mandy's eye, she grinned. Mandy grinned back. Underneath the rather startling appearance was a very sweet girl, she decided.

After waving goodbye to the Dillons, Mandy headed back inside. She wondered how Grandad was getting on. Before she had a chance to find him, her phone rang. She was on call this afternoon, and for a moment, her stomach gave a familiar lurch. When she answered the phone, it could be anything from a foaling horse to a hamster with a nose bleed. Her job was rarely boring, that was for sure.

It was Molly Future from Six Oaks Stables. Back in the summer, she had rehomed Bill, the ancient Shire Mandy had rescued. 'Hi, Mandy.' The voice on the other end was fizzing with brisk cheerfulness as usual. 'Nothing urgent,' she went on. 'I was just wondering if you'd come over and rasp Bill's teeth, please?'

'Of course.' Mandy's heart rate returned to normal. 'One day next week?'

'Well . . .' There was a brief pause. 'That's fine if it's convenient. But I wondered if you'd like to come for a ride as well? You said last time you were out that it was ages since you'd been on a horse and you sounded so wistful. The forecast for tomorrow's good.' She sounded as if she was smiling.

'Wow!' Mandy felt a wave of excitement. She had indeed mentioned that she wished she could take up riding again on an earlier visit to Bill. How lovely that Molly had remembered. Mandy wouldn't normally carry out such a routine visit on a weekend, but the carrot Molly was holding out was very tempting. 'I'm a bit out of practice,' she warned Molly.

'You'll be fine,' Molly promised. 'It'll all come back to you.'

Through the window, the low winter sun bathed the fells in a golden light. Mandy couldn't resist the thought of cantering up one of the tracks that criss-crossed the moorland. 'In that case, I'd love to.'

'Great.' Molly still sounded as if she was smiling. 'I'll see you tomorrow.'

Chapter Eleven

By the time Mandy tracked down Tom Hope, he had cleaned out the guinea pigs as well as the rabbits. 'Any of the dogs still need exercising?' he asked.

'Not really,' Mandy replied. 'Though I cut Melon's session a bit short. Maybe we could play with him a few more minutes.' She glanced at her watch. James was coming round later. There would just be time to sort out Melon and the cats. Then she would have to go in and help her parents prepare dinner.

At the thought of food, Mandy frowned. The Harper's delivery still hadn't arrived. She was sure she had booked it for Saturday morning and now it was two o'clock. Not only did she need cat and dog food, but she had been waiting for some specialised donkey feed for her two new charges. They weren't young enough for replacement milk, but they did need a special diet until they were fully grown. 'I'm just going to call Harper's,' she told her grandfather.

He took a flask out of his rucksack and went to sit down on the small sofa that stood in the reception area. 'I'll take a breather,' he said.

Pulling the phone from her pocket, Mandy dialled the number. It was most unlike Harper's to get the order wrong. Did she forget to call them? But she distinctly remembered the conversation. They had talked about the donkeys. She had spoken to Sally Harper herself and Saturday had been the earliest they could manage delivery.

Mandy was relieved when she heard Sally's voice on the other end of the line. 'Harper's Supplies, Sally speaking.'

'Sally!' Mandy began. 'This is Mandy Hope from Hope Meadows.'

'Hi, Mandy.' Sally's voice was warm. 'What can I do for you today?'

Mandy had half expected a swift apology for lateness, or regret that there was a problem, but Sally sounded as cheery as she always did. Was it possible there had been a misunderstanding about the date?

'I think I was expecting an order this morning?' she said. 'Cat and dog food and a special for the baby donkeys?'

There was a moment of silence at the other end of the line, then Sally answered with a hint of surprise. 'Oh. Yes. I remember you calling the other day, but there was nothing on the manifest this morning. How odd! Just let me check, will you?' There was a scuffling sound and the clicking of keys on a keyboard. Voices in the background. Mandy leaned over the counter, propping herself on her elbow.

'Hello again.' It was Sally.

'Hi.'

'I've got the details on screen. You did place the order, but it was cancelled two days ago. Wasn't it you who cancelled it?'

Standing up straight, Mandy shook her head. 'No. Definitely not.' The silence this time was longer. Distant voices again. Mandy's eyes wandered to the window. She could see Holly and Robin standing together under an apple tree. Their fur was almost the same shade as the weathered grey bark. Holly had her head on Robin's back.

There was a click on the other end of the phone. 'It wasn't me who took the call.' Sally had returned. 'It was our assistant Janice. She didn't get a name I'm afraid, but the order was definitely cancelled. I'm sorry if there's been a misunderstanding.'

Mandy stifled another sigh. It wasn't Sally's fault, but she needed that feed. 'Can I speak to Janice, please?' she asked, trying to keep the irritation out of her voice.

'Yes, of course. I'll just get her.'

Outside, the donkeys shifted. Robin had turned around and was nuzzling Holly's ear.

More muffled chat came down the phone line, then a new voice. 'Hello, Miss Hope.' Mandy felt a stirring of sympathy for Janice. The assistant sounded nervous as well as apologetic. 'I'm so sorry about your order,' Janice went on.

'Thanks.' Mandy gathered her thoughts. Janice hadn't taken a name, but perhaps she could recall something. 'I know you don't know exactly who it was that cancelled my order,' she said, 'but do you remember anything about the call, please?'

'Oh.' There was a pause. 'Well, it came in after lunch on Thursday. I'd just come back from the sandwich run and there were a couple of people waiting at the till. The phone rang while I was serving but I picked it up. It was a man, but he didn't give his name. I can't remember exactly what he said but I know he told me he was from Hope Meadows. He asked if we were due to deliver anything and I told him just the Saturday order. He told me it wasn't needed any more. Just like that. It wasn't needed any more.' Janice stopped to draw breath. 'I asked him if there was anything wrong and he said you'd got the food cheaper somewhere else. He said you wouldn't need anything else now. I was a bit surprised because there's only Gosling's and that's miles away. And they're definitely not cheaper, not if you add in delivery fees and everything . . .' Her voice trailed off.

Mandy found herself wondering whether Janice was always so chatty or whether it was just nerves. The story seemed odd, too. Hope Meadows had been mentioned by name. And why suggest she wouldn't be using Harper's again? Why would he do that, whoever he was? A million questions whirled in Mandy's head. What exactly had she learned from all Janice's chatter? The only useful thing seemed to be that it was a man who had called.

'It was definitely a man's voice?' she checked.

'Dcfinitely.'

'Did he mention me?'

'No. He said Hope Meadows. No other names at all.'

'And you don't remember anything else about him? Accent or . . . did he sound young or old?'

Mandy's eyes wandered over to Grandad. He had found a catalogue for cat accessories and seemed engrossed. 'He might have been youngish,' said Janice, 'but I'm not sure. I really am sorry.'

Mandy shifted her feet. Her legs felt stiff. 'Never mind,' she said. 'Can I speak to Sally again, please?'

'I'm so sorry for all this.' Sally's voice came down the line loud and clear. 'I'm afraid there's nothing we can do today. The van's already left. I'll have a look at the list though.' Another interval, more clicking. 'We could get it to you first thing Tuesday,' she announced. 'Sorry I can't do anything sooner.' She did sound truly apologetic. Mandy couldn't help but feel a bit guilty for her interrogation. None of this was Sally's or Janice's fault.

'Thanks, Sally,' she said. 'When are you open till? I'll have to come in and get a couple of things to tide me over.'

'We shut at five.' Sally sounded relieved. 'See you later.'

As she ended the call, Mandy stared out of the window and frowned. From what Janice had said, it didn't sound like there had been a mistake. The man, whoever he was, had mentioned Hope Meadows. But why would anyone do that? Were they trying to cause trouble? Even if there had been rumours about the barking, it was a big step from moaning in the Fox and Goose to deliberately phoning the store to cancel a food delivery.

Grandad put down the catalogue and looked at her, eyebrows raised. 'Problems?' His voice was sympathetic. When Mandy nodded, he patted the seat on the sofa beside him. Putting the phone back in her pocket, Mandy walked over and sat down.

'It's very odd,' she said. 'Someone phoned Harper's and cancelled my feed order.'

Grandad Hope raised his eyebrows. 'On purpose?' he asked. 'That doesn't make sense. It must have been a mistake, surely?'

Mandy shook her head. 'It didn't sound that way.' She stared at her hands. 'It's not just that,' she admitted. 'I found a hole in the hedge yesterday. It was just the right size for a dog to escape.' She glanced up at Tom, whose blue eyes were troubled. 'I thought at first an animal must have made it, but it didn't look right,' she told him. 'It was too high up, and too round.'

Grandad looked shocked. 'You think someone made it on purpose?'

Mandy lifted one shoulder in a half shrug. She didn't know what to think. 'It just seemed odd,' she said.

Her grandfather put one of his warm, weathered hands over hers. 'If you think someone might be doing these things maliciously,' he said, 'you should keep a record. If anything else happens and you go to the police, it'll help if you have everything written down.'

'The police?' It hadn't crossed Mandy's mind that this might be a legal matter. Surely no one wanted to commit a crime against the rescue centre?

Tom Hope pursed his lips. 'It probably won't get that far,' he said, 'but it's worth being prepared.' His expression softened. 'I'm sure it'll be fine,' he said. 'Whatever's going on, you've far more allies than enemies.' Putting his arm around her, he pulled her into a hug and Mandy let herself relax against him. At least her family were on her side.

Releasing her, Tom Hope pulled himself to the edge of the couch. 'We should finish up,' he suggested. 'After that, I can pop to Harper's for you. How would that be?'

'That would be amazing,' Mandy told him.

Grandad followed her into the dog room. Melon was sitting by the door to his cage, perched on his haunches with his head on one side. 'You're one persuasive little animal,' Mandy told him as she opened the cage and clipped on his lead. 'I have a feeling he won't be with us much longer,' she said. 'I think he made a rather unlikely friend today!'

Mandy threw her arms around James when he arrived, shortly after six o'clock. Squeezing him tight, she was relieved to feel that he had gained some weight, and he wasn't quite as bony as before. She had already planned to load his plate with food full of healthy fats and carbs. James was going to eat with them, then return to sleep at his parents' house overnight.

'You're squashing me!' James puffed. Mandy let him go and he wrestled off his overcoat.

'How are you?' The words still caught in Mandy's throat, as if the only possible reply could be, 'My husband died. How do you think I am?'

But James was more generous than that, which was one of many reasons why Mandy loved him so much. 'A bit better each day,' he said. 'How about you? Are you getting into the Christmas spirit?'

Pushing aside the thought of Flame's escape, the hole in the hedge and the cancelled food delivery, Mandy managed to laugh. 'Hardly!' she replied. 'It's not even December yet.'

James hung his coat on a spare peg. 'It will be in two days,' he reminded her. 'Then you'll have to start facing up to it. You can't stop December 25th from coming round.'

It would be his first Christmas without Paul, Mandy thought. Turning away, she blinked fiercely and took a deep breath. She led the way to the kitchen. 'There won't be much time for festivities if I'm on duty all day,' she said.

'It might be fun to have a completely different sort of Christmas.' James sounded wistful. Mandy wondered if he was wishing he could be at work, too. She knew the busy café he ran in York kept his mind occupied. But he never opened over the Christmas period because all his customers were busy with their families. 'I'm going down to spend Christmas with Paul's parents,' he told her, as if he could tell what she was thinking.

'That sounds like a great idea,' Mandy said, with a

flash of relief that he wouldn't be on his own. Though of course she would have insisted he spend the day at Animal Ark if he hadn't made other plans. 'Now, brace yourself. Dad's made chilli. There's soured cream and mashed avocado and everything.'

The scent of tomatoes met them as they walked through to the kitchen. James rolled his shoulders and cracked his knuckles. 'I'm braced,' he reported to Mandy, and Adam and Emily stared at them baffled as they dissolved into giggles.

Two hours later, waistband straining, Mandy followed James to the front door to say goodbye.

'I hope you sleep well,' she said, taking his coat down from the hook and helping him into it. 'When are you heading back?'

'Tomorrow evening.'

Mandy pulled open the door. Dense fog had crept over the village and the streetlights on the far side of the field shone through halos of drizzle. Stepping outside, James turned up his collar. 'Are you free tomorrow morning?' he asked. 'I want to visit Paul's grave. I . . . I'd like the company, if you don't mind.'

The simple way he said it tugged at her heart. Mandy knew him so well, but his dignity, the way he was bearing up in spite of everything, made her love him more than ever. 'It would be an honour,' she told him.

They clasped hands for a moment, then James turned and tramped off into the mist, his overcoat giving him an unusually bulky silhouette.

'Good night!' Mandy called after him, and he raised a hand in return.

The square church tower loomed above them below the overcast November sky. The earth on Paul's grave was still bare, though it no longer looked newly-dug. Autumn rains had smoothed the clay soil and there were a couple of tiny blades of grass sprouting from the mound. James seemed calm, though there was a bleak edge to his gaze that made Mandy want to reach out to hug him, but simultaneously warned her to hold back. Neither of them had worn black, though James's charcoal mac and Mandy's brown wool trenchcoat were in keeping with the sombre mood.

Mandy stood beside the grave with her head bowed. James was silent. Raising her head an inch, Mandy risked a glance at her friend. His left arm hung at his side, his hand forming a tight fist, the knuckles white. In his right hand, he clutched a Christmas rose in a pot. The greenish white flowers seemed insubstantial against his dark grey coat. When Mandy lifted her gaze to his face, she winced at how pale he looked. His dark eyes were huge behind the rimless glasses and his cheeks looked hollow, but when he caught her gaze, he managed a small smile. 'Thanks for coming,' he said.

'Thanks for inviting me,' she murmured.

Brown leaves littered the churchyard. James crouched down to clear the few that clung to the mound at his feet. Then he carefully placed the pot on top of the soil, pushing down until it sat securely.

Mandy reached into her pocket and felt the smooth coolness of an ornament that had been in her bedroom since their childhood. When she had come across it again emptying a drawer just a few weeks earlier, she had been reminded so strongly of James's dog Seamus that she wanted James to have it. Pulling it out, she held it out to her friend. His fingers were chilly as he took it from her.

'Seamus?' There was a spark of amusement in his eyes. 'Gosh, I remember this! Where did you find it?'

Mandy grinned. 'It fell out of a drawer when I was having a clearout. I couldn't resist saving it for you. I can't even remember where it came from originally.'

James was turning the little brown shape over and over, gazing at the narrow muzzle and shining black eyes. 'Can I leave it here with Paul?' he asked. 'Along with the rose?'

'Of course. It's yours.'

Bending down, he placed the ornament beside the plant.

'Where are the dogs?' Mandy asked.

'They're at Mum and Dad's,' he admitted. 'I wasn't sure it was appropriate to bring them.' He thought for a moment and his eyes lit up. 'Remember when you brought them to the hospital in York?'

How could she forget? Mandy gave a half-laugh, feeling her ears grow warm. 'Yup. I'm never one to worry about whether something's appropriate.'

James reached out a hand and squeezed hers. 'Thank goodness someone doesn't,' he said with meaning. For a moment, Mandy felt cheered, but James let go of her hand and she heard him sigh. Looking round, she could see pain in his face. 'It's so hard,' he said quietly. 'I want to talk about Paul all the time. But it's as if everyone's terrified I'll fall apart if I mention his name.' His jaw clenched. 'I do get it,' he went on. 'I wouldn't have known what to say either, before . . .' His voice trailed off.

Mandy took hold of his hand again and squeezed his fingers. 'You can talk to me,' she said. 'I'll make time, any time.'

The wind was rising, the leaves on the ground shifting and whirling. She felt the first drops of rain on her cheek, and heard a creak from the yew tree as it bent to the breeze.

'I loved him so much.' James's eyes were fixed on the mound of earth which marked the final resting place of the love of his life. Eventually, he looked up, across the graveyard, over the wall. There were tears in his eyes. Mandy's gaze followed his to the war memorial on the village green. Other young men were remembered there. They had died long ago, but they too had been loved.

'At least we had the wedding,' James said. Still holding hands, they left the graveside, walking through the gate and over the road to the green. 'What a cracking day that was.'

'It really was,' Mandy agreed. James and Paul had been a model of happiness and romance, despite the tidal wave that was rushing towards them. 'Seamus and Lily were the best ringbearers I've ever seen, that's for sure.'

'I was so worried they would find a way to prise open those little boxes and swallow the blasted rings,' James admitted, managing a smile, though there were tears on his face.

'Really?' Mandy stared at him. 'That hadn't even crossed my mind.' She grinned. 'It wouldn't have been the end of the world. You would have just had to put the wedding back a few days.'

James pulled a face. 'What a pleasant thought.'

Side by side, they headed over to stand beneath the bare branches of the oak tree where the marriage ceremony had taken place. The green looked very different now, but the village and the fells were as they had always been.

Lowering his eyes back to Mandy, James found a smile. 'How about the handsome Jimmy Marsh?' he asked. Mandy felt the heat rising in her face. 'Have you seen much of him lately?'

James's eyes had brightened and he was looking at her as if he already knew the answer. He could read her far too well, Mandy thought. 'There do seem to be some developments in that direction,' she confessed.

'I'm so glad for you. You deserve nothing but happiness, do you know that?' Without warning, James put his arms out and hugged her. The droplets of rain cooled Mandy's warm cheeks as she closed her eyes and hugged him back.

Chapter Twelve

After waving James off to Sunday lunch with his parents, Mandy rushed upstairs. It was time to head over to Six Oaks Stable. It was almost three months since she had seen Bill, the charismatic Shire she had rescued in the summer. Donning a pair of stretchy jeans and pulling out her old riding boots, Mandy found her old riding hat at the bottom of the cupboard. Though the boots still fitted, when she tried to pull on the helmet, it was much too small. Hopefully Molly would be able to lend her one.

She thought back to the summer, and the unexpected disappointment she'd felt when she had seen Molly and Jimmy in the Fox and Goose. That had been the first time she had truly recognised her own interest in Jimmy, she thought. Helen had told her Jimmy and Molly had dated and that they must have been back together.

Mandy had been taken aback to feel so aggrieved, though she'd never had any reason to dislike Molly herself. It was the same day Paul had died, Mandy remembered. The familiar wave of pain passed through her at the memory. So many things brought her back to Paul. She stood for a moment, lost in thought, then pulled herself back to the present, walked downstairs and climbed into her car.

Drawing up in the immaculate stable yard, she stepped out of her SUV. Overhead, the sky was clearing at last and the wind was easing. Mandy admired the revamped yard. The stable doors were freshly painted in royal blue paint. Wooden tubs suggested floral displays in summer, and hooks beside each stable held colourful headcollars with their ropes neatly coiled. There were far more horses than in the days Mandy had attended the somewhat ramshackle riding school. To her left, a handsome bay with a wide white blaze was gazing at her with interest. From the far side of the yard, there came a sound of shuffling straw and a black face emerged, all liquid eyes and ears alert. What an intelligent head, Mandy thought. Walking round to the back of the car, she pulled out the long tooth rasp and the Hausmann's gag that she would need for Bill's dental treatment.

'Hello!' called a voice and Mandy turned, expecting to see Molly, but a long-legged girl of about fifteen was approaching. She wore her long blonde hair in a plait and her blue eyes shone in the emerging sunshine. 'You're Mandy Hope.' Not stopping to explain how she knew, the girl went on, 'Molly has asked me to take you to Bill.' She offered a rapid smile with an appealing hint of shyness, then turned away to stride across the yard and round a corner, leaving Mandy to trot behind.

Bill the Shire horse was tied up outside a short row

of stables, resting one hind leg. He looked in great shape, even better than Mandy had dared to hope. He had been so thin last summer that his ribs had stood out and the hollows in his face had been deeply shadowed. Now his dappled grey coat was thick and fluffy for winter, but his belly was healthily rounded beneath the hair and his face looked about a million years younger, despite his age. Mandy turned her body sideways and allowed the old boy to stretch out his nose to her in his own time. It didn't take him long. The gentle gelding nuzzled at her hair and snuffed in her ear, making her laugh.

'He's so lovely,' said the girl who had greeted Mandy. 'Molly told me all about your rescue last summer. The photos of Bill on your website are lovely, though he's even more handsome now he's rounded out a bit.'

'He's clearly in the best place,' Mandy agreed. 'What's your name?' she added.

'I'm Nicole. Nicole Woodall.' The girl was hanging her head again, her face pink as if she was embarrassed to be asked about herself, though she seemed happy to talk about the horse. She untied the lead rope attached to the metal ring and reached up to smooth Bill's forelock. 'Would you like me to hold him while you examine him?' Nicole offered.

'That would be great, thanks,' said Mandy. She studied Bill, thinking hard. She often gave horses a small dose of sedative when she wanted to do a thorough check inside their mouth. But Bill's age meant that she was reluctant to take the risk, and Mandy had seen enough of him to know that he was exceptionally quiet and unfussed about being handled.

Nicole undid Bill's headcollar and buckled it around his neck, leaving his head free. Mandy held up the rather daunting-looking equine gag and the metal rasp so that Bill could sniff them.

'Nothing to worry about, old chap,' Nicole murmured, smoothing her palm down Bill's neck on the other side. Mandy smiled. Nicole reminded her of herself at the same age, infinitely comfortable around animals but not quite so sure about people.

Running her hands over Bill's face, she checked for lumps and bumps. The temporomandibular joint felt fine. Bill's breath smelled sweetly of hay, as it should. Hoping her fingers weren't too stiff from the cold, Mandy tucked herself close to Bill's head. Moving very slowly, she eased the gag into his mouth and buckled it behind his poll. He tossed his head experimentally, but Nicole kept a contact on the lead-rope and he stood still again, blinking his long-lashed eyes. Once he seemed settled, Mandy cranked the ratchet attached to the gag so that Bill's mouth opened wide. He looked a bit startled, but kept still.

'Good boy,' Mandy praised him. Reaching into her pocket, she pulled out her headtorch and put it on.

Bill stood as steady as a rock while she carried out a careful inspection inside his mouth. There were no signs of decay on his teeth, no cheek ulceration. After a thorough visual check, Mandy slipped her hand into Bill's mouth. The metal gag was cold against her arm as she felt right to the back. As she had expected from his age, there were a few jagged edges on his cheek teeth. Picking up the rasp, she slid it into position and with Nicole holding the old horse's head still, she worked it backwards and forwards against the rough edges of the lower teeth until they felt smooth.

Repeating the action on the upper teeth, Mandy could feel her arm tiring. Bill was tall enough that she almost had to stand on tiptoe to reach, and working above your head was always difficult. She was relieved when another check of his teeth with her fingertips revealed the sharp edges had gone.

'I think that should do,' she said to Nicole as she set the rasp down on the windowsill. After a final glance inside the dark cavity of Bill's mouth, she closed the gag, allowing his teeth to come together. Then she unbuckled the leather strap. With a grunt of relief, Bill let the gag drop into Mandy's hand. He opened and closed his mouth a few times, as if enjoying the release of pressure. Mandy leaned her head against Bill's neck. With her left hand, she stroked his thick coat, enjoying the softness of the hair and the solid feel of his muscles.

When she looked around again, Nicole was smiling at her. 'He's such a special horse,' she said.

Mandy nodded. 'And he's landed on his feet here – or should I say hooves?'

'Would you like to see my boy?' Nicole asked with a hint of hesitation.

'I'd love to,' Mandy replied. Giving Bill a last pat, she opened the stable door to let Nicole walk him in. She emerged a moment later with the headcollar in her hands. Leaving the headcollar on a hook, she led Mandy back to the main yard.

'He's called Braveheart.' Mandy could hear pride in the girl's voice. No wonder, she thought when she saw where Nicole was taking her. Braveheart was the horse she had admired earlier. Jet black, with a huge noble head and tidy hogged mane, his ears pricked forwards as he listened to Nicole's voice. 'He's half Irish Draught and half Thoroughbred,' the girl told Mandy. She reached up to smooth her horse's ears. 'We've started doing some eventing this year, and he's going really well.'

Mandy could see that the gelding would be ideally suited to competing, with his inquisitive, thoughtful gaze and sturdy build.

'Hello, Mandy.' This time, the voice was definitely Molly's. Mandy turned to see Molly approaching across the yard. 'I see you've been introduced to Braveheart.'

'I have.' Mandy smiled. 'He's fabulous,' she added.

'He is,' Molly agreed. She turned to Nicole. 'Have you finished mucking out Sasha?'

Nicole glanced across the yard. Following her gaze, Mandy could see a skewbald horse with one blue eye watching them. 'Yes,' she replied. 'I made a start on Moon-dance, too.'

'That's great,' Molly told her, then to Mandy,

'Nicole's a great worker. I'd take her on fulltime if I could!'

'Do you like working with all animals, or just horses?' Mandy asked, with the seed of an idea growing.

'All animals, definitely,' said Nicole. 'I love horses the most, but dogs, cats, rabbits, fish . . . I think they're all amazing.' She paused and her cheeks reddened. 'I love your website,' she added. 'I think it's wonderful that you've opened Hope Meadows.'

Perhaps that was why Nicole had recognised her instantly when she arrived, Mandy thought. Her photo was on the website as well as Bill's. It was a relief to hear something positive. Negative thoughts had been swirling in her head more often than she liked after the recent events. 'Would you like to help out with the animals sometimes?' Mandy asked. Maybe she had found an answer to at least one of her difficulties. 'If Molly can spare you, that is?'

'It'd be fine with me if you wanted to,' Molly said to Nicole. 'It would be great practice for you to deal with different animals.'

Nicole was gazing at Mandy with shining eyes. 'I'd love to,' she said. 'I don't live too far away. Just on the edge of Graylands.' That was the oldest of the new housing estates that spread along the valley. 'I could cycle to you easily.' She straightened up, one hand still resting on Braveheart's neck. 'How often can I come?'

Mandy wanted to laugh. She was absolutely looking in a mirror at her teenaged self, desperate to do anything to spend time with animals. 'Could you do a couple of evenings a week?' she said. 'What about Tuesday and Thursday?'

'Can I come on a Saturday too?'

Mandy grinned. 'Of course,' she said. Coming down to earth, she added, 'I can't afford to pay you for now. Are you sure that's okay?'

'It's definitely okay,' Nicole said. 'I wasn't expecting you to pay me anyway.'

Mandy felt a surge of gratitude. As soon as she could afford to give the girl some pocket money, she would. She was sure her rescue animals would love Nicole, and it would do them good to see a different face sometimes.

'Well, that's settled.' Molly looked pleased too. 'Are you still keen to ride? We should probably get on.' With a last nod to Nicole, Mandy followed Molly across the yard. 'How did you get on with Bill's teeth?' Molly threw the question over her shoulder.

'They were fine,' Mandy replied. 'A few sharp edges, but nothing serious.'

'That's good.' Molly stopped beside the stable with the skewbald horse. 'This is Sasha,' she said. 'She can be a bit spooky, but if you're firm with her, she goes well.'

Mandy looked at Sasha. Her blue eye gave her a lopsided look, but her face was broad and intelligent. 'She's lovely,' Mandy said. 'I need to borrow a hat, though. Mine was too small. If you have one, that is?'

Molly looked amused. 'We've got plenty.' She led

Mandy to a well-stocked tack room. 'There.' She pointed at a shelf which had a line of hats of all different sizes.

Mandy picked up a plain black helmet and tried it on. It was too big, but only slightly. Pulling it off, she replaced it and selected one that was half a size smaller. This time, it fitted well. Walking back outside, she found Molly was already more than half way through tacking up Sasha.

'Just about there,' Molly announced, tightening the girth. 'I'm going to ride Georgie.' She pointed out a tall chestnut mare watching them from over a stable door. She was already wearing a saddle and bridle. 'She's a retired eventer,' Molly said. 'She and Sasha go well together.' Gathering Sasha's reins, she led the mare out into the yard. 'Will you need a mounting block?' she asked.

Mentally crossing her fingers, Mandy shook her head. She watched as Molly moved around to tighten the girth another hole, then pulled the stirrups down. Sasha wasn't enormous. About 16 hands, Mandy guessed, but it was still a long stretch to get her foot up into the stirrup. With muscles that she hadn't used in years, she swung herself up and to her relief, landed lightly in the saddle. She was glad when Molly continued to steady Sasha while she adjusted the stirrup lengths. The mare was quite fidgety.

Molly was smiling up at her. 'How do you feel?' she asked.

Mandy wriggled her feet in the stirrups, pushing her heels down. They felt comfortable on both sides. 'Fine,' she told Molly. Shuffling forwards slightly, she gripped with her knees and adjusted her reins. Molly let go of the bridle and Sasha bounced sideways, her hooves clattering on the concrete. Resisting the temptation to cling on with her legs, Mandy relaxed her weight a little more into the saddle and shortened the reins very slightly. On the far side of the yard, Molly had mounted Georgie from a stack of breeze blocks.

Nicole opened the gate for them. 'Have a good ride!' she called, waving.

Mandy nodded, not wanting to take one hand off the reins to wave back. Sasha was certainly responsive. She had a choppy walk, with a tendency to veer sideways, but once she was tucked alongside Georgie, she seemed to calm down a little.

Molly grinned down at Mandy from the chestnut mare. 'Sasha goes best if you keep her on a light contact,' she said. 'Use your legs to keep her moving forward, and keep her focussed with your hands.'

For the first few minutes, Mandy found herself concentrating hard. Through the reins, she could feel the mare was keen to get a move on. But the walk, though brisk, was steady and easy to sit in to, and Sasha didn't even blink when a pigeon flew out of the hedge beside them. Mandy straightened her back and started to relax.

By the time they reached the gateway that led to the track up the fellside, Mandy was feeling thoroughly at home. Molly was very chatty. The conversation had moved from Hope Meadows to Christmas and then back to Welford.

'What made you move here?' Mandy finally got a chance to ask a question. She was half hoping that Molly would tell her something about Jimmy, but she didn't want to be the one to bring him up in conversation. Part of her wanted to tell Molly she was seeing him. But any relationship they had was at such an early stage that she didn't want to mention it. Also, for all she knew, Molly could still be feeling hurt by the split.

'I heard about the stables coming up for sale and knew I wanted to buy them as soon as I saw them,' Molly replied. 'Mrs Forsyth was retiring, so she sold me a lot of her tack and field equipment. I had Georgie and Sasha already. Coco was Mrs Forsyth's gelding and I agreed to keep him on.'

'So it wasn't Welford that really drew you?' Mandy suggested.

Molly, who had stopped to open the gate that led out onto the fellside, gazed back at the village. They had already climbed high enough to see over the roofs of the houses. 'Not exactly,' she said, 'but as soon as I arrived, I knew I wanted to live here.' She grinned. 'And there are definitely a few great perks to living in the Yorkshire countryside, aren't there? Though I seem to have a preference for men from the Lakes.'

Mandy stared at her for a moment. Jimmy had grown up in the Lake District and Molly and he had dated a couple of years ago. Had Molly found another man from

Cumbria to swoon over?' Molly's smile was so wide that Mandy couldn't help but feel pleased for her. Whoever it was, he was certainly making Molly happy. The gate was open. Steering Sasha through the gate, Mandy tightened the reins. The mare's ears were pricked, her body tense. She would ask Molly more later, Mandy thought. For now, Sasha needed her full attention.

'Want to go for a run?' Molly had closed the gate and was smiling. Mandy could see that Georgie had raised her head, ready to go.

'Love to!'

She barely had time to draw breath before Georgie spun round and raced up the grassy track. Sasha needed no encouragement. The muscular body tensed and surged beneath Mandy, and suddenly the only sounds she could hear were hooves thudding on the firm earth and the wind rushing past. Leaning forward, Mandy relished the chill of the air on her face, a tingling sensation, fresh and exhilarating: she felt truly alive. She kept her hands close to Sasha's neck, among the thick brown and white mane. The mare felt full of running, but Mandy didn't feel out of control. She could tell that Molly was having to keep tighter control of Georgie, who was plunging against the reins as if they weren't going fast enough for her taste.

Ahead of them, the path stretched from the tree-lined valley right up to the ridge that overlooked the village. They were halfway already, the fell rising steep and green to their left, walled fields falling away to the right.

The sky seemed to draw closer as they crested the ridge. Even Georgie slowed down when they reached the top. Sasha returned to a walk in a couple of strides, snorting. Mandy leaned forward to pat her neck, and gave her a loose rein. It was colder up here and the horses' breath made white plumes of steam in the air. Relaxing back into the saddle, Mandy felt like laughing out loud.

'That was amazing!' she gasped.

Molly twisted in the saddle to grin at her. 'Better than anything in the world!' she agreed.

Mandy suddenly felt as if she was being watched. At that very moment, a voice called, 'Hello!'

She would know that voice anywhere, she thought. When she looked around, she felt her already glowing cheeks flush an even deeper shade. Jimmy stood beside the track, flanked by a group of people in waterproof walking gear, ranging from a grey-bearded older man, who was breathing hard, to a glamorous young woman. Several of them held cameras and mobile phones to take pictures, though whether they wanted to photograph the horses or the view, or indeed both, Mandy didn't know.

Jimmy beamed up at Mandy. 'I see you've gone over to the dark side,' he said. 'Hillwalking is much easier with four legs.'

'Technically six,' Mandy pointed out.

Jimmy's grin widened as Molly halted Georgie and looked back. 'Don't forget about Friday,' she called.

For a moment, Mandy wondered who Molly was speaking to, but Jimmy was nodding. 'I won't,' he replied.

Mandy blinked. Jimmy had mentioned spending the weekend with his children and his corporate clients when they had been in the Fox and Goose. He hadn't said anything about Molly.

For a moment, she toyed with the idea of asking outright, but Jimmy had already turned to his troops and was rallying them for the journey back. 'Better get moving,' he was saying. 'It's not good for our muscles to stand around too long in the cold.' The mobiles and cameras were being secreted away.

'We should go too,' Molly said. 'We'll need to take the horses down more slowly and we don't want to run out of daylight.'

She guided Georgie towards a clump of trees, where a stony path led back down to the valley. Mandy glanced back as Sasha headed across the grass. Jimmy's hiking group had disappeared as if they had never been there. She pushed away disquieting thoughts about Jimmy and Molly, and let her gaze drink in the spectacular view. Far below, smoke was beginning to rise from chimneys. People would be sitting in their living rooms, Mandy thought, feet stretched out towards the fire. She would much rather be out here, with the wind on her face.

The scent of warm horse filled her nose. Her hands were nipping and she tucked them under Sasha's mane. She was enjoying herself too much to dwell for long on the mystery of Molly and Jimmy. She and Helen had jumped to the wrong conclusion before, hadn't they? Jimmy had given her no reason to mistrust him.

They arrived back in the yard as the sun started to dip behind the fell. Hooking her leg over Sasha's back, Mandy slid to the ground with a thud. She was pleased when Nicole came over and took the reins from her. 'I can see to Sasha,' the girl offered.

For a moment, Mandy considered objecting, but instead she bent over and rubbed her aching thighs. Since returning to work with farm animals, she had become used to finding unexpected aches and pains, but this particular brand felt like an old friend.

'Thanks so much,' she said to Molly, who had also dismounted and was standing with Georgie. 'That was fantastic.'

Molly grinned. 'Come any time,' she said. 'There are always horses to exercise.' She ran a hand down Georgie's neck, then looked back at Mandy. 'Definitely a fair exchange for Bill's care.'

It was, Mandy thought. She hadn't known Molly for long, but her new friend's love of horses and generous care for Bill made Mandy feel she was someone to be trusted.

Mandy pulled herself up straight. She could feel her knees protesting. Nicole returned from Sasha's stable with the saddle in her arms, the bridle hanging from her shoulder. 'I'll see you on Tuesday,' she said to Mandy with a shy smile.

'I'll look forward to it,' Mandy replied. 'I just hope Molly doesn't miss you too much!'

Chapter Thirteen

There was a knock on the door of the consulting room. Before Mandy had a chance to call out, it opened a crack. Helen's head appeared through the gap. 'Phone call for you,' she said. Her head disappeared.

Mandy smiled at Susan Collins, who had brought her cat in for vaccination. 'Sorry,' she said. 'I'll be back as soon as I can.'

Susan smiled. Her son Jack stood beside her and his dark eyes gazed up at Mandy. Susan had been at school with Mandy and they had become firm friends since Mandy's return to Welford. Jack often visited Hope Meadows with his mum. 'We can wait a few minutes,' Susan said, then looked into the cat basket, from which the round eyes of a ginger cat were staring at her. 'We'll be fine, won't we, Marmalade?' Marmalade made no reply, though to Mandy he almost looked as if he was shrugging. The cat was in no hurry to see her, she was sure of that.

Helen was sitting at the reception desk when she went through. For now, the waiting room was empty. The telephone receiver was in its cradle, but the light for line 1 was flashing.

'Who is it?' Mandy spoke in a low tone to Helen. When a client rang up and asked for her by name, she liked to be prepared before she lifted the phone. There were few things worse than facing an emotional query, only to realise she couldn't remember the intricacies of a complicated history.

'It's the solicitor,' Helen whispered back. 'He tried your mobile but it was switched off, of course.' The mobile was always off when Mandy was dealing with clients. It seemed incredibly unprofessional to field calls or check messages when she was supposed to be concentrating on an animal's care. 'I know you don't like to be disturbed except in an emergency, but I thought you'd want to take this one,' Helen added.

Mandy lifted the receiver and pressed the button that would put her through to line 1. 'Amanda Hope speaking,' she said.

Five minutes later, she set the phone back in its cradle and leaned her weight against the counter, feeling breathless. Helen was watching her with a look of amusement. 'Good news?' she hazarded.

'Yes!' Mandy wanted to throw her arms in the air and do a jig. 'Yes!' she said again. 'My mortgage for Lamb's Wood Cottage has been approved! The contracts are ready and I can pick up the keys tonight!' She shook her head. After all this time it was hard to believe.

Helen's smile was as wide as Mandy's. 'Congratulations!' she exclaimed. 'Will you be going up there tonight? Only I'm free, if you'd like some company.' She paused and winked. 'Though I'll understand if you have someone else in mind for your first official visit.'

Mandy knew that Helen was referring to Jimmy. The nurse had expressed her approval when Mandy said that she had changed her mind about taking things slowly with Jimmy after their evening in the Fox and Goose. Helen thoroughly approved of 'Mandy's new relationship' as she'd taken to calling it. Mandy had told Helen she intended to let him know and the nurse had encouraged her. It was good to know her friend thought she was doing the right thing.

'I might just text Jimmy,' she conceded.

Helen's eyes gleamed with triumph. 'Go for it!' she said.

Pulling her mobile from her pocket, Mandy switched it on. After a moment's thought, she texted a short message. 'Mortgage approved. Can get the keys to Lamb's Wood Cottage today. Are you free this evening?' She pressed 'send' and switched the phone off with a pleasant feeling of anticipation. She had missed having someone to share good news with. Mum and Dad and Helen were lovely, but sharing with Jimmy was quite different.

When she returned to the consulting room, Susan was sitting down with Jack on her knee. 'Thanks for being so patient,' she said.

'No problem,' Susan assured her, leaning forward to drop a kiss on Jack's dark head. 'I don't think Marmalade is in any hurry to get his jabs, anyway!'

★   ★   ★

Half an hour later, morning surgery was at an end.

'Fancy a coffee?' Helen offered as Mandy closed the door behind the last client.

'Yes, please.' Although coffee sounded good, what Mandy really wanted was a chance to gather her thoughts. She had been more than a little distracted through the past thirty minutes. Even as she had worked through the complicated process of calculating the dosage of wormer to treat a budgerigar, there had been a tiny part of her mind holding on to a seed of excitement.

Tonight would be her first proper visit to Lamb's Wood Cottage since she had carried out the rescue in the summer with Seb Conway. This evening, she would be visiting it as her first ever home. She wanted Jimmy with her. It was short notice, but already she had a picture in her mind of exploring together. They would push through the overgrown front garden. Perhaps they would kiss inside the front door. Not the fleeting kind of goodbye kiss they had shared after the Fox and Goose, but something more intense. She could still remember the delicious whirling feeling when he had kissed her in the copse beside the rope course. This time, she wouldn't pull away.

When she switched on her phone, she was disconcerted to find that, as yet, Jimmy hadn't responded to her message. He had read it just after she'd sent it. And then nothing. Not even a thumbs up or a smiley face. She stared at the tiny letters. 'Read 09.30'. Trying to quell the swoop of disappointment, she shoved the phone back into her pocket. Probably her text had arrived at exactly the same time as one of his clients. Or maybe his phone had run out of power. She'd give him till lunchtime. If she still hadn't heard, she would give him a call.

As she was about to join Helen in the kitchen, the phone in Mandy's pocket rang. Her heart jumped, but when she pulled the mobile out, it was an unknown number. Trying not to sound too disheartened, she answered. 'Amanda Hope.'

'Hello.' The voice sounded familiar but she couldn't place it. 'Is that Hope Meadows?'

'Yes, it is.' Mandy held her breath. It could be anything from a complaint to a request for help. But to her pleasure, the caller introduced himself as Peter Dillon, the father of the family who had visited the rescue centre on Saturday morning.

'How can I help?' Mandy asked.

'We were really taken by Melon, the little Westie,' Mr Dillon told her. 'Can you tell me if he's still available?'

Mandy let her head fall back against the wall with a thrill of satisfaction. Hadn't she said to Tom Hope that she thought they had been interested in Melon? 'He's definitely available,' she said.

'Well, in that case, we'd like to adopt him,' Mr Dillon announced. 'I think you mentioned a house visit? What would that involve?'

The door of the clinic clicked open. Mandy was about to ask Mr Dillon if she could put him on hold when she saw it was Gran. Mandy gestured to Dorothy Hope that she should go into the cottage. 'It just means I'd come and have a look round your home,' she explained to Mr Dillon. 'I need to check everything's safe and that you have as much information as possible before you agree to take Melon on.' She always tried to describe the home visit as something positive and exciting. The last thing she wanted was for people to be nervous and over-prepare, or change their environment completely. She wanted to get the truest possible picture of the home that was on offer.

'Okay. That seems a good idea.' Mr Dillon sounded thoughtful. 'What about Wednesday afternoon?'

Moving behind the desk, Mandy checked the appointment lists for Wednesday. There was nothing too onerous at the moment. 'That would be fine,' she replied. 'Is two o'clock all right?'

'Perfect. Thanks very much. We'll see you then!' Mr Dillon sounded excited, and Mandy realised she was smiling as she ended the call.

Mandy glanced at the screen on her phone. There was no reply from Jimmy. Still, it looked as if she had a new owner for Melon. She added the visit to Wednesday's list. Then with a glance around the empty waiting room, she headed for the door that led into the cottage.

When she arrived in the kitchen, she was greeted by the wonderful smell of pastry. Helen had sat Gran down and given her a coffee. Both of them looked up when Mandy came in.

'What is that lovely smell?' Mandy gazed around the

kitchen. On the side, Gran had placed a box of fluffy golden pastries. 'I've brought some cheese and onion pasties,' Dorothy Hope explained. 'I was having a practice run for the WI Christmas Fair. Thought you might like them.'

Mandy breathed in deeply. The whole kitchen was filled with the delicious aroma.

'You could sit down,' Helen suggested.

'I could indeed.' Mandy laughed as she pulled out a chair.

'Grandad sends his love,' Gran told her, lifting her cup and taking a sip. 'He enjoyed himself ever so much on Saturday.'

Mandy smiled. 'He's welcome any time,' she said. 'And while I remember,' she leaned over and gave her grandmother a hug. 'Thank you so much for your wonderful gift.' She was gratified to see the contented look on Dorothy Hope's face.

'I know you can manage,' Gran said, 'but every little helps.' She smiled. 'Speaking of which, I had a brainwave about the WI. One or two of them are always talking about you and all the good you do. I wondered whether you might think about having an open day at Hope Meadows? I'm sure several of them would love to have a look inside. You could ask for donations or charge a small entry fee. Maybe we could provide some baked goods for sale. What do you think?' The blue eyes in the wrinkled face were filled with love.

'That sounds like a great idea,' Mandy told her. Perhaps

they could get some publicity as well. Mandy was sure the local paper could be persuaded to cover the event. The more local people who understood the good she was trying to do, the better they would accept it, she thought.

'And how are things going with all your lovely charges? Should your grandad come round again to help out?'

Mandy grinned, remembering Tom Hope's suggestion that Gran wanted him out from under her feet. 'Actually, I've found a new volunteer called Nicole. She's helping Molly Future at Six Oaks and she's agreed to do a couple of evenings at Hope Meadows.'

'That's great.' Helen beamed across the table at Mandy.

'Do you mean Nicole Woodall?' Gran said. 'The one who moved into the house on the edge of Graylands?'

Mandy looked at Gran, caught somewhere between astonishment and hilarity. She had no idea how Gran kept up her supreme knowledge of Welford's inhabitants, despite the fact that the village now extended miles down the Walton road. 'That's the one,' she agreed. 'I thought I should take on someone before social services came calling. They might want to know why Hope Meadows is staffed by octogenarians,' she added and was pleased when Gran let out a peal of laughter.

Despite being hungry, Mandy didn't enjoy Gran's pasties as much as she had hoped. Not that they didn't taste good. They were delicious. But she couldn't help being troubled by the continuing silence from Jimmy. If he hadn't got back to her by one thirty, she would have to call him. Adam was still out when they sat down to lunch, but Emily had returned. She was looking paler than ever, Mandy thought. It seemed stupid, but until she heard from Jimmy, she didn't feel she could tell her mum about the solicitor's call. All through lunch, she was willing the phone to ring, but when it reached one forty-five, she pushed her chair out.

'I'm going upstairs for a minute,' she said.

To her relief, Mum just smiled. 'See you soon,' she said.

Even though she told herself she was being daft, Mandy's fingers were shaking as she pressed the buttons to dial Jimmy's number. She wondered if his phone was switched off, which would explain why he hadn't replied. She perched herself on the edge of the bed and stared out of the window at the orchard. On the other end of the line, Jimmy's phone was ringing. So it was turned on, thought Mandy.

After what seemed an age, she heard his breathless voice. 'Mandy! Sorry I didn't get back to you.' He sounded as if he was running. 'It's been crazy up here this morning.'

Mandy frowned. Even if there had been a lot going on, couldn't he have found time to respond to her text? It would only have taken a minute. He must have known it was important to her. 'I was wondering whether you'd like to come with me this evening?' she said, cringing at the note of hope in her voice.

'I'm afraid I can't,' he said. 'Not tonight.' Mandy could

hear voices in the background, then Jimmy's voice again, filled with tension. 'Hope it goes well. I'll call as soon as I can.' The phone went dead.

Mandy could feel the wooden edge of the bed pressing into her thighs. Had something happened at Running Wild, she wondered? If there had been an accident, it would explain Jimmy's strange tone. But wouldn't he have told her? Putting her hands behind her on the bed, Mandy leaned back. Had it really been necessary to be so short with her? She had been so excited. Now she just felt worried.

Pulling herself upright, she crossed the bedroom floor, walked over the landing and into the bathroom. After splashing her face with cold water, she felt slightly better. She knew what it was like to be rushed off her feet; she wasn't such a sensitive snowflake that she had to take Jimmy's response personally. She would ask Helen to come to Lamb's Wood Cottage instead. And it was about time she told Mum as well.

Emily was delighted. She hugged Mandy and congratulated her. Adam too was excited when he returned. But Mandy's own happiness was tempered by a worm of unease about Jimmy. He hadn't even congratulated her. What could possibly have been so urgent that he didn't care about her purchase of Lamb's Wood Cottage?

'You had a good time the other night, didn't you? Nothing went wrong, I mean?' Helen frowned as she sat down behind the reception desk. So far, evening surgery had been quiet. With a bit of luck, they would get away early.

Mandy thought back to Friday evening in the Fox and Goose. You could hardly say it had been a night of romance and starlight, but she and Jimmy had got on well, hadn't they?

'It wasn't the best evening ever,' she conceded. 'It was busy because of the Christmas light thing, but . . .' She shrugged. 'It was fine.'

'What about the end of the night?' Helen's eyes studied her. 'He walked you home? What did he say? Did you talk about seeing each other again?'

'Yes.' Mandy thought back to those few minutes when Jimmy had asked her if she would change her mind about going on a real date. What had she replied? Had she been definite enough? She thought she had. 'He said something like . . .' She rubbed her forehead. 'Could I be persuaded to go on another date . . . something like that. And I said maybe I could.' She rolled a Biro across the counter. 'It sounds a bit feeble when I say it like that, but I'm sure it didn't come across that way.'

'Did he say anything after that?'

Mandy closed her eyes, trying to remember. She had suggested something else to him, hadn't she? A picture of Holly and Robin came into her mind and she smiled. 'I told him he should bring Abi and Max round to meet the donkeys,' she said. 'Don't you think they'd love that?'

But Helen's expression was ambivalent. 'I'm sure they would,' she said. Her mouth had stretched to a straight line and her eyebrows were raised. 'But perhaps he thought that was rushing things? When my sister and her husband split and she met someone else, it took ages for her to introduce their kids to her new boyfriend. Even though she liked him very much, she wanted to be absolutely sure. She was really mad when her ex introduced her two girls to a whole series of girlfriends. It caused no end of trouble between them.'

Mandy stared at Helen in confusion. 'But I've already met the twins,' she pointed out.

Helen nodded. 'Wasn't that when you were still with Simon? Even if Jimmy liked you back then, he wouldn't have been introducing you as a girlfriend.'

Mandy frowned. Was it really possible that her question had offended Jimmy? He talked about the twins often enough, but it was true he had never suggested that they all hang out together. She ran her hands through her hair. He had kind of brushed off her question without answering, but she still didn't believe it was enough to have put him off calling her back. He'd told her he'd ring her afterwards.

'Mandy?' She was jolted out of her reverie by Helen's voice. Almost at the same time, she heard the door opening and turned around to welcome the next client.

It was Roo Dhanjal. As Roo pulled open the door, Mandy felt a shock of alarm. Roo's beautiful face was crumpled with worry. Was something wrong with one of the young cats she had adopted in the summer?

'What's wrong?' Mandy blurted out. 'Is it one of the kittens?'

Roo viewed her for a moment with surprise. 'No,' she said, 'they're fine. It's . . .' She paused and fiddled with the strap of her bag. 'We've had a really bad review,' she confessed. 'On TripAdvisor. About the campsite.'

Poor Roo. Mandy was sympathetic. 'I know most people are lovely,' she said, 'but there are a few who're not so nice. You shouldn't take it to heart.'

Roo shook her head. 'You don't understand,' she said. 'Someone wrote that their stay was ruined by barking and dog mess from Hope Meadows. They mention it by name. I'm sorry. I thought you should know.' Her mouth twisted with unhappiness. 'We've asked TripAdvisor to take it down,' she said. 'They've removed it, but it was there for two days before we saw it.'

Mandy felt a surge of nausea wash through her. Behind the desk, Helen looked horrified.

Roo shook her head 'I don't understand it,' she went on. 'We've never heard the dogs barking. Even outside. And there's no mess that we know of. I know you tidy up after yourself.'

Mandy glanced down at her hands. They were shaking. Is this what Grandad meant when he talked about things escalating?

'I'm not sure what it was,' Roo was saying, 'but it seemed so *personal.*' She pursed her lips, her dark eyes on Mandy's face. 'You don't think . . .' She stopped, then started again. 'You don't think someone might be trying to cause trouble, do you?'

Mandy couldn't speak. *There must be. But who could hate Hope Meadows so much?*

'What about the hole in the hedge and the cancelled food order?' Helen put in. She started to tell Roo. Mandy wanted to clap her hands over her ears, shut out the list of mishaps and coincidences that were piling up.

Instead, she rested her hands on top of the counter, willing them to keep still. 'Why would anyone have a problem with the rescue centre?' she said calmly when Helen had finished. 'It doesn't make any sense.'

'What about Mr Powell, with the donkeys?' Helen suggested. 'You said he was raging.'

'He was,' Mandy agreed, 'but the hole in the hedge appeared before I met him.'

Grandad had been right, she thought. She needed to write everything down. The order things happened in might be important. 'I did wonder about Geoff Hemmings,' she admitted. 'He was very angry when Flame went after his rabbits, understandably, but she didn't actually do any harm.' Mandy pressed her lips together as she remembered something else. 'He told Ellen Armstrong that someone was complaining about Hope Meadows in the Fox and Goose,' she said.

Helen stood up and put her arm around Mandy's shoulders. 'I know it seems awful,' she said, 'but there are loads of us who think Hope Meadows is brilliant. If you like, I can do some detective work. We could try and find out who's behind it.'

She sounded so enthusiastic that, despite everything, Mandy laughed. 'You can try if you like, Miss Marple,' she said. 'But I think I might ring Ellen.' It had seemed ridiculous when Tom Hope had suggested going to the police. Mandy would give it a day or two, she thought, to see if Helen unearthed anything obvious. Then if nothing was resolved, she would give Ellen a call.

'I'd better get back,' Roo told them. 'I left Josh in charge of the children, the cooking, and the campsite. It's a bit much, even for him. I'm so sorry, Mandy.' With an apologetic wave, she let herself out of the surgery.

Helen followed Roo to the door and locked it behind her, then turned off the main light. 'Come on,' she said to Mandy. 'Even if there is some nutjob on the loose, there's still your lovely new cottage to explore.' Mandy beamed. She had completely forgotten that she was a homeowner!

'Lucy! Sky!' Opening the door to the kitchen, Helen called to her beloved Flat Coat as well as to Mandy's much loved collie. Lucy and Sky stood up from where they had been lying curled together in front of the stove. They trotted over. 'I'll drive,' Helen offered.

'Let's take the Land Rover,' Mandy suggested. 'The track will probably be very overgrown.'

It was thoroughly dark outside. As Helen steered the vehicle down the lane, Mandy noticed that more of their neighbours had put up Christmas decorations. Curtains had been left open to reveal fir trees laden with baubles and twinkling coloured lights. They were three days into

December, Mandy realised. Wouldn't it be wonderful if she could have Lamb's Wood in a habitable state by Christmas? It wasn't long, but she had never been afraid of hard work. A few months ago, Simon had been trying to railroad her into leaving Welford to tie herself to him and to Leeds forever. For the past few months, she had been back with her parents. Although she loved them and was happy to be surrounded by her family again, the purchase of Lamb's Wood Cottage felt like a positive step towards being a fully independent adult.

The track up to the cottage was indeed becoming overrun. The Land Rover lurched over the ruts and Helen had a job to keep the wheels straight. Brambles lashed the windscreen and dragged at the tyres. At times, the headlights seemed to be shining into an impenetrable hedge between the ancient trees. But Helen ploughed on and eventually the foliage released them in front of the tumbledown barns.

Pushing open the door, Mandy climbed down and waited while Helen loosened the seatbelts for Sky and Lucy. The two dogs erupted from the car and disappeared into the darkness. Mandy grabbed the torches she had put in the glove compartment and handed one of them to Helen. It was a chilly night and for a moment, they stood there in the gloom, letting their eyes adjust. The sky above was a clear velvet blue. A full moon hung low over the trees, its cold light illuminating stark winter branches and the hunched outline of the fell on the far side of the valley. Sky was only away for a few seconds before she reappeared, but when Lucy didn't immediately return, Mandy felt a swell of nervousness. What if there really was a 'nutjob on the loose', as Helen had put it? Could he have followed them here?

Shivering, she called, 'Lucy!' and was relieved when a crescendo of rustling culminated in the black dog emerging from the shadows, her whole body wagging.

The path through the front garden was almost invisible, but some of the weeds had died back with the onset of winter and Mandy was able to bash a way through. Sky and Lucy could be seen in flashes as they rushed in and out of the torch beams. Both had their noses to the ground and their tails high in the air. Their enthusiasm for every outing, no matter how unusual, always made Mandy smile.

She reached the front door. Helen stood back and nodded to Mandy, her eyes sparkling with excitement. 'Welcome home!' she whispered.

With an odd feeling of reverence, Mandy pulled the key from her pocket. For better or worse, the cottage was hers. Although the key was stiff, she twisted it with her cold fingers and finally, with a grating noise, the door was unlocked. Gripping the handle, Mandy turned it and with Helen's help, she pushed open the door.

As Mandy stepped inside, she felt a rush of emotion. She had first set foot in the house years ago with James, when they had come to help Robbie with his ferrets. Even then, the little cottage had felt welcoming. When she had been here in the summer, the circumstances had been awful, with Robbie Grimshaw being taken away and neglected animals in every corner. But the house had still felt special. It was where she had found Sky, after all.

She had been meaning to visit Robbie for ages. Now, standing inside his old house making plans, it felt even more important to see him. After his spell in hospital, he had been moved to a residential home. It was only in Walton. She would try to find the time very soon, she thought.

As her torch cast a pale line across the hallway to the carved wooden spindles of the staircase, Mandy felt a nudge behind her knees. It was Sky. The collie's ears were back and her eyes looked nervous in the torchlight. Mandy crouched beside her, her hand caressing the soft fur. 'It's okay,' she murmured. She wondered what memories Sky held from living in the cottage. Robbie had never done anything to mistreat his dog, but her life had been very limited and unhappy. Sky would have known that her owner was sick and unable to care for his animals.

Sky's tail flickered on the stone floor. When Mandy stood up and walked into the kitchen, Sky stayed beside her, an anxious, feather-footed shadow. The last time Mandy had been in here, there had been overflowing bins and rotten potatoes all over the floor. Someone had been in since then and roughly cleaned up, but the ancient oak table still stood under the window. The moon shone gently into the room, picking out the old-fashioned cupboards and rickety stove.

Mandy ran her hand over the cupboard doors. They

seemed more or less intact, so perhaps she could get away with cleaning them and rubbing them down rather than replacing them. The stove stood near the centre of the wall opposite the window. It was made of cast iron, and looked heavier than Bill the Shire horse. The top was flat with a solid ring where a kettle could be boiled. She wouldn't be cooking a three-course Christmas dinner, Mandy realised with a wry inward smile.

Raking up the wall, Helen's torch picked out a flimsy wire that crossed the ceiling and dangled a bare light bulb above their heads. Mandy found herself ducking instinctively. She would need to get an electrician here as a priority.

'It could be really cosy in here,' Helen declared. She was being generous, Mandy thought, but she couldn't help being relieved that Helen saw potential in the little house, too.

She directed the beam of her torch at the oak table and chairs. 'I know they're filthy, but I like these,' she said. 'If I can get them clean, I think I'll keep them. It'd be difficult to find one to fit better.'

Helen let out a sigh. 'It really will be lovely,' she said. Mandy walked over to the sink. Although it was rusty, she managed to turn on the cold tap. The water that spluttered out was rusty looking as well, and after a few seconds it stopped.

'Maybe there's a stopcock somewhere,' Helen suggested. For a moment, Mandy considered going down on her hands and knees to search under the sink, but it would be better to investigate in daylight, she decided. Anyway, if there was a cold snap, it was just as well that the water was switched off.

They explored the rest of the cottage. The room opposite the kitchen had a lovely brick fireplace. The green wallpaper would have to come down, but there were spaces on either side of the chimney breast where Mandy could put bookshelves. Sky's basket would lie in the corner on the far side of the fire. In her mind's eye, she pictured a big L-shaped sofa and comfy chairs covered in soft tartan throws.

The staircase seemed sturdy enough, so it just needed some paint and a new carpet. Mandy would ask James what he thought about colour. Something warm, perhaps, like russet. Helen climbed the stairs and turned left into the little bedroom that looked out across the valley from under the eaves, but Mandy turned right into the master bedroom. This was where she had found Sky. When she stopped, the little collie sat down beside her. She looked up at Mandy and her thick black tail started to wag, sweeping across the floorboards. Bending down, Mandy buried her face in Sky's coat. She smelled of hay and leaves, sweet and clean.

'What do you think, girl?' she whispered. Sky put her head on one side. Her soft ears pricked as she listened. 'Would you like to come home? I know you've slept here before, but this time, we'll be together.' The tail twitched again. Reaching up, Sky licked Mandy's ear.

'I'll take that as a yes,' Mandy said.

Chapter Fourteen

Mandy glanced at the clock on her dashboard. There should be just enough time, she thought. She was on her way to visit Robbie Grimshaw. It would be the first time she had seen him since that awful day in the summer when she had helped the police to disarm the confused old man.

Mandy had left Sky behind with her parents. She had a feeling Robbie would enjoy seeing Sky at some point, but she needed to check it was okay to bring a dog into the home. And that Robbie was mentally clear enough to understand that he couldn't keep Sky with him. Mandy's heart skipped. She couldn't imagine the pain of having to give up your beloved animals because you were too old to care for them. Poor Robbie.

The Rowans turned out to be an impressive double-fronted Victorian house, set back from the road in its own grounds. There were extensive lawns to the front, dotted with evergreen trees and bushes. An elderly lady, well wrapped up, was walking on a pathway between the trees, using a zimmer frame to steady herself. Beside her, a nurse in pastel trousers topped by a padded jacket and hat hovered attentively.

Outside the front door, in a covered porch, a smartly dressed man in a wheelchair seemed to be enjoying the winter sunshine. He nodded to Mandy as she approached. 'Nice day for December,' he remarked.

'It's lovely,' Mandy agreed.

The front door was closed so Mandy rang the buzzer. The door was made of white-painted wood with a large window of textured glass. On the far side, she could see a graceful arched hallway.

An auxiliary, dressed in a uniform the same colour as the nurse's trousers, came and opened the door. A wave of warm air hit Mandy accompanied by the unmistakeable smell of overboiled cabbage, but the auxiliary's smile was welcoming. A name badge showed her name was Linda. 'Can I help you?' she asked, pulling the door wide to let Mandy inside.

'I'm Mandy Hope. I've come to see Robbie Grimshaw, if that's possible,' Mandy said.

From an open doorway on the right, she heard a sudden wail, which rose to a crescendo, then fell to a quiet sobbing. 'It's okay, Mrs Outhwaite,' came a voice. 'I can pick it up for you. Here you go.' A shuffling sound, then the voice again. 'It'll be fine now.' After a few moments, the sobbing stopped.

'Robbie Grimshaw?' The auxiliary regarded her with a smile. 'Of course you can see him. He can be a bit confused sometimes, but he's very gentle and loves watching the birds outside his window. He's got a visitor already today. His nephew comes quite often. I'm sure he won't mind if you join them.'

Mandy was relieved to hear that Mr Grimshaw had found some kind of peace here. He had seemed so hostile and terrified when she had seen him in the summer. Not only that, but there was a nephew visiting. Mandy hadn't realised he had family nearby. He had seemed so alone.

With directions from the auxiliary, Mandy found her way up a broad staircase and along a wide corridor to Robbie's room. It was a beautiful building, and well maintained. The walls were freshly painted in warm colours and the carpet looked brand new. Through an open doorway, she caught sight of another auxiliary seemingly deep in conversation with one of the residents.

She stepped through the open door of Mr Grimshaw's room. It too was thoughtfully decorated in a soothing shade of green. A door in one corner was ajar to reveal an en-suite bathroom. The room itself was spacious and airy, with a double bed in the centre and a large window overlooking the front garden. Two armchairs stood by the window, each with an occupant. In one sat Robbie Grimshaw himself. Mandy was pleased to see he was neatly dressed in trousers and a long-sleeved polo shirt. A young man sat opposite. He was tall and thin with dark hair, and was so engrossed in his phone that he didn't look up when Mandy entered.

'Hello,' Mandy said.

Hearing her voice, the young man lifted his head with a sharp intake of breath. He had the most brilliant blue eyes she had ever seen. They were huge and striking, rimmed with lashes so dark he might have been wearing eye-liner. If Mandy had hoped to avoid startling him, she failed spectacularly. The expression on his face mirrored that of a fox caught raiding a bin. He launched himself out of the chair, then paused just long enough to reach down and squeeze Mr Grimshaw's hand. 'I have to go now, Uncle Bob,' he muttered.

'It's fine,' Mandy said. 'You don't have to. I could get another chair,' she suggested, giving him what she hoped was a reassuring smile. He must be terribly shy, she thought.

But the young man shook his head. 'I have to go,' he said again. He glanced down at the phone, gripped in his long pale fingers. 'Goodbye,' he said, and with a nod of his head, he strode out of the room.

Mandy looked after him, feeling rather sorry. She was delighted that Robbie had someone to visit him, and she wished she hadn't scared him away. She would have liked to speak to a member of Robbie's family and tell them how honoured she was to be the new owner of Lamb's Wood Cottage.

Robbie didn't seem to notice that he had lost one visitor and gained another. He was gazing out of the window as if his head was filled with peaceful thoughts. Mandy felt a pang as she looked at his tidy hair and realised that it had been combed in a different direction than the one she remembered. She told herself that Robbie was being well cared for, which was all that mattered.

'Hello, Mr Grimshaw,' Mandy said. She might as well sit down in the seat Robbie's nephew had vacated, she thought. The old man still seemed oblivious to her presence. Mandy followed his gaze through the window. Beyond the grassy garden, there were glimpses of other large houses among well-maintained trees. The roofs of Walton stretched away as the land started to slope up, and behind them, in the distance, the fells were visible. Was Mr Grimshaw remembering long ago days when the dales were his playground, Mandy wondered?

'Can you see Norland Fell from here?' she asked out loud. There was no reply. Moving her chair a little, she spotted the long ridge that topped the high moor. 'I can't quite see High Cross Farm,' she went on, 'but I passed by a couple of days ago.'

High Cross was where Mr Grimshaw had helped Mandy and James with some rabbits many years ago. 'Remember you went there with your ferrets?' she prompted.

For the first time, Robbie reacted. 'Kirsty?' he said, turning with wide eyes to look at her.

'That's right. Kirsty,' Mandy echoed. She pictured Robbie cradling his favourite creature, Kirsty's beady eyes fixed on his.

The old man gazed at Mandy, his head on one side. 'Who are you?' he said and then, 'Where's Kirsty?' He stretched his hand towards Mandy. Reaching out her own, she grasped it. It felt as brittle as a bird and the thin skin was flecked with age spots, but the old man's grip was surprisingly firm.

'Kirsty is safe,' Mandy assured him. It was sort of true, she thought. Kirsty was long past any harm. 'All your animals are safe,' she said. 'The cows and the sheep, your lovely Shire horse. Your dog Shy.' She used the original name that Robbie had given her beloved dog.

'Shy?' There was a look on Mr Grimshaw's face as if he was trying to remember and he squeezed Mandy's hand. For a moment, she thought he was going to say something else, but his shoulders dropped and the pressure on her hand faded. 'Kirsty,' he said again, just as the auxiliary Mandy had spoken to earlier bustled into the room.

'Who's Kirsty?' the woman asked Mr Grimshaw, but the old man made no sign of answering. 'She was one of Mr Grimshaw's ferrets years ago,' Mandy explained to the woman. 'He used to have a smallholding.'

'Oh.' Linda's eyes were compassionate as she looked from Mandy to the old man. 'It's lovely that you've brought back some happy memories for him.' If Robbie Grimshaw was following the conversation, he showed no sign. 'And I'm sorry, Mandy, but Mr Grimshaw has an appointment with the physiotherapist in five minutes. I came to get him ready.'

'No problem,' Mandy replied. She glanced at her watch. It was nearly time for afternoon surgery. She rested her hand on top of Robbie Grimshaw's. 'I'll come back another day,' she promised, but the old man was looking out of the window again and did not respond.

'It was nice of you to come,' Linda told her. 'I'm glad you and he had a chance to talk about his animals and it would be lovely to see you back again.'

Mandy managed a smile. It was impossible to tell whether her visit had been good for Robbie. The feeling of melancholy that had threatened on the way intensified as she walked back down the stairs. Lovely as it was here, she was sure Robbie must miss the animals and the space he'd been used to all his life. Mandy recalled the young man she had disturbed. At least Robbie had someone who loved him enough to visit. Mandy made a mental note to come again soon, this time with Sky. Perhaps they could take her for a walk in the garden, and remind Robbie of old, happy times. Maybe some of the other residents would like to be introduced to some of the rescues. She knew there were many homes where dogs were encouraged to visit. Next time, she would try to find out whether the Rowans ran such a scheme. The more Hope Meadows could do to become a positive presence in the local community, the better it would be.

'Do you have anything planned for tonight?' Adam asked Mandy as they were clearing the dinner table.

For once, Mandy didn't have to rush back to the rescue centre to finish her chores. Nicole had visited for the first time that afternoon and proved to be a quick learner, as well as willing to tackle the least glamorous tasks. She had single-handedly cleaned out the rabbits and guinea pigs, and then helped Mandy with some donkey handling before grooming the cats. Like Mandy's dad, Nicole had been very taken with Tango, and had gone back several times to give him an extra cuddle.

Mandy slotted the last of the plates into the dishwasher. 'No plans at all,' she said. 'Why?'

Adam walked over to the stereo in the corner and slipped his mobile into the socket that connected his smartphone to the speakers. 'We're going to write Christmas cards,' he said. 'Since you're a member of the practice now, we thought you should join us.'

Mandy smiled. 'It would be an honour! Shall I put the kettle on?'

Adam was fiddling with the smartphone. The pure sound of a chorister's voice came through the speakers. 'Once in royal David's city . . .'

Adam turned to look at Mandy. 'I have something better here,' he said with a wink. Opening a cupboard, he pulled out a bottle and showed it to Mandy. 'An early present from Mrs Anthony,' he explained. Mrs Anthony was one of their regular clients, who had a garden full of treasured rabbits.

'*Murgatroyd's Mulled Wine.*' Mandy read out the name on the side of the bottle.

'I'm on call tonight,' Emily announced. 'None for me, I'm afraid.'

Adam was grinning at Mandy. 'Just us then,' he said. 'Oh and . . .' he held up a finger. 'Wait here.' He rushed out of the kitchen, reappearing shortly wearing a headband with a pair of red plastic antlers. Looking pleased with himself, he reached up and pressed a tiny switch. The antlers began to flash and a tinny rendition of *Rudolph the Red-Nosed Reindeer* competed with the choir on the stereo.

Mandy shook her head. Her dad always threw himself wholeheartedly into the festivities at this time of year. Christmas in Welford wouldn't be the same without him.

'How did Nicole get on?' Emily asked, setting out pens alongside piles of Christmas cards.

Mandy sat down and shuffled her cards into a tidy stack before taking one to sign. 'Really well,' she said. 'I'll have to be careful not to monopolise her time. I have to share her with Molly Future!'

As she wrote her name beneath the printed message, Mandy's mind wandered back to the work they had done with Robin and Holly that afternoon. The two donkeys were becoming far easier to handle, and Holly even let Nicole pick up each of her tiny hooves and tap them gently with a hoofpick. They had taken Flame out as well, and the lurcher had been fascinated with the foals, staring at them with her tail wagging gently until Nicole had joked that perhaps Mandy should consider rehoming the three of them together.

Lifting her glass, Mandy took a mouthful of mulled wine, savouring the flavours of cinnamon and clove.

Adam had warmed it up on the hob. He had slipped in a cinnamon stick and several slices of orange, and it was delicious. The kitchen smelled wonderful too. Whoever Murgatroyd was, he knew what he was doing.

Adam stood up. 'Another glass?' he offered.

She was feeling distinctly cheerful. 'That would be lovely,' she said.

'How about you, Emily?' Adam looked over at her mother, who was leaning her head on her hand as she wrote. 'Would you like some more orange juice?'

Emily looked up and shook her head. 'Not just now thanks,' she replied.

Moving over to the pan of still-warm wine, Adam wielded the ladle and returned with a brimming glass. 'Hey Mandy,' he began, his eyes sparkling. 'What do you call a law that calls for the banning of Father Christmas?'

Mandy put down her pen. There came a time every year when Adam would begin to regale her with ridiculous Christmas jokes. Obviously this year was to be no exception. She wracked her brain trying to think of an answer. A law banning Father Christmas? 'I have no idea,' she admitted.

Adam looked triumphant. 'An anti Santa Clause,' he declared. With a flourish of his hand, he made a low bow. Mandy's groan turned to a laugh as her dad knocked his antlers against a chair, snapping them in half. 'Oh!' He stood up looking embarrassed, one antler flashing at a crazy angle behind his left ear.

'Are you all right?' Mandy asked, once she had managed to control herself.

'I'm fine.' Grabbing the antlers, Adam switched them off and tossed them onto the kitchen counter. 'So much for Rudolph,' he said.

'Well, if we're going for cheesy jokes . . .' Mandy warned. She waited a moment until her father had settled himself back in his seat and was looking at her, eyebrows raised. 'What do Santa's helpers create for him every year on the first of January?'

Adam held up his hands to admit defeat. 'Go on, tell us,' he said.

'An Elf and fitness plan,' she flashed back with a sheepish grin.

Adam rolled his eyes. 'Now that is truly awful,' he said. 'Ten out of ten for cheesiness. You win. Christmas is officially here!' He looked delighted and Mandy thought he might stand up and do a celebratory lap of the kitchen. But her father's gaze had fallen on Emily who was sitting at the end of the table. She had been very quiet through their silliness, Mandy thought. Usually she would have joined in. 'Are you all right, love?'

To Mandy's horror, Emily's face was ashen. 'I just need a glass of water,' she mumbled. Pushing her chair away from the table, she tried to stand up but her legs gave way. She slumped to the floor with a faint yelp.

Thrusting her own chair aside, Mandy rushed across. 'Lie down, Mum,' she urged. 'Lie down, please.' She put her arm around Emily's shoulders and lowered her down so she was lying on her back. Pulling the chair round, she gently lifted Emily's feet up so they were resting on the seat. A modicum of colour returned to Emily's face. Mandy's hands were shaking.

Adam crouched down beside his wife and stroked her hair. 'Emily?' he said, his voice hollow. 'It's all right. We're here.' He looked up at Mandy. 'Can you get the phone? We need to call an ambulance.'

Emily shook her head, her hair brushing the carpet. 'I don't need an ambulance. I just felt a bit faint. I'll be fine in a minute.'

Mandy studied her mother. Emily was less pale now, though her pupils were still huge and her eyes were shadowed. 'I'm going to call 111,' Mandy said. 'Let them decide.' Walking out into the hall, she felt a tightness across her chest and shoulders. She had been worried about her mum for ages. Why hadn't she had done something before now? With a lump in her throat, she dialled the number.

'They're going to call back,' she told her dad, returning to the kitchen. Adam had helped Emily to her feet and was steering her into the living room. He settled her on the sofa and covered her with a blanket, then stood gazing down at her, his brow furrowed. Mandy winced. Her father had always seemed infinitely strong and capable, whatever happened. But this seemed to be more than he could bear. Emily was lying still, her eyes closed, but she was breathing evenly and her cheeks were a little pinker.

It felt like an age before the callback came. After

answering what felt like hundreds of questions, Mandy handed the phone to Emily. 'They want to talk to you,' she said.

She listened to her mum's half of the conversation. It all seemed far too casual, with Emily dismissing her collapse as a mild dizzy spell. 'Thank you so much. I'll do that,' Emily said finally. She passed the phone back to Mandy. 'I don't need an out-of-hours appointment,' she said. 'I'll go to the GP first thing.' She lay her head back on a cushion, looking exhausted. 'Don't worry about me, I'm fine,' she murmured, shutting her eyes again.

'You're not fine,' Adam told her briskly. 'But we'll do everything we can to get you better. Come on, let's haul you up to bed.'

Mandy blinked back the tears that stung her eyes. Biting her lip, she helped her dad steer Emily up the stairs, then made her way to her own bedroom. She lay awake a long time.

Chapter Fifteen

Mandy was glad nothing complicated came in next morning. Her father had taken Emily along to the GP clinic while Mandy covered surgery, and she was finding it nearly impossible to concentrate.

Helen Steer, predictably, had been wonderful as soon as she heard the news. The nurse had arrived that morning laden with Christmas decorations, but as soon as she had seen Mandy's face, she had stowed them away.

'What's wrong?' she'd demanded, and Mandy had poured out all the details. About Emily being tired and pale for so long; about her terrifying collapse last night. Helen had been neither dismissive, nor hysterical. She had agreed that Emily had looked tired recently, and then had set about sorting out the workload. She called a client whose dog had been booked in to see Emily for a non-emergency dental and another whose cat was due for sterilisation. Mandy had been relieved when the dental client had been happy to postpone. She could deal with the cat herself. There was at least one call she would have to attend later, but for now, she just wanted to know what the GP had said.

She was relieved to see Emily in the car when her dad pulled into the drive. Mandy had half-expected her mum to be referred straight into hospital. By the time she had washed her hands and gone through to the kitchen, Emily was sitting at the table. Adam was outside, moving the car away from the door. It was raining hard so he'd spared Emily a soggy walk to the back door.

'Mum?' As soon as Mandy spoke, Emily turned and held her arms out. Mandy flew over to hug her. 'What did they say?' Letting go, she pulled out a chair and sat close beside her mum, holding her hand.

'They weren't sure.' Emily's voice was husky. 'They think I'm a bit anaemic, but they want to check if there's anything else going on. They took a load of blood samples.'

Adam walked in and smiled at his wife and daughter. 'They really did.' He kicked off his shoes. 'If she wasn't anaemic before, she certainly will be now.' It was just like her dad to try to lighten things with a joke, Mandy thought. Even Emily raised a faint smile. 'Mandy?' Adam looked apologetic. 'Would you be able to look after Mum for a few minutes? I have to phone Mr Hapwell at Twyford about his bull.'

'Of course,' Mandy said as Emily protested, 'I'm not an invalid!'

Adam walked over, put his hand on Emily's shoulder and gave it a squeeze. 'I'll be back as soon as I can,' he told her, bending to kiss her forehead. With a final worried glance, he disappeared.

'What can I get you, Mum?' Mandy still had hold of Emily's fingers. They felt cold. 'Would you like to lie down? I could help you up to bed and bring you a cup of tea, if you'd like.'

'That sounds very indulgent,' her mum said. 'Thank you, love.'

Mandy held on to her mum's arm as Emily pushed herself up from the chair and walked slowly upstairs. It was all wrong. Emily never allowed anyone to help her. Tears pricked at Mandy's eyes when she came back down, but she blinked them away. Even Sky seemed worried, clinging to Mandy's heels as she prepared the tea and carried it up to the bedroom. Emily was almost asleep. Leaving the mug on the bedside table, Mandy tiptoed downstairs and went through to the clinic.

'How is she?' Helen asked as soon as Mandy appeared. 'Your dad rushed out here, made a call, then rushed back into the house,' she added. 'I didn't like to disturb him.'

Mandy sighed. 'We don't know much more than before,' she admitted. 'They've taken blood. The results won't be back till after the weekend.' It seemed an impossibly long time to wait.

Perching herself on one of the chairs at the reception desk, Mandy looked at the work list. There was nothing on until this afternoon, when she was due to carry out the Dillons' house visit. 'Is there really nothing to do?' she said to Helen. 'I could use the distraction, to be honest.'

Helen pushed her heavy ponytail over her shoulder and shrugged. 'I was going to put up the decorations, but it doesn't seem right when your mum's not well.'

Mandy looked around the waiting room. Despite being clean and well lit, the room seemed dull as the winter rain hammered against the window. It wasn't as if Emily would mind a few festive ornaments, she thought. Mum loved Christmas as much as Adam did.

'Where did you put the decs?' she asked Helen.

'In the cupboard with the cleaning equipment. Your dad got the tree down and put it in there yesterday.'

Mandy stood up and opened the door to the cupboard. Helen came and peered over her shoulder. The tree and its ornaments lay in a sad pile in the dark. 'Maybe we could put the tree up at least,' Mandy suggested, picking up a strand of tinsel that was trying to wriggle free. 'It would cheer the place up.'

'One Christmas elf reporting for duty!' Helen responded with a grin. She leaned into the cupboard and grabbed the trunk of the artificial tree. 'Can you bring the base?' she called over her shoulder as she hauled the tree out.

Lifting the plastic feet from the box, Mandy followed Helen back into the waiting room. Between them, they slotted the base together and began unfolding the fluffy green branches. Mandy had a moment's wistful pang for the fresh spruces that she and her father used to fetch from the Christmas tree farm near York. Nothing could beat the scent of real pine needles. But they weren't good for dog paws, and cats were less likely to nibble artificial branches, so Animal Ark went with the health and safety festive option.

It didn't take long to hang up lights, silver tinsel, and a whole host of baubles, some of which Mandy remembered from her childhood. 'I think it looks lovely,' Helen declared, tapping a glittery gold bauble with her fingertip so that it spun slowly.

Mandy rummaged at the bottom of the cardboard box of decorations. She pulled out a heap of white tissue paper and unwrapped it to reveal a lamp in the shape of a star. 'I can't believe this thing still works,' she murmured, placing it on the reception desk and plugging it in.

Helen beamed. 'We'll have the three wise men here in no time.' She started to tidy away the bubble wrap where the baubles had been stored. 'Did you get in touch with the police about the weird things that have been happening?' she asked. 'Roo Dhanjal called in while you were with your mum. They haven't had any more strange reviews, but she asked after you.'

Mandy felt her shoulders droop. She'd had so much on her mind, what with the visit to Robbie Grimshaw and then Mum being ill, that she'd forgotten she had to call Ellen Armstrong. She shook her head.

Helen regarded her with sympathy. 'I know it's probably the last thing you want to think about,' she said. 'But I really do think you should phone.'

A wave of apathy washed over Mandy. 'I'll do it later,' she said. 'When I get back from the house visit.'

Helen, brisk as ever, put out her hand and rubbed Mandy on the arm. 'I think you should do it now,' she said. 'Get it over with.'

Mandy sighed. 'Okay then.' She looked round the room at the newly dressed tree and the star on the reception desk. Christmas was supposed to be a time for celebration. This year, it was hard to feel overwhelmed with good cheer. She took her phone into the cottage and up to her bedroom. She wanted some privacy for this call.

As she ran through the list again – the hole in the hedge, the sabotaging of her food order and the TripAdvisor review – she found herself wondering whether Ellen would dismiss her concerns. But the police officer seemed to take her seriously at once.

'Don't forget about the gossip in the Fox and Goose,' she reminded Mandy. 'If there were fewer things, it could just have been bad luck, but it's starting to look like some kind of campaign.'

A campaign? Really? Mandy walked over to the window and looked out at the donkeys. Holly and Robin were standing nose to tail in the field shelter. Robin was chewing a thistle. *Are you pretending to be Eeyore?* Mandy thought. *He only ate thistles.*

Ellen's voice interrupted her musings. 'Can you think of anyone who might have a grudge against you?'

It was still raining. The stone and wood-framed rescue centre looked sturdy and secure against the dark sky. Mandy thought of the animals inside that were safe now.

Why would anyone want to harm them? 'I can't think of anyone,' she said.

'What about Geoff Hemmings?' Ellen suggested. 'Or Mr Powell?'

Mandy had already discussed this with Helen. 'The hole in the hedge was before Mr Powell,' she pointed out. 'And Mr Hemming?' She paused, picking a bit of dirt off the window pane. 'Could he really feel so strongly?' she asked. 'It's not as if Flame actually did any damage.'

She heard Ellen sigh. 'These sort of whispering campaigns can be very hard to deal with,' she warned. 'Keep a note of everything that seems odd, however small. I'll get in touch with the Dhanjals and TripAdvisor to see if that sheds any light on who left the review. And in the meantime, let me know at once if anything else happens.'

Mandy thanked her and ended the call. It was almost lunchtime but she didn't feel remotely hungry. Making her way downstairs, she found Adam in the kitchen. 'How's Mum?' she said.

Adam smiled. 'She's been asleep most of the morning,' he said. 'I'm going up in a minute or two to see if she wants lunch.'

'I'll go,' Mandy offered. At least she felt as if she was doing something useful by looking after Emily. There seemed to be nothing she could do about her invisible enemy, unfortunately.

★　★　★

Just before two, Mandy loaded her bag into the RAV4 and drove to the Dillons' house for the home inspection for Melon the Westie. She very much hoped that Melon would soon be in a lovely new home. Mum had still been asleep when she had gone up to see her, and lunch with Adam had been subdued. The Dillons lived on the far side of Walton, not far from the residential home where Mandy had visited Robbie Grimshaw. Mrs Dillon opened the door wearing blue linen trousers and a fluffy mohair sweater. The delicious smell of homemade biscuits greeted Mandy as she stepped inside.

'Hello,' she said. She glanced down at the paperwork she had brought with her. Despite having done a few of these visits, she liked to have a basic plan to follow.

'Hello again.' Mrs Dillon ushered Mandy through into the kitchen. The house seemed very neat and tidy, and very quiet. 'Sam and Buddy are at school,' Mrs Dillon explained. An image slipped into Mandy's head of Sam with her statement haircut and piercings, paired with a school uniform. She wondered what the teachers thought, and hoped they had seen through to the gentle girl underneath. 'Where do you want to start?' Mrs Dillon asked.

Mandy spotted that the kitchen had a door to the garden. 'Maybe we could have a look outside first,' she suggested. The rain had stopped, though the grass was still wet. Mrs Dillon followed her outside and stood on the patio as Mandy paced around, making notes. A well-kept lawn was surrounded by flowerbeds with a few shrubs. It only took a few moments to check that there was nothing poisonous to dogs if Melon fancied an al fresco nibble. Mandy walked around the perimeter. There was a wooden fence made of upright spars, quite close together: too small for Melon to get his head through.

'Is the fence tall enough?' Mrs Dillon queried. She was looking rather nervous, Mandy noticed with a stab of sympathy. Hopefully, she would be able to relax soon. From what she had seen so far, the house and garden were perfect.

'It's definitely tall enough,' Mandy assured her. 'I'm checking for small gaps at the base. Melon is a typical terrier,' she added. 'If he thinks can burrow under something, he'll give it a try.'

Mrs Dillon smiled. 'I'll watch out for signs of digging!'

'There's a couple of places where the ground dips right to the bottom of the panels.' Mandy bent over, pointing out the risk points. 'Those'll need filling with a bit more soil.' She straightened up. 'But everything else is great. I'll give you a list of recommendations and if you still want to go ahead with the adoption, you can sort them out and I'll come back in a few days to check.'

She peered through the fence at the garden next door. 'Do your neighbours have dogs?' she asked, and was relieved when Mrs Dillon shook her head. She usually recommended that any rehomed dogs should go for a walk with the neighbour and their dogs but that was one less thing for Mrs Dillon to worry about. 'If any do move in,' she said, 'it's a good idea to socialise them together. Try to take them out for walks and so on. That way Melon is less likely to react when they make a noise. You don't want to set off the Twilight Barking in Walton!'

With a final mark on her notes, Mandy led the way back inside. 'Do you have an idea where Melon's bed will be?' she asked. 'He'll need somewhere that's just his, somewhere he can get some peace if he feels like being on his own.'

Mrs Dillon frowned. 'We've already got him a bed,' she said, 'but I hadn't really thought about where it would go. Is there anywhere you'd recommend?'

Mandy opened a door and discovered a small utility room next to the kitchen. 'What about in here?' she suggested.

'I'm in and out of here quite often.' Mrs Dillon went in and looked around the little room. 'But there's space in the corner by the tumble dryer, if you think that would be okay. I don't want him to feel like he's been banished to the scullery.'

Mandy smiled. Mrs Dillon was fast becoming a dead cert for Melon's new mum. 'I think it would be fine,' she said. 'Will you be able to feed him in here as well?'

'We could put his food bowl beside his bed,' Mrs Dillon said. 'But perhaps his water bowl should go by the door in the kitchen, so he can always get to it?'

'That sounds great,' Mandy agreed. 'Now, I know Sam and Buddy will be excited to have a new pet, but will you explain the importance of letting Melon have his own space if he looks like he needs it?'

'Absolutely. I won't let them bug him, I promise.'

'And when you go out, he'll be able to stay in here with water and a few toys to keep him entertained. I can recommend some of his favourites if you like.'

Mrs Dillon nodded. 'Would you like a cup of tea?' she offered. Walking back into the kitchen, she picked up a pair of oven gloves. 'Must get these out,' she said. When she opened the oven door, the delicious scent of biscuits that had greeted Mandy on her arrival grew stronger.

Mandy sat down at the table and filled in another form as Mrs Dillon set the kettle to boil.

'Have you thought about furniture?' Mandy asked. 'Yours, I mean. Do you think he'll go on your sofa, or would you prefer him to stay on the floor? We can talk about training him, if that'd help. Some dogs have a special blanket they know is theirs which you can put out when you want them to join you.'

Mrs Dillon poured hot water onto teabags in two mugs and set one of them in front of Mandy. 'Would you be able to go through that at the second visit?' she asked. 'I'll talk to Peter and then you can go over it with the children when we collect Melon, if everything's okay, of course.' She deftly slid the biscuits off the tray onto a cooling rack. 'Would you like one?'

'I would love one! Thanks.' Mandy found her mouth was watering. 'I'm happy to go through some training tips when everyone's together.' She took a bite of the biscuit and chewed for a moment, glancing down at her paperwork. Looking up again, she smiled. 'There are only a few things to do,' she said, 'most of which we've already discussed. If you've got any questions, just ask. I'll come back in a few days for a final check, and you should have Melon by Christmas! How does that sound?'

'It sounds wonderful.' Mrs Dillon beamed. 'It's been years since I've had a dog,' she said. 'I'm really looking forward to the company. And Melon is a very special little soul, I think.'

Mandy held up her cup of tea. 'I'll drink to that,' she said.

Chapter Sixteen

'That was the last one,' Helen told Mandy as the final clients led their enthusiastic spaniel out into the darkness.

Mandy had returned from the Dillons' feeling much more cheerful. Before evening surgery, she had seen to the donkeys, dogs, cats, rabbits and guinea pigs in a whirl of energy, buoyed up by the possibility that Melon would soon have a new home. Despite all the worries, or perhaps because of them, it was important to feel that the work she was doing at Hope Meadows was making a difference in the right way.

When the waiting room door burst open, Mandy looked up, expecting to see a late-running client. She was pleased to see Seb Conway in the doorway, clutching two white plastic bags.

'Surprise!' he called out. Rubbing his feet on the mat, he strode across the room to kiss Helen. 'Surgery finished?' he asked, dumping the two bags on the counter.

'It has,' Helen replied. 'What are you doing here?' She looked confused. 'You didn't tell me you were coming.'

Seb looked sheepish. 'I heard Emily wasn't well. I thought you might be too busy to cook,' he explained, looking at Mandy. 'I hope you don't mind. I brought enough for everyone, but if it's inconvenient . . .'

'It's not,' Mandy assured him. What a thoughtful guy. Lucky Helen. For a moment, the thought of Jimmy popped into her head. He hadn't called yet. Mandy had been tempted to call him to tell him about Emily, but given his odd reaction to her news about the cottage on Monday, she had postponed it. Pushing that particular niggle aside, she sniffed the air. From the scent that was emanating from Seb's bags, it seemed he had brought some of Roo Dhanjal's wonderful food. Mandy invited him through into the kitchen.

'I'll set the table,' Helen offered, following them.

'Thanks,' Mandy said. She was about to go up to check on her mum when to her surprise, Emily walked into the kitchen. Although Adam was hovering close behind her, she was looking much more herself, and she smiled when she saw Seb and Helen in the kitchen with Mandy.

'What a lovely surprise,' she said. With Adam still shadowing her, she made her way over to the table and lowered herself into her chair. Helen had already set out knives and forks and was opening the cupboard to pull out some plates.

'What have you got in those bags, Seb?' Adam was sniffing the air like a hungry Labrador. 'I was about to make beans on toast, but that smells way better.'

Putting the two carrier bags on the table, Seb began to pull forth a series of plastic boxes. 'They're from the Dhanjals' takeaway,' he explained. 'Actually, Roo gave me a call and suggested I could bring them round.' He glanced at Mandy as he set the last of the containers on the table. 'She said she wanted to help out.'

'That's really kind of her.' Mandy hoped Seb wouldn't say anything more. Emily didn't know about the strange TripAdvisor listing and right now, Mandy didn't want to tell her.

'Roo's lovely,' Seb said.

'We should eat it while it's hot,' Helen interjected. Mandy looked at her gratefully. She and Helen had discussed PC Armstrong's reaction earlier. Helen had been pleased to hear the police constable had taken Mandy seriously, but she seemed to understand that now wasn't the time to share the news with Emily.

To Mandy's relief, her mother managed to eat a portion of the curry and rice along with some of Roo's delectable naan bread. After dinner, Emily insisted on seeing the newly decorated waiting room.

'All we need now is some gifts under the tree,' she said. 'What about you, Mandy? Would you like another box of plastic gloves? We could wrap you up a new calving jack, perhaps. What do you think?'

Mandy was relieved that her mum was feeling well enough to tease her. And she was amused to be reminded of her gift of a box of plastic gloves from the staff at Thurston's, where she had worked before coming back to Animal Ark. 'I was hoping for a new hoof rasp,' she joked. 'I've worn mine out already!'

Emily had wandered over to the reception desk and was checking the appointments book. 'Ah, I see the dental has been postponed. Thanks, Helen.'

'No problem,' said Helen. 'Mr Hodges was happy to wait until next week to make another appointment.'

Mandy waited for her mum to protest that she'd be back to work long before then, but instead Emily surprised her by yawning and heading for the door. 'I'm going back to bed,' she announced. 'The GP told me to rest and I'm not going to argue. Thank you, all of you, for taking care of everything.'

'It's what we're here for, Mum,' said Mandy, giving her a hug. 'Sleep well.'

Adam appeared in the doorway to steer Emily upstairs, and Helen and Seb pulled on their coats. 'See you in the morning!' Helen called as they let themselves out.

'Goodnight!' Mandy called back. The clinic was very quiet when everyone had gone. She pulled out her phone. She hadn't given up hoping to find a message from Jimmy, but there was still nothing. He'd said he would call as soon as he could and it had been two days now. The confidence Mandy had felt about their burgeoning relationship at the end of last week was beginning to drain away. Had Helen been right about his reluctance to allow her to hang out with the twins? Had she put too much pressure on him?

With a sigh, she flicked through her contacts. She needed to take her mind off Jimmy Marsh. Maybe she could call Jenny from Thurston's, she thought, prompted by the mention of the ridiculous box of gloves. Mandy could wish her a Merry Christmas, see how things were going over in Leeds.

Finding Jenny's number, she tapped the screen to dial.

'Mandy! What a lovely surprise.' The warmth in Jenny's voice made Mandy smile. 'How are you?'

'I'm well, thanks.' Pulling out a chair, Mandy sat down and leaned her elbow on the reception desk. She gazed at the star lamp, which glowed with a soft yellow light. 'How about you?'

'Oh . . . busy, busy. Same old routine, with added Christmas spirit!' Jenny laughed. 'Angela's being strict with all the clients and going mad when dogs cock their legs on her desk. Peter still moans every time he gets an unusually sized animal in. Bossy boss Amy is bossing as normal. Nothing ever changes at Thurston's,' she commented. 'Oh, except . . .' Her voice tailed off.

'What is it?' Mandy was dying to hear whatever had brought Jenny to a halt. Up until six months ago, Thurston's gossip had been a huge part of her life.

Jenny sighed. 'I suppose I might as well tell you. It's not a secret. Samantha has moved in with Simon.'

Mandy was glad she was sitting down. Although she and Simon were ancient history, there was still a shock that ran through her and left her legs wobbly. 'Gosh,' she said. 'That was fast.' She took a breath and let it out, feeling the immediate confusion pass. The idea didn't sting as much as she had expected.

'As far as I know, nothing started before you left,' Jenny said quickly, as if she was trying to reassure Mandy.

Mandy found, perhaps against the odds, that she believed what Jenny had said, at least as far as Simon was concerned. She thought back to six months earlier, when she had left Simon behind to come to Welford. Simon and Samantha had become closer the moment the door shut behind her, that had been obvious. The pair of them had even gone out together to look at practice premises for Mandy and Simon to start a clinic. Mandy wanted to laugh at her naivety. It seemed obvious in hindsight that Samantha had been interested in snagging her boyfriend. There had been a flattering picture of Simon on the fridge in their shared flat that Samantha had put there. And she had been annoyingly flirtatious one night they had all been out during the summer. But there had been no sign back then that Simon was reciprocating.

'How about you, then?' Jenny's voice broke through her thoughts. 'Any new love interest in sunny Welford?'

Mandy hesitated for a moment, but what harm could it do? 'Actually, I have been seeing someone,' she admitted. 'It was all going well up until Friday, but we've both been really busy since then so we haven't been in touch.' It didn't sound too bad when she said it like that. It was only a few days after all, and Jimmy had sounded very stressed on the phone. Something must have come up.

'Perhaps something came up!' Jenny's words echoed

what she had been thinking so closely that Mandy jumped. 'Does he have family in the area?'

'He has two children,' Mandy admitted, suddenly wondering if something unfortunate had befallen one of the twins. She knew Jimmy well enough to guarantee that he would drop everything else if his son or daughter needed him. Jenny's reaction had given her a different perspective on his radio silence, though Mandy very much hoped nothing bad had occurred.

'I should probably go,' Jenny said. 'I'm supposed to be going round to walk my mum's dog and it's getting late.'

Mandy smiled. She should be getting on, too. She had to do the final check of the rescue animals. Tuck them into their beds before falling into her own. 'Bye, Jenny,' she said. 'It's been great talking to you.'

'And you. Don't forget about us down here!' Jenny called, and the line went silent.

As Mandy stood up to go outside, the door opened and Adam walked in. 'Mum's asleep,' he said. 'She seems miles better already.'

'That's good,' Mandy said. 'I'm just heading out to check everything's okay.'

She was pleased when Adam replied, 'I'll come with you.' He seemed much more cheerful, to Mandy's relief. Hopefully the doctor would find something in Emily's blood tests and she would be treated and everything could get back to normal.

'I just spoke to Jenny at Thurston's,' she told him,

opening the back door and stepping outside. The air was sharp and cold, and the sky was scattered with stars. As they crossed the grass to look at the donkeys, Mandy could feel the ground was already firmer, as if it had started to freeze.

'How is Jenny?' Adam asked. Although he had never met them, apart from Simon, Mandy had often talked about her colleagues in Leeds.

'She's fine.' Holly and Robin were standing close together in their shelter. With their thick coats, full of healthy oils, they didn't seem to be concerned at the change in the weather. Mandy gave them each a piece of carrot. They nuzzled up to her, resting their heads against her body, closing their eyes with pleasure as she ran her hands through the thick grey fur behind their ears. They were adorable little creatures, and Mandy knew she would miss them.

'Simon is going out with Samantha,' she told her dad. She spoke the words almost as a test to see how they would feel, but she found that they didn't hurt too much. She could see Adam looking at her in the dim light of the shed. 'I'm fine with it,' she added with a shake of her head. 'I'm just glad I'm back here in Welford.'

Her dad reached out and patted her arm. 'That's wonderful to know,' he said.

They headed into the rescue centre to check the dogs, cats and small furries. Mandy watched Adam carefully as they went through to the cat area; just as she had expected, he made a beeline for the old cat Tango.

'Have you heard anything more about Roo's awful TripAdvisor review?' Adam had opened Tango's cage and was stroking his ear, but he was looking over at Mandy. 'I wanted to ask earlier when Seb mentioned she'd sent the food, but I didn't know whether your mum knew.'

'Thank goodness you didn't,' Mandy said. 'I haven't told Mum and I'm not going to until we know what's wrong with her.' She opened the door to one of the female cats, a delicate silver tabby with white paws. She stroked the soft fur and listened with pleasure to the purr before closing the cage. 'I did call Ellen Armstrong earlier though,' she admitted. 'You know, the police-woman.'

'And what did she say?' Adam was still tickling Tango behind the ear.

'She seems to be taking it seriously,' Mandy said, joining her dad. Tango was pressing his head against Adam's hand, his eyes closed, purring so loudly that the whole cage was vibrating. 'I think that cat likes you,' she teased. For a moment, she toyed with the idea of telling her father that he should just get on and rehome the little animal, but she wanted the decision to be Adam's.

'I know it's worrying,' Adam said, finally withdrawing his hand and closing the door of the cage. 'But I'm sure whoever it is making this trouble, they won't do any real harm. We're here for you. Our clients are, too. Someone tells me every day how much they love having the rescue centre in the village.'

As they walked back through the chilly air, he put his arm around Mandy's shoulders and gave her a hug. Mandy leaned into his sturdy warmth. She hoped, rather than believed, that her dad was right when he said it was all going to be okay.

Chapter Seventeen

Outside the huge glass window, the grass was frosty white and tiny ice crystals clung to the apple trees. The temperature had plummeted overnight. Inside Hope Meadows, everything was running smoothly, though Mandy had to carry out a couple of buckets of water for the donkeys as their trough had frozen over.

Emily was continuing to take it easy but morning surgery was so quiet that Adam had suggested that Mandy could go over to the rescue centre for a while. She was happy to have an opportunity to update the website with photos of the cats and a very cute picture of Holly and Robin sharing a piece of turnip.

A movement through the window caught Mandy's eye and she looked up to see a tall, slim figure glide past on a bicycle. She parked her bike against the wall and removed her helmet to shake out her blonde hair. It was Nicole. Mandy was puzzled to see the teenager on what surely was a school day.

'Hi, Mandy!' Nicole sounded breathless as she pushed her way through the door. 'Burst pipes at school! I came to see if you needed a hand.'

'You angel.' Mandy felt touched that Nicole was so keen. 'I was just about to put up some Christmas decorations.' That wasn't strictly true, but it would be fun to do it while Nicole was here. Mandy had bought a tiny artificial Christmas tree and Nicole set to work, adding miniature tinsel and tiny baubles while Mandy draped tinsel around the pictures on the walls and the information board. By the time they had finished, the reception area looked very festive, especially with the wintery scene outside the window. Despite the fact that Mandy didn't feel particularly like celebrating right now, she wanted the centre to feel seasonal and welcoming for any clients who turned up.

'What's next, boss?' Nicole looked at Mandy, head on one side and eyebrows raised. Yet again, Mandy felt as if she was looking in a time-travel mirror. Nicole had a true gift with animals, as well as the ability to listen to Mandy and follow her instructions. Mandy already felt she could trust Nicole with all the residents, even the inmates that were more difficult to handle.

'Would you be able to take the dogs out?' she asked. 'You know what we've been doing with each of them.' That would mean Mandy could get on with cleaning out the other animals. She wasn't going to leave all the unpopular chores to Nicole.

'I'd love to,' Nicole said with a dazzling smile. Mandy almost wanted to hug her.

While Nicole headed outside with Melon, Mandy went through to the cat section. She wanted to take a closer look at Tango. Although the old cat was very friendly, especially when Adam visited, he had worried her over the past few days. Despite regular brushing, his coat was looking dull and patchy, and though Mandy had tempted him with different foods, he wasn't eating properly. He still seemed delighted to see her. He purred so loudly when she stroked his head, it sounded as if he might take off and buzz around the ceiling.

Lifting him out, Mandy held him against her chest. He nuzzled under her chin as she carried him to the examination table. She wasn't reassured when she studied him under the lights. As well as his coat being out of condition, Tango's aged-cat face was bonier than ever. Under his coat, she could feel ribs and the ridges of his spine. With a sigh, she put him on the small weighing scales that she kept especially for cats. He weighed half a kilo less than when he'd arrived. His condition score wasn't awful, but he couldn't afford to get any thinner. She would have to do a blood test, she decided. Once Nicole had finished with the dogs, she would ask her to help.

By the time Mandy had cleaned out the kennels, Nicole had been outside with all four of the dogs. Mandy stuck her head round the door of the dog room as Nicole was returning Flame to her bed. 'I need a hand with one of the cats, please.'

By the time Nicole came through, Mandy was hoisting Tango back onto the table. She had treated herself to a warming cabinet for clean towels, and she had laid one out for Tango. When she lowered him down, he kneaded the towel once or twice with his front paws, then snuggled down and rested his chin on the cosy fabric. Mandy gently folded the edges of the towel around his body. When they had time, she thought, she would treat Nicole to her special tutorial: *101 ways to wrap a cat*. For now, she was hoping they could manage using minimal restraint.

'I want to take a blood sample,' she explained, 'from the jugular vein that runs down his neck here.' She showed Nicole the depressions down the sides of Tango's neck where the veins lay. 'I'd like you to hold him for me like this.' Walking round behind Tango, she leaned over the table. She placed her index fingers under the cat's chin, with her thumbs reaching round behind his ears, and lifted his head so that his neck was extended. If he didn't sit still in that grip, there were loads of other things they could try, but the less they upset him, the better.

Nicole carefully moved into position and took hold of Tango's head. To Mandy's relief, Tango just yawned from inside his towelling robe. This new game they were playing was fine with him, his face seemed to say. Mandy picked up a small pair of cordless clippers. They were much quieter than the old type that had been used when she was younger. She switched them on at a distance from the cat, only bringing them to his neck once he'd had time to get used to the noise. Although some vets advocated not clipping, she found it easier to find the vein first time if she removed the fur.

'If he starts to move,' she told Nicole, 'you can distract him by rubbing behind his ears.'

With her left thumb pressing at the base of the jugular groove, Mandy spotted the line of the vessel under the skin. With her right hand, she wielded the syringe with its stubby needle, sliding the bevelled edge through the skin and into the vein. It only took a couple of seconds to draw the blood.

'That's brilliant,' she told Nicole a moment later. 'Can you press here?' Leaving Nicole putting pressure on the vein, she decanted the fluid into two test tubes, inverting the one with anticoagulant a few times to ensure it was mixed well. She would send it off to the lab later, which would offer more information than the tests she could run here.

Mandy watched as Nicole lifted Tango back into his cage, stopping for a cuddle on the way. Her blonde hair fell over Tango's head, and a wisp puffed up when he breathed. Nicole laughed and kissed the tip of the old cat's ear.

'Fancy a bit of donkey whispering?' Mandy suggested.

'Yes!' Nicole seemed keen to help with anything. 'I'll fetch my coat.'

The air was literally freezing, Mandy thought, trying not to gasp. Even with gloves on, her fingers were nipping. Her heart lifted when they walked out onto the crisp grass, carrying a halter apiece, and Robin and Holly rushed over to investigate. It was a joy to see how much they had progressed in one week. Each foal stood still while their headcollars were buckled on. Holly walked obediently beside Nicole, responding to the slightest pressure on the rope and drawing a huge grin from the teenager. Robin was still inclined to dig his heels in and lean back against the rope, but he too was beginning to get the idea.

'I'm so glad these two are here,' Nicole told Mandy, halting under a tree to wait for Robin to inch forward. 'I've never worked with baby donkeys before. They are the sweetest things ever.' Bending down, she rested her cheek on the soft fur on the side of Holly's head. The young donkey flicked her ears and wrinkled her top lip as if she was smiling.

'Let's have some hoof-picking practice,' Mandy suggested. Nicole held both lead-ropes while Mandy worked her way round, lifting each of the neat little hooves in turn. After they had done a little more leading and had a few more cuddles, they led the donkeys into their straw-lined shelter and let them go. Holly made a beeline for the pile of hay but Robin hung around Nicole, trying to nibble her sleeve.

'I think hay tastes better,' Nicole laughed, detaching him from her coat.

'Just the feeds to prepare now,' Mandy declared.

As they stood side by side in the small food prep area, Nicole turned to Mandy, looking thoughtful. 'Do you think it would be okay for more people to come and see the rescue centre?' she asked.

Mandy was surprised. Was Nicole hoping more of her

friends could visit? 'Generally yes,' she replied. 'So long as they are respectful to the animals. Was there someone in particular you wanted to invite?' It would be good to have a little more help, but Mandy wasn't about to start a crèche for stray teens. Collecting a handful of small carrots, she put them on the board and began to chop them into slices.

'It wasn't that.' Nicole used scissors to open a bag of cat food and picked up a plastic scoop. 'I just wondered if we could offer charity vouchers as a Christmas present. Like people buying a goat for someone in Africa, but more local.' She took out a neat measure of feed and poured it into a metal bowl. 'If the person receiving the voucher could come and see where the money was going, that would be fantastic. Stroke the donkeys, walk with you and the dogs, that sort of thing.'

What a wonderful suggestion, Mandy thought, pausing from her chopping to look at Nicole, then out of the window at the donkeys, then back to her carrot.

'I could design a voucher on my computer at home if you like,' Nicole added. There were spots of pink on her cheeks, and Mandy realised she had never heard Nicole say so much in one go.

'I think it's a great idea,' Mandy told her warmly. 'If you could design something, that would be wonderful. We'll chat through some ideas before you go home.'

Nicole looked as if Mandy had just offered her a baby donkey of her very own. She carried the bowls of food off to the cats, whistling a Christmas carol. Mandy smiled as she scraped the pieces of carrot into a dish. Never mind invisible enemies lurking behind the hedge. Nicole was the best ally she could have asked for!

Mandy spent the first part of her lunch hour going through the Hope Meadows accounts. Until this month, she had put quite a lot of her Animal Ark wages into the centre, but even with that, the error over the Harper's invoice had brought it home to her that things were a little too precarious. Now that she would be paying a mortgage and fixing things up at Lamb's Wood Cottage, it was essential that she should find another source of income. She raised a small amount through rehoming fees and donations. Nicole's voucher idea was brilliant, but even with that, the figures wouldn't add up for long.

Mandy closed the Excel spreadsheet and sighed. As much as she loved Hope Meadows and all the animals in it, she didn't have the energy for this at the moment. Looking up, she spotted one of the pictures on the wall that James had donated when Hope Meadows had opened. Maybe he could help, she thought. He had always been better than her at finding solutions in the murkiest circumstances. She could drive over to York to see him. It would be lovely to have a day away, and she could do some Christmas shopping in the bookshop section of his café.

Her mood lifting, she walked through into the cottage. Emily joined Mandy in the kitchen for lunch. When

Mandy asked her how she was feeling, she responded vaguely. Other than 'Not too bad,' she refused to be drawn.

She still looked pale, Mandy thought. 'Would you like a cup of tea?' she offered, finishing the last mouthful of her sandwich.

'Yes, please.' Emily smiled.

Mandy took a deep breath and turned away, busying herself with the kettle and mugs. There was an exhausted edge to her mum's features that frightened her. Though Mum was trying to act normally, it was as if a shade of the wonderful warm person that Mandy had known all these years had taken over. Once or twice, she had caught her mum looking baffled, as if Emily herself couldn't understand what was happening.

It had been ages since her mum had looked really well. She had even looked tired at James and Paul's wedding, Mandy recalled. Again the thought of Paul made her wince. She had always assumed her parents would carry on into serene old age like Tom and Dorothy, but that safe vision of the world had been cast into shadow. She should have urged Mum to go to the doctor's months ago.

But would she have gone, Mandy wondered. She turned and placed Emily's mug on the table, managing to dredge up a smile. There was nothing to do but wait for her results and let the doctors decide the next step.

★   ★   ★

Afternoon surgery was far busier than the morning had been. Mandy was relieved when Mrs Gill, who had brought Muffy in to have her teeth checked, made another appointment at the desk with Helen and left. Muffy the little terrier seemed to regard coming to the vets as a treat these days. Despite everything that was going on, Mandy's heart lifted each time she could see that her training had paid off and the animals she handled felt safe and secure in her care.

There was just time to walk to the post office, she thought, before the last collection of the day. She wanted to send off Tango's samples. It would be nice to chat to Gemma, who ran the post office as well. She always knew everything that was going on in Welford.

Helen had already packed the test tubes in protective wrapping. 'There you go,' she said, putting the thickly padded envelope in Mandy's hand. 'Tell Gemma I'll see her at Six Oaks, would you?'

Mandy knew that Helen and Gemma sometimes rode together, Helen on her grey mare Moondance and Gemma on Jarvis, her palomino gelding. 'Will do,' she replied. Calling to Sky, Mandy let herself out of the clinic and strode down the lane. She was glad of her warm jacket and woolly hat. The leafless hedges provided little shelter from the arctic wind.

She stopped outside the post office. She had come here so often as a child, sending off samples for her parents. She had even paused in front of the window to check her reflection before James's wedding in the summer. Through the glass, she could see Gemma behind the counter, reading a piece of paper. Her long blonde hair was tied back, but wisps were escaping onto her cheeks. She was wearing a sweatshirt that read, 'Warning: moody mare!' over a pair of skintight jeans and high-heeled boots. She was so different from Mrs McFarlane, who had run the post office years ago. Mrs McFarlane had always worn a blue gingham overall and thick tights with sensible flat shoes. Pressing down the shiny brass thumb plate that opened the catch, Mandy pushed the door inwards.

Gemma looked up as the door swung open. Her face looked surprisingly warm, and there was a flustered expression in her eyes. 'Mandy!' she exclaimed. 'I was just . . .' She tailed off.

Mandy frowned. 'Is everything okay?'

Gemma blew out her breath through pursed lips, looking pained. 'I've just found a petition on the notice-board,' she said. 'I'm glad you came in. I didn't know what I should do about it.' Her eyes dropped from Mandy's face to the paper on the counter and back up again.

'What does it say?' Mandy's chest felt suddenly tight. The petition could be about anything, she reminded herself.

Gemma's face crumpled with distress. 'I'm afraid it's about Hope Meadows,' she said.

'Can I see?' Mandy held out her hand. She had to concentrate hard to stop it from shaking.

Gemma turned the paper towards her.

'WE THE UNDERSINED CALL FOR THE CLOSEING OF HOPE MEADOW'S ANIMAL CENTER.' Bile rose in Mandy's throat. She swallowed. There were poorly printed lines underneath, though there was only one signature, which was quite illegible. The whole thing was badly produced, but its intent was crystal clear.

'Did you see who put it up?'

She looked at Gemma, hoping against hope that she could give Mandy a description, but Gemma shook her head. 'I'm afraid not,' she said. 'It wasn't there first thing this morning. I think it must have been added when I was dealing with the dairy delivery. I'm going to throw it in the bin of course,' she added, her voice suddenly fierce. 'Who would do such a thing? It's horrible.'

Mandy felt a rush of gratitude, but it didn't make the situation less ghastly. 'Please don't throw it in the bin,' she urged. 'It's not the first thing that's happened. Someone wrote a review on TripAdvisor complaining about me. They messed up my food order, and someone made a hole in the hedge.' The hole was the worst of all, Mandy thought. One of the animals could easily have been hurt on the road or even killed.

'That's awful.' Gemma looked even more dismayed. 'Have you been to the police?'

'I've spoken to them.' Mandy took a deep breath. 'That's why I don't want you to throw the petition away. PC Armstrong might want to come out and speak to you.'

Gemma twisted her hair in her hands. 'It's hard to take in,' she said. 'So much hate. I don't understand it. Everyone's always loved Animal Ark, and Hope Meadows is wonderful. Why would anyone do that?' She shook her head again, as if trying to make the logic fit. 'What was it you came in for, anyway?' she prompted.

Mandy had almost forgotten Tango's sample. She handed over the package. 'Next day delivery, please,' she said. 'I'm not too late, am I?'

'No, you're not,' Gemma assured her.

Retrieving Sky from her position outside the door, Mandy set off to walk back. Her legs felt heavy. She thought of Robin and Holly, of Melon and Flame, the other dogs, cats, rabbits and guinea pigs. How could anyone be offended by them? Risk hurting them? She was no nearer to reaching an answer by the time Animal Ark hove into view.

Looking down at Sky, Mandy sighed. 'Who on earth hates the rescue centre so much?' she wondered out loud. Sky wagged her tail. Mandy just wanted to cry.

Chapter Eighteen

She had been putting it off for long enough, Mandy decided when she woke on Friday morning. She was going to have to get in touch with Jimmy. She desperately wanted to speak to someone other than Helen about her awful trip to the post office yesterday. Mum and Dad already had enough to worry about.

She hesitated with her hand outstretched. Should she wait until later? It was too early to call, but she could text him. She might get a message straight back. It would put her mind at rest. If she didn't get a text, she could always call later.

She should get it over with. There could be lots of good reasons why Jimmy hadn't called. Lifting her phone from the bedside table, Mandy tapped out a text. 'Are you free for dinner tonight? I would love to see you.' She looked at it for a moment before pressing send. Should she be more circumspect? More angry he hadn't been in touch with her? It was difficult to do those things in a text message. If Jimmy had lost interest, it would soon be obvious. If it wasn't already . . . Taking a deep breath, Mandy pressed the send button. Then she slid out of bed and reached for her dressing gown.

The phone beeped before she reached the bedroom door. Feeling breathless, she checked her inbox. 'Not available tonight,' the message read. 'Can do tomorrow. Lots to tell you.'

A feeling of relief washed through her. Jimmy hadn't forgotten about her. *Something must have happened.* Tomorrow night wasn't long to wait.

'First ever dinner party at Lamb's Wood Cottage?' she typed.

'I'll bring veggie burgers and chips if you bring the champagne.' The response came winging back.

Mandy sat back down on the bed and allowed herself a smile. The tension she had felt earlier had vanished like frost in sunshine. She should have just texted Jimmy much sooner, rather than allowing doubts to fill her head. 'Sounds perfect,' she texted back and was pleased when a picture of two thumbs-up pinged onto her screen. They were seeing each other tomorrow night. Whatever else was going wrong, at least that was resolved.

After last night's dinner, Mandy hadn't expected to see Seb Conway again so soon, but he called in just after morning surgery. 'How are things with Holly and Robin?' he asked.

'They're fabulous,' Mandy replied. 'Feel free to go over to the paddock and have a hug.'

Seb fiddled with the council laminate that was clipped to his belt. 'I came to tell you that Mrs Powell called,' he said. 'Apparently, the delightful Mr Powell has invested in mini-motorbikes. To paraphrase, Christmas is no longer ruined and could we please keep the donkeys?' He rolled his eyes theatrically.

Mandy wanted to laugh at his expression and his careful choice of words. 'That's nothing but good news,' she said. 'It's no hardship to keep them a bit longer. Just a pity Mr Powell didn't think before he bought the poor donkeys in the first place.'

Seb looked relieved. 'I hoped you'd say you could manage,' he said. 'It'd be almost impossible to find some-where else for them right now. I've been trying to chase up the breeder, too. He's in Sheffield, so I've passed the information on. Sorry, must dash. I'm on my way to pick up a stray cat.' Calling out to Helen, who was tidying one of the consulting rooms, that he would see her later, Seb sketched a wave and rushed back out.

Mandy decided to update the website to say that the donkeys were available to be rehomed. They would benefit from some more handling but by the time she'd carried out all the usual checks on a possible owner, they would be ready to go. Booting up her laptop, she added the donkeys to her rehoming list and turned to her e-mails. She was pleased to see that Mrs Dillon had sent confirmation of a second appointment for a home visit for Melon. There was only one other e-mail in her inbox.

'*Dear Hope Meadows,*' it read. '*I have been looking at your website and would be very interested in taking the two rabbits you have advertised as a Christmas present for a friend. Please could you let me know if they are still avail-able?'*

Mandy closed her eyes to think. On the face of it, the e-mail was a standard request. Normally she would reply asking for more information, with an electronic form to fill in. Now, with all the problems she'd had, she found her suspicions rising. What if this was someone trying to catch her out? With a sigh, she typed back a response, explaining that animals were not generally suitable to give as presents. It was a difficult juggling act, she thought. For all she knew, the query might come from someone who had always wanted pets and was ready and prepared for the commitment. She left her message open enough that she hoped the sender would feel able to get back to her.

Pushing herself upright, she went through to see the small furries. As ever, the guinea pigs greeted her with a flourish of squeaks and whistles, their funny little faces peering out, hoping for some leaves. In spite of everything, her miniature tenants still made Mandy smile.

'Your lives are so straightforward,' she told them. 'I hope you know how lucky you are!'

'Anything planned for this evening?' Helen asked Mandy much later. 'Seb and I are going to try out that new bar on the edge of Walton. Would you like to come?'

Mandy pondered the invitation. She needed some distraction and Seb and Helen were fun, but would she feel like a gooseberry with just the two of them? 'Gemma and Luke are coming too,' Helen added.

Mandy's doubts scattered. Gemma was always fun, though Mandy hoped she wouldn't want to talk too much about the petition. She wanted to get away from her problems and it would be lovely to see the new bar, which had only been open a few weeks. Luke, Gemma's husband, also knew Jimmy well. Both volunteered for the local mountain rescue. Mandy would be interested to hear about their latest call-outs. 'I'd love to join you,' she said. With a burst of energy, she finished writing up her final case notes. 'I'll just get changed,' she told Helen.

When Mandy had swapped her stained jeans for a clean pair, and her sweatshirt for a striped sweater, the two of them walked to the centre of Welford, where Gemma and Luke were already waiting. A few minutes later, Seb arrived and within two minutes, the taxi Luke had ordered was driving them along the Walton Road. It was cold outside, but quite fun, all squeezed together in the minicab.

The driver decanted them outside the rather modern building that stood a little way down the road from the school that Mandy had attended for so many years. Brightly lit lettering over the door announced that its name was 'Sheep from the Goats.' It all looked very smart.

Inside, it could not have been more different from the old-fashioned Fox and Goose. There were curved white leather seats ranged around small circular tables in a row in the centre and along one wall, raised booth seats were set around more of the black-lacquered tables. They made their way over to the last of the booths. Mandy was the first to sit down. Luke grinned at them, his dark-brown hair looking very shiny under the blue coloured lights. He took out his wallet. 'What can I get everyone?'

To Mandy's relief, Gemma didn't seem inclined to broadcast the latest attack on Hope Meadows. Luke brought a tray of drinks to the table and they were soon deep in discussion about the freezing cold weather and their plans for Christmas.

'We're going to spend the day together,' Helen announced, glancing at Seb as she reached out to squeeze his hand. How contented she looked, Mandy thought. Six months ago, Helen and Gemma had sat in the Fox and Goose, gossiping about Jimmy Marsh. Now Helen and Seb seemed so close it was hard to imagine they hadn't been together forever.

Mandy had a wonderful view over the rest of the bar from her seat in the corner. Gemma and Luke had slipped into the booth beside her. Helen was sitting opposite, with Seb to her left. There were a lot of people coming and going. The chrome stools at the bar filled and emptied. Helen had just finished telling Seb the latest update on Holly and Robin when the nurse's eyes seemed to be caught by someone or something at the door. A puzzled frown appeared on Helen's usually serene face. Feeling curious, Mandy turned her head to see who had come in.

It was Molly Future. Behind her, his hand on the

small of her back, walked Jimmy Marsh. He guided Molly to a quiet table almost at the other end of the room. Pulling out one of the curved white chairs, he sat down with his back to Mandy.

Helen's eyes were wide, though Seb had pulled out his wallet and was peering into it, oblivious to the unfolding scene. Helen leaned forward and spoke to Mandy across the table in a low voice. 'Did you know Jimmy was coming here with Molly tonight?' she asked.

Mandy shook her head. Though it was something of a shock to see Jimmy and Molly together, she had known for a long time that they were friends. Back in the summer, she had seen them together in the Fox and Goose and they had obviously been planning something when they had met up on the fell a few days ago. She should go over and say hello, she thought, but when she looked round, Gemma and Luke seemed to be deep in conversation and she didn't want to disturb them by asking to slide past.

Her eyes swivelled back to Molly and Jimmy. As she watched, she couldn't help but feel a little uneasy. Why hadn't Jimmy told her what he was doing tonight? He and Molly seemed to be getting very cosy for friends. Molly was gazing intently at Jimmy. A moment later, she had reached out a hand to take Jimmy's, which was lying on the table. Mandy's stomach dropped as she saw Molly entwine her fingers with his.

From somewhere a long way away, Seb was asking if anyone wanted another drink.

'I'll give you a hand.' That was Luke's voice. Neither of them seemed to have noticed anything.

Gemma stood up. 'Just going to powder my nose,' she announced and walked off towards the ladies. Though her way out was now clear, Mandy felt as if she couldn't move.

Her mind was working overtime. She knew Molly and Jimmy were supposed to be friends, but their intimacy was obvious. They were still holding hands, gazing at one another, deep in conversation. Even as she watched, Molly got up from her chair walked around the table and put her arms round Jimmy. She dropped a kiss on his dark head, before detaching herself and walking over to the bar.

Was this was why Jimmy had not called this week? Surely it couldn't be, she thought. Jimmy was too decent to leave her without telling her. And if he was two-timing her, he would have to be mad to see Molly in such a public place. Opposite her, Helen was bristling like an angry rabbit. 'What's he playing at?' she hissed, but Mandy had no idea what to say. Her almost empty glass was still in her hand. The dregs of wine quivered as she reached over and set it down on the table. She was finding it difficult to breathe.

'Are you okay?' Helen was peering at her.

Mandy shook her head. If she hadn't seen them together, she would never have believed it, but Molly's every action had screamed of an intimacy with Jimmy that went way beyond friendship.

'Do you want to leave?' Helen asked.

Mandy clenched her fists, trying to stop the trembling. 'Can you make my excuses?' she stumbled. Her tongue felt thick, the words clumsy.

'Do you want me to come with you?' Helen's eyes were filled with sympathy, but it would be easier to leave now before the others returned and Mandy wasn't sure she could bear anyone's company.

'Can you apologise to Seb about the wasted drink?' Somehow that seemed important to Mandy. She had upset enough people already.

Helen shrugged. 'He won't mind,' she said. 'He really won't.'

Head down, Mandy slid out from the booth. Molly was still waiting at the bar and Jimmy hadn't moved. A moment later, she was outside in the cold streetlight. She was going to have to call a taxi.

She pulled her mobile from her pocket. The texts from this morning would still be there, if she wanted to call them up, she thought, feeling sick. Her fingers trembled as she selected the number for Walton Minicabs. When was Jimmy planning to tell her about Molly, she wondered. Tomorrow night, over champagne and veggie burgers? He and Molly must have arranged tonight's cosy dinner before last Sunday, she realised with a horrible lurch. Molly had mentioned it in front of Mandy when they had been out riding and he had answered quite casually. Mandy let out a little yelp. How could anyone be that brazen? Or had they planned something platonic, but been pulled back together? The image of Molly kissing Jimmy's tousled hair was etched on Mandy's brain.

Her thoughts jumped back again to something Molly had said when they were out riding together. What had she said? The words floated into Mandy's mind. 'I do seem to have a preference for men from the Lakes.' Molly had mentioned it so casually. Mandy had assumed she had met someone new, but she must have been referring to Jimmy.

On automatic pilot, she pulled open the door of the cab when it arrived. To her relief, the driver didn't try to talk beyond asking for their destination. He dropped her off in the driveway of Animal Ark. Her mind was still in turmoil as she pushed open the door of the rescue centre and walked from room to room. Everything inside was peaceful, orderly, exactly as Mandy wanted it to be. The dogs looked up sleepily. The rabbits and guinea pigs were hidden in their sleeping quarters. One of the cats yawned and stretched. How could her rescue project be under perfect control when the rest of her life was crashing wildly off the rails, she wondered bleakly.

Tears welled into her eyes but she pushed them away with her fingers. If Jimmy could treat her this way, he wasn't worth crying over. Everything that was important was right here, in the rescue centre and in the cottage next door. Nothing else mattered. Mandy clenched her teeth together, trying to convince herself.

When she went back to the cottage, Adam was in the

sitting room alone, watching the television. On the screen, an eagle was soaring in a blue sky over a frozen mountain range.

'You're home early.' He looked at her with a smile and only mild interest. He was tired and distracted by Mum.

'Yes.' Mandy shrugged off her coat. 'Bit of a headache,' she added. 'Thought I'd have an early night.'

'Can I get you anything?' He was looking at her properly now. She was glad she hadn't given way to the threatened tears.

'No, thanks,' she said. To her relief, her dad didn't ask any more questions. Calling to Sky, she headed upstairs. The landing light was on and Emily's bedroom door was open. Mandy tiptoed past.

Without turning on her light, she undressed and slipped under the duvet. She had gone out that evening in search of some distraction from her worries about Emily and the campaign against the rescue centre. That plan had backfired spectacularly. Molly and Jimmy, Jimmy and Molly. An image of the two of them sitting clutching hands across the little black table whirled in Mandy's head, interspersed with pictures of Simon and Samantha in the house where Mandy had once felt so welcome.

What did he think he was doing, she wondered. Had he always secretly wanted Molly back? Had he been confused and unable to choose? He had seemed so stable. It was she who had been rocking the boat.

Mandy heard her father come upstairs, then silence. She shut her eyes and forced her mind to empty. She couldn't afford to lose a night's sleep. She had far too many things to do tomorrow.

She wasn't sure if she was dreaming when she heard a dog bark outside. She sat up, her heart racing, ears straining. But there were no more sounds and after a few minutes, she lay back down. Beside her on the floor, Sky snored gently. Mandy lowered her hand and rested her fingers on the collie's soft fur. Eyes wide open, she stared into the darkness.

Jimmy and Molly. Molly and Jimmy. It was a long night.

Chapter Nineteen

By the time Mandy stirred from a restless sleep, grey morning light was spilling past the half-closed curtains. Lifting her head from the pillow, she saw it was already past eight. For a moment she considered turning over and going back to sleep, but there were animals to feed. She dragged herself upright and pulled on jeans and a baggy sweatshirt. Downstairs, she opened the fridge. Was she hungry? There was nothing she fancied. With a sigh, she closed it again and walked over to pull on her boots.

Inside the rescue centre, the Christmas decorations looked garishly out of place. Their fake promise of joy needled Mandy and she resisted the urge to put them all back into their boxes. As Mandy was finishing the breakfast rounds, Nicole burst in through the door. Mandy had forgotten the teenager had said she would come on Saturday. At least Mandy would have a bit of company and unlike Helen, Nicole knew nothing about the events of last night.

'Morning!' It was heartening to be greeted as if there was nowhere Nicole would rather be right now. Dredging up a smile, Mandy led her though into the dog area. They would start with some exercise sessions.

Flame was in a good mood as well. Although her recall wasn't much more reliable, she seemed to like Nicole. The girl had all the patience in the world, watching for the right moment to engage Flame's attention and call her. The lurcher still seemed fascinated with Robin and Holly too. They stood on opposite sides of the fence, the two grey animals with their long ears, peering through at the smaller golden brindle one. When Flame bowed down on her front paws, asking them to play, the donkeys jumped backwards. Robin shook his head with a snort, but Holly turned her head to one side, studying Flame.

Mandy had expected it to be freezing this morning, but during the long night, clouds had rolled in. She could see them hanging over the fells, dark and threatening. It was much milder than yesterday and she and Nicole soon shed their coats as they followed first Flame, then Melon, then Twiglet and Arthur around the paddock. It was only when Nicole had set off home and Mandy picked up her jacket to return to the house that she realised she had received a text.

It was from Jimmy.

'Dinner tonight at Lamb's Wood Cottage. Vinegar or ketchup? Don't forget the fizz!'

Mandy had to read it twice to believe it. Last night, he had been cosying up to Molly. Now he had sent this offhand message. There could be no doubt now about his deceit. 'Don't forget the fizz' was insulting. There was absolutely nothing to celebrate.

What on earth was going through Jimmy's mind, she wondered as she pulled the door of the rescue centre closed behind her. Was it possible he thought he could hang out with Mandy when Molly wasn't available? Okay, so there had been nothing 'official' between her and Jimmy. They hadn't had a specific conversation about exclusivity. But they had been heading in that direction, hadn't they? Jimmy had been serious about Molly before. If he had started seeing her again, he should have the decency to let Mandy know. She had never been into the idea of casual dating. If Jimmy had asked her, she would have said no. He hadn't given her that choice.

She shoved the phone back in her pocket. How was she supposed to reply? She had no idea, but she was not going to pretend everything was fine. As she walked back across the field to the cottage, the heavens opened and she launched herself in through the door at a run. She would have to send him something, she realised as she stood in the kitchen shivering. Angry as she felt, she wouldn't leave him hanging. Pulling her mobile back out, she began to type. 'No longer available tonight,' she typed. 'Please do not contact me again.' She clicked send and was left standing there, looking at the screen. With a last painful look at his message, Mandy switched off her phone.

By three thirty it was almost dark and the storm had picked up. Adam had gone out with Tom Hope to a farm sale, leaving Mandy and Emily together. Her mum was still too quiet, Mandy thought, though they had joked about what kind of rural bric-a-brac the two men would come home with. She badly wanted to talk to someone about Jimmy. She wanted to try to understand what he might be thinking. But Emily's white face reminded her that her mum had enough on her own plate without Mandy adding to her worries.

Mandy had lit the fire and she and Emily sat with their feet stretched out as the rain hurled itself against the window. Sky snuffled in her sleep, pedalling her paws as if she was chasing a rabbit. Emily looked like she was drifting off into sleep too. There was nothing Mandy could do about Jimmy other than ride out the sadness, she thought. What would he do tonight, she wondered. Would he stay at home, huddled in front of his own fire? Or would he have called Molly when he realised Mandy wasn't going to make herself available? Pushing the rather morbid thought from her mind, she picked up the remote and switched on the TV.

The coal shifted in the grate. Mandy had piled it high and despite the awful weather, the room was cosy. Bing Crosby's mellow tones crooned from the TV as black and white images flickered across the screen. She would get up in just a minute, Mandy decided. Her body felt heavy. She really was very tired after last night. In a while, she needed to start dinner, but she was so comfortable sitting here, with Sky at her feet and her mum dozing beside her.

She was startled into wakefulness by a volley of thuds at the back door. Sky was sitting up, her ears pricked. She gave a low growl, looking at Mandy as the banging noise began again. Mandy glanced at her mum. Emily was still sleeping.

Scuttling into the kitchen, rubbing her eyes, Mandy opened the door to find Jimmy standing on the step. There had been no let-up in the rain. His hair was flat to his head and rivulets of water were running down his face. For a moment, Mandy considered slamming the door, but he looked so wet and cold that she couldn't bring herself to leave him in the storm. Opening the door wider, she let him step into the kitchen.

'Wait there,' she said in a low voice. Being as quiet as possible, she slipped through and closed the door to the sitting room and then the hall. The last thing she wanted was for Emily to listen.

When she returned, Jimmy was still standing on the doormat. His coat, his hair, his trousers, everything was soaked. Pulling a hand towel from the hook on the wall, Mandy tossed it to him and watched as he gave his face a cursory rub. With his hair darkened, his half wild countenance, he looked, annoyingly, more appetising than ever.

Jimmy took a step towards her. 'Is everything all right?' he asked. He gave a slight shiver as his green eyes searched her face. 'I tried to phone. I couldn't get through,' he said.

Mandy found herself trembling, though not with cold.

'Yes,' she said, clenching her fists to stop her fingers from shaking. 'I switched it off.'

He took a step nearer to her. 'Why?' he said. 'I don't understand. Is something wrong?'

Mandy stood her ground. Was he really going to pretend not to know? Didn't he have more respect for her than that? 'I think you know what's wrong,' she said. Her face felt tight. She shouldn't have to spell it out for him, she thought.

He stared at her. 'Well I don't,' he said, his brow wrinkled. 'I'm totally confused, if I'm being honest. First you said you wanted to take things slowly, then everything seemed fine – and now this.'

Mandy closed her eyes and took a deep breath, trying to clear her head. Was he laying the blame at her door? The image of Molly gazing at Jimmy across the blue-lit table flitted through her mind. She should have listened to her instincts, she thought. It had all moved too fast and now reality was kicking in. He couldn't even admit what he'd been up to last night. She should end this now, she thought. She needed someone she could trust.

'I think we should stop this,' she said.

Jimmy's eyes darkened. 'You want to stop?' he said, incredulously. 'Why?'

The words were on the tip of her tongue, but somehow Mandy couldn't bring herself to mention seeing him with Molly. Instead, she found herself reeling off other reasons, the ones which had stopped being so important once she'd truly acknowledged her feelings for Jimmy. 'There's

. . . there's just too much going on,' she said. 'I've got too much to do here with sick animals and rescues and all kinds of problems cropping up all over the place.'

'What problems?' He was frowning.

Mandy shook her head. She didn't want to get into a conversation about the campaign against Hope Meadows or her mum being ill. About previously unpaid bills and the cost of winter bedding for the kennels. Was it only last week that she had thought it would be lovely to have him to share news with? How naïve she had been. 'It's not easy starting a new business.' She had to drag the words out.

'Tell me about it.' Jimmy raised his eyebrows. 'I know that you're busy, Mandy, but you're not the only one with things going on,' he said. 'If you'd asked for help, don't you think I would have dropped everything and come over? You're so determined to do everything yourself that you push people – push me – away.' His voice was shaking.

Mandy started to feel hot with rage. So now it was her pushing people away? Had she pushed him so far that he had landed in Molly's arms? 'I may push people away,' she said, 'but at least I'm not a cheat.'

Jimmy's eyes flashed. 'I've never cheated on anyone in my life!'

'Are you sure about that?' The words were flowing from her now as if she could no longer control them. 'Were you, or were you not, in Walton last night with Molly Future?'

An unreadable look flashed into the green eyes. Was it guilt? 'Yes, I was.' For the first time, Jimmy sounded less sure of himself. 'But . . .'

Mandy cut him off. 'That's all I need to know.' She pulled herself fully upright as she ground the words out.

'Wait, that's not what . . .'

The sound of a door opening caught her ear. 'Mandy?' Emily's voice was weak.

'Just go!' Mandy reached past Jimmy and pulled open the back door. There was no way she wanted to explain what was going on to her mother. Not now, not ever.

'But . . .'

'Go!' Holding the door wide, Mandy came close to pushing him out. Her whole body was shaking.

For an instant, Jimmy stared straight into her eyes and then without another word, he turned and was swallowed in the rain and darkness. Mandy closed the door just as Emily walked into the room.

'Was someone at the door?' she asked.

'Just a client,' Mandy lied. 'I've sorted it out.'

'Has something happened?' Emily looked puzzled. 'Is everything okay?'

Gripping her fingers into tight fists, Mandy shook her head. 'Everything's fine,' she insisted. 'I need to go and check the animals.' She grabbed an umbrella and before her mum could argue, opened the back door. Gripping the plastic handle in the gusty wind, she rushed down the path.

Moments later, she was inside the rescue centre.

Without switching on the light, Mandy leaned against the wall. She closed her eyes, but somehow a tear slipped out and ran down her face. Rain lashed against the huge window. Mandy slid down the wall until she was sitting on the floor. Despite the weather, Sky had followed her outside and the little dog tucked herself in close to Mandy, a solid furry source of warmth.

She wanted Jimmy, Mandy realised. She wanted the Jimmy she'd thought she had known. The anchor in the storm, who would hold her tightly and tell her everything was going to be all right.

Another tear slid down her cheek. Sky licked it away. Mandy reached out an arm and Sky slid under it. Her coat was wet, but Mandy didn't care. 'Bloody men.' If she said it often enough, would it make her feel better? 'Bloody Jimmy. Bloody MEN!' Her face was wet. She rubbed the tears away with her sleeve, but they were replaced in an instant. With a gasping sob, she let her head fall back against the wall.

Chapter Twenty

In the end, Mandy slept better than she had expected. It was as if the storm of emotion had cleared her mind and she woke in the morning feeling much calmer. Her spirits rose a little, as she looked forward to the day. She had arranged for her dad to look after the animals so that she could visit James in York.

It had only been a week since Mandy had seen him, though it felt much longer. So much had happened. Lots of positives to tell James about, she reminded herself as she negotiated the roundabout on the way to his flat. She'd had good news about Lamb's Wood Cottage. Nicole's arrival at Hope Meadows was a bonus, too. And James would want to hear all about the donkeys' training.

James was waiting for her on the doorstep with Seamus and Lily, who bounced around Mandy as if their paws were ping pong balls. Sky crouched behind Mandy for a minute before remembering that she had met these crazy hounds, and leaped out to join in.

'I thought we could go a walk,' James suggested, and Mandy nodded as she stroked Lily's velvety brown ears.

With the dogs swirling at their feet, they headed into

the centre of York and made their way down to the river. A whole box of Christmas had exploded throughout the city. There were trees and tinsel in all the shop windows, and coloured lights festooned the ancient buildings. Down by the Ouse, the riverbank was quiet. The three dogs trotted ahead, noses to the ground, as Mandy and James strolled along the leaf-strewn pathway.

A student cycled past wearing a pair of light-up antlers. They reminded Mandy of her dad and their card-writing session, which had begun so well but had ended with Emily's collapse. She sighed.

'Not feeling very festive?' James prompted.

'Not really,' Mandy confessed.

'I'm not either,' James said. 'I keep thinking about this time last year.'

Last year, James had spent the festive season with Paul in a hotel near Whitby. Paul had been well enough for Christmas with all the trimmings, and James had told Mandy all about their windswept walk on the beach and huge Victorian-themed lunch. Now, Mandy looked at the pain carved on James's face. How she wished she could ease her friend's grief.

A grey squirrel jumped onto the path in front of them, glanced around and then scampered off up one of the trees. Mandy watched as it disappeared. Too late, Seamus caught the squirrel's scent and strained to the end of his lead, paws scrabbling on the stones.

'So what's wrong?' Bending down to disentangle Lily, who had wrapped her lead around her paws, James looked up at her. 'Is it Jimmy? You said you'd been seeing him, but you don't seem full of the joys of romance to me.' He stood up and started walking again. Ahead Mandy could see bright blue railings: a bridge over one of the tributaries to the river.

'We were meant to be going out last night,' she admitted. 'Only I was out on Friday and I saw him in a bar in Walton with his ex.'

'His ex?' James echoed as they reached the bridge. They stopped at the apex, leaning on the railings. Upstream the brick flood barrier remained open despite yesterday's rain.

'Well, she *was* his ex, until last week,' Mandy corrected herself. 'Now they seem very much back together.'

James's eyes were sympathetic. 'That sucks,' he said. Pushing themselves off the railings, they carried on walking.

'There's been some other stuff going on, too.' Though she hadn't meant to trouble him, Mandy realised she needed to talk to someone before her head exploded.

'What sort of stuff?'

They were passing houses on the left. In the distance, Mandy could see the Millennium Bridge with its distinctive arch. 'Weird things,' she said. 'A hole appeared in the hedge so the dogs could have got onto the road. Someone called Harper's and cancelled my food delivery. A horrible review of the campsite on TripAdvisor about barking from the centre and a stupid petition in the post office. It's as if someone is determined to close down

Hope Meadows!' She stopped, slightly horrified by how long the list had become.

James was silent, and Mandy felt the rush of guilt she always felt these days if she unloaded her problems on him. 'I'm sorry,' she said. 'I know you have enough on your plate.'

But James was staring at her in dismay. 'No need to be sorry.' Putting both dog leads into one hand, he reached out and hugged her. 'That's awful.' He let go and began walking again. 'Nobody got hurt, did they? From the hole in the hedge. None of the animals managed to escape?'

Typical James, Mandy thought. Like her, he always had animals at the forefront of his mind. 'None of the dogs got out,' she assured him. 'Nobody's been hurt.'

'Still awful though.' His voice was intense. 'Have you been to the police?'

Mandy admitted that she had.

'You will make sure they're following it up?' James urged her. 'Keep in contact with Ellen Armstrong. It sounds like some kind of hate crime.'

Mandy winced. Put like that, it seemed as if she had got off lightly. So far.

James seemed to read her mind. 'It sounds as if things are escalating. You have to find out who's behind it before some real damage is done.' He stopped at the entrance to a bridge and looked at her, his brown eyes serious behind his glasses. 'No wonder you're not in the mood for Christmas.'

Halfway across, they leaned over the wall to look down at the dark, swirling water. James reached down to rub Seamus's head. 'About Jimmy and his ex,' he said. 'Is there any chance it could be a misunderstanding?'

Mandy shook her head. 'I did wonder about that,' she admitted. 'I knew they were still friends. I'd seen them out together once before, back when I was still going out with Simon. But they were holding hands across the table. She even kissed him as she went up to the bar.' She clenched her teeth to stop herself talking.

'I'm sorry you had to find out that way.' James reached out a hand to give her shoulder a squeeze. 'Whatever happens, it's better to know the truth, don't you think? If Jimmy's not the one, you'll be free to find someone else.'

'What about you?' They were still leaning on the wall. The water slid beneath them, flowing steadily south to the North Sea. 'Do you ever think about finding someone else?'

Beside her, Mandy felt a deep shudder run through her friend. The muscles in his jaw bunched. 'Sorry,' she said, cursing her insensitivity. 'One day I'll learn to keep my big mouth shut.'

James managed a pained smile. 'Please don't,' he said. 'So many people don't know what to say that they don't say anything at all. There's nothing you could say that will offend me.'

They wandered on. 'How are your mum and dad?'

James called as he waited for Seamus to finish sniffing a lamp post.

Mandy felt the colour drain from her face. She had been hoping James wouldn't ask. It didn't seem fair to spring the massive question mark over Emily's health on him so soon after Paul. James loved Emily like a favourite aunt. Mandy knew she could try to lie, but he would see straight through her.

Their steps suddenly seemed very loud on the path. Beside them a boat chugged upstream, struggling against the current.

'Mum's not well,' Mandy admitted, when the silence had stretched so thin that the air felt like glass. 'She collapsed on Tuesday.' James kept walking. His face was white, but he glanced expectantly at Mandy, waiting for more information. 'She's at home,' Mandy went on. 'Getting lots of rest. We're waiting for blood results.' She stopped, holding her breath. How would James react?

'I'm so sorry.' It sounded as if James was finding it hard to speak. 'I do know . . .' He trailed off, his jaw set.

He knew better than most. There were tears in his eyes, and Mandy felt her face starting to crumple. Her relationship with her parents was unusually strong. She had been adopted as a baby, but both Mum and Dad had loved her so unquestioningly, with such steadiness, that she had never felt like anything other than their precious daughter. Dad was Dad, the best father in the world, hardworking, teasing and full of fun. The easiest person in the world to be with, a source of everything that was positive in life.

Mandy's relationship with Emily had been more subtle: harder to define. Mum had trusted Mandy. Shown faith in her judgement, given her space to be ruled by her own conscience. She was, on some level, the person who had influenced Mandy most. Without her, Mandy would have been a very different person.

'There's nothing I can say that will help.' James's voice broke through her thoughts, steadier than Mandy expected. 'I hope you get some answers soon. Try not to worry.'

Good advice. Almost impossible to apply. James reached for Mandy's hand and gripped it so hard, it was almost painful. 'Don't jump to conclusions,' he urged, then, 'you will let me know, won't you?'

Mandy swallowed. 'Of course I will.'

For several long moments, they walked onwards. In front of them, the dogs trotted side by side, fur brushing together. Mandy envied them their innocence, their trust in the humans closest to them to keep everything safe and as it should be.

James picked up the pace. 'We should go back via the bookshop,' he suggested. 'I've got something to show you.'

'That sounds good,' Mandy said, trying to pull herself together. She adored James's little bookshop-café, with its nooks and crannies and tumbling heaps of utterly readable books.

They made their way back along the riverbank, through Rowntree Park. A few barges were moored close to the narrow road that ran along the riverside, though there was little life to be seen. Mandy began to feel calmer as they walked through the city centre. They threaded their way past tourists and shoppers until they reached James's shop. Mandy stopped outside to admire the decorations in the window. The space behind the glass had been transformed into an animal-themed snow scene, complete with sledging kittens as well as a tasteful miniature tree, hung with little animals and white lights that shone warm in the softly lit interior.

'Sherrie's done a fantastic job,' James said as she peered in. 'Come on in.' He opened the door. 'We can put the dogs in the staffroom,' he added, leading Lily and Seamus through and taking off their leads. Mandy and Sky followed.

'What did you want to show me?' Mandy asked. 'Was it the window?'

'It was not.' For the first time since Paul had died, James's eyes were properly twinkling. He led her round into one of the cosy alcoves further back in the shop. 'Look.' He held out his arms.

A table stood in the recess holding an array of animal books, non-fiction as well as classic stories, beautifully arranged. Above the display, straight in front of Mandy, there was a poster on the wall. Mandy glanced at it, then stared. It was a picture of two young donkeys who looked very familiar. Behind them, she recognised the unmistakeable lines of her rescue centre. It was Holly and Robin, she realised. On her left, she saw a photo of Sky that she had taken back in the summer on top of Norland Fell. When she turned to her right, she felt herself turn red. She was looking at a photograph of herself, beaming with a newborn lamb in her arms. She hoped that wasn't a smear of poop on her cheek.

A notice was pinned to the front edge of the table: '*All proceeds from the sale of these books will be donated to Hope Meadows Rescue Centre.*'

'What do you think?' Sherrie had come over and was standing beside James. Her white-blonde hair was tied back in beaded dreadlocks, and she was wearing patched turquoise dungarees over a handknitted purple sweater.

'It was Sherrie who made the posters,' James explained. 'Using photos from your website.'

'I hope you don't mind.' Sherrie sounded a little anxious.

'Mind?' There were tears in Mandy's eyes. She shook her head in disbelief. 'I definitely don't mind.' She looked at the posters again, then back down at the books. There was a small spotlight in the corner illuminating the table. The books looked appetising for every age and preference of animal lover, from picture book stories to a guide to endangered feline species in Asia. 'It's wonderful,' she said. 'Thanks so much.' She turned and squeezed James's hand, then Sherrie's. 'Thanks, both of you.'

'We've been selling Hope Meadows biscuits too,' Sherrie told her. Mandy followed her round to the counter.

Glass jars ran the full length, containing different-shaped animal biscuits. There were cats and reindeer, rabbits and sheep. There was even a tortoise. All of them were cheerfully iced.

Sherrie traced her finger along the side of a jar of rabbits. 'My niece India helped me with these. She's only ten, but I can tell you that her icing skills are far better than mine! It was her idea to use chocolate chips for the noses.'

'May I buy one?' Mandy asked. *Is James telepathic,* she wondered? She had been planning to ask him about fundraising ideas, and he was several leaps ahead already. The proceeds from biscuits and books wouldn't make much of a dent in her overdraft, but they would definitely feed several animals for a while. Mandy pressed her hand against his cheek. 'I can't believe you've done all this.'

James grinned at her. 'Isn't this what we've always done?' he said. 'We help animals as a team. You didn't think I'd leave you to do it all on your own, did you?'

She wanted to hug him, but the door opened and a customer came in, and then another.

'Give us a hand?' Sherrie suggested.

As the afternoon rush started and the café filled up, Mandy found herself feeling properly festive for the first time. The animal biscuits sold well, especially the rabbits with chocolate noses. Sherrie had made some special Christmas soup of sprout and parsnip. Despite sounding awful, it was warming and delicious. 'It's tastier than it sounds,' Mandy told people as they came in. She could feel her grin grow wider each time she said it.

'Merry Christmas!' she called out as the last customers, an elderly couple in matching pom-pom hats, made their way to the door.

'You too,' they replied.

Together, the three of them began to tidy up the last of the crockery. Mandy wiped the tables while Sherrie sorted out the till. James was washing a few glasses by hand. When they were finished, Mandy looked round the room. It had been an amazing afternoon, and her worries felt dimmed in a haze of goodwill. A couple of people, recognising her from the photo, had asked about the rescue centre. There had been nothing but positivity from everyone she had spoken to.

'Here!' As she pulled on her coat to leave, Sherrie held out a piece of paper. It was a cheque for £600. 'To buy Christmas food for your animals,' Sherrie said.

'It's an ongoing project,' James told her. 'There'll be more to come.'

Feeling the prickle of grateful tears behind her eyes, Mandy reached out and hugged Sherrie and then James. 'This has been the best day I've had in a long time,' she said. 'Thank you both so much for everything.'

Calling to Sky, clutching the precious donation, she set off back to the car for the long drive home.

Chapter Twenty-One

'You know you have two wonderful fairy godmothers in York?' Mandy addressed the dogs in the kennels. Flame looked through the bars, her long tail switching from side to side. Twiglet tilted her head. Her ears pricked as she listened to Mandy's voice. 'Though hopefully *you'll* be having Christmas in a lovely new home,' she said to Melon. His button eyes were bright and he gave the tiniest bark in return. Mandy sighed. If she won the lottery, she would build a dozen rescue centres and keep all the animals for herself.

Or would that bring even more hostility from Hope Meadows' invisible enemy?

Mandy shook her head. She wasn't going to think about that, she reminded herself. Until they knew who was behind the attacks, there was nothing she could do, other than stay vigilant for any signs of trouble. Closing the door behind her, she headed into the cottage for breakfast. Adam was in the kitchen, making toast. Emily was sitting at the table with a cup of coffee in front of her.

'I'm due at the doctor's this morning,' Emily said. As

if she could forget, Mandy thought. The time was imprinted on her brain.

'You know I've got to be at Twyford.' Adam's glance was filled with worry. He hadn't been able to put off a critical tuberculosis test so that he could take Emily to the surgery.

'I know.' There was no resentment in Emily's voice. Veterinary practice had moulded their life for too long now.

'I could come with you,' Mandy suggested, though she suspected her mum would say no.

'Would you?'

Mandy was taken aback. She looked closely at Emily. There was a trace of fear in her blue eyes. If this was difficult for her, how much harder must it be for Mum?

'Of course I will.' She made her voice as reassuring as she could. Monday mornings could be busy, but one way or another, she would get through everything in time. Squaring her shoulders, she stood up. 'Better get on then,' she said.

It looked as busy as she had feared, though when she studied the list closely, most of the work was routine. There was a spay she could do when she got back. Two vaccinations. One coughing dog. 'Did you remind Mrs Jenson to stay in the car with Boysie?' she asked Helen, who nodded. Ears. A skin follow-up for Demodex mites; Mandy hoped the treatment was working. Then one more vaccination. Unless anyone phoned with an emergency, she should be able to get through those by ten thirty.

Letting herself into the consulting room, she checked the first patient on the screen. Damocles Jamieson for a routine vaccination. Damocles? That was quite a name for a French Bulldog. Mandy grabbed a syringe from the drawer and the vaccine from the fridge. She checked the room. The stethoscope was on a hook on the wall: thermometer and covers in the drawer. There were wormers in the cupboard. Hearing the clinic door, Mandy went through to watch as Helen booked the first client in. Contrary to his warlike name, Damocles was a meek little pooch, all soft skin and soulful eyes. Mandy relaxed. She would take this as a good omen that the morning would run smoothly, she decided.

Damocles proved to be a reliable lucky mascot. The last patient left on the dot of ten thirty and Mandy changed in double-quick time to drive her mum to the surgery. It wasn't far, and they could have walked it, but Mandy didn't want to test her mum's fragile reserve of energy. Mum sat beside her in the car, looking out of the window. Mandy's fingers felt stiff as she changed gear. She rolled her shoulders back, fighting the anxiety that threatened to take over.

When they walked into the waiting room, three other patients looked up. Mandy glanced at the clock on the wall. It was five to eleven. Maybe some of them were waiting to see the nurse. She sat down with Emily just as the door to the nurse's room opened.

'Mr Abbot?' The nurse was dressed in a dark blue uniform with white piping. She was gazing expectantly at the only man in the room. Mr Abbot looked about ninety, but he stood up as if he was much younger. The door closed again.

Mandy's gaze wandered. There were blue chairs with wooden armrests, a busy notice board, two plants in large pots on the floor. There was nothing austere about the surroundings, but it was too quiet, sitting there. Mandy was glad when the door opened and the doctor called them in. Dr Grace had short brown hair in a no-nonsense cut and calm brown eyes. It was hard to read her expression. Mandy felt a tingling sensation in her fingers. She tried to slow her breathing. The last thing her mum needed was for her to start freaking out. Taking a deep breath, she sat down and concentrated on the doctor's face.

'Well, we've had the results back,' Dr Grace said calmly, 'and as well as being a little anaemic, you're very low in vitamin B12. You must have been feeling poorly for a while.' There was a steady smile now, to match the eyes. For a moment, Mandy felt as if she was weightless. Beside her, she could feel Mum shaking. She leaned towards her, pressing her shoulder against Emily's as her mum's fingers reached for her hand.

'There are some further tests you should have,' Dr Grace went on, 'but we'll start you off with some iron tablets and a vitamin injection.'

'What might have caused it?' Emily sounded as if she feared worse news.

Dr Grace was reassuring. 'It can be dietary or there are a number of stomach problems that can trigger it. Mostly it's nothing serious.' The trembling slowed, though the hand that was gripping Mandy's was still chilly. 'I'll just get the injections ready, then I'll get you a prescription,' the doctor said. 'You should start to feel better quite soon.'

There was a lump in Mandy's throat as they walked back out to the car a few minutes later. Her mum was going to be okay. She was going to be okay!

'Was it true, what the doctor said?' she prompted. 'That you'd been feeling bad for a while?' There was a tiny atom of frustration behind her relief. What if it had been something awful? 'Wouldn't it have been better to go sooner?'

Emily sighed. 'It has been a while,' she admitted. 'But it came on so gradually, I couldn't work it out. I just felt tired.' Mandy drove out of the car park and stared out of the windscreen, concentrating on the road. 'Then I started to feel like I wasn't really myself. It was hard to remember things. I couldn't understand what was happening to me. I wondered whether this was just what it felt like to get old.' Mandy risked a glance at her mum. Emily had closed her eyes again. A single tear escaped and ran down her pale cheek. Mandy pretended not to see as her mother lifted a hand and brushed it away.

'You're not old.' Mandy reached out and squeezed her mum's shoulder. 'You're not going to be old for years.' She felt a surge of protectiveness. If it had been frightening for her, it must have been unbearable for Emily.

Back at the clinic, with Helen's help, Mandy performed the spay that had been booked in. It was a lurcher that looked so much like Flame it was uncanny. Though the slimness of the patient made the operation easier, the anaesthetic for such a muscular dog required a cautious approach. It was a relief when the operation was over.

'I'm going over to the rescue centre,' she told Helen when she had finished scrubbing her hands. She knew she would be able to relax properly in her beautiful glass and stone building, among the animals that trusted her with nothing less than their lives.

It was time to do some kitten training. Mandy was in the process of teaching them to open their mouths to be tableted. Forking a small quantity of tuna into a bowl, she went through to the cat area and took the first kitten out. He was black and white like his mother, with large golden eyes. He was already used to having his head and ears examined. The little animal was interested enough in what was happening to sit still. Now Mandy set to work, getting the kitten used to having his mouth opened manually. Each time she successfully held his head, she rewarded him with a flake of tuna.

By the end of the session, Mandy could grasp the kitten's head, open his mouth wide and slip a finger in to deposit a sliver of tuna on his tiny pink tongue. Potential new owners would be taught how to practice so that when they eventually needed to give the cat a tablet, it would think it was a game. So long as there was something tasty to slip in as soon as the tablet was swallowed, then it would be far easier than starting out with the medicine itself. Mandy repeated the process with the second kitten, a larger female tabby. Both of them were so sweet. Repetitive as it might be, this was one of the best parts of the job.

Next, she spent some time with Tango, encouraging him to eat. His blood sample had come back clear, so it was possible he was just depressed. Some cats found it hard to settle in to kennel life. Mandy now took him out every day into reception and let him meander around while she did other work. He seemed to eat better when he could wander free.

When she had put Tango back, she pulled her mobile from her pocket. She should give Sally Harper a ring, she thought. The last order had eventually arrived, but she would need to make another before Christmas. Sally was very attentive. 'If anyone tries to change the order this time,' she said, 'I'll speak to them myself. And don't worry, I won't cancel or change anything unless I hear it directly from you.' Mandy felt grateful as she ended the call.

She must ring James, she thought, to tell him about Emily. He was predictably relieved. Mandy was happy to be able to give him some good news.

As she was putting her phone back in her pocket, the door of the rescue centre swung open. Helen stood in the doorway.

'Your dad's back from Twyford and I've brought you some cake,' she announced.

'Ah, just the kind of visitor I like.'

'It's great news about your mum.' Helen had brought a slice of chocolate Yule Log for herself and one for Mandy. 'Has Jimmy been in touch yet?'

Mandy blew out her cheeks. 'He turned up in that awful storm on Saturday, dripping all over the place. We had the most awful row.' The memory made her feel sick.

'I heard something bad happened at Running Wild,' Helen told her. 'I don't know the details, but someone was taken ill.'

Mandy didn't know what to say. Last week, when she had been waiting for Jimmy to call, this information might have made sense. But after Friday night, and then the appalling visit on Saturday, she couldn't see that it made any difference. A tape played in her mind: the image of Jimmy's hand on Molly's back. The two of them holding hands across the table. 'Was the person okay?' Her voice sounded flat, even to herself.

Helen shook her head. 'I'm not sure,' she said. 'The person I spoke to didn't know much. Didn't Jimmy mention it? You said you had a row on Saturday, but didn't he explain anything at all?'

'Not about that,' Mandy admitted. 'He admitted he had been with Molly.' She paused to look at Helen, who had just taken a mouthful of cake. 'He told me I was so determined to do everything myself that I pushed people away.'

Helen swallowed, then shrugged. 'There may be a grain of truth in that,' she said, 'but it wasn't you who pushed him to Molly. He did that all by himself. I hope you gave him a piece of your mind. If I see him, I might give him a piece of mine too.' She grinned. 'You should try this cake though. It's delicious.' Mandy found herself smiling. It was hard to feel down when Helen was around.

Afternoon surgery came and went and at the end, Seb Conway arrived.

'What can we do for you today, Seb?' Mandy came out from her consulting room on hearing his cheerful voice. Really, Helen and Seb were ridiculously well-matched.

'I've got a present for you,' Seb replied. 'In the van.'

Together, they went out to the vehicle which was parked at the side of Animal Ark. When Seb opened the door, a tiny terrier was shivering inside. She cringed away from Mandy's hands at first, but with time and coaxing, Mandy was able to draw her out of the cage. She could feel the dog's ribs through her wet fur, and when Mandy picked her up, she weighed almost nothing.

'She was found this morning,' Seb explained. 'She was in a ditch with a brick tied round her neck, poor little thing.' He reached out a finger and stroked the matted coat. Now she was out of the cage, the little terrier seemed less distressed. Carrying her inside, Mandy examined her. Other than a wound on her neck, and her extreme thinness, the little terrier seemed in good health.

'She's only young,' Mandy said, pulling back the dog's lip to reveal healthy pink gums and clean white teeth. Fetching the chip reader, she ran it over the terrier's neck, but there was nothing.

Helen sighed. 'Probably someone going away for the Christmas holidays and couldn't be bothered to find a kennel,' she said. It was the only time Mandy heard Helen sounding bitter, when she learned that an animal had been maltreated. Mandy knew how she felt. *Utter, utter bastards.*

With Seb's help, she set about cleaning up the dog's fur. When she was dry and fluffy, and her neck wound had been seen to, she looked very sweet. Her newly washed coat was a delicate shade of silver.

'She's a lovely colour,' Helen commented.

'I'm going to call you Birch,' Mandy told the little dog. Birch pricked up her rather long ears as if she approved. 'We'll take you out to meet the other dogs,' Mandy said.

Whenever she had a new inmate, she tried to introduce him or her to the other dogs as soon as possible, especially the ones in the neighbouring cages. There was a small kennel beside Twiglet, but as she carried Birch into the room, her attention was caught by Flame. The golden lurcher stood up, her tail wagging, and gave a single loud 'wuff'.

Mandy looked at Flame in amazement. Though some of the dogs barked frequently, Flame had never, ever joined in. Now she was staring at the little silver bundle in Mandy's arms, her tail waving faster than ever. For a moment, Mandy wondered if Flame thought Birch was some kind of prey, but Flame bowed down her front end in an invitation to play. Then, as if realising she had to be quiet to be introduced, she lay down in her kennel.

With Birch in her arms, Mandy let Flame out and together they went through into the reception area. Once it seemed that they were friends, Mandy set Birch down. She watched, ready to interfere if Flame showed any sign of predatory behaviour, but the two dogs, one lanky, one miniscule, greeted one another nose to nose. Within moments, Flame was licking the newcomer as if she was a puppy. After a few moments of playing, Mandy took the two of them back through to the kennels. They squeezed into Flame's cage and lay down together on her bed. Mandy could hardly bring herself to move Birch. She would take them outside together tomorrow, she decided.

With a feeling that Birch's arrival might be a good thing for Flame, Mandy scooped up the little dog and popped her into the smaller kennel opposite. They settled quickly, looking at one another across the passageway.

Seb, who had accompanied Mandy out to the rescue centre, had watched all this with delight. 'You really are working wonders with these animals,' he said.

Mandy sighed. 'They're working wonders for me,' she replied. It was true. There was nothing she could imagine that would give her more pleasure. If only everyone was as happy to have a rescue centre near them.

As if reading her mind, Seb spoke. 'I know you've been having some trouble,' he said. 'Helen told me.' Mandy hoped Helen had only divulged her problems about the centre and not about Jimmy.

'I've already spoken to Ellen Armstrong,' Seb went on. 'I'll give her any help I can with the investigation. She told me she'd found out about some kind of rumour in the Fox and Goose, but I've not heard anyone say a word against you.' He scratched his head, running his fingers through the spiky hair. 'There are some odd people around,' he concluded.

That was the truth, Mandy thought. Anyone who tried to sabotage what she was trying to do must be very odd indeed.

Chapter Twenty-Two

Mandy rose early on Sunday morning. Outside her bedroom window, there was thick frost on the grass. Everything in the paddock seemed to be sparkling. Holly and Robin were standing nose to tail, basking in the morning sunshine. Mandy felt equally sunny, with the good news about Emily's diagnosis and the donation from James's café. Although she was still sad about Jimmy, she was starting to accept he was no longer in her life. Molly deserved better, she thought, but she wasn't going to interfere. And there hadn't been any signs of sabotage for a while now. She was starting to hope that whoever it was, they had got bored and gone away.

Susan Collins was due round later with her son Jack. Over the past months, Susan and Jack had been visiting the animals on a semi-regular basis, to Mandy's delight. She and Susan got on well, and Mandy wanted her rescue animals to be socialised with people of different shapes and sizes. Mandy was careful to keep Jack away from any animal that seemed distressed, or might put him at risk, but most of them adjusted well. There was no objection from Jack. He seemed thrilled with the whole enterprise. He was surprisingly good, especially with the kittens, who needed gentle handling. Today, he had asked especially to come and see the donkeys.

As Mandy walked downstairs, she heard a chirp from her phone. Halting halfway, she pulled it from her pocket. The message was from Jimmy, the first since the stormy night last weekend.

Avoiding him forever wasn't possible. He was an Animal Ark client with his dogs, for one thing. And he worked so close to Upper Welford Hall that Mandy was bound see him sooner or later. But right now, she was trying to ignore him. With a feeling that she could be entering a minefield, she clicked on the message.

'*I think there's been a misunderstanding,*' the message read. '*Can we talk?*'

Mandy gripped the bannister and continued downstairs. The kitchen was empty. Pulling a croissant from a packet on the side, she put it in the oven to warm and set the kettle to boil. Sitting down at the scrubbed pine table, she pulled her mobile back out of her pocket. What should she reply? She didn't know what to say.

It was difficult after the row they'd had. Not just because of Molly. His words haunted her. *She couldn't accept help and pushed people away.* Even Helen had admitted she thought there was some truth to them.

She didn't want to do everything on her own, she thought. Was that the impression she gave? She sighed. She knew how much her family helped her. Friends too.

They were all wonderful, but to have had Jimmy as a partner would have been even better. He was someone she could have shared her worries with. Yet he wasn't who she thought he was. He had let her down, just when she needed him most.

For a moment, she toyed with the idea of calling him. He had asked to talk. Her thumb hovered over the screen for a moment, but she couldn't bring herself to press call. With a sigh, she texted back, 'Sorry, but I don't want to yet. I will get back to you when I'm ready.' She looked at the message for a moment, then clicked send. He would wait, she thought. He would understand that she needed time.

Standing up, she opened the oven and pulled out her croissant. Wrapping it in a piece of kitchen roll, she pushed her feet into her boots and made her way out to the centre.

A few minutes before Susan and Jack were due to arrive, she went out to the donkeys. Whenever they saw her, they came racing over, though Mandy rarely took titbits of fruit and veg for them now. They seemed to enjoy her attention without any food. Both of them were quite willing to put their heads into their headcollars. Within a couple of minutes, she had them both caught and tied up. This was a new skill they were learning. Robin quickly got tired of standing still so Mandy didn't leave them for long, but they needed to learn that they should wait patiently when they were put somewhere.

Mandy was walking round Holly, lifting up the

donkey's feet, when she heard voices. It was remarkable how much Jack's speech had come on in the last six months. As he rounded the corner, Mandy could see that Susan was holding his hand to prevent him from rushing over. Mandy unclipped the donkeys so they were loose in the paddock, then joined Susan and Jack on the other side of the gate.

'Donkeys!' Jack was jumping up and down in his little red wellington boots and blue woolly mittens.

Susan, also in wellingtons and a warm hat, smiled at the excitement in the little boy's dark eyes. 'Donkeys indeed,' she agreed. 'This one is called Holly and this is Robin,' she added.

'Holly and Robin,' Jack echoed. He always seemed solemn when he came near the animals. However excited he was at a distance, as he approached he became calm. A lot of adults could learn from him, Mandy thought.

'Mary rode a donkey to Bet-lem,' he announced, looking up at Mandy.

'That's right.' She nodded.

'She was pregmant. With Baby Jesus.'

'Pregnant,' Susan told him. 'He's going to be in the nativity,' she explained to Mandy.

'I'm the innkeeper,' Jack said. He held up his little hands. 'No room! No room!'

Mandy grinned. 'I bet you'll be a great innkeeper,' she said. 'Do you want to stroke Holly?'

Jack's eyes opened wide. 'Yes please,' he said.

Taking him by the hand, Mandy led him through the

gate. Holly regarded Jack for a moment with one ear back. 'Stand very still.' Mandy crouched down beside the small boy. 'Don't stare. Wait for her to come to you.' They stayed together until Holly put her ears forwards and took a step towards them. 'It's very important with donkeys and horses that you don't stand behind them,' Mandy told Jack.

''Cos they can kick,' Jack told her.

'Very good.' He had been listening, Mandy thought with amusement. Holly padded delicately over to them. Reaching out her smooth, light coloured muzzle, she sniffed at Jack's hair.

Jack's face transformed with delight. 'Can I touch her?' he whispered.

'Yes.' Mandy stood up and scratched Holly in her favourite place, below her ear. 'Stroke her here,' she said. 'She likes it.'

The small hand reached out. Mandy watched Jack's eyes grow huge as he touched the soft fur. 'Why doesn't Father Christmas use donkeys for his sleigh?' he asked Mandy.

She wanted to laugh. He was so sweet. 'I think reindeer have special feet so they can run on snow,' she told him. 'Donkeys just have tiny feet. Look.' Together, they inspected Holly's hooves. They were indeed very small.

'I saw Father Christmas,' Jack said. 'There were no reindeers *anywhere*.' He sounded crestfallen.

'It must have been exciting to see Father Christmas, wasn't it?' Mandy prompted.

'Sort of.' Jack's face brightened. 'He gave me a present,' he told her. 'It was a horsey.'

'Well, that was lucky,' Mandy said. 'I bet not everyone gets a horse for Christmas. Is it going to live in your garden?'

Jack frowned. 'It wasn't a real one, silly.' His voice was stern. Mandy wanted to laugh again.

Pulling herself upright, she opened the gate and Jack trotted back to Susan. 'Would you like to come in and see the rabbits?' Mandy offered.

'Yes!' Jack shouted gleefully. Had she been the same when she was that small, Mandy wondered.

'He was quite disappointed with Father Christmas,' Susan told her as Jack fed the rabbits and then the guinea pigs. 'We went to the grotto at the garden centre and there were no animals. The only thing he wants for Christmas at the moment is to feed the reindeer some carrots. No idea how I'm going to organise that one on Christmas morning. We've been going on "reindeer hunts" in the meantime. We've been all round Welford without any success.'

Mandy laughed. 'Sorry,' she said. 'I can do dogs and cats, rabbits and guinea pigs. I can even do donkeys, but I've never seen any reindeer in Welford.'

Susan gave her a mock glare. 'Really,' she said, 'I don't think you're trying hard enough.'

'Do you think they might be out on the moor, Mummy?' Jack had turned his head to look at them.

'Maybe they are,' Susan called, suppressing a grin.

Jack turned back to the cage, holding out a small piece of carrot. Snowy the white guinea pig pushed her stubby nose towards him and took it, shuffling backwards and watching him with her shining eyes as she munched her way down the stick. Bubble, who was chestnut brown with a smooth coat except for two rosettes on his midriff, came over. Jack gave him a carrot stick as well.

'I think it's time to go now,' Susan told him as he crouched down cooing at the two friendly creatures.

He turned his dark eyes to her. 'Must we?' he asked. Then he stood up and dusted off his knees, looking like a tiny old man. He sighed with the weight of all three of his years. 'Okay then, Mummy,' he said.

'Come back soon,' Mandy told him.

'What do you say to Mandy?' Susan prompted.

'Thank you, Mandy.' Jack stretched up to offer his cheek for a kiss. Mandy pressed her lips briefly against his cool, soap-scented cheek and straightened his woolly hat. She opened the door for them and waved as they walked down the path. Jack was skipping beside his mum, chatting about the donkeys.

Mandy was sitting at the desk when she heard the door open and close again. Looking up, she expected to see Jack and Susan, returning to find something they'd forgotten. But to her surprise it was Brandon Gill, Rachel's fiancé.

'Hello, Brandon.' Mandy stood up.

As ever, Brandon looked faintly awkward, standing in his overalls among the Christmas decorations. It wasn't like him to come in at the weekend and it was even more unusual that he had come to the rescue centre. So far as Mandy knew, Adam and Emily were both in the cottage.

'What's up?' she asked. 'Is it one of the pigs?'

Shuffling his feet while simultaneously gazing at them, Brandon eventually managed to glance her way. 'It's about the guinea pigs,' he muttered.

Mandy frowned. 'The guinea pigs?' She hadn't known he had any.

'I want to adopt them.' He paused, clearing his throat. 'For Rachel,' he added. 'For Christmas.'

Mandy opened her eyes wide. 'That's a lovely idea,' she said. Normally, she was cagey about animals for Christmas. Animals needed so much care that they shouldn't generally be given as gifts. The recipient might not care for them properly. But Rachel loved Snowy and Bubble, and she had years of experience in caring for cavies. She would be the best owner Mandy could have asked for. 'Would you like to see them?' she offered.

He followed her through into the room where the small animal cages were stored. 'I'll buy a cage this week,' he said. 'Food and sawdust. We've already got hay.'

'When do you want to collect them?' Mandy asked. Opening the cage, she took out Bubble and handed him to Brandon.

Like most farmers, he knew how to handle the little animal gently. He smiled as he gazed down at the small face. Bubble made happy burbling noises as Brandon stroked him. 'I could come for them on Christmas Eve,' he suggested. 'If that's okay,' he added, flushing his trademark shade of puce.

'That would be perfect,' Mandy said.

Once he was gone, she started up her computer. Navigating to the 'Animals for Rehoming' page, she marked the guinea pigs 'Reserved'. Brandon's gift idea was adorable and perfectly judged. He obviously knew Rachel well.

Mandy sighed as she added some video of Flame to the website. Much as she loved Flame, the lurcher had so much energy that Mandy wondered whether anyone would want to rehome her. Although her recall was much better, she still required a great deal of handling. Only someone very active could manage her. Closing down the computer, she went through to the dog area, remembering the promise she had made last night.

'How would you like to go out with Birch?' she asked Flame when she opened the kennel. As if in reply, the lurcher bounded out of her cage and rushed straight to Birch's door. The two dogs stood gazing at one another, nose to nose, wagging their tails.

Mandy unlatched Birch's cage and the little dog trotted out. The contrast between the leggy golden lurcher and the tiny silver terrier was almost painfully funny. To Mandy's surprise, Birch led the way, walking to the door in a steady fashion. Instead of her usual dash, Flame trotted behind the little dog, the expression on her face as close to adoration as anything Mandy had witnessed.

Outside in the orchard, the same thing happened. The silky little body trotted round with the lanky lurcher stalking behind.

'Birch, come!' Mandy thought recall was worth a try. Many dogs arrived with at least some training. Even if she didn't know the terrier's original name, she might still respond to the tone of voice. To her amazement, not only did Birch come, but Flame did too. 'Come, Flame,' Mandy added, when she saw the lurcher was heading towards her. When the two of them arrived, she was as encouraging and enthusiastic as she could be. Was this the secret to Flame's training, perhaps?

Taking out her phone, Mandy took some videos and then several pictures of the strangely-matched pair. This was something she would have to show Helen and Rachel, she thought. Flame and Birch might be an odd couple, but Mandy had a hunch they were going to be an unbreakable team.

Chapter Twenty-Three

As she drove towards Walton on her way to Melon's second home-check, Mandy's thoughts were with Rachel. She'd accidentally-on-purpose left the Hope Meadows website open on the 'Animals for Rehoming' page in reception. Rachel had sighed so heavily about the guinea pigs that Mandy had to stop herself from grinning.

'Something wrong?' she had asked.

If Mandy's innocence was suspicious, Rachel hadn't noticed. 'Someone's reserved Bubble and Snowy,' she said mournfully.

'We'll get more guinea pigs in soon, I expect,' Mandy said.

Drawing up outside the Dillons' house, she grabbed the checklist she had prepared. This time, Mr and Mrs Dillon opened the door together. They looked very serious, and Mandy realised how important it was to them that they passed the house-check. She wanted to hug both of them and point out that this just made them even more perfect for Melon.

The gaps at the bottom of the fence in the garden

had been filled in and the utility room had been arranged as Melon's private space. There was a heap of toys in different shapes and textures to keep him entertained.

'This is all great,' Mandy said warmly. 'Melon is going to be in doggy heaven!'

'You mean we can have him?' Mrs Dillon looked as if she was about to throw her arms around Mandy.

Mr Dillon's grin was so wide it nearly split his face in half. 'Brilliant!' he said.

'I promise it's my pleasure,' said Mandy. 'Will you be able to bring Sam and Buddy along when you come to collect him? It would be good to give you all the training and feeding information at the same time.'

'We will,' Mrs Dillon assured her.

'How about coming over on Saturday?' Mandy suggested.

'Perfect. The kids will be thrilled!' Mr Dillon opened the front door. 'Thanks very much,' he told Mandy, beaming again. 'Hope Meadows is giving us the best Christmas present ever!'

Mandy drove home feeling warm inside. This must be how Father Christmas felt, she thought. There was no doubt about it. She had the best job in the world.

Helen greeted her on her return. 'I just had Seb on the phone,' she told Mandy. 'Asking how Birch was getting on. She's fine, isn't she?'

'She's more than fine.' Mandy pulled her mobile from her pocket. 'I made a video,' she said. 'Look.' She handed over her phone and watched over Helen's shoulder. The video ended with Mandy calling Birch and Flame, and both of them running to her.

'Wow!' There was surprise in Helen's voice. 'That's amazing. I was starting to think Flame didn't even know her own name.'

Mandy pulled up a couple of photographs. 'Aren't they sweet together?' she said, holding out a picture of the two dogs curled up in the same kennel. Flame looked a bit squashed with her legs folded under her, but her long nose rested on Birch's back and her eyes were half-closed with delight.

'You should put that on the website,' Helen suggested. 'Maybe they could be rehomed together?' She flicked through the rest of photos again. 'Birch seems to have a very calming effect on Flame.'

'I've been wondering if Flame's lack of response to us is down to nervousness,' Mandy said. 'Maybe she feels more secure when Birch is there.'

'Because Birch keeps her calm, she doesn't get so easily distracted by other things going on around her, you mean?' said Helen.

'Exactly.' Mandy pushed a strand of hair behind her ear and studied the photo of Flame and Birch again. She wasn't usually a fan of rehoming animals in pairs unless they had always been together. It limited the number of potential owners, for a start. But in Flame's case, it might be worth a try.

'Have you seen the weather forecast?' Helen asked.

Walking into the kitchen, she put the kettle on. 'Coffee?' she added, opening a cupboard and grabbing two mugs before Mandy had a chance to reply.

'Yes,' Mandy said. 'And yes please.' She had indeed seen the announcement last night. An area of low pressure was moving in and heavy rain was forecast, with snow over high ground. Mandy knew from past experience that Welford, high up the dale and surrounded by the fells, lay above the winter snowline. There could be heavy falls in Welford, while York, only an hour away, could be snow-free.

'Do you need to get more feed in?' Helen asked. 'Just in case.'

Mandy smiled as the nurse handed over the mug. 'Thanks. And you're right. I'll go along to Harper's as soon as I've finished this.'

The country store's window was festooned with animal-themed decorations, including a toy lamb masquerading as Baby Jesus in a manger filled with haylage. It was already beginning to get dark and brightly coloured lights on the bushes outside were cheery in the gloom. Mandy pulled up in the gravel car park and picked her way around the puddles to the front door. Inside, the shop was brightly lit and chiming with the sound of Christmas carols.

'Hello!' She called out a greeting to Sally Harper, who appeared as soon as the door opened. Sally was dressed in her usual red Harper's sweatshirt, accessorised with a flashing reindeer badge. As ever, she came out with a smile, but when she saw it was Mandy, she frowned.

'Is something wrong?' Mandy asked, feeling her heart sink. It had been so long since the last attack. *Please don't let it be starting again*, she thought.

'I'm afraid we had another call.'

Mandy's head felt heavy, as if her neck could barely support it. She looked at Sally. 'You mean from the person who's causing all the trouble?'

Sally nodded. 'I think so,' she said. 'This time he was trying to order tons of extra feed, everything from equine conditioning cubes to a full lorry-load of brewers' grains. Don't worry, I would never have sent it out without checking. He must be unhinged.'

Mandy nodded, feeling stunned. What was it Helen had called him? *A nutjob.* 'Was it Janice who spoke to him again?'

'It was me,' Sally replied. She folded her arms and leaned on the counter, facing Mandy. 'He sounded odd.' She pursed her lips, thinking. 'Kind of hoarse, but it didn't sound like he was ill. Like he was trying to disguise his voice. Not a Welford accent . . . Yorkshire I think, but not local.'

Mandy felt her anger rising. 'Would you call the police?' she asked. 'Speak to PC Ellen Armstrong if you can. She's dealing with it.'

'Of course I will.' Sally nodded. 'I'll give them any help I can.' The store owner wasn't tall, but she looked so ready to do battle that Mandy almost laughed.

'Hope Meadows won't go down without a fight,' Mandy declared.

'Go you!' Sally leaned over the counter to high-five her. 'Just so you know,' she went on, 'I told him we wouldn't change the order. And I told him to leave you alone. You're doing good things at Hope Meadows. Loads of people have said so.'

The wave of defiance lasted all the way home. In the headlights, Mandy could see tiny snowflakes beginning to swirl in the air. Was it possible, she wondered, they would have a white Christmas? There had been a time in her childhood when there had been several in a row, but for the past few years there had been mostly rain from Christmas to New Year. It would be lovely to be knee-deep in snow, though it might make even getting to Lamb's Wood Cottage difficult. She had given up all hope of moving in, but it would be lovely to have a few mince pies and a cup of coffee there, boiled on the stove. Maybe Adam and Emily would celebrate there with her. Christmas was only a few days away.

Emily was waiting for her when she returned to the cottage. In the week since Mum had received the diagnosis and the injections from the doctor, Mandy had noticed a change. Already, Mum seemed more like her old self. Though there was still little colour in her cheeks, she had more energy than she'd had for months. The worry lines around her eyes had faded, and she was much more ready to laugh. Mandy was torn between relief and kicking herself for not insisting her mum should seek help much earlier.

'Did you get everything you needed?' Emily called.

Mandy kicked off her boots and stood them by the door. 'I did,' she said. She had decided that she wasn't going to worry her parents with Sally Harper's news. Sally was phoning Ellen. Mandy would follow up with a call tomorrow. There was nothing her mum and dad could do right now, except get more worried.

'Come and look at this,' Emily urged. She had her iPad open on the kitchen table.

Walking over, Mandy pulled out a chair and sat down. 'Standish House Hotel, Kilchrennan,' she read. 'Luxury hotel on the banks of Loch Awe.'

Emily's blue eyes were sparkling. 'Your dad's taking me there for Christmas,' she announced. 'He told me while you were out that you'd agreed to take care of Animal Ark over the break. He said you'd told him when I was ill. We're taking you up on the offer.' She looked so happy that Mandy reached out and hugged her. 'Thank you so much,' Emily whispered in Mandy's ear.

Mandy took a deep breath. She was going to be in sole charge of Animal Ark over the holidays. Her dad must have faith that she would manage, and the look on her mum's face made everything worthwhile. 'Thank *you*,' Mandy replied, pulling away from Emily. 'Thanks for trusting me.'

Emily raised her eyebrows. 'Have I ever not trusted you?'

Mandy laughed. 'I guess not,' she admitted. 'I'm so glad you're feeling better, Mum.' Standing up, she opened the fridge and took out a carton of milk. 'Shall we push the boat out and have a hot chocolate to celebrate?'

Emily grinned. 'I thought you'd never ask,' she said.

Chapter Twenty-Four

A dusting of snow stippled the fellside by morning. The sky had cleared, though extreme weather warnings were still being read out in dire tones on the radio. Mandy sat in the reception of Hope Meadows looking out of the window. She was waiting for the Dillon family. They were due to collect Melon at eleven o'clock.

She felt a beat of excitement when their car drew up five minutes early. Standing up, she went and pulled the door open. Mandy was pleased to see that Sam and Buddy were with their parents. Both of them looked so thrilled it gave Mandy's heart a lift.

'Come in,' she told them. A blast of cold air followed them inside and she closed the door quickly. She had set out chairs in a circle. She wanted to talk to all of them before they saw Melon. Hopefully, they would take in more if they weren't distracted by their new dog bouncing around. As she went through various aspects of Melon's behaviour, and how to continue the training she had been doing, the family listened closely. Sam in particular had several questions that showed she was very interested.

Mandy knew there was nothing more she could do

to make this rehoming a success. Melon had well and truly landed on his paws. She stood up to fetch him from the kennels, asking the Dillons to stay in reception. When she entered the dog room, the little Westie was standing on his hind legs with his paws on the bars. His stubby tail thrashed from side to side and he made a little sound of excitement as if he understood exactly what was going on.

'It's a big day for you, Melon!' Mandy wondered if he had recognised the Dillons' voices. She opened the door to his cage and clipped his harness on. Forgetting his training, he bounded ahead, pulling on his lead, and for once, Mandy didn't have the heart to make him stop and wait.

To her dismay, she felt tears prick her eyes as she watched the joyous reunion. She was supposed to be a professional, she told herself. The Dillons didn't notice. All of them were crouching on the floor, stroking Melon, ruffling his ears, telling him that he was a good boy and that he was coming to live with them forever. Melon gambolled between them like a spring lamb in sunshine. His button eyes were bright. Just once, he came back to Mandy and pressed his damp nose against her leg as if to say thank you, before returning to give Sam an extra lick.

'I suppose we'd better let you get on,' Mr Dillon announced, standing up.

'It'll be brilliant to get him home,' Buddy said. 'Won't it, Mum?'

He looked at Annie Dillon, who smiled down at him. 'It will,' she said. She turned to Mandy. 'Thank you so much for everything,' she said. 'We will look after him.'

'I know you will.' Mandy swallowed the lump in her throat. Following them out to the car, she saw a sticker on the rear window: *A dog is for life, not just for Christmas.* The Dogs Trust slogan was still relevant, even though it was almost forty years old. Mandy already knew a few pets would be abandoned when the first holiday after Christmas came round. But right now, her thoughts were with Melon. He leaped into the Dillons' car with delight and was strapped in between Buddy and Sam on the back seat. As Mandy waved them off, she could see the fluffy ears on the little white head were pricked as he gazed through the windscreen, ready to begin his new adventure.

'Go well, Melon,' she whispered.

Walking back inside to clear out his kennel, she saw Albert and the other dogs gazing hopefully at her. 'Don't worry,' she assured them. 'I'll find homes for the rest of you too.' Albert wagged his tail and lay back down with a sigh.

Back in the clinic, Emily was dealing with a cat which had turned up without an appointment. It had a chicken bone stuck across the roof of its mouth. It only took Emily a few moments to grasp the bone with some forceps and pull it away. Mandy was so pleased to have her mum back in Animal Ark. The few days she had been away hadn't been overly busy, thank goodness, but the clinic hadn't been the same without Mum's calm presence.

'Are you going to do something nice this afternoon?' Helen asked Mandy, closing the door behind the cat's relieved owner.

Despite Mandy's insistence that she didn't need a half day, Emily had been firm. 'Don't forget Dad and I are going away for a few days,' she had told Mandy. And although Mandy had suggested that Emily should still be taking it easy, Mum had not backed down.

'We could do something together,' Helen offered. 'It's Rachel's afternoon on reception.'

Looking out of the window, Mandy noticed clouds starting to pile up over Norland Fell. 'I think I might go up to Lamb's Wood Cottage. I was hoping to have it partly habitable by Christmas.'

Helen's eyes widened. 'Do you really think you might try to move in? You know there's snow on the way? And that cottage hasn't been lived in for months, right?'

'I've abandoned the idea of moving in,' Mandy admitted. 'I thought about taking Mum and Dad up there for a mince pie, but they're going away. It's going to be just me and Sky on Christmas day. I thought we might try to have some lunch there. Just something simple.'

Helen put her head on one side, studying Mandy's face. 'You're serious, aren't you?' she said.

'Yes, I am.'

'In that case, I shall come and help you.'

Mandy tried not to laugh. Helen was wearing her determined face. If anyone could get the cottage whipped into shape, it was her. 'Are you absolutely sure? It'll be messy.'

Helen pursed her lips. 'Look around you,' she said. 'Do you think I'd let a little bit of mess get in my way?'

'Good point,' Mandy said. Almost every day, animals came into the waiting room. Some were bleeding, some had diarrhoea. Many of the dogs cocked their legs on the reception desk. Yet Helen made sure the place was always spotless. 'In that case, I gratefully accept your offer. And in return, I shall take you out for a drink.' It was about time she went back to the Fox and Goose, Mandy thought, even if it brought back memories of her last visit. If she was in a mood for facing demons, she might as well put that one to rest. If Jimmy was in there with Molly, then so be it.

The last time Mandy and Helen had visited Lamb's Wood Cottage, dusk had turned the house rather beautiful in the half-light. This time, in the cold light of a December afternoon, the cottage looked very grim indeed. Although the roof had been mended, Mandy had forgotten just how blistered and awful the paint was on the front door and how green the once-white weatherboarding had become. Dead weeds in the guttering poked through the ribbon of snow. For a moment, Mandy had a sense that nature was taking over, that if she sat down for too long, weeds would cover her too.

She shook herself. The cottage was neglected, that was all. It just needed a bit of attention.

The key to the front door was still difficult to turn. She would bring some WD40 next time, Mandy decided.

As they entered the hallway, the house felt damp. There were little piles of white dust on the flagstones, showing where the ceiling plaster was crumbling. A worrying patch of black mould had appeared at the foot of the stairs, and one of the window frames had started to disintegrate into splinters. Mandy tried not to show her dismay. Given the state of the place, there was no way she would be moving in properly for a while. But having lunch here on the big day felt like a demonstration of intent. The cottage had once been a home. For now it was a shell, but with a new bathroom, refurbished kitchen and lots of stripping and redecorating, it could be lovely again.

'Where should we start?' Helen stood in the hallway gazing around. To their left was the sitting room, to their right the kitchen. 'It's a huge job.'

Mandy went back through into the kitchen. ''There's no way we can do it all,' she said. 'But I'd love one room to be clean enough so I can eat there, even if I can't cook. It'll have to be the kitchen or the sitting room. That way I can light a fire.' She would have to look into central heating to combat the damp. It could be done at the same time as the decoration. After Christmas, she would formulate a proper plan.

Together, they inspected both rooms. While the

kitchen was filthy, the room on the other side of the hallway had rain damage from the previously missing roof tiles. Though it was now more-or-less dry, the room had a musty smell. There was also a nasty-looking carpet on the floor. Even though Mandy, like most vets, had a strong stomach, she tried not to think about what might be growing underneath. But the kitchen tiles, once cleaned, would be serviceable.

'I think we should start with the kitchen,' Mandy said after they had been into both rooms twice.

'I think you're right,' Helen agreed.

Two hours later, with the light fading, Mandy rubbed her aching back and surveyed the newly-cleaned kitchen. The floor had been swept twice, stirring up all kinds of ancient grime. It needed a good scrub with hot water, but that would have to come later when the boiler was working. At least Helen had found the stopcock and switched on the supply of cold water, which seemed to be working. Mandy planned to switch it off and drain the system before they finished for the night. The last thing she needed was burst pipes if there was a hard frost.

They had filled several black plastic bags with the dregs of Robbie Grimshaw's grocery supplies. Mandy felt sad as they emptied out the cupboards. His existence must have been pretty miserable towards the end. She wondered why his nephew hadn't done more to help him; from the looks of it, Robbie had lived off tinned pilchards and the occasional potato. Couldn't his relative have done a proper food shop for him? Mandy decided to visit Robbie again in the New Year, she thought. She would take Sky next time. Even if he couldn't remember his dog, he had always loved animals. He would be happy to see her. And at least his nephew seemed to be around now. Perhaps he had just moved to the area, Mandy thought charitably. Hopefully the young man would visit his uncle over Christmas.

Most of the cupboards were now empty. There was only one left and then the wood stove. Mandy would have to clean that out before she could light a fire. Even after hours of hard work, Helen still seemed to be full of energy. She was standing in the centre of the floor, sporting a thick pair of rubber gloves and a hairstyle that would not look out of place on a scarecrow. 'It's not too bad now,' she declared. Her voice held its usual certainty. 'Just the one cupboard to go.'

'Would you mind getting it?' Mandy asked. 'I want to have a look at the stove.'

'Of course.' Helen crossed to the corner cupboard and opened the door wide. To Mandy's surprise a pile of beer cans fell out, tumbling onto the tiles. A single can rolled across the floor landing at Mandy's feet and she lifted it up. Unlike everything else in the kitchen, the can looked brand new and only recently emptied. Though she knew aluminium didn't rust, Mandy could smell ale. Surely after all these months, any dregs would have dried out. Upending it over the sink, a few drops of beer made their way over the lip of the can.

'That's strange.'

She looked at Helen, who shrugged. 'Maybe they haven't dried out because the cupboard is damp?' the nurse suggested. She didn't look convinced. She started pulling out the remaining cans and shoving them into the rubbish bag.

Mandy crouched down and opened the door to the stove. There was a bunch of crumpled plastic inside. She drew it out. It was a bag from the local bakery. Inside it, she found a screwed up ball of greaseproof paper and some brown bags. There was no way these were old. There were crumbs as if from a bread roll and a slice of tomato that had obviously been removed from a sandwich. Holding the bag in her fingertips, she stood up.

'Someone's been here,' she said to Helen. There was an uneasy feeling in the pit of her stomach.

The nurse came over and peered into the carrier. 'You're right,' she said. 'I expect a tramp must have sheltered here overnight. It has been very cold.' She frowned. 'I wonder how they got in.'

Despite Helen's calm words, Mandy felt a prickling sensation at the back of her neck. A shiver ran down her spine. 'I'll go and look,' she said. Her breathing quickened as she moved through to the back of the house.

There was a small bathroom to the left, opposite the staircase. To her horror, the window had been shattered and most of the glass removed. Some of last night's snow had made it inside. Nobody had been in or out since then, at least. There were no new footprints. To Mandy's disgust, someone had also used the toilet. Without water, there had been no way to flush it. Thanking Helen silently for turning on the water today, Mandy tugged on the ancient chain. Yellowish water swirled around the bowl, accompanied by a startling clatter from the cistern above her head. Mandy retreated before the ancient contraption fell off the wall, and decided to check the rest of the house for signs of her uninvited visitor.

Mounting the stairs, she could feel a surge of anger rising. She knew that people were homeless for all kinds of reasons. They needed somewhere to shelter. But there was a centre in Walton. Why would someone traipse all the way out here, to a draughty cottage? She dreaded to think what would have happened if they had tried to light a fire.

She popped her head into the small bedroom to the left at the top of the stairs. It was as empty as it had been on her last visit. Nothing seemed to have been disturbed. As she crossed the landing to the master bedroom, she tried to get her thoughts under control. Whoever it was didn't seem to have done too much damage. She would board up the window downstairs and get a glazier to come out. Perhaps tomorrow, if she was lucky.

But in the main bedroom, Mandy stopped dead and stared in horror at the message scrawled in black paint. 'GET OUT BITCH.'

Despite the dimness of the light, the huge letters on the wall were as stark and horrifying as fresh blood. In her shock, Mandy let out a scream.

A moment later, Helen cantered up the stairs. 'Are you okay?' she called.

Mandy was shaking from head to foot. She couldn't answer.

Helen stopped. Her eyes were fixed on the wall. 'I'm calling the police,' she said.

Mandy watched as the nurse dialled 101. There was a roaring noise in her ears that made it impossible to hear what Helen was saying.

'I spoke to Sergeant Jones,' Helen told Mandy when the call had ended. She touched Mandy's arm, her hand warm and comforting. 'He's coming over to take a look. Are you okay?'

Mandy shook her head. *Who had been in her house?*

'Shall we go and wait in the car?' Helen steered Mandy gently out of the room and down the stairs. Together they went outside and climbed into Mandy's RAV4. Mandy put the engine on and locked the doors. Helen turned up the heater. She found a can of juice in the glove compartment and they shared it. Mandy was relieved when a set of headlights appeared, bouncing over the humps of the rough track.

The liveried police car came to a standstill beside them and Sergeant Dan Jones climbed out, broad-shouldered and reassuring in his uniform. Brandishing a powerful torch, he came and stood beside the Toyota as

Mandy and Helen got out. They made their way back inside the house. It was dark now, and the graffiti looked even more eerie in the beam of yellow torchlight.

'As I told you, we found some rubbish downstairs that suggested a tramp had stayed here for a while,' Helen said. 'But this doesn't look like something a tramp would do.' She gestured towards the wall. 'This feels . . . personal.'

Mandy closed her eyes, willing herself not to cry.

Sergeant Jones nodded. The whites of his eyes were very bright in the dusk. 'I've read PC Armstrong's notes on your recent problems, Mandy,' he said. 'I think we have to assume there's a connection between this and the attacks on Hope Meadows.' He looked sympathetically at her. 'I'll take away some of the cans. There might be fingerprints.'

Mandy felt sick. It was so cold. Chances were, anyone spending time here would be wearing gloves. Even if they hadn't, to have fingerprints on file, the person would have to have a criminal record. *What kind of enemy had the rescue centre made?*

Somehow this was worse than the meddling that had been done before. '*Bitch*' lifted everything to a whole new level. If Lamb's Wood Cottage had come under attack, then it wasn't just Hope Meadows that was threatened. It was Mandy herself.

Chapter Twenty-Five

The light in Mandy's bedroom when she dragged herself out of bed in the morning was a strange shade of pewter. Opening the curtains, she gazed at the scene outside. The snowstorm had arrived overnight. The orchard and the rescue centre were enveloped in whirling flakes. The sky seemed far away and somehow both white and black at the same time. Beyond the hedge, the fellside stretched away, a white counterpane reaching into an invisible sky.

Emily and Adam had been horrified to hear about the graffiti when Mandy had returned from Lamb's Wood Cottage. It had been a relief that she could share everything with them, now that her mum was on the mend. But Mandy wasn't a child any more: her parents were still wonderful people, but she couldn't rely on them to make everything right. She had to figure out who hated her with such a passion, and why.

Sky had followed her over to the window. She seemed to sense Mandy's anxiety and was staying very close. They walked down the stairs together and headed into the kitchen. Snow had gathered on the ledge outside the window and when Mandy opened the door, a small avalanche tumbled onto the doormat. Mandy kicked the snow back outside and cleared the doorstep before stepping into the drift.

Sky seemed puzzled by the snow at first, snapping at the spiralling flakes as if it was some huge game. Her fluffy coat looked like it had been dusted with icing sugar by the time she followed Mandy into the rescue centre. Mandy took Birch and Flame from their kennels. Birch was still underweight so Mandy put a fluorescent coat on the little dog, both to keep her warm and to ensure she was visible in the deepening snow.

As soon as they were released in the orchard, Flame and Sky raced away from Mandy, chasing round and round the paddock with spurts of snow flying up from their paws. Birch seemed equally enthusiastic about the strange white stuff, though for most of the time, she could only take flying leaps with her short legs. She cleared the snow in short bursts, sinking in past her elbows, then bounding forwards again. Flame stopped beside her little friend on every circuit, pausing to lick Birch's head before zooming off again. After only a few minutes, Birch struggled back to Mandy, who took her back inside and dried her fur before putting her back in her warm kennel. Despite her doubts, Mandy had already received a couple of expressions of interest about rehoming Birch and Flame together. She felt a glow of satisfaction as she thought of the odd pair spending the rest of their lives together.

The cats seemed comfortable in their lovely warm room. Mandy checked the thermostat, moving it up a notch with a burst of gratitude to her parents for their generosity. Thanks to them, the animal housing was warm and easy to heat. The original wooden structures she had planned would have been far less sophisticated, and a real challenge in this extreme weather.

Despite the frenzied happiness of the dogs, Mandy couldn't shake the heavy feeling from her chest. With her invisible enemy still raging, was she going to have to turn Hope Meadows into a fortress? There were locks now on all the windows. Adam had insisted on fitting them as soon as the attacks had begun to look more serious. Mandy was glad of them, but she was starting to check them obsessively. It felt so strange to be worrying about someone trying to get in, rather than the usual concerns about the animals getting out. She couldn't help hoping, as she checked the tiny window in the toilet, that whoever it was that was carrying out these attacks would reveal him or herself soon. She hated the feeling of being watched from the shadows by someone she could not see.

'It's quiet this morning,' Helen declared as Mandy walked into the clinic. 'So many people have cancelled, there's almost nobody left.' Mandy couldn't blame them. Most of the appointments were non-urgent anyway. They could be rescheduled when the roads were clear.

'I think it's time to clean out the cupboards,' the nurse announced. Mandy smiled. Helen would never take advantage of an empty schedule to relax. Mandy decided to help her. Too much time doing nothing just fed the troubling thoughts inside her head.

When the door clicked open twenty minutes later, both Mandy and Helen were up to their elbows in soapy water. Pulling her head out of the cabinet she had been scrubbing, Mandy dropped her cloth into the bucket and walked through into reception.

Susan Collins was standing at the desk, ashen-faced and clutching a pair of gloves.

'Susan! What's wrong?' Mandy asked. 'Is it Marmalade?' Susan's cat had been in a few times, but never for anything serious.

Susan shook her head. There was fear in her eyes. 'Is Jack here?'

She must have known the answer would be no. If Jack had turned up on his own, Mandy would have called Susan immediately. Mandy could see her friend was on the edge of a terror she didn't want to face. 'What's happened?' she prompted gently.

'He's gone missing from nursery. Someone left the gate open. I know he loves it here. I thought he might have come to see you.'

Susan's eyes were pleading, but Mandy could only shake her head. 'He hasn't been here. Is there anything we can do?'

Susan swallowed. 'Can you come and help look for him?' she begged. Her voice was high and quavering. 'There are loads of people searching, but he knows you.'

Tears welled in her eyes and started to run down her cheeks, but Susan didn't seem to notice.

Mandy was already pulling on her coat and boots. She couldn't begin to imagine what Susan was going through, but she would do whatever she could to help. 'Helen will stay here in case he turns up,' she told Susan. The nurse had appeared behind her, then vanished again. 'Where have you already looked? Where would he go?'

Susan took a deep breath. 'There are people all over the village,' she said. 'But no one out this way. I'm worried he might have gone looking for reindeer with all the snow. He's been going on and on about hunting for them. It was just meant to be a bit of fun . . .' She stopped for a moment, her face stricken. 'Please can you . . . and if anyone else could . . .' she trailed off. She was shaking from head to foot and her tears were starting to stain her snow-flecked coat.

Helen bustled into the room brandishing two chocolate bars, handing one to Mandy, one to Susan. 'For when you find him,' she explained, handing them over. 'Susan, can I get you a hot drink . . .' But the terrified mother had thanked her for the chocolate and was already rushing out of the door.

Helen reached out and squeezed Mandy's arm. 'I'll call Seb, in case he's out this way,' she said. 'Don't worry about a thing here. I'll let your parents know what's going on. Just find that little boy, okay?'

Mandy nodded, unable to speak. She followed Susan

outside. The snow was falling thicker than ever, swallowing up the countryside. Mandy hoped that Jack would turn up somewhere safe and sound in a cosy little hiding spot. If he was out in this, it didn't bear thinking about.

Susan had run back down the drive to the road, and Mandy could see her woollen hat bobbing along on the other side of the hedge, heading to the village. Much as she wanted to stay close to her friend and support her, Mandy figured she would be better off striking out on her own, to cover the greatest distance.

Where to look first, she wondered? Was there any chance Jack could have found his way here without her noticing? She walked along the drive and turned up the lane, peering over the gate into the paddock. There was no sign of Jack in the donkey field. Pulling her mobile from her pocket, she dialled the Animal Ark number.

'Helen,' she said, when the nurse answered the call, 'could you have a quick look in the donkey shelter and the far side of the rescue centre, please? Give me a shout if you find him.'

'Will do.' The phone went dead. Helen never wasted any time.

Mandy was alone in the lane. The tarmac was blanketed in snow, and there were no footprints, no tyre tracks. No indication anyone had been this way at all.

She would walk up the lane away from the village, Mandy decided. She could see if anyone from the outlying cottages had seen him. Twenty minutes later, she had drawn a blank. Gran and Grandad were away visiting friends overnight. There was no way they would come back until the weather had cleared. There had been no reply in Jasmine Cottage and Mrs Jackson, who answered the door of Rose Cottage, had not seen him. Mandy had spent a couple of wasted minutes convincing Mrs Jackson, who was suffering from a heavy cold, to go inside and get back to bed. Further up the lane, she could see Manor Farm in the distance. She would walk as far as the gate that led onto the fell. If the gate was closed, she would retrace her steps and search on the other side of Main Street.

Despite being fit, it was tough going through the drifts. Though she was wearing walking boots and gaiters, in some areas the snow was so deep it came up to her knees, clinging to her legs like a dead weight. Mandy started sweating inside her heavy coat, and she pushed lank pieces of hair out of her eyes. The lane was eerily silent apart from the sound of her breathing. She stopped in the shelter of the hedge to stamp the snow off her gaiters, and realised that the flakes, which had been falling thick and fast, had slowed. A few wisps hung in the air, but the dense clouds had lifted, revealing the distant peaks against a pale sky. Mandy loved the fells in every season. She loved their space and the sense of freedom they gave her. In the snow, they had a beautiful austerity. But today they seemed threatening. A vast empty wilderness. If Jack was out there, how would they ever find him?

Mandy was almost at the gate to the main path. Another few steps and she would be there. It seemed to be closed, but she decided to go right up to check.

As she reached the gate, she saw something that chilled her to the bone. There, caught in the hedge, almost but not completely covered by snow, hung a small blue mitten. Pictures filled her mind: Jack Collins, standing in the paddock playing with two baby donkeys. Jack, with his sweet red wellingtons and woolly blue mittens, talking about reindeer. 'Do you think they might be out on the moor, Mummy?' Mandy felt sick.

She decided to do what she should have done right at the start, when Susan first showed up. She would phone Jimmy: call out the mountain rescue team and their dogs. If Jack had any chance of survival, it was down to them. Her fingers shaking, she dragged off her right glove and pulled her mobile from her pocket.

Jimmy answered the phone at once. 'Mandy?' His voice sounded the same as ever.

'Hi Jimmy. I'm calling for Susan Collins.' Mandy spoke as clearly as she could, convinced Jimmy would hear her heart thudding. 'Her three-year-old son Jack has gone missing. I've found one of his gloves at the moor gate. The one that leads off from Manor Farm Lane.'

'The moor gate on Manor Farm Lane.' He repeated the words back to her, loud and clear.

'We need the mountain rescue team,' Mandy stated. 'Can you come?'

'I'll call the others.' Jimmy's voice was reassuring.

'Jared Boone is helping with an accident on Walton Road. They'll join us as soon as possible. Are you still at the gate? I'll come straight there.' He rang off.

Mandy stood for a moment, the phone in her hand. Jimmy was on his way. Despite everything that had happened, she felt a sense of relief. Jimmy had sounded so calm and organised. If anyone could find Jack, it was him. She looked again at the tiny glove. She could make a start by opening the gate. It was a barred wooden gate which rested on the ground due to old hinges and rain-swollen spars. Not easy to open, even in summer. If Jack had come this way, he must have climbed it. Standing right beside it, Mandy peered over and studied the ground. Was there a slight indentation where little wellies might have landed? Regardless, the gate would be better opened for the dogs to go through safely. Unhooking the string that was looped around the post at the end, Mandy tried to shove the gate open, but it wouldn't budge. Climbing over, she began to kick the thick snow out of the way. By the time she had the gate open far enough to admit a dog, Jimmy's Jeep was coming up the lane. Climbing out, he grabbed a rucksack from the seat beside him then went round to unclip the dogs.

'Thanks for coming,' she said. How good it was to see him and he smiled his old smile for a moment as the dogs rushed over to greet her. Zoe, his husky and Simba, his German Shepherd, trotted at his heels, each wearing a bright orange waterproof jacket bearing the mountain rescue logo.

'What was it you found?' Jimmy wasted no time with unnecessary chat, but his voice was kind.

'His mitten is on the bush there.' Mandy pointed. 'I didn't touch it.'

Jimmy went over and pulled the mitten down. He offered it to Zoe to sniff. 'It's a bit of a long shot,' he said to Mandy. 'Too much snow, but Zoe's a good trailing dog.' Zoe pricked her beautiful silver ears as she sniffed at the tiny mitten. Jimmy had her on a halter. Once she had inhaled the scent of the mitten, Zoe put her nose to the surface of the snow, searching for the trail. She cast about, turning her body this way and that, but she didn't seem to be having much success.

In contrast to Zoe, Simba was not on a lead. 'Go on, Simba,' Jimmy urged. 'Simba's trained to air-scent,' he explained. 'She'll home in on any human scent she can detect.'

Suddenly Simba slipped through the open gate and started to plunge into the snow. Her tail left a faint line behind her, and her long legs made light work of the drifts. Unlike Zoe, whose nose was to the ground, Simba's head was at normal height. She zig-zagged up the fellside, a slim black and brown shape in her high-viz coat. Mandy marvelled at the ability of a dog to pick up scent molecules from the air.

Following the dogs, Mandy and Jimmy ploughed up the path, pausing frequently to call Jack's name into the echoing whiteness. Every time they stood still, straining to listen, but there was no reply.

The trail led across the shoulder of the fell, plunging into drifts and climbing slopes that were almost sheer. It was heavy going and Mandy could feel herself turning scarlet, but there was no way she was going to slow down. Beside her, she could hear Jimmy breathing hard but his face was determined and his eyes were fixed on Simba as if he was sending her on with the strength of his will.

Simba stayed ahead of them, barely slowed by the deepest drifts. Zoe ran a few paces behind, nose to the ground, occasionally circling around as if Jack had lost his way for a moment. *That's if we have picked up Jack's trail*, Mandy thought grimly. The scent on the mitten would have been very faint after being left in the wet hedge, and how much could Zoe detect from the ground when it was buried by snow?

While she was pondering, Mandy suddenly lost her footing and landed waist-deep in a hidden cleft. Jimmy grabbed her wrist, then took her hand helping her gently back to her feet. His green eyes met hers, and she was conscious of the closeness of his warm, solid body.

'Are you okay?' he asked.

Breathless, Mandy nodded. Jimmy released her hand and turned back to the trail. Simba had disappeared into a spiky copse of bare trees. Mandy peered between the trunks, then suddenly Simba was back, running straight towards them, ears pricked, tongue lolling out. She raced to Jimmy and barked twice.

'Show me,' Jimmy told her, and the beautiful Shepherd

turned and began to hurtle back up towards the trees. 'She's found something,' Jimmy panted to Mandy as side by side they rushed up the hill.

By the time they reached the trees, Simba was lying beside a large snow-covered rock, overhung by a stunted birch tree. As Mandy approached, a cleft opened up between the rock and the gnarled silver trunk. The hole was squarish and lined with crumbling timber, and Mandy guessed it had once been the entrance to an old mine. *Oh god, Jack. What have you done?*

'Show me?' Jimmy spoke again to Simba, who barked just once.

'Someone's down there,' Jimmy told Mandy. 'Can't be sure it's Jack, but we're going to have to take a look.' Removing his backpack, he pulled out a torch. Mandy stared down at the gap in the snow in alarm. The edges of the hole were uneven and treacherous. It was impossible to see where the rocks were solid and where the snow had formed a fragile overhang with nothing underneath.

Seemingly oblivious to the cold, Jimmy lay down, shining the powerful torch into the abyss.

'Looks like an old mineshaft.' He twisted his head to look up at Mandy. 'I thought I knew where all of them were on this part of the fell, but I didn't know about this one.'

'So what do we do?' Mandy was starting to feel strangely numb, as if this was all just a dream and any minute now she and Jimmy would plunge into the hole like Alice in Wonderland. She lay down beside Jimmy, sinking into the snow. The freezing chill stung, whisking her back to reality. If she was cold, what must it be like for whoever was in the hole? And how far down did it reach? Had Jack fallen?

'We can't wait for the rest of the team,' Jimmy said, flicking off the torch, rolling over and standing up. 'I'm going to have to go in.'

Chapter Twenty-Six

Jimmy opened his rucksack and pulled out a coil of rope. Tying one end around the thickest part of the birch tree, he stepped into an abseiling harness, then clipped himself on to the rope. He wrapped a second length of cord around the tree and handed one end of it to Mandy before snapping the other end onto his harness. 'Let this out as I go down,' he told her. 'When I need you to pull, I'll shout. If it's Jack, you might have to pull him up on his own. I'll try to guide him, but it depends on the climb.'

Lying on her front, Mandy wedged herself more deeply into the snow and took hold of the rope as Jimmy shuffled backwards to the edge of the hole. After a few false steps, when he dislodged chunks of snow without getting any purchase with his feet, he managed to wedge himself against the side wall. He sat back into the harness, letting the rope take his weight. Simba whined as she saw Jimmy disappearing. 'It's fine, Simba,' he called to her. 'Stay there.' Simba lay down beside Mandy and Zoe joined her, resting her elegant face on Simba's back.

Mandy was glad of their company and the warmth she could feel radiating from them.

'Can you try and give me some light?' Jimmy called as he started to lower himself into the mineshaft. Mandy let out the rope with one hand and tried to hold the torch steady in the other. The cold ground was pressing into her stomach. Snow was falling again. She could feel it landing on her neck. Flakes drifted into the shaft, twisting and turning in the torchlight. Trying not to shiver as the cold bit deeper, Mandy watched the top of Jimmy's head inch down. Sounds drifted up to her: the scrape of his boots on the side wall, an occasional clatter of falling pebbles. Then finally, the crunching of feet on gravel, and Jimmy's voice, like an echo. 'He's here.'

Mandy held her breath. *Here and alive?* Her ears strained, but there were only scraping sounds and light tugs on the rope: movement, but no voices.

'Now PULL!' When the yell came, Mandy felt a sense of panic. How could she hold the torch and haul in the line at the same time? It wasn't possible. She needed to brace herself and use two hands on the rope. Jimmy would have to be in the dark for now. She hoped enough daylight would shine down the shaft to allow him to see a little. Flipping onto her back, she braced her feet against the birch tree. Somewhere behind her, she could hear Jimmy climbing up the shaft, even faster than he had descended. Mandy half hauled herself up the rope, half reeled it in. Unseen, shrouded in darkness, Jimmy was bringing Jack up from the depths.

'Mandy.' When his voice sounded close beside her, she almost let go of the rope. Wrapping it around her left hand, she flipped over to see him staring at her over the edge of the shaft. His eyes were wide and his face etched with strain.

'Can you take him?' Jimmy managed through clenched teeth.

Gripping the rope so tightly it burned her palm through her gloves, Mandy edged closer to the hole. Jack was curled in Jimmy's arms. His face was deathly pale, but as Mandy watched, his eyelids fluttered. He was alive.

Breathless, Mandy knelt on the ground, reached down, and wrapped her right arm around the sleepy-eyed toddler. Alive he may be, but as she felt his skin, she was shocked at how cold he was. Shuffling backwards, she lifted him clear of the hole. A moment later, Jimmy was beside her, coiling up the two ropes, repacking his bag.

Mandy cradled Jack in her arms. He was heavy, but she should be able to carry him. Opening her jacket, she hugged the little body close to hers and wrapped her arms as far round him as she could. Jimmy nodded his approval, adding an extra layer in the form of a foil blanket from his bag, which he laid around her shoulders, tucking it in around the small boy in her arms. Pulling his mobile from his pocket, he called Susan and asked her to arrange for an ambulance crew to meet them. Then calling the dogs, they set off.

It was snowing again in earnest as they made their

way back down the hill. Jimmy walked in front of Mandy while she was carrying Jack. When she began to stumble under the weight, Jimmy took the boy into his own arms, tucking the small body into his jacket as Mandy had done before him. His face was grave as he looked down at the little white face and he doubled his pace, moving so quickly it was all Mandy could do to keep up through the deep snow.

By the time they reached the lane, it was full of people. The mountain rescue Land Rover was there, with a paramedic crew. Jack was lifted from Jimmy's arms by a female paramedic dressed in red overalls, her brown hair tucked into a fleece cap. 'We'll take it from here,' she said. 'The ambulance is down in the village so mountain rescue gave us a lift.' Her voice and face were reassuring.

There was a commotion among the knot of people and Susan broke through, her face crumpling when she saw Jack. She bent over her son as the paramedic cradled him, her long hair falling over Jack's face. Mandy felt a lump in her throat and tears prick her eyes.

Susan looked up. 'You found him,' she whispered. 'Thank you. Thank you.'

'Simba found him,' Mandy managed to say. 'And Jimmy rescued him.'

The paramedic started to carry Jack towards the Land Rover. 'Come on,' she said gently to Susan. 'Let's get this little chap to hospital for a check up.'

As the Land Rover drove away, Mandy suddenly felt weak and shivery. Exhaustion and cold were beginning to catch up. Someone took her arm, and Mandy realised it was Gemma Moss. 'Come on, hero,' Gemma said with a smile. 'Can you walk back, or shall we wait for Luke?'

'I can walk,' Mandy said, forcing her feet to move. She looked around for Jimmy, but he was several metres away, tending to the dogs. As she watched, he stood up and looked round as if searching for her. He took a step in her direction, but then Luke, appeared, taking hold of her other arm, and he and Gemma steered her down through the crushed snow towards the village. For a moment, she though that Jimmy would come to her still, but then Gary Parsons from the Fox and Goose appeared. Then Jimmy too was walking among his own band of human props. She watched his head bob with each step, a shade taller than his helpers. She wanted so badly to feel his arms around her. Her head was spinning with weariness, and she was dimly aware of people chattering around her.

'Such a relief.' 'Hats off to Mandy.' 'Thank goodness.' 'Wonderful dogs.' Mandy wanted to put her hands over her ears. The only voice she wanted to hear was Jimmy's, but he might as well have been on the moon.

Suddenly they were back in the village. They must have walked straight past Animal Ark, Mandy realised. She hoped someone had let Helen and her parents know that Jack had been found. The Christmas tree on the green was smothered in lights and swathed in snow. Although it was only early afternoon, the lantern above the entrance to the Fox and Goose was lit, adding a

Victorian charm to the Christmassy scene. Mandy found herself carried into the pub on a wave of humanity. The fire was burning brightly, stinging her cheeks and making her blink. She realised she was perched on a chair right by the fireplace. Her fingers were painful. They had been numb, but when she pulled off her wet gloves, they turned red and started to swell.

'Mulled wine all round,' announced Bev. Someone called, 'One over here for Mandy.'

A warm glass of red wine was pressed into her hand, wafting the scent of cinnamon and cloves. Mandy took a mouthful and felt the liquid warmth slide down inside her. Beside her, the coals shifted, sending sparks up the chimney. Mandy lifted her head and looked around.

The bar was full. There were people at every table. Half the village must have turned out to look for Jack and most of them had ended up here. There was Brandon. Rachel was with him. Gemma and Luke had ended up on the far side of the room. They were talking to Jimmy, Mandy realised. She felt as if she was hemmed in by the fire, toasting like a marshmallow. With a stab of unease, she noticed that Geoff Hemmings was on the other side of the fireplace. He glanced at her, then turned to talk to a bearded man she didn't recognise. Were they talking about Hope Meadows? Now the other man was looking over at her. The tense feeling that had filled Mandy for days returned with a vengeance.

Somewhere near the window, an older lady dressed in hiking trousers and an Icelandic sweater was tapping her glass. As the room fell silent, she held up her phone.

'I've had a text from Susan,' she called out. 'Jack is suffering from mild hypothermia, but he's recovering well and should be allowed home today. She sends her love to Mandy and Jimmy, to all the members of the mountain rescue team and to everyone else who helped.'

There was a wave of congratulatory noise. Glasses were raised. 'A toast to Mandy and Jimmy!'

Bev yelled that she had put a donation box on the bar for the Mountain Rescue service.

It should have been wonderful, Mandy thought. She was steadily getting warm and dry. A second glass of mulled wine had been pressed into her hand. Everyone wanted to tell her how wonderful she was. But the one person she wanted to talk to was as out of reach as Jack had been at the bottom of the mineshaft.

Mandy's seat was almost opposite the door of the pub, so when it swung open, she saw immediately who had arrived. It was still snowing outside, but rushing in, pulling off her scarf, shaking snow from her flame red hair, came the person Mandy least wanted to see. It was Molly Future. Spotting Jimmy at the far side of the room, Molly rushed over, bending to give him a kiss on the cheek and hugging him. 'Well done!' Mandy saw her mouthing the words. She looked . . . Mandy searched for the word. Elated? Ecstatic? Jimmy was smiling. They looked so good together.

She couldn't take her eyes off them. A feeling of sadness welled up inside her. She had worked so hard to accept the fact that they were together, but for a short while this afternoon, she and Jimmy had been a team again. She wanted to be able to walk over and hug him, but it wasn't her place.

Molly was standing close to Jimmy, she was looking round the room as if searching for somebody. When her eyes reached Mandy, she smiled and waved. Mandy had the sensation of being crushed, bodies pressing around her, the walls of the pub closing in . . . Then she saw Molly again, pushing her way through the crowd. She was coming over.

Mandy stood up, almost sending the table beside her flying. 'Let me through, please.' Her urgent request, three times repeated, was successful. A few moments later, she was outside the pub, stumbling through the churned snow at the side of the road. She had taken only a few steps when she heard the door open and close.

'Mandy?'

It was Molly's voice. For a moment, Mandy contemplated ignoring her. But Molly had done nothing wrong, and Mandy had to face her sometime. Steeling herself, she turned and dredged up what she hoped would pass for a smile.

'Are you okay?' Molly was peering at her in the dimming light.

Pressing her mouth together, feeling a prickling behind her eyes, Mandy was unable to answer.

'I can see you're not,' Molly went on. 'Come on, I'll take you home.'

Her voice was practical, yet sympathetic. How could Mandy tell her that she didn't want her pity?

Molly took her arm and started to steer her in the direction of Animal Ark. 'I'm sorry if you're not feeling well.' Molly's voice was inexorable. 'Shouldn't you have asked Jimmy to take you home? I know you and he are . . .' Her eyes widened and she broke off. 'Is that what's wrong? Has something happened to you and Jimmy?'

Mandy's feet had stopped moving. Her mind was finding it hard to focus. 'Me and Jimmy?' She turned and looked straight into Molly's eyes. 'But I thought you and he . . . I saw you together. Out in the new bar in Walton.'

There was snow settling on Molly's hair. She shook it off and frowned. 'You mean the Friday after we rode out together?' She shook her head. 'I passed my Senior Equitation and Coaching Exam. He promised me ages ago he'd treat me when I got it. I'm so glad we managed to stay friends after we broke up. Romantically, Jimmy and I are ancient history. Didn't you know? You should have asked me if you were worried.'

Why didn't I, Mandy wondered. 'You said . . .' She was having trouble thinking. 'You said you had a preference for men from the Lakes when we were out riding. I thought . . . I thought . . .' She trailed off.

'I've been seeing Aira. Aira Kirkbryde,' Molly said. 'We met the day of the Running Wild opening.' Her face was still puzzled. 'Didn't Jimmy tell you that either?'

The man from the Lake District, Mandy thought with a sense of shock. It was Aira Kirkbryde, not Jimmy at all.

Molly was gazing at Mandy. 'I know he meant to tell you he was taking me out, but then everything else took over, I guess . . .' A wave of realisation passed over her face. 'Something terrible happened at Running Wild. Didn't you know that either?'

Mandy shook her head. She was shivering again.

'One of his clients died.' Molly's voice was bleak. 'He was crazy busy that week with all the fallout. But I don't understand why he wouldn't have told you eventually.' Her blue eyes were anxious.

Mandy's head was spinning slowly, as if snow had clogged the space behind her eyes. Someone had died? Helen had said someone had been taken to hospital from the Outward Bound Centre. But died? Dear God.

Wait.

Jimmy had come to talk to her that weekend. Rushed through the storm. And she had turned him away.

She got her breathing under control. 'I think it was my fault,' she whispered. 'Jimmy did come round, but I didn't listen . . .' she trailed off.

Jimmy standing on the doormat with rain running down his face. She had shouted at him. Shame filled her.

'Hey.' Molly patted her arm and tugged her forwards. Mandy followed, feeling as if she had fallen down the mineshaft after all and was wading through an alternate universe.

'Don't worry about it,' Molly said. 'Jimmy'll listen if you talk to him. It didn't work out with him and me, but he's a nice guy. He's playing his cards close to his chest, but I definitely get the feeling he's into you. He kept on mentioning you, then changing the subject.' She sent Mandy a gentle smile. 'It'll be fine, really it will.' She stopped at the turn-off to Animal Ark. 'You'll be okay from here, will you?' she checked. 'I should be getting home.'

'Of course I will.' Mandy managed a weak smile.

'Do talk to Jimmy,' Molly urged. 'He seemed kind of sad today.'

Poor Jimmy, Mandy thought as she trudged under the old wooden Animal Ark sign. It was half obliterated by clinging snow, the words obscured. Someone had died at Running Wild. It must have been awful. Mandy should have been there for him, and instead she had jumped to all the wrong conclusions. Was there any way he would forgive her? Molly seemed to think she should try, but Molly had no idea how furious Mandy had been with Jimmy when he appeared on her doorstep.

She would have to speak to him, she decided, mentally squaring her shoulders. Even if he wouldn't forgive her, she needed to apologise. She couldn't do it now, but she would do it as soon as she had the chance. Stamping the snow from her boots, she followed the familiar path down the side of the cottage and round to the back door.

Chapter Twenty-Seven

Mandy dealt with the morning's work on autopilot. As the professional parts of her mind concentrated on dental patients and heart murmurs, the knowledge that she was going to have to talk to Jimmy bubbled underneath. Her heart beat faster whenever she pictured his puzzled, hurt face in the rainstorm. She was glad she was no longer a new graduate. Even with only half her mind on the job, she was able to deal with the routine tasks she performed on an almost daily basis.

Helen was sympathetic, but she encouraged Mandy to go ahead and clear the air. 'He'll understand, you just wait and see.' The nurse was so positive, Mandy almost started to feel optimistic herself.

But as she drove up to Upper Welford Hall in her lunchtime, all the doubts resurfaced. Those fateful few days replayed in her mind. Jimmy had told her he would ring after their dinner at the Fox and Goose. When he hadn't, instead of calling him, she had waited and worried. She had thought she trusted him, but she hadn't trusted him enough. When she had seen him with Molly, she had jumped to conclusions. He'd wanted to talk, wanted it so badly he had rushed out in the rain. And she had yelled at him and turned him away.

As she parked her car outside the steading and walked through the courtyard, she barely registered the festive shops and stalls. Was she asking too much of Jimmy? Helen didn't seem to think so. Nor did Molly. She had to try.

Jimmy was in his workshop, mending a net. For a moment, he didn't notice Mandy. His strong hands were nimble as he spliced and knotted the ropes. His broad shoulders stretched the black material of the polo neck he was wearing: the same one he had worn that night in the Fox and Goose, when they had gone there together. Mandy could feel her heart beating almost painfully in her chest.

'Jimmy?'

Hearing her voice, he spun round. If he had looked tired yesterday, today his green eyes seemed exhausted and empty.

'Mandy.' His cheek twitched, as if he was about to smile, but then his features settled back into resignation. He looked so sad that Mandy wanted to reach out and hug him, but there were things she needed to say. Steadying herself, she took a deep, shuddering breath.

'I'm so sorry,' she began. 'When you didn't phone me, I was worried, and then I saw you and Molly and I thought . . . I thought you were back together, only she told me you weren't and that she'd passed an exam and she said something awful had happened and I . . . Oh, I don't know, I'm just so sorry.'

Jimmy blinked. His expression had changed. There was confusion in his eyes now, diluting the tiredness. The hint of a smile twisted his features. 'I have no idea what you just said,' he confessed, 'but does this mean you're willing to talk to me?'

Mandy let out a strangled sound: half laugh, half sob. She pressed a hand to her mouth until the moment passed, then straightened up. 'I'm willing to talk,' she replied.

Where to begin, she wondered? For the first time that day, her brain began to clear. 'Molly said someone died?' She blurted out the most pressing question.

Jimmy's face creased with pain. Pulling out a chair, he offered it to her and sat down himself. He pushed the unfinished net away to the far side of the bench. 'I think you saw the man,' he told her, 'that day up on the ridge. An older gentleman with a beard?'

Mandy could only vaguely remember, but she nodded. 'We were up at the high-wire course, you know, where we rescued the deer?' Mandy nodded again. She could see Jimmy was struggling to speak. He swiped a knuckle across one of his eyes. 'He got ill really suddenly. Crushing sensation in his chest. Pain in his arm. He was sweating and clammy. I could tell it was something bad.' His jaw clenched as he glanced down to the floor, then back up to Mandy's face. 'I had to decide what to do,' he told her. 'There was no way a helicopter could get to us in the trees. It would take ages for an ambulance crew to get there. So I decided we should try and walk out. He died on the way.'

Jimmy's eyes were on the ground again. Without thinking, Mandy reached out and took his hand. She had to deal with death at work, but not like this. A human being. A terrible situation beyond anyone's control.

'There was nothing else you could have done,' she murmured. 'If it was so quick, it would have happened anyway.' She squeezed his fingers as another tear escaped from his eye and fell to the matting on the floor. 'Nobody could blame you.'

It wasn't true. She knew it, even as the words left her lips. People who were grieving often looked for someone to hold responsible. It was one of the hardest things she had to face in her chosen career. 'It wasn't your fault,' she insisted.

'I know.' Jimmy's voice was so quiet, it was hard to hear. 'They told me after that he had a heart condition. He hadn't declared it on his form, so I couldn't have taken it into account. There's still going to be an inquest, though. So many people descended on me. I had the police and someone from his company. I visited his family. I should have called you, but there was so much to do . . .' He trailed off, his tired eyes searching her face.

Mandy shook her head. 'It was my fault,' she said. 'When you didn't get in touch, I should have called you. And then I jumped to all sorts of conclusions. Molly told me last night why you were out together. I'm so sorry I didn't listen when you came round.'

Jimmy let out a groan. 'I shouldn't have come that

night,' he said. His mouth twisted. 'I came to your door and had no idea what to say.'

Mandy felt tears prick her own eyes. Poor Jimmy. His hand was still in hers. He hadn't let go. 'Can we try again, please?' she ventured. 'I know I always jump into everything with both feet. But I really am sorry.'

Jimmy found a smile, his green eyes gazing into hers. 'It's one of my favourite things about you,' he admitted. 'I just need to learn to manage it better. I think I can improve with practice.'

'Are you sure you still want to?' Mandy made a rueful face. 'Practise, I mean?'

The fingers holding hers tightened. He nodded. 'Definitely.'

The heavy lines around his brow had lifted. The old smile, the one that made her heart swoop, was back in place. He sat back with a sigh, but then he frowned. 'There was something I wanted to ask you about,' he said. 'Some rumour I heard that Hope Meadows had been attacked. Did something happen?'

Mandy had not meant to tell him about her strange battle with an unseen enemy, but once she started, everything came pouring out. As she spoke, some of her fear and loneliness began to lift. Sharing the information with Jimmy was enough to lighten the load.

Jimmy, on the other hand, looked aghast. When he heard about the awful message on the wall in Lamb's Wood Cottage, Mandy felt his fingers jerk against hers, then grip almost painfully. 'You won't go back on your own, will you?' he asked her, his voice urgent.

Mandy shook her head. 'I won't,' she promised.

'I'm glad the police are taking it seriously,' he said, then in frustration, 'I wish there was something I could do.'

Mandy sighed. 'Me too. I just don't know what.'

He looked at her, his eyes serious. 'You will be very, very careful won't you?'

'Of course I will,' she replied. 'Trust me, Hope Meadows is battened down like a medieval fortress, thanks to my dad. It's a miracle I can get in to feed the animals!'

'I think we should do something to take your mind off it.' Jimmy's face brightened. 'How about dinner tomorrow night. My place. Seven thirty?'

His hand was warm, the fingers strong. The workshop was brightly lit. Mandy caught the scent of sawdust and aftershave. Taking a deep breath, she felt strength and comfort just from being close to him. He had rescued Jack. Perhaps he could rescue her from her troubles, too? 'That would be wonderful,' she said.

It turned out to be a brilliant evening, uncomplicated, full of simple good food and shared humour. Jimmy had driven to Ripon and brought back mushroom paté and an asparagus quiche from Booths, which they had eaten with salad. As well as the food, he had bought a bottle of Wiston Estate Rosé 2011, an English sparkling wine. After two glasses, Mandy felt relaxed and more cheerful than she had done for days.

Better still was the text that Mandy received at the end of the meal from Susan Collins.

'Jack is allowed to come home today. He told me he had found the reindeers' lair, but then he'd fallen and he doesn't remember anything after that. I've told him he's never to go hunting without me again. He seems fine thanks to you and Jimmy. Hope to see you at the nativity. Susan.'

She showed it to Jimmy as they sat together in front of the fire, snuggling on the sofa.

'What does it mean?' Jimmy regarded the message with his head on one side. 'About the reindeers' lair?'

Mandy smiled at his bewildered expression. 'He was obsessed with Santa's reindeer,' she explained. 'Susan and he were playing a game, trying to find them.' A thought crossed her mind. 'I hope Susan isn't feeling bad. No one could have predicted he'd go looking on his own.'

'I'm sure Susan is too sensible to be worrying now he's safe.' Jimmy's voice was comforting.

'Safe, thanks to you.' Mandy told him.

'And you.' Jimmy said with a grin.

The three dogs were snoring in a pile before the blazing fire. Mandy felt like a teenager when he wrapped his arm around her. When he leaned in for a kiss, there were butterflies in her stomach.

'I've got something to show you,' he said a little later. He pulled away and stood up. He went out into the hall, returning a moment later with something that resembled a small camouflaged box with a number of lenses. 'It's a video camera,' he explained as he sat back down, 'with night vision.' He handed it to her and Mandy inspected it, feeling a little puzzled. It was just a camera, right? If Jimmy had taken some film of wildlife, why not show her that? 'I've used it before for otters and badgers,' Jimmy went on. 'It's motion triggered. I've two of them and . . .' he paused as if for a big announcement . . . 'the other one is, at this very moment, attached to a tree up at Lamb's Wood Cottage.' He grinned. 'If there's anyone hanging about up there, there's a good chance we might manage to get a picture of him.'

Mandy felt her heart beginning to race. If they filmed the intruder, maybe someone would be able to identify him or her. What a great idea. She thought back to her evening there with Helen. There had been a lot of beer cans. Perhaps he or she had been coming and going quite often. 'It might work,' she said, feeling suddenly breathless. Reaching out, she put her arms around him, pulling him into a tight hug. 'You really do think of everything,' she said.

Chapter Twenty-Eight

For the next two days, there was nothing to report from Lamb's Wood Cottage. Jimmy checked the camera each day and texted Mandy to keep her updated, among the flurry of other messages they pinged back and forth.

They had talked a great deal during their evening together. Mandy had told Jimmy she wanted to take things slowly, but that she was committed. Jimmy had assured her they would take things at a pace where she was comfortable. He had also told her that for now, he didn't feel ready to bring the twins over to Hope Meadows. They would meet officially when their relationship was more established. Mandy was more than a little relieved. There was so much going on that she didn't think she could string a coherent sentence together when it came to spending time with Jimmy's children.

On the third day, she stood in the orchard watching the sun come up as the dogs raced around. She heard the car before it came into view. When she saw it was the Jeep, her heart began to race. That Jimmy had come so early meant he must have news. Hustling the dogs inside, she locked the centre and met him coming round the corner.

He greeted her with a kiss on the cheek. 'I haven't downloaded it yet,' he said in a rush. 'I came straight here. But we've recorded someone. Yesterday evening.'

'Come inside,' she told him. They made their way to the kitchen door. Adam was cooking scrambled eggs and Emily was filling the kettle, but they gathered round as Jimmy connected the camera to Mandy's laptop.

The video footage was black and white, but Mandy was amazed at how clear it was. The first run of film showed a red deer as it wandered through the bushes. It seemed like a false alarm, but then the images became more chilling. A figure appeared in shot. From the size, gait and shape of the head, it was definitely a man. He was wearing a hooded jacket and dark trousers. He walked up the front path, turned left and disappeared round the back of the house. Mandy's heart sank. The hood had obscured the person's features. Unless he came out with it down, they were no further forward. At least, she thought, the bathroom window where he had got in before was sturdily boarded up. It was unlikely he would get in that way again and the windows at the front of the house were a good deal higher. Climbing into them would be more difficult.

The film stopped, then started again when the figure reappeared. To Mandy's disappointment, the hood was still firmly in place. From the timing on the footage, he had not been round the back of the house long, so he hadn't managed to break back in. Mandy realised she was holding her breath. Was this her invisible enemy at long last? The figure paused for a moment, staring at the house, then began to amble across the lawn. He was going to leave.

When he was almost level with the camera, the man stopped. What was he doing, Mandy wondered? There was a small clump of rocks in the garden that might have been part of a wall. The topmost stones protruded from the snow. The intruder had stopped and was looking down. Then, bending, he lifted one of the rocks. Tossing it in his hand, he made his way over to the sitting room window. Mandy felt sick as she watched the series of images: the arm drawn back, the thrust, the smash. She half expected him to go and knock the rest of the glass out so that he could climb in. Instead, he returned to the pile of stones. Again, he reached down, but seemed to stumble and lose his balance. As he straightened up, the loose hood of his jacket fell back. Just for an instant, his face was visible. In the next shot, he had pulled it back into place. The sequence continued as he broke the kitchen window as well. After surveying his handiwork, he turned and swaggered back down the path and disappeared.

'That's the lot,' Jimmy said. Disconnecting the camera, he flipped back through the film and showed it to Mandy. There was one single shot of the man's face. It was remarkably clear. 'We'll have to take this to the police,' Jimmy said.

But Mandy was gazing at the image. She had seen this man before. 'Wait,' she told Jimmy, holding out her hand. 'I think I know him from somewhere.'

Everyone looked expectantly at her. Mandy wracked her brains. He hadn't been in the rescue centre. Could he have been an Animal Ark client? But Mandy couldn't picture him with an animal.

'It's Robbie Grimshaw's nephew!' she gasped. 'I saw him the day I visited Robbie in the home.'

'Robbie Grimshaw's nephew?' Adam was frowning. Emily, too. 'Why would he have a grudge against the rescue centre?'

'Not the rescue centre.' Jimmy's voice was grim. 'He's attacking Mandy herself. Maybe in some crazy way, he blames Mandy for Robbie being moved into the home?'

It seemed a thin excuse. It was not as if Mandy had driven Robbie away and stolen his house. She had helped the police get Robbie to a safe place when he was in a really bad way. She had only bought the cottage when he had moved out. Not everyone was rational, she reminded herself. Robbie's nephew could yet turn out to be a 'nutjob' as Helen had predicted.

Emily looked at Mandy, her face worried. 'Would the staff at the home have some details for Robbie's nephew?' she asked.

'Maybe,' Mandy admitted. They hadn't asked for her address when she went in, but the auxiliary she had spoken to had entered her name in some kind of log, she remembered. She'd had to sign out when she left.

If she was lucky, the nephew might have given them his name too.

She had to look up the number for the home. Tapping it in, she heard a pleasant voice on the other end of the line.

'The Rowans Care Home, how can I help you?'

Mandy's mind was working furiously. She had dialled without planning what she wanted to say. 'I was wondering,' she paused for a moment, then rushed on, 'I was in a couple of weeks ago, visiting Robbie Grimshaw,' she said.

Three sets of eyes were on her. It was hard to think. Walking over to the window, Mandy looked out at the snow-covered garden. A Christmas rose was flowering defiantly in the shelter of the hedge. 'I met a young man,' she explained. 'Robbie's nephew. He seemed ever so nice. I was wondering if . . .' She paused infinitesi-mally, her eyes on a blue tit that had landed on one of the bushes. '. . . I'd like to send him a Christmas card,' she invented, keeping her voice casual, though it was an effort. 'Would you have his details there, please?'

There was a moment's silence. Outside in the garden, the tiny bird flitted away. Then the voice came again. 'What a lovely thought. I'm afraid I don't have an address, but I have his name here. Maybe you can look him up. It's Stuart Mortimore.'

Raising her eyes skyward in silent thanks, Mandy told the woman how grateful she was for her time and rang off.

'His name is Stuart Mortimore,' she told Emily.

Her mum frowned. 'Mortimore?' she said. 'That rings a bell. I think there was a family over in Walton called Mortimore. There was something about them. Some trouble. I can't remember what.'

'I guess I should call PC Armstrong,' Mandy said heavily. Suddenly everything felt very real. What if she was wrong, and she was about to accuse Stuart Mortimore of a crime he hadn't committed? She dialled the number for Walton police. Ellen Armstrong answered, to Mandy's relief.

'I'll come over right now,' Ellen told her. 'I'll bring Sergeant Jones as well.'

Mandy ended the call and sat down at the table. Was she doing the right thing? Was the film on Jimmy's camera admissible evidence? She wasn't sure if that was even the correct term.

'It'll take them a few minutes to get here.' Adam glanced round as the first client of the day drew up outside. 'I'm afraid I'm going to have to make a start on surgery,' he said.

'I'll have to go too,' Jimmy added. 'I said I'd give Jared a hand.'

Mandy stood up and followed him to the door, stepping outside to kiss him before he left. 'Thank you so much for this,' she said, meaning it. 'I'll let you know how it goes.'

'Please do.' For a moment, he held her tight. She could feel his heart beating. 'You will look after yourself?' His eyes were anxious. 'I'll come back at lunchtime,' he promised.

'You don't need to.' Mandy couldn't help smiling at his earnest, worried face. 'I will look after myself,' she assured him. 'And the place is going to be crawling with police in a moment!'

He managed a grin, then raised a hand in farewell and jogged over to his Jeep. Mandy watched him drive off, feeling her smile vanish. Had Robbie Grimshaw's nephew really launched a hate campaign against her and her rescued animals?

Twenty-five minutes later, a police car drew up. The two officers came into the kitchen. Sergeant Jones looked at the image on the screen of Mandy's laptop. 'Nice and clear,' he commented. 'Stuart Mortimore was known to us when he was younger. Right tearaway, he was. Always in some sort of trouble. He disappeared a couple of years ago and we lost sight of him. I heard he'd moved to Leeds. But that's him right enough.' He sighed.

PC Armstrong tapped something into her phone. 'We've got his mother's address. I know she's still there. Nice woman.' She gave Mandy a wry smile. 'We should be able to pick Stuart up soon enough. He has some friends locally that we can look up as well. Hopefully we'll have him in a day or two.'

'Really?' Mandy could hardly believe that her troubles might be over so soon.

Sergeant Jones nodded. 'We'll cross-reference with Leeds to see if they have any outstanding warrants for him. Even if they don't, if we can show Stuart was involved in all of the attacks against you, he might get a custodial sentence.' He smiled. 'Well done for identifying him,' he said. 'I haven't picked up someone using a wildlife camera before. I'll keep that in mind!'

Mandy felt slightly uneasy, wondering if Sergeant Jones realised it was his wife's ex-husband who had set up the camera at Lamb's Wood Cottage.

The police officers left, assuring Mandy that they would keep in touch. 'Just keep an eye out in the meantime,' Ellen warned her.

'I will,' Mandy replied. She certainly had no intention of going to Lamb's Wood Cottage without Jimmy until Stuart Mortimore was found. Jimmy answered his phone after only two rings. 'The police think they should be able to pick him up quite quickly,' she said.

'Good.' Mandy had never heard his voice sound so grim.

Morning surgery was almost over by the time Mandy and Emily made it out to the clinic. The snow and the nearness of Christmas seemed to have put more people off making routine appointments, making it a quiet morning. After they'd all had a coffee, Mandy went out to vaccinate a horse, and by the time she returned, Emily and Adam were also out.

Helen had put some festive music on in the waiting room. For the first time in ages, Mandy felt calm. It was only a few days to Christmas. Her mum was back to normal. She and Jimmy were back on track. And if PC Armstrong and Sergeant Jones were right, they would soon have Stuart Mortimore in custody. That would be a relief. Until they had him, Mandy had decided to put her ideas about visiting Lamb's Wood Cottage on hold. She didn't want to spend her first Christmas in her new home cowering behind the kitchen door with a rolling pin.

Helen stood up and grabbed her coat. 'Can you take the phones?' she said. 'I want to meet Seb for lunch.'

'Of course.' *Oh Holy Night* was playing through the speakers. Mandy smoothed out a piece of tinsel on the desk. 'Have a good time,' she told her friend.

'Back at two,' the nurse assured her. 'I've diverted the phone to your mobile.'

When Helen had gone, Mandy went outside. The snow crunched under her feet as she walked over to the paddock. The fellside was sparkling white and the orchard trees stood black and stark against the blue sky. There was just enough time to do a bit of work with Holly and Robin before lunch. Her mobile would ring in her pocket if anyone needed to contact the surgery

Mandy spent several minutes grooming Robin, trying to get a sheen on his fluffy grey-brown fur, and now it was Holly's turn. The young donkey seemed to enjoy the attention as Mandy brushed her hair, methodically working towards her hindquarters. Sky was lying in the sunshine at the edge of the field shelter. With her thick coat, she seemed oblivious to the cold.

Although it was still freezing, grooming was warm work. Mandy stopped to take off her jacket and hung it on a fence post. When she turned around, she noticed that Sky was sitting up. Her ears were pricked and her head was on one side.

'What is it?' Mandy smiled at the collie's intent expression. Inside the rescue centre, one of the dogs began to bark, and then another. Mandy frowned. She had been working hard with all the dogs to keep them calm if they heard something outside. It was rare for them to make much noise. Sky's ears had gone back. Her hackles were raised. To Mandy's surprise, she growled.

A shadow fell across the paddock, black on white. A figure rounded the end of the field shelter. Holly jumped, her little hooves slipping in the trodden snow. Mandy felt the pulse throb in her temples. A pair of startling blue eyes glared at her from inside a thick hood. She would have recognised them anywhere. It was Stuart Mortimore.

Everything seemed to go into slow motion. Mandy took a step back, her fingers reaching for the phone in her pocket. Stuart was wearing the same tracksuit he'd had on when she had seen him at The Rowans. It looked grubby, as if he had been wearing it for days. His hair was greasy, straggling across his forehead under the hood.

'What can I do for you?' Mandy's voice was high,

trying for normality: failing badly. She took another step backwards. Her phone was between finger and thumb. She struggled to pull it from her pocket.

'You can give me my inheritance back.' The voice was low and angry. 'You sent my uncle to that home. I was going to move in.' He took another step.

Mandy held up her right hand, her body leaning away from him. Her left hand was still half in and half out of her pocket, fingers trying to press the right numbers. She twisted further, hoping Stuart wouldn't see what she was doing.

'I didn't know that. I didn't know you existed.' It was hard to breathe, but she managed to get the words out. Her eyes were latched on his. Her mind was racing. There was nobody near: no point in screaming.

Stuart advanced on her. Step by step, crunching in the snow. 'He's my uncle.' The voice was louder now. The eyes were bulging. 'I was going to inherit. You put him in a home, you bitch! They're spending my money. That house was MINE!' He was flat out yelling now, fists clenched.

His shouts were too much for Sky. She darted along the ground, body low, then launched herself at Stuart. His eyes caught the snarling black streak and his howl of rage turned into a gasp.

Mandy half thought that he would kick the collie aside, but Sky's attack knocked him off balance. Stuart teetered on his heels, arms flailing. His head hit the side of the field shelter as he went down.

Terrified by the commotion, Robin snapped his lead-rope and made a dash for freedom, bolting out from behind Mandy and leaping over the prone body. A careless hind foot landed on Stuart's stomach as the young man tried to roll out of the way.

For a moment, the pathetic figure lay clasping his abdomen. His breath came in wheezing sobs. When he lifted his head, he looked dazed. He fell back onto the snow with his eyes shut. Mandy could tell he was still conscious because he was moaning.

Mandy had the phone in her hand. Barely taking her eyes off Stuart, her fingers found the redial button. Walton Police was the last number she had called. She prayed that PC Armstrong would answer and figure out what was going on fast.

The body on the floor was moving again. To Mandy's amazement, as Stuart started to get up, Sky leaped forward. The collie stood closely over him like a sheep-dog with an aggressive ewe. Her ears were flat against her head, eyes boring into him. Every time Stuart tried to move, she darted towards him, baring her teeth.

'Call your dog off!' Stuart shouted, lying in the churned-up snow. Mandy ignored him. He would have to take his chances with Sky, she thought. On the other end of the phone, she heard someone answer. It sounded like Ellen, but before Mandy could say anything, Stuart started to speak, his voice so low it was difficult to hear.

Mandy took a step towards him and held the phone so that it would pick up his words. She hoped Ellen could hear, and would come straight back. Mandy didn't want to interrupt Stuart, not if there was a chance he was going to explain himself.

'What did you say, Stuart Mortimore?' Mandy prompted clearly. *Please Ellen. Please be listening.*

'You know what I said.' His voice was louder now. 'You stole my inheritance.'

'Was it you?' she asked. 'Who did all those things to the rescue centre?'

And now, despite his prone position, despite Sky beside him, Stuart Mortimore managed to laugh. 'Course it was.' His face was filled with spite. 'Enjoyed it, too. Thinking about you, all scared and pathetic.'

He sneered at her, his mouth twisting. 'It was me who made the hole in your fence. I got the idea from some idiot in the pub. He was whining about you, said your dogs were running around the countryside, terrifying his rabbits.' He gave another short laugh. 'I told him I'd had trouble with you too. Knew he'd pass it on, make sure everyone knew you weren't welcome. And then I made the hole.' He smiled with satisfaction.

'Why would you do that?' Mandy demanded faintly. His words sickened her, but she wanted to keep him talking.

'I hoped another of your dogs would escape,' he boasted. 'I hoped they'd cause an accident. If someone died, you'd have been in real trouble.' His head was twitching from side to side, as if he couldn't talk fast enough to keep up with his memories. 'I did other things too. A complaint to the campsite, some calls to your supplier.'

While he spoke, his body was still. But as he spat the last word, he rolled. Tucking his legs beneath him, he lurched upright in a single motion. Mandy staggered backwards. For a moment, she thought he was going to kick her. He paused with his foot in the air, then turned to run. Sky took off after him like a bolt from a gun.

Mandy lifted her head. In the distance, she heard the sound of a police siren and squealing tyres. By the time she had pulled herself together and walked unsteadily to the front of the rescue centre, the police car was parked slantwise across the drive and Stuart was being handcuffed.

'Are you okay?' Ellen Armstrong seemed out of breath. She had hold of one of Stuart's arms and Dan Jones was on his other side.

Mandy gave them a shaky nod. For the moment, she didn't trust herself to speak.

'That's some dog you've got there.' Sergeant Jones nodded at Sky, who was slinking about the yard as if wondering who to round up next.

Blood dripped from one of Stuart's hands. He seemed to have given up the fight and his head drooped. Mandy expected to feel contempt for him but for the moment she felt nothing, as if her brain had been wiped.

'The dog had him by the hand,' Dan went on. 'She wasn't for letting go, that's for sure.'

She leaned on the wall. Sky slunk over, looking up as

if unsure of her reception. Legs buckling, Mandy sank down to the ground. She was trembling. Sky shuffled up beside her, and Mandy wrapped her arms around her beloved dog.

A shadow came between her and the sun. Looking up, she saw Dan Jones gazing at her. 'I'm really sorry,' he said. 'We have to go. Will you be okay? Is there anyone we can call?'

Mandy realised she was sitting in the snow in her jeans, but the shivers running through her body were nothing to do with cold. 'Please don't call anyone,' she said. 'Not just yet.' In a few moments, she would go indoors but for now, she wanted to sit here with Sky.

'Are you sure?' His dark eyes were filled with concern. 'We could get you inside. You must be freezing.'

'I'm fine.' She could see doubt in Dan's eyes, but he just nodded. Checking that the prisoner was secure in the back seat, he climbed into the police car and drove off.

Mandy was still there a few minutes later when her mum drew up. She could feel tears on her face but she couldn't wipe them away. Her body felt drained of energy.

Emily's eyes opened wide with alarm when she saw Mandy sitting there. Mandy opened her mouth but nothing came out. *Alice in Wonderland again*, she thought dimly. *Falling down the mineshaft*. Jack would be back home by now. She should go and see him.

'Mandy?' Her mother's worried voice jerked Mandy back to the present. 'What's happened?'

'Stuart Mortimore,' Mandy whispered.

'He was here?' Emily almost shrieked, then visibly steadied herself. She closed the car door, walked over and sat down in the snow. Without a word, she wrapped her arms round Mandy and Sky. It was a stretch for Emily, but she held them tight, filling Mandy with warmth and love. 'Is it safe now?' Emily asked gently against Mandy's hair. 'Do you want to talk about it?'

Mandy sighed. How precious and gentle she was, this wonderful woman who had taken Mandy as a daughter. She would never stop feeling grateful that her parents had chosen her. Never.

'He was taken away by the police,' she said. 'I don't want to talk now.'

'Whenever you feel ready, I'll be here.' Emily reached up a hand, smoothing a stray lock of hair from Mandy's eyes. Simple words, a promise made. The tears were taking over again. The loving arms surrounded her and Mandy leaned into her mum's embrace feeling comforted to her core.

Chapter Twenty-Nine

'You really do need to leave.' It was the twentieth time Mandy had said it. Despite feeling nervous, she didn't want to keep her parents from their much-needed Christmas break. It had been a long time since they had been off duty over the festive season. After everything that had happened, they deserved to get away for a long rest.

'But are you sure you'll be okay?' Emily's eyes held love and concern in equal measure.

Stuart Mortimore was in custody. Ellen Armstrong had called to let Mandy know that the police from Leeds had some outstanding arrest warrants for him, too. With that and the evidence of Mandy's phone call, it wasn't likely Stuart would be on out on bail before the hearing.

But Mandy was still jittery. 'I'll be fine,' she told her mum. If she repeated it often enough, it would probably be true.

Adam sighed. 'Come on, love,' he said to Emily. 'Mandy's right. If we want to get to Loch Awe before it's dark, we really have to set off.' He turned to Mandy. 'Look after yourself.' He held out his arms and she flung herself into them for one last hug. 'Before I go,' he added as he released her, 'I've got a present for you. You can open it now.'

He reached out and picked up the mysterious gift from the windowsill that had been tantalising Mandy all morning. Tearing off the festive wrapping, she found a green plastic food bowl and a smart black cat collar. Mandy frowned at her dad.

He smiled at Emily, then back at Mandy. 'Assuming you approve,' he said, 'Mum and I would like to adopt Tango. We thought you might let us, given that the rules on adopting rescued animals have already been broken.' He grinned as he looked down at Sky. 'Though Tango might not be quite as useful as Sky when it comes to rounding up criminals.' On hearing her name, the collie sat up, ears alert and head on one side.

In reply, Mandy hugged first Adam and then Emily. 'I can't think of anyone better,' she said, looking from one to the other. 'He's such a sweet old thing.'

'Are you calling me old?' Adam narrowed his eyes. 'And sweet?' He bared his teeth.

Mandy laughed.

'I'm glad you approve.' Emily was smiling.

'How could I not?'

Adam opened the door. 'Look after yourself,' he said again.

Despite the chilly air outside, Mandy stayed on the doorstep until the sound of the car faded into the distance. She sighed as she closed and locked the door.

The house seemed terribly silent. Saturday afternoons were often quiet at Animal Ark. Mandy had already been out to tend to her rescues twice. There was really nothing else she needed to do. Having made herself a cup of hot chocolate, she sat down in front of the television, but after only a few minutes, she found herself back on her feet.

Sky followed at her heels wherever she went. Since Stuart's attack, the little collie seemed to have decided that Mandy needed close protection at all hours of the day. Mandy stood in the kitchen, looking out of the window at the clinic and the rescue centre in the paddock. Before Stuart was behind bars, she had altogether given up the idea of spending any part of Christmas at Lamb's Wood Cottage. Now she was so far behind with her renovations that even the prospect of having lunch there was less than enticing. The electrician was unable to carry out the rewiring work until after the New Year. The plumber had fixed the toilet, but the boiler wasn't working. It rankled that Stuart Mortimore with his stupid scheme had prevented Mandy from achieving something she wanted so badly.

Outside the window, there was still snow on the ground, but the afternoon was bright and sunny. Holly and Robin were outside, nosing at the ground. Remembering Robin's part in tackling Stuart, Mandy felt a surge of determination. She would spend the next couple of days in her new home working to get the kitchen into shape. She was not going to let him stop her. The décor might not be up to scratch in time for the big day, but she could warm up the ground floor and cook soup on the wood stove. She had plenty of candles. She could make the kitchen cosy. It would hardly be the height of luxury, but it was her home. She had the perfect right to be there at Christmas.

Before she could change her mind, Mandy changed into some old clothes and began to load all the things she would need into the back of her SUV. She piled in buckets and sponges, disinfectant and soap and an old radio. Strapping Sky in, she drove the short distance up to the cottage.

After the brightness of Animal Ark, the cottage seemed dimmer than ever, despite the sunshine that was making its way into the kitchen. Mandy walked around the house, trying not to wince at how much needed to be done. The bathroom window which had been boarded up was flapping loose again. She should secure it before she left. But for now, she would make a start with cleaning down the walls in the kitchen. She would start the stove later, she thought. She might as well get on with some of the other tasks while it was still light enough. Setting the radio on the side, she found some Christmas music and set to work.

An hour later, she had begun to regret her decision. Despite the hard work, her hands were freezing from dipping in and out of cold water as she scrubbed down the surfaces. It was starting to get painful. After an hour and a half's work, she had only managed half the room.

Even the dirt on the cupboards was impossible to clean. For a moment, Mandy quailed. Should she give up now? Admit defeat and crawl back to Animal Ark? She took a deep breath and put the cloth on the mantelpiece.

She decided to light the stove. Maybe if it was warmer, things would seem more possible and at least she could heat up the water she was using. It was already dusk outside. Before setting up the fire, she should get some candles out. She would light them when she got back from collecting the wood.

By the time she had set up the candles and run out to fetch the logs, Mandy was very cold indeed. She was glad she had brought a pack of firelighters with her. With hands that were now trembling as well as red with cold, she opened the stove door. She set several fire-lighters on the grate and stood the logs around them. Hoping against hope that the fire would catch quickly, she struck a match. It blew out before she reached the firelighters.

Trying to steady her shivering, she fumbled another match from the box. This time, by cupping her hand around the light, she managed to get it to the flammable white sticks. Mandy watched as the tiny orange flame spread blue, licking upwards towards the logs. As it reached the wood, a choking cloud billowed towards her. She waited a moment, but the smoke continued to pour out. Checking that the air inlet below the grate was open, she pushed the door shut. For a moment, she listened for an encouraging roar as the flames took hold, but when she edged the door open two minutes later, the lighters had burnt themselves out. The wood, though blackened, was unlit. Rancid fumes filled the room and Mandy started to cough.

She needed to light the candles before carrying on. It was too dark to see enough to set up the fire again. At least those lit easily, though from the way they flickered, the room was so draughty that she would need a really good blaze to get the area warmed.

Mandy refilled the stove with firelighters. Another three matches wasted. More smoke. When the fire went out for a second time, she was beginning to feel desperate.

Clearing out the logs, she rolled up some newspapers she had found in the woodshed. Twisting them into knots, she set them around the firelighters until she had a good base. Another trip out to the woodshed. There had been an axe there. Perhaps, unlike the stove at home where the logs seemed to light easily, she was going to have to make some kindling. Aiming at the end of one of the logs, Mandy drove the blade into it, then tapped the combined axe and log up and down until the wood split. Repeating her actions, she soon had a small pile of splintered sticks.

Back in the kitchen, some of the smoke had cleared. Mandy opened the stove and set a few more lighters on top of the paper, balanced some kindling around the pile, then added some logs.

This time, the smoke was even more intense. Despite

the door being closed, fumes poured out through the air inlet. When Mandy opened the door to see what was happening, she was engulfed in a choking cloud. Slamming the door shut again, she sat back on her heels. She had known it was an uphill task, but if she couldn't get the stove lit, it would be impossible.

Sky growled. She had been pressed against Mandy's side, trying to offer comfort. A moment later, with a tiny whine, she broke free from Mandy's grasp and rushed towards the door. Half panicking that Stuart had somehow returned, Mandy was scrabbling backwards when a man's shape appeared in the candle light.

It was Jimmy. 'Sorry I startled you,' he said.

She laughed at his worried expression. 'I'll get over it,' she said. 'Do you know anything about stoves? I think maybe Santa's already stuck in the chimney. There's certainly something blocking it.'

'Don't worry,' he said with a grin. 'The chimney probably needs sweeping.' Glancing round the room, taking in the cloths and bucket, the radio and candles, he frowned. 'Why are you here anyway? Isn't it a bit late?'

'Well, I was planning to have everything ready for Christmas,' she joked, 'but I think it might need a bit more tinsel.' He laughed, but she said more soberly. 'I was hoping to have some lunch here on Christmas day with Sky. Mum and Dad are away and I'm on my own. But if I can't get the fire lit, it'll be cold soup with the crackers.'

Jimmy rubbed her shoulder. 'There's a lot to do,' he said, 'but if you're willing to wait till after Christmas, I can give you a hand.'

'As for Christmas dinner in your new home . . .' He pursed his lips, then one side of his mouth twitched up. 'How about you spend the whole of Christmas in my home instead?' To Mandy's amazement, he dropped down on one knee. 'I hereby propose,' he said, 'that you spend Christmas with me at Mistletoe Cottage.' He reached into his pocket and pulled out a bar of chocolate. 'We can seal the deal with this.'

Mandy stared at him, then laughed. He was so corny. And so exactly, perfectly what she needed at this moment. Wrapping her arms around Jimmy, she hugged him, then was surprised by Sky, who barked and thrust her nose between them.

'You really will need to teach that dog of yours that I'm one of the good guys,' Jimmy said as Sky glared up at them.

Mandy shook her head. 'I think she knows,' she told him. 'You should have seen Stuart Mortimore after she'd finished with him.'

Mandy ate half of the chocolate bar. When she was finished, Jimmy found her some gloves and a hat and helped her pull them on.

'There's a window round the back that needs to be secured,' Mandy remembered. 'It was boarded up, but Stuart must have loosened it that night he was here.'

'Do you have tools?' As ever, Jimmy was briskly practical. Mandy reached into the tool box she had brought, handing over a hammer and nails. The chocolate and extra clothes were already working their magic. She no longer felt as if her blood was freezing. 'Can you bring the torch?' Jimmy suggested. Together they crunched their way through the snow, round to the back of the house.

Mandy held the torch steady as Jimmy hammered each nail home with the efficiency she still found mesmerising. When he had finished, she reached her arms around him from behind, kissing his ear. 'You know, the very first time I saw you here, you were hammering in nails,' she whispered. 'You really are very good at it.'

He laughed. 'Everybody's good at something,' he said, turning towards her, pulling her in close.

'It was the first time I noticed how attractive you were,' she admitted, feeling her face turn red. Her arms were wrapped round his waist. His cheek felt warm against hers.

Finding her mouth, he began to kiss her, gently exploring to begin with, then more deeply as Mandy relaxed into his embrace. His aftershave mingled with the frosty air. She could feel the weatherboarding against her back, the cold air on her cheeks and his warm body tight against hers. By the time he let her go, she was breathless.

Hand in hand, they walked back round to the front of the house. Mandy couldn't quite bring herself to let go and he seemed quite content to have her fingers in his.

They drove first to Hope Meadows. 'Shall I take the dogs out while you see to the cats?' Jimmy offered.

Mandy nodded. No doubt, in time, he would get used to the cats and for now, she was happy to spend a little extra time with Tango. 'As soon as I come back after Christmas,' she promised the old cat, 'you'll move in to the cottage. And it'll only be a couple of days until Dad comes back.' The gaunt ginger tom purred loudly, reaching his head towards her hand.

It felt strange to close up the rescue centre and leave when there was nobody at home. Climbing back into her car, Mandy followed Jimmy along the lanes and pulled up in front of Mistletoe Cottage. She would need the SUV to have easy access to the road if she was called out.

Jimmy had gone ahead while she locked up Animal Ark. By the time Mandy walked in, he was in the sitting room lighting the fire. Sky seemed delighted to be back. Within moments, she, Simba and Zoe were rushing around in circles, dashing round and round the room, almost knocking over the Christmas tree that had been set up in the corner.

Having lit the fire, Jimmy stood up. He smiled as he watched Mandy looking round the room, taking in the tree, the tinsel, and the holly that decorated the mantel-piece. There were homemade snowflakes on the window and paper chains criss-crossing the ceiling.

Mandy shook her head in amazement. 'I had no idea you were such a festive elf.'

'It was Abi and Max,' Jimmy explained. 'They blitzed the place. You're going to have to put up with streamers and fake snow in the bedrooms too, I'm afraid.'

'It's lovely!' Over the top it might be, but it felt like a warm and cosy piece of paradise after the chill at Lamb's Wood Cottage.

'I wasn't sure about, er, overnight arrangements.' Jimmy's words were tentative. 'You said you wanted to take things slowly. You could always sleep in Max and Abi's bedroom, if you need your own space?'

Mandy grinned. 'I don't think I'll need quite that much space,' she told him. She looked around again. 'There are an awful lot of streamers,' she said, raising an eyebrow, 'but did anyone remember to hang up any mistletoe?'

Jimmy laughed. 'I don't think anyone brought any indoors,' he said. 'If you feel the need, there's more than enough in the garden.' He shrugged, his eyes dancing. 'But from what you said earlier, we won't need any. I'll just find some DIY to do and you won't be able to resist me.'

'You do that,' Mandy advised, flinging herself down on the sofa. 'When you're done, I'll be here waiting. Or if you prefer, you could just come and sit down beside me.'

'Perhaps that would be easier after all,' he said. With a grin, he threw himself down beside her.

Chapter Thirty

The church looked like something out of a Christmas card, Mandy thought as she walked through the ancient oak doors. There were garlands of holly and ivy and thick candles on the window ledges. To the side of the altar, a towering fir tree had been decorated with paper hearts and stars which were gently shedding glitter onto the flagstones. The children from the nursery school were already massing in the vestry when Mandy arrived. When Jimmy had left her at the rescue centre earlier, he'd asked her to meet him at a quarter past six for the seven o'clock performance. Mandy wasn't sure why, but she had come early as requested.

The nursery nativity, with its mince-pie supper, had become a staple Welford event, but this was the first time it had been held in the church. Soon half the village would arrive to watch their children and grandchildren, nieces, nephews and friends. But for now, all the chatter was emanating from the room at the back of the church.

Walking down the side-aisle, Mandy squinted past the small group of parents outside the vestry door to the tumble of tea towel headdresses and tinsel crowns beyond. Susan Collins, her smart trouser suit offset by a sparkling bow on her head, was marshalling the children into some kind of order, though to Mandy's inexperienced eye it seemed chaos was not far from the surface.

A small girl, dressed in what looked like a blue nightie, was having a white scarf draped around her head. 'I think that's you almost ready, Angela.' Taking a step back, Susan surveyed the effect. 'Do you know where baby Jesus is?' The little girl nodded. Turning, she pointed to the doll that was lying on the table in the corner.

'And now you, Gavin.' Susan moved on to the young boy in a brown dressing gown who was presumably playing Joseph.

'Please, Miss Susan, I need the toilet!'

Mandy wanted to laugh. At least he had piped up before the performance. She wasn't sure if the stable in Bethlehem offered bathroom facilities.

'I'll take him.' One of the smartly-dressed mothers from outside the door stepped into the room and held out her hand. 'Come on, Gavin.'

'Thanks.' Susan threw the woman a grateful glance. She looked surprisingly calm, Mandy thought. In the same situation, she would be tearing her hair out. For a millisecond, she considered going in and offering to help. Then one of the children, dressed as a lamb and bleating loudly, bounded past her, followed closely by a cow wielding a pair of long plastic horns. It was tough enough wrangling real animals, Mandy thought. Better leave these critters to people who knew what they were doing.

Despite insisting that she arrive early, there was no sign of Jimmy. Turning her back on the young cast, Mandy made her way back out to the churchyard. She dug her hands in her pockets against the biting cold and walked across the well-gritted path. The graveyard looked tranquil under its blanket of snow. There was still a covering on the village green as well, though children had been playing there with sledges, leaving dark green scores in the pristine white. When Mandy stopped and looked up, the sky above was filled with stars.

From a long way off, she heard the roar of a vehicle. A few moments later, a pair of round headlights appeared. It was a Land Rover towing a livestock trailer. To Mandy's surprise, it came to a halt in front of the church gates.

The door on the far side of the vehicle opened and closed. Booted footsteps rang on the road, walking round to the back. A tall figure in a green jacket with a jaunty red hat appeared under the yellow streetlamp. It was Jimmy. He grinned when he saw the look on Mandy's face. 'Hello,' he said.

Mandy looked from his amused face to the trailer and back again. There was a scuffling noise from inside, followed by an odd grunting sound. Mandy stared. 'What on earth have you got there?'

If anything, the grin on Jimmy's face widened. 'Just you wait and see,' he said.

He slipped off the catches at the back of the trailer. As he lowered the ramp, Mandy peered past him. In the darkness, she could make out two short white tails above two pairs of slim hind legs. When one of the creatures turned its head to peer at them, revealing velvety brown antlers, she gasped. 'Reindeer?' She looked at Jimmy in amazement.

'I've borrowed them,' Jimmy announced, 'from Father Christmas. Aren't they fabulous? Mandy Hope, meet Dancer,' he gestured towards the smaller of the pair, 'and Blitzen.'

Mandy looked back at the beautiful animals. 'What exactly are you planning to do with them?'

Jimmy stepped up onto the ramp. 'They're going to be in the nativity,' he said. 'I did discuss it with Susan,' he added. 'I know it's not *completely* traditional.' His voice was tight with suppressed laughter.

Following Jimmy, Mandy climbed into the trailer for a closer look. How sweet they were, with their shaggy grey bodies and fuzzy antlers. Both were wearing red-trimmed velvet halters. She wanted so badly to touch them.

'Where are they really from?' she asked. Unable to resist, she ran a hand down Dancer's shoulder. Her fur was thick and soft, reminding Mandy more of the baby donkeys than any native species of deer.

'They belong to some friends of mine who moved to a place near Walton a couple of weeks ago,' Jimmy said. 'They own a small herd. They've had to pop into

Harper's, but they'll be here soon.' He too seemed unable to stop himself stroking them. 'So what do you think?' Jimmy prompted. He had his head on one side, looking for her approval.

'Quite mad . . .' Mandy replied, watching as his grin faltered, '. . . and yet absolutely brilliant,' she added, raising her eyebrows at him as he growled and shook his head at her.

For a moment, she thought he was going to lean over the back of Dancer and kiss her, but the headlights of another car drew up behind the trailer, illuminating them. Mandy blinked in the bright lights, then a moment later, they went out. The doors on either side of the car opened. A woman climbed out of the driver's seat and walked towards them. Her long blonde hair was tied on top of her head and she was wearing a Scandinavian-style sweater. A man in a matching jumper approached from the other side of the car.

Jimmy ushered Mandy out of the trailer towards them, nodding a welcome. 'Mandy Hope, meet Ed and Ania Legg,' he said. 'Proud owners of the Rydal Reindeers.'

Ania held out her hand. 'Good to meet you,' she said.

'Absolutely. We've heard all about you.' Ed shook hands with Mandy and slapped Jimmy on the shoulder.

'We should get the reindeer inside,' Jimmy said, 'get them settled before everyone starts to arrive.'

Ed and Ania clipped ropes onto the velvet halters and led each reindeer neatly down the ramp. They walked calmly beside their handlers, their huge limpid eyes looking curiously at the snowy graveyard and the sparkling church.

Mandy tried to imagine getting Robin and Holly up the steps of the church and in through the porch. It would cause a battle royale with her baby donkeys. But Dancer and Blitzen seemed to take everything in their stride, even as a host of miniature angels descended upon them, coming to a wide-eyed halt in a circle around the two animals. Susan Collins was obviously waiting for them. She walked down the side-aisle with a smile on her face, leading Jack by the hand and followed by sundry kings and shepherds, now fully costumed and ready to go.

'How wonderful,' she said. 'Thank you, Jimmy. And thanks to you.' She nodded at the Leggs with a friendly look. 'You must be Ed and Ania.'

Ania smiled at the children. 'This is Dancer,' she put her hand on the distinctive withers of the smaller reindeer, 'and this is Blitzen.'

The look of wonder on the children's faces brought an unexpected lump to Mandy's throat. And how wonderful for Jack, she thought. Finally getting to see his reindeer. Jimmy too was watching the small boy.

'Where did they come from?' Jack's voice was barely more than a whisper. He was staring as if he could hardly believe his eyes. Mandy was thrilled to look at his pink cheeks and bright eyes. He clearly hadn't suffered any lasting effects from his fall down the mineshaft. She suspected Susan knew how lucky he had been.

'I've borrowed them from Father Christmas,' Jimmy announced in a serious voice. 'Tomorrow night, they'll be very busy indeed, so we'll have to look after them, won't we?' There were wide eyes and nods all round.

Ania Legg pulled something out of her pocket. Bending down, she beckoned Jack over. 'Would you like to give Dancer a piece of carrot?'

Jack seemed almost unable to breathe. 'Yes please.' It was little more than a sigh. Mandy wasn't sure whether to laugh or cry. She put a hand over her mouth as the small boy, his dark eyes huge in the dim light, approached the two reindeer. With reverence, he held out his hand, the piece of carrot flat on his open palm as Mandy had shown him with the donkeys. When Blitzen put down his head and snaffled up the morsel, Mandy found herself smiling. Jack's face blazed with delight. His dream had come true. He had met some of Father Christmas's reindeer.

Jimmy winked at Mandy. She guessed he felt pretty much like Father Christmas right now. The children had begun to whisper amongst themselves and jostle to get nearer the reindeer, but before they grew too restless, Jimmy crouched down and held up his hands. 'You'll have more time to speak to them afterwards,' he said, 'but right now, they have to go into their pen. Otherwise they won't be ready when all your mums and dads get here.'

'Back into the vestry,' Susan urged them. With several longing backward glances, the children shuffled away.

To the right of the altar, a small area had been set aside. In addition to props indicating an 'inn' and a manger in the middle of the chancel, temporary wooden fencing had been put up and straw had been spread on the floor. The two reindeer looked so sweet, standing with their heads facing the pews. At Jimmy's suggestion, Mandy sat close to the animals at the front of the church, though she made sure she was sitting near the aisle. The clinic had been quiet today, but emergencies could come in at all hours. She switched her phone to vibrate.

The audience began to arrive, a trickle of people at first, rising to a flood of near-Biblical proportions. Mandy saw many, many faces that she knew. Reverend Hadcroft was there in his dog collar. Mrs Ponsonby had arrived in a smart blue coat and her best church hat. For once she didn't have her Pekinese with her, to Mandy's relief.

Despite the influx of friends and acquaintances, all wanting to say hello and wish her season's greetings, Mandy found it hard to take her eyes off the reindeer. Blitzen didn't seem to be bothered by the noise and movement at all, but Dancer was restive. Stretching out her neck, she gave the strange croaking, grunting noise that Mandy had heard coming from the trailer outside. Her liquid eyes seemed wary, and she didn't seem able to stand still, pawing with her front legs at the straw, shifting from foot to foot. It wasn't surprising, Mandy thought. The chatter of excited voices and clatter of footsteps was loud enough to upset any animal.

She glanced at her watch. Seven o'clock. Silence fell over the audience as, in the background, someone switched on a recording of *Little Donkey*. From the back of the church, the lights began to go out until only the altar was brightly lit. The two children dressed as oxen walked out with the noisy lamb Mandy had seen earlier. One of the oxen, a boy with huge blue eyes and strawberry blond hair, seemed transfixed by Dancer and Blitzen in their pen. The other ox had to nudge him in the ribs to steer him into position.

Jack trotted onto the stage dressed as the innkeeper in a scarlet shirt and black leggings covered by an apron that was slightly too long. He was also finding it difficult to stop staring at the pen. Mandy followed his gaze. Dancer still seemed uneasy. Lifting a hind leg, she kicked at her belly and again stretched out her head to make the odd lowing sound.

On the far side of the tableau, there came the rattle of hooves. Mandy looked over to see one of the nursery teachers standing in the doorway of the vestry, banging two coconut shells together. Mandy was enchanted when Angela, in full Mary garb, cantered onto the scene, riding a hobby horse. Looking over her shoulder as she galloped towards the inn, she called out, 'Hurry up, Joseph!' There were titters of laughter all around the church.

Mandy was just wondering how many times Mary would circle the altar before the hapless Joseph caught her up, when she noticed that Dancer, who had been scraping and scuffling more than ever, was making moves to lie down. Mary had finally come to a stop in front of the inn, but Joseph, whose attention should have been on his pregnant wife, was staring with wide eyes at Dancer in her pen. Raising his hand, he pointed to her back end.

'She's doing a wee!'

The girl playing Mary, whom Mandy recognised as the daughter of one of her farm clients, let go of her hobby horse with one hand and swung round to look. Having inspected the situation, she stuck out her chin and turned to Joseph. 'No, she's not,' she said in a voice that brooked no questions. 'She's having a baby!'

The audience let out a collective gasp and several small heads appeared at the vestry door, trying to look. Reverend Hadcroft stood up from the other end of Mandy's pew and faced the audience. Holding his hands up, he said loudly, 'Is there a vet in the house?' and with a slightly nervous air, he turned to look at Mandy. 'Would you mind stepping in, please, Mandy?'

Standing up, Mandy felt very self-conscious under the spotlights. This was the first time she had ever examined a reindeer. And almost all of Welford was there to watch.

Mary had been right, she realised a moment later. There was a tiny hoof protruding from under the doe's shaggy tail. As Mandy watched, the animal lay down on the straw with a grunt. Her flank bulged as she began to strain. But although the little foot poked out each time the doe heaved, whenever the contraction ended, it was sucked back in. Despite her efforts, the doe was making no progress.

Several children had crowded round the pen, but Jimmy moved them back. 'We have to give Mandy and Dancer some space,' he told them. Then he asked Mandy, 'What do you need?'

'My lubricant and some ropes,' she replied. 'I've got them in the car.' She let herself out of the pen. It was just as well she was on call and had the car with her, she thought. Hurrying outside, she opened the boot of the Toyota and took out the sterilised ropes that she usually used for calving cows. There was an almost full bottle of lube. Finally, she pulled on some arm-length gloves, slammed the boot shut and made her way back into the church.

The children were a little further back from the pen, herded competently by Susan and her staff but the adult audience were all on their feet as they watched Dancer straining and straining. There was still only one foot visible. There should have been another by now, and ideally a tiny nose as well. Climbing into the pen, Mandy dropped to her knees.

When Mandy inserted her hand, she could feel the warmth of the doe's body. There was very little space in the birth canal, hardly more than a large sheep. As she had suspected, as she moved her hand further inside, she could feel only that single limb. The shoulder was pressing against the bony ring of Dancer's pelvis. The head and the second leg were twisted back inside the uterus. There was no way the little creature could be born while it remained in that position.

Withdrawing her hand, Mandy lubricated it again and set to work. She had to push back the calf's shoulder to allow her to guide the second leg and then the head into place. To get into the correct position, she lay down on the floor. She waited as the doe strained again, then as the contraction ended, she pushed the bony shoulder back, reaching her hand in through the pelvic opening. The movement triggered another tightening of the uterus and for a long moment, Mandy felt a bruising pressure on her wrist as she prevented the calf from moving forwards. In the brief pause that followed, she reached in almost to her shoulder and found the second cloven hoof. Gripping it, she drew it forwards, just as the next contraction began.

There were now two feet in the passage. Mandy could feel herself beginning to sweat. Her head was almost touching the reindeer's tail as she waited, panting, for the contraction to stop.

It was time to bring the head round. Extending her arm once more, she wriggled her fingers past the legs, feeling down the side of the calf's body. From the angle of the neck, she could tell that it was twisted to the left. As she moved her hand, past the ear, past the eye, right along to the slim muzzle, the straining began again. Gritting her teeth, Mandy waited until the agonising pressure diminished, then in a smooth movement she gripped the tiny nose and drew it towards her. As the next contraction began, the little head swung round into place. This time, as Dancer strained, two small cloven hooves appeared beneath a miniature nose.

There were one or two gasps from the audience as the head began to emerge. Mandy had no need of the ropes. As Dancer groaned and pushed again, and Mandy assisted, the calf surged forwards, nostrils, eyes, ears, shoulders. And then with a final heave, the hips were through the birth canal and the newborn calf was lying on the straw, still half encased in the birth sac.

It wasn't breathing. Mandy cleared the membrane from the nose. The small body lay still. Looking up, Mandy saw Jimmy standing close beside her. 'Help me,' she said. Together they lifted the little creature up by its hind legs. With Mandy's guidance, they swung the calf gently from side to side and to Mandy's relief, the fluid that had been filling its airways flooded out. Laying the animal back down on the straw, she cleared its nose again. The little chest jerked and the calf took its first gasping breath.

'Attagirl,' Jimmy whispered, and Mandy wondered if he was talking to her or the calf.

It took only a moment for Dancer to scramble to her feet. Turning, she sniffed at the calf and began to lick. Tiny grunts of contentment came from her throat as the calf lifted its head, instinctively reaching for its mother. Mandy heard a collective sigh from the audience, as if they were watching a particularly satisfying firework.

Even the children watched in enthralled silence as the reindeer mother encouraged the little calf to stand for the first time. It tucked its tiny soft hooves underneath it, then in stages, the hind end rose. Mandy watched the weight of the little body swing forwards onto the front knees. The calf tried to extend one of its front feet, but fell back twice. Then, with a swift motion, first one front leg then the other straightened, and the calf was wobbling on all fours, as Dancer continued the sweet grumbling noise that seemed to indicate her delight.

The crowd stayed quiet. Mandy was aware of Reverend Hadcroft beaming over the heads of the children, and of Jack's face reduced to two huge eyes and a mouth like an O. Dancer seemed oblivious to the fact that she was the centre of so much attention.

The boy playing Joseph raised his hand. 'Can we call the calf Jesus? Please?'

Mrs Ponsonby, who had been behind Jimmy in the pew next to Mandy, seemed to swell into sight like a balloon. 'You cannot possibly call a baby reindeer Jesus,' she insisted in a loud stage whisper. 'It's not right.'

Mandy tried not to laugh. She thought Jesus would be a fabulous name for a reindeer. But she took pity on Mrs Ponsonby, who had her heart in the right place.

'Don't worry, Mrs Ponsonby,' she said, then turned to the children. 'Lovely as the name Jesus is,' she told them, 'I'm afraid I don't think it would suit this new baby.' She tried to hide her grin as there came a chorus of 'Why not?' and 'Awww, Miss.' Holding a finger to her lips, she hushed them. 'It wouldn't suit this new baby,' she said, 'because Jesus is a boy's name. And this little calf is actually a girl.'

A murmur of laughter ran through the audience. Jimmy's face was split in two by his broad grin. 'Why don't we call her Mary?' he suggested. There was a chorus of assent from the children.

'What a lovely name.' Ania Legg smiled at Jimmy. 'What do you think, Ed?' She turned to her husband.

'I think it's perfect,' he said. 'And that we were very lucky that Mandy was in the audience to help out.' He smiled his thanks. 'But I also think we should get Dancer and Mary home, so they can get to know one another in peace.' Mandy looked at Dancer, who was starting to look distracted by the rows of faces watching. Mary the calf needed to start feeding, but Dancer's milk would only come down if she was relaxed.

Ed was frowning. 'I think we're going to have to make two journeys,' he said. 'We can't take all three of them in the trailer.'

Mandy stepped forward. 'If it would help,' she said, 'I could take Blitzen back to Hope Meadows for the night. He'd have to share the paddock and field shelter with some donkeys, but I'm guessing he wouldn't mind.'

Ania smiled at Mandy. 'That would be great,' she said. 'If you're sure. We can collect him any time it's suitable.'

Reverend Hadcroft ushered the children aside as Ania and Ed guided Dancer and Mary back up the aisle. Mandy, Jimmy and Blitzen followed. Behind them, the crowd closed in like the Red Sea, following them all the way to the door and into the snowy churchyard.

'Merry Christmas, everybody!' Ed and Ania turned and waved once doe and calf were safely loaded. There was a chorus of greetings in return, then the crowd of nativity goers turned to filter back into the church. There was still the rest of the performance to see, minus the reindeer guests.

'I guess we're going to miss the mince pies this year,' Jimmy said, his words making puffy cloud breaths in the clear night air. Beside him, Blitzen seemed perfectly calm as they made their way up the lane.

'Actually, Gran brought me some round yesterday,' Mandy said. 'We can take them back to yours, if you like.'

The Milky Way glittered overhead as the two of them released Blitzen into the paddock. Holly and Robin trotted over to greet the newcomer, fascinated by this new creature with his fur-covered nose and velvet antlers.

Jimmy filled the rack in the field shelter with hay. 'I hope Santa doesn't mind missing a couple of his reindeer,' he joked.

'Maybe next year Holly could be in the nativity,' Mandy suggested as she watched the three animals start pulling at strands of hay. 'She'd be better behaved than the hobby horse Mary was riding.'

Jimmy grinned. 'Shall we head off?' he suggested.

Mandy took a last glance around the field shelter. The ground was strewn with clean straw. The two donkeys and one reindeer looked very comfortable as they ate side by side, a row of fluffy grey-brown backs, two pairs of tall ears matched by a spectacular set of antlers.

Without Adam and Emily at home, the cottage seemed very quiet and Mandy was glad she wasn't going to spend the night there. Jimmy clutched Gran's tin of mince pies on his knee as Mandy drove up the lane. It felt right to be heading back to Mistletoe Cottage. Tomorrow would be Christmas Eve. Jimmy was seeing Abi and Max. Not wanting to get in the way, Mandy had arranged to spend the evening with James, who was popping in on his way to stay with Paul's parents. Mum and Dad had arrived safely in Scotland and Stuart Mortimore was behind bars. For the first time in weeks, Mandy could properly relax.

Chapter Thirty-One

It was lovely to wake up slowly and naturally. For once, Mandy hadn't set the alarm. Opening her eyes, for a moment she wondered where she was, but then Jimmy stirred beside her. Sitting up in bed, she gazed out of the window. Christmas morning and there was still snow on the ground. Bunches of living mistletoe hung heavy from the apple tree in the garden. Beyond the fence, a black-thorn hedge sloped away, following the line of the lane.

'Merry Christmas.' Jimmy's sleepy eyes held a smile, as if he was amused and delighted to see her there. He opened his arms for a hug. 'Ooof!'

Sky, whose bed had been placed in the corner, took a flying leap onto the bed, landing on Jimmy's midriff. He laughed as the excited collie dashed straight over him and into Mandy's arms, licking her face.

'Typical!' Jimmy said, rolling his eyes. 'Using me as a trampoline and then stealing my hug, just to add insult to injury.' He looked hard at Sky. 'Dogs these days,' he grumbled. 'You should know your place, young Sky.'

Hearing her name, the collie stopped fussing over Mandy and stretched over to lick Jimmy's ear.

'She does know her place.' Mandy reached over and pulled Sky back into her arms. 'Her place is right next to me at all times.'

Jimmy grinned. 'I guess we'd better get up,' he said. 'The way that dog's trying to eat you suggests to me she's hungry.'

It was all still very new. Standing downstairs in her dressing gown and slippers, Mandy had to wait while Jimmy grabbed his keys from a bowl in the kitchen and let the dogs out. She would find her way around soon enough, but for now, she watched out of the window as the three excited animals raced around the garden and Jimmy put the kettle on for coffee.

Her mind wandered back to yesterday evening. James had been delighted with the present she had given him. She had commissioned a portrait of him on his wedding day, with Paul, Seamus, and Lily. His eyes had filled with tears when he had seen it.

The dogs pattered back into the kitchen, their tongues lolling out, tails wagging. Carrying a tray with coffee and cream, Jimmy led Mandy into the sitting room. To her surprise, there were three bulgy hiking socks hanging at the side of the fireplace. She was even more amazed, when Zoe and Simba rushed over to the stockings, sniffed them, and then rushed back to Jimmy. Simba let out a single 'Wuff!'

'Okay, okay!' Jimmy held up his hands as the two dogs glanced up at him, then rushed back over to inspect the stockings again. Following them, he took down the stockings. 'One for you.' He lay Simba's down on the rug. 'One for you.' Zoe examined the sock from end to end, then began to try to burrow inside. 'And this one,' Jimmy's eyes were laughing as he gazed across the room, 'this one's for you, Sky.'

Mandy glanced down. Sky was standing close to her, looking up as if requesting permission. 'Go on, then,' Mandy told her. Zoe and Simba seemed to know exactly what to do with their stockings, but Mandy had to help Sky to retrieve the gifts inside hers. There was a hide chew toy, some healthy snacks, and a fluffy mallard which quacked when it was squeezed. Sky seemed a bit puzzled. Mandy wondered if she had ever had a present before. Maybe next year she would rush in to her stocking, as Zoe and Simba had done.

Jimmy had heated up some Danish pastries to go with their second cup of coffee. When he came back from the kitchen, he was clutching something under his arm. Setting the tray down on the coffee table, he held out the package towards Mandy. 'For you,' he said, sitting beside her on the sofa.

It was immaculately packed in red and gold giftwrap. Mandy removed the Sellotape and unfolded the paper to reveal a book. '*British Birds of Prey*,' she read. On the front was a photograph of a red kite, its wings outstretched. 'Thank you.' She reached over and kissed Jimmy on the cheek. 'It's beautiful.'

Handing over her presents for him, she watched as he ripped them open. He laughed when he saw what she had bought him. 'Thermal underwear,' he said. 'To keep me warm when you're not here . . .' He unwrapped the second. 'And a vegetarian cookbook for when you are. Just what I always wanted.' His voice was teasing and he continued to smile as he kissed her in turn.

They all went together to Hope Meadows. To Mandy's pleasure, Nicole had left presents for all the animals. Pull toys for the dogs, little balls for the cats to bat around. She had even left plant-based chew toys for the rabbits. Mandy missed the sweet sound of the guinea pigs, but she had no doubt they would be having a wonderful Christmas with Rachel and Brandon.

Holly and Robin seemed delighted with the extra Christmas carrots Mandy had brought them. She and Jimmy stayed for a while, just making a fuss of them. How different they were from a few weeks ago, when they would have run away as soon as anyone arrived. Mandy found herself wishing they had red velvet collars like the reindeer.

Ania and Ed had called in yesterday to take Blitzen home. Mary was doing very well, they said. Dancer too.

Lastly, Mandy took the rescue dogs into the orchard. For once, she let them all out together. Albert, Twiglet, Flame and Birch galloped round and round with Simba, Zoe and Sky. It was a wonderful sight as they dashed around in the snow, bowing and leaping, chasing and playfighting. Their coats were shiny. Birch's ribs were no longer standing out.

'They are a credit to you,' Jimmy told her as Sky

bounded up to them, then raced away again after Birch. 'You should be very proud of yourself. The last few months can't have been easy. Lots of people would have given up.'

'I had a lot of help,' Mandy protested, but he just put his arm around her and gave her a squeeze.

'Well, whatever you say, I'm proud of you,' he insisted.

Mandy looked round the paddock for a change of subject and soon found one. 'Look at Zoe,' she said with a laugh. The husky had dug her nose right in under the snow and had pulled out an old carrot that must have been buried. She was now parading round the orchard, looking very pleased with a large clump of snow balanced on her nose. The orange vegetable hung at a rakish angle from her teeth.

'Maybe she's going to build a snowman and she needed a nose,' Jimmy suggested. They stood there a long time. When Birch started to look a bit shivery, Mandy took them all back inside for a special dinner with hot salt-free gravy and some pieces of potato. It was almost too difficult to leave them, but Mandy satisfied herself that all her charges were comfortable before heading back up to Jimmy's house.

When the phone rang on the way back, Mandy jumped. With all the festivities, she had almost forgotten that she was on call. Pulling in to the side of the road, she stopped the car. Her heart sank a little as she pulled the phone from her pocket, but it was Emily's number. With a sigh of relief, she pressed the button.

Emily had the phone switched to loudspeaker. 'Merry Christmas,' she said and Adam called, 'From me too.'

'How are you getting on?' Emily sounded worried, but then she laughed, saying, 'Stop it, Adam! I'm allowed to ask!' Mandy could imagine her father making faces at the question.

'Everything's fine,' Mandy replied. 'Quiet so far.'

'That's good. How are all your charges doing? How's Tango?' Her dad sounded as if he was still grinning.

'Tango is just fine, Dad. He'll be waiting for you when you come back.' Mandy had pulled into the side of the road beside the hedge. She could see a sparrow among the bare branches outside the car window.

'I'm sorry you're working over Christmas.' Emily's voice again.

The sparrow flitted off. In the back of the car, Sky stood up, her head on one side as if she was trying to listen to the voices on the other end of the phone.

'There's nowhere else I'd rather be,' Mandy assured her mother. 'And I've got a very useful assistant to help me.' Beside her in the car, Jimmy grinned. 'So how about you?' Mandy asked. 'How's the hotel?'

'It's absolutely wonderful.' Emily was enthusiastic. 'We've got a view of the loch from our room. There's a peat fire in the lounge and a wonderful library. I'm going to read until my eyes squint.'

'Sounds lovely,' Mandy said.

'Maybe we could come back in the summer. Is Jimmy there?' her mum asked.

'He's here. We're just on our way back from Hope Meadows.'

'Well, I'm glad everything's going well. Please give my love to Jimmy.'

'They send their love,' Mandy told him, after the call was ended.

Back at the cottage, Jimmy led Mandy into the kitchen. Opening the fridge and then the freezer, he showed her the food he had bought. There were frozen roast potatoes, cabbage and swede mash, Yorkshire puddings, onion gravy, vegetarian sausages, and a roast, which declared it was handmade from pistachios, lentils, and porcini mushrooms. They had been planning to make lunch when they returned, but the weather was so lovely that Mandy found herself wishing they could spend some more time outside instead.

As if reading her mind, Jimmy closed the door of the fridge and turned to face her. 'I know we said we'd cook when we got back, but it's such a lovely day. What would you say if I suggested a walk and we'll cook later when we get back?'

'That would be wonderful' Mandy found herself beaming up at him. 'I can't go too far from the car, just in case a call comes in, but we could take the Land Rover up and go for a wander up towards the Beacon?'

'Sounds perfect,' Jimmy told her.

'I'll just go and get changed.' Galloping up the stairs two at a time, Mandy grabbed her walking boots, waterproof trousers, and a jacket. She put two lightweight fleeces into a rucksack for good measure.

Despite her warm clothes, it was bracing as they made their way through the snow. It had crusted over, after yesterday's sunshine. In places it was firm, but in others it had softened in the sunshine and they sank in, as if walking on sand. It was hard going, but the view as they climbed was stunning. Mandy stopped to catch her breath. Behind her, Jimmy also halted, though the dogs continued to explore, trotting up and down the track, searching for scents on every clump of heather which poked through the icy layer.

Far below them, snaking across the valley floor, Mandy could see the dark lines of drystone walls peeping out from under their caps of snow. The church with its arched windows and square tower seemed to have an almost reddish tone as it bathed in the light from the sun, which hung low in the winter sky. Beyond the village green, the river was a faint silvery line through snow-heavy banks.

On the far side of the valley, Mandy could see Lamb's Wood. The roof of the cottage was barely visible, covered in snow and hidden among branches. She caught herself sighing and pulled herself up. This was no time to be sad.

'It's a pity you didn't manage to get it ready for Christmas.' For the second time that day, Jimmy seemed to have divined her thoughts.

'I'd hoped to be much further on with renovations,' Mandy admitted.

'It is a massive project. And impossible to tackle in this snow.' Jimmy's voice was philosophical. 'I'll help you when the weather changes, if you like.'

Mandy reached out and took his gloved hand in hers, giving it a squeeze. 'Thanks,' she said. She sighed again. 'I know I should be happy, because everything has worked out okay,' she told him. 'But so many things seem to have gone wrong there. Robbie getting ill and the state his animals were in was bad enough, but then with his nephew and all the things he did . . .' She trailed off. 'It's not how I pictured finding my first home would be,' she confessed.

Jimmy stood very still, gazing over in the direction of Lamb's Wood. 'You could make a new start,' he suggested. 'What about a new name? And all the bad things you mentioned are over now. There can be new memories. You and Sky. You'll make some together.'

For a moment, Mandy felt uneasy. Could she really rename the cottage? Wouldn't it be disloyal to Robbie Grimshaw? Would it be like erasing all the memories he had left? Closer to home, she realised it bothered her that Jimmy had mentioned her and Sky making memories, but not himself. She might not wish to rush anything, but if they were to have any future, they would have to create it together.

She reached out, wrapping his hand in both of hers but keeping her eyes on the landscape. 'We'll make new memories together,' she said. 'You and me, Sky, Zoe and Simba. All of us. And yes, I think I would like to rename the cottage.'

Though she was not looking at his face, she could tell he was pleased. His gloved fingers squeezed hers. 'We'd better think of a perfect name, then,' he said.

Turning back onto the track, they began to climb again. The pathway was strewn with rocks and Mandy had to pick her way carefully. For several minutes, neither of them spoke.

'It's not easy, is it?' Jimmy said eventually. He stopped to look back at her, his hands on his hips. 'What sort of thing were you thinking? Some kind of tree name? Birch Cottage? The Spinney?'

Mandy frowned. Birch Cottage sounded cosy, but too tame somehow. The Spinney? There were a lot of bushes and trees. 'They sound a bit too . . .' She searched for the right word. '. . . humdrum.' She stopped as well and bent down to rub Sky's fur, feeling the breath catch in her lungs. It was too difficult to talk and scramble at the same time. 'Maybe something more quirky?'

Jimmy grinned. 'Quirky?' he echoed. 'What, like Simba's Hide or Sky's-the-Limit?'

Mandy made a growling noise in her throat. 'You know what I mean,' she said, baring her teeth at him, then laughing. 'I don't know. Something like Wild Winds or Aerial Acres.' She frowned. 'Those aren't right either, they're a bit twee, but that sort of thing.'

The amused expression had left Jimmy's face and

now he looked thoughtful. 'What about combining those two?' he suggested. 'What about Wildacre?'

'Wildacre?' Mandy let the word roll around her tongue. It wasn't humdrum, that was certain. It suited the little cottage. It had been left to run wild and now it needed to be tamed. 'Wildacre.' She said it again. Jimmy was standing on a rock, watching her. She smiled up at him. 'It's a lovely name.' He held out his hand and she took it and he steadied her as she clambered over the final rocky outcrop.

They had reached the summit. Mandy had expected to look at the view for a few minutes, then turn and go back down, but Jimmy had taken the rucksack off his back and set it down in the snow. After rummaging for a moment, he pulled out two brightly coloured folding mats. Handing one to Mandy, he set his down beside the cairn that marked the summit and sat down. Mandy unfolded the green foam mat and lowered herself onto it. It was wonderful insulation against the snow. Hugging her knees, she gazed at the magnificent scene that was laid out before them. The snow had melted from most of the village roofs, and the grey slate stood clear against the white backdrop. Smoke drifted from a few of the chimneys. Mandy pictured her neighbours, bulging with Christmas dinner, stretching their feet towards blazing fires. In the churchyard, the scattered bushes were dark smudges among the higgledy-piggledy gravestones. The blue sky arched overhead.

Jimmy was rooting in his rucksack again.

'Here.' He had taken a box from his bag. Inside it, wrapped in layers of foil, were four of Gran's mince pies. Mandy pulled off her glove. When Jimmy handed her one, she could feel it was still warm. He must have heated them up before coming out.

He pulled a flask out of one of the outer pockets. Unscrewing the two lids, he filled them both, handing the larger one to Mandy. It contained hot coffee made with milk.

The three dogs, realising there might be crumbs to clear up, gathered round. They lay down in the snow, tongues lolling. Sky looked as though she was grinning, Mandy thought.

'I think we should have a toast!' Jimmy raised his steaming coffee cup. 'Here's to Hope Meadows, to Running Wild, and to making new memories at Wildacre.'

Mandy grinned back at him. 'I'll drink to that,' she said, raising her own cup.

'But most of all,' he said, 'here's to us. Merry Christmas, Mandy!'

'Merry Christmas,' she echoed.

Summer at Hope Meadows

Lucy Daniels

Newly qualified vet Mandy Hope is leaving Leeds – and her boyfriend Simon – to return to the Yorkshire village she grew up in, where she'll help out with animals of all shapes and sizes in her parents' surgery.

But it's not all plain sailing: Mandy clashes with gruff local Jimmy Marsh, and some of the villagers won't accept a new vet. Meanwhile, Simon is determined that Mandy will rejoin him back in the city.

When tragedy strikes for her best friend James Hunter, and some neglected animals are discovered on a nearby farm, Mandy must prove herself. When it comes to being there for her friends – and protecting animals in need – she's prepared to do whatever it takes . . .

HODDER

Springtime at Wildacre

Lucy Daniels

In the little village of Welford flowers are blooming, the lambing season is underway . . . and love is in the air.

Mandy Hope is on cloud nine. Hope Meadows, the animal rescue and rehabilitation centre she founded, is going really well. And she's growing ever closer to handsome villager Jimmy Marsh. What's more, James Hunter, her best friend, is slowly learning to re-embrace life after facing tragedy.

But when an unexpected crisis causes Mandy to lose confidence in her veterinary skills, it's a huge blow. If she can't learn to forgive herself, then her relationship with Jimmy, and the future of Hope Meadows, may be in danger. It'll take friendship, love, community spirit – and one elephant with very bad teeth – to remind Mandy and her fellow villagers that springtime in Yorkshire really is the most glorious time of the year.

HODDER